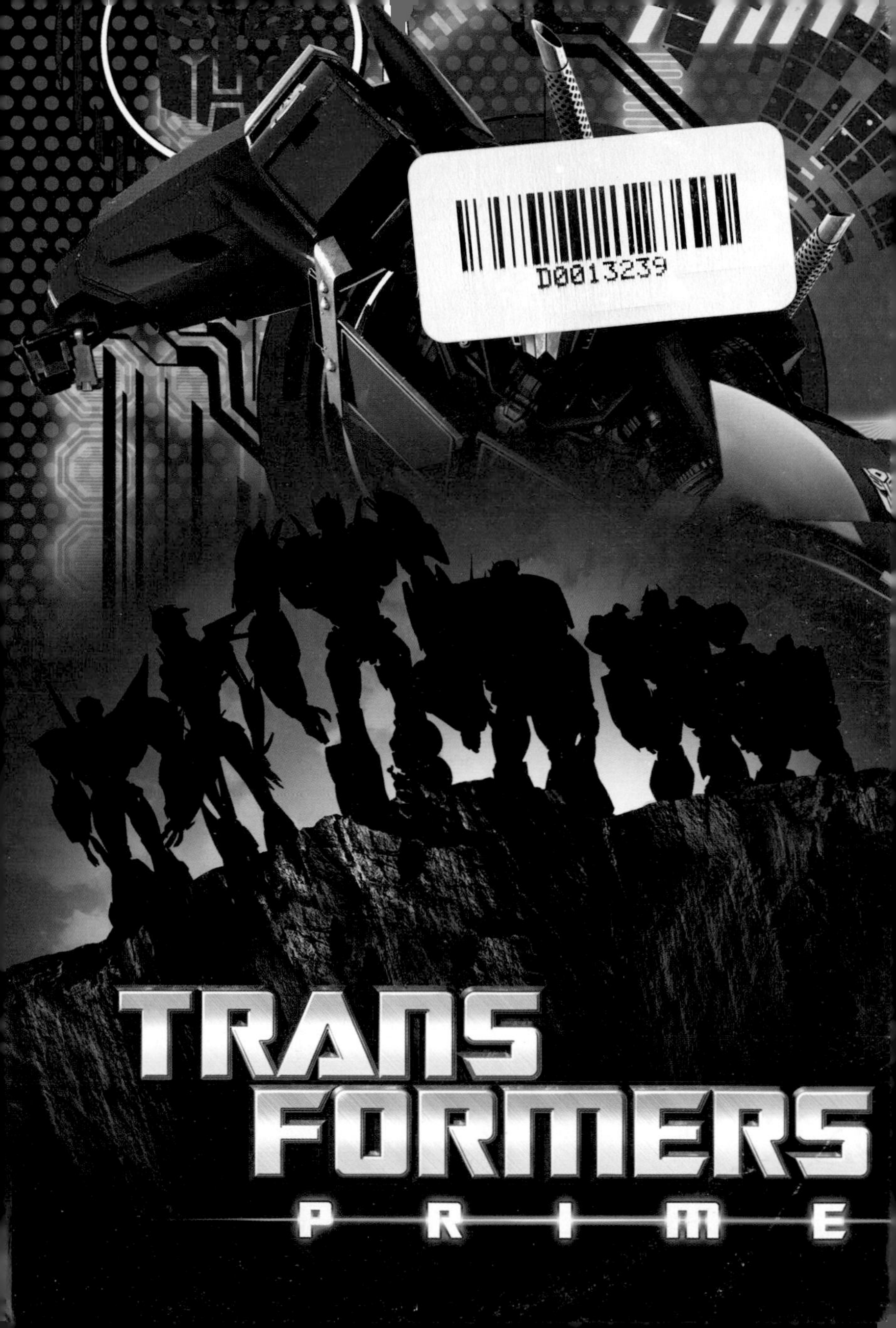
TRANSFORMERS
PRIME

TRANSFORMERS
PRIME

ADAPTATION BY:
JUSTIN EISINGER

EDITS BY:
ALONZO SIMON

LETTERS AND DESIGN BY:
TOM B. LONG

Special thanks to Hasbro's Aaron Archer, Jerry Jivoin, Michael Verret, Ed Lane, Joe Furfaro, Jos Huxley, Andy Schmidt, Heather Hopkins and Michael Kelly for their invaluable assistance.

ISBN: 978-1-61377-540-0
15 14 13 12   1 2 3 4
www.IDWPUBLISHING.com

Ted Adams, CEO & Publisher
Greg Goldstein, President & COO
Robbie Robbins, EVP/Sr. Graphic Artist
Chris Ryall, Chief Creative Officer/Editor-in-Chief
Matthew Ruzicka, CPA, Chief Financial Officer
Alan Payne, VP of Sales
Dirk Wood, VP of Marketing
Lorelei Bunjes, VP of Digital Services

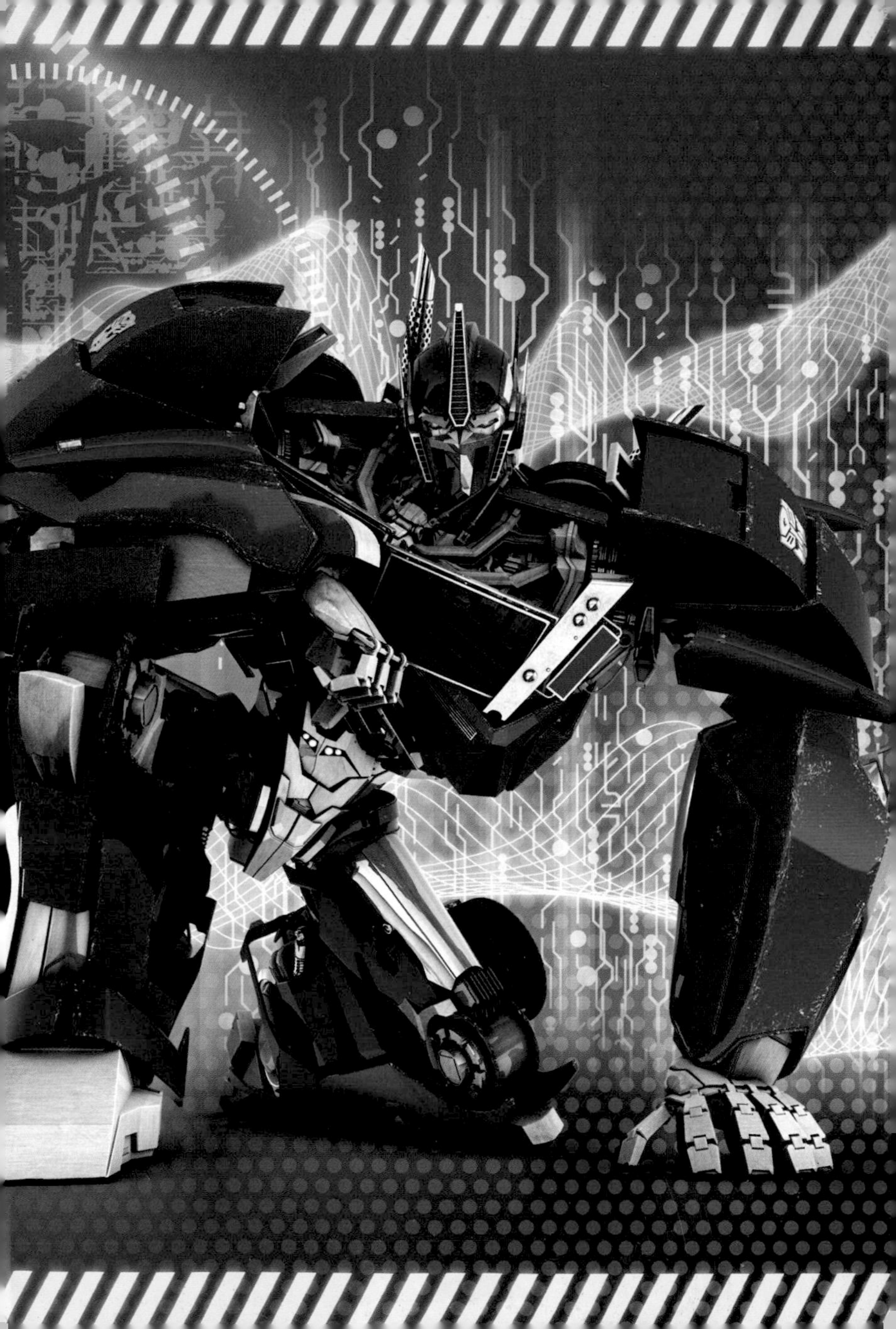

PREVIOUSLY ON

TRANSFORMERS PRIME

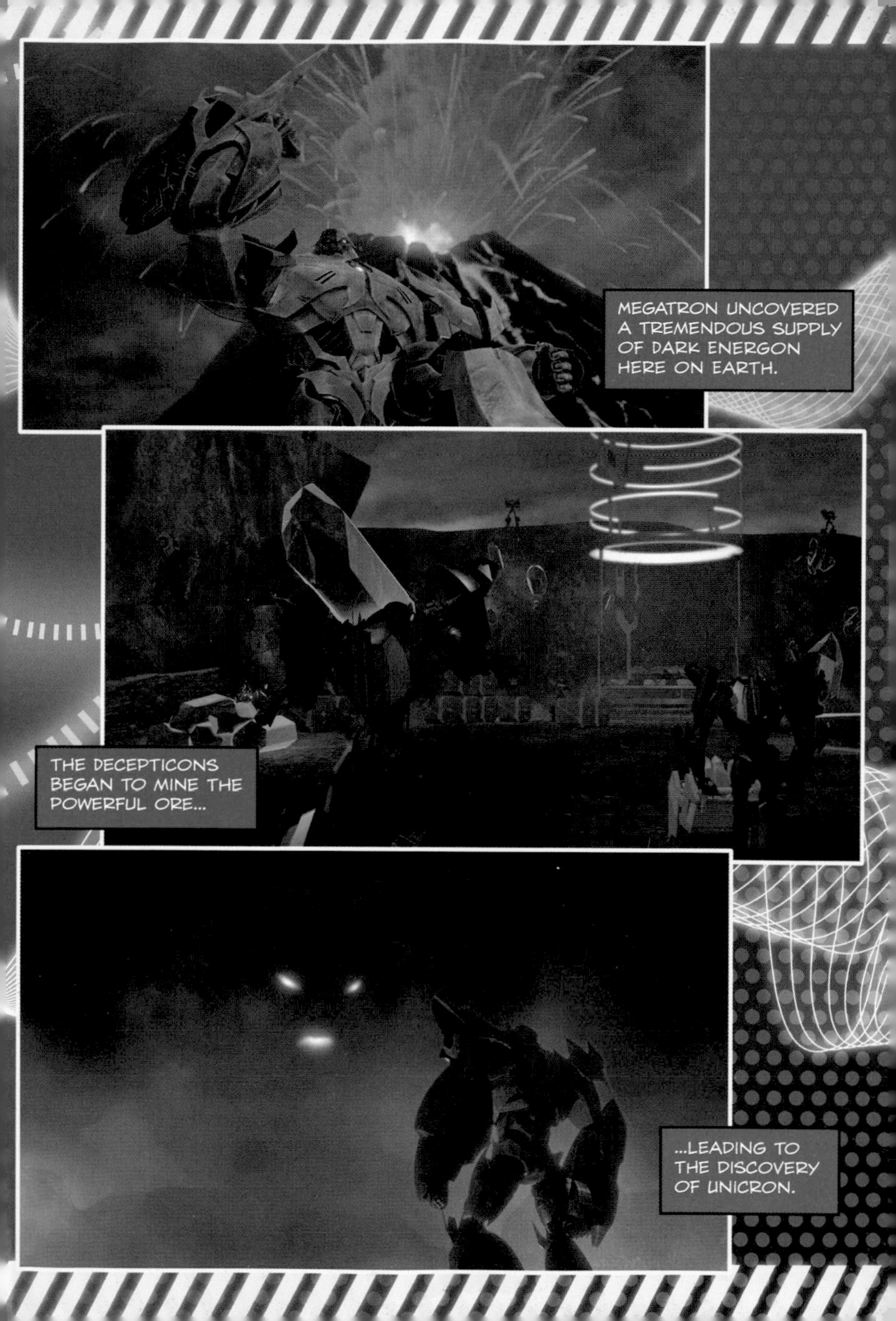
MEGATRON UNCOVERED A TREMENDOUS SUPPLY OF DARK ENERGON HERE ON EARTH.
THE DECEPTICONS BEGAN TO MINE THE POWERFUL ORE...
...LEADING TO THE DISCOVERY OF UNICRON.

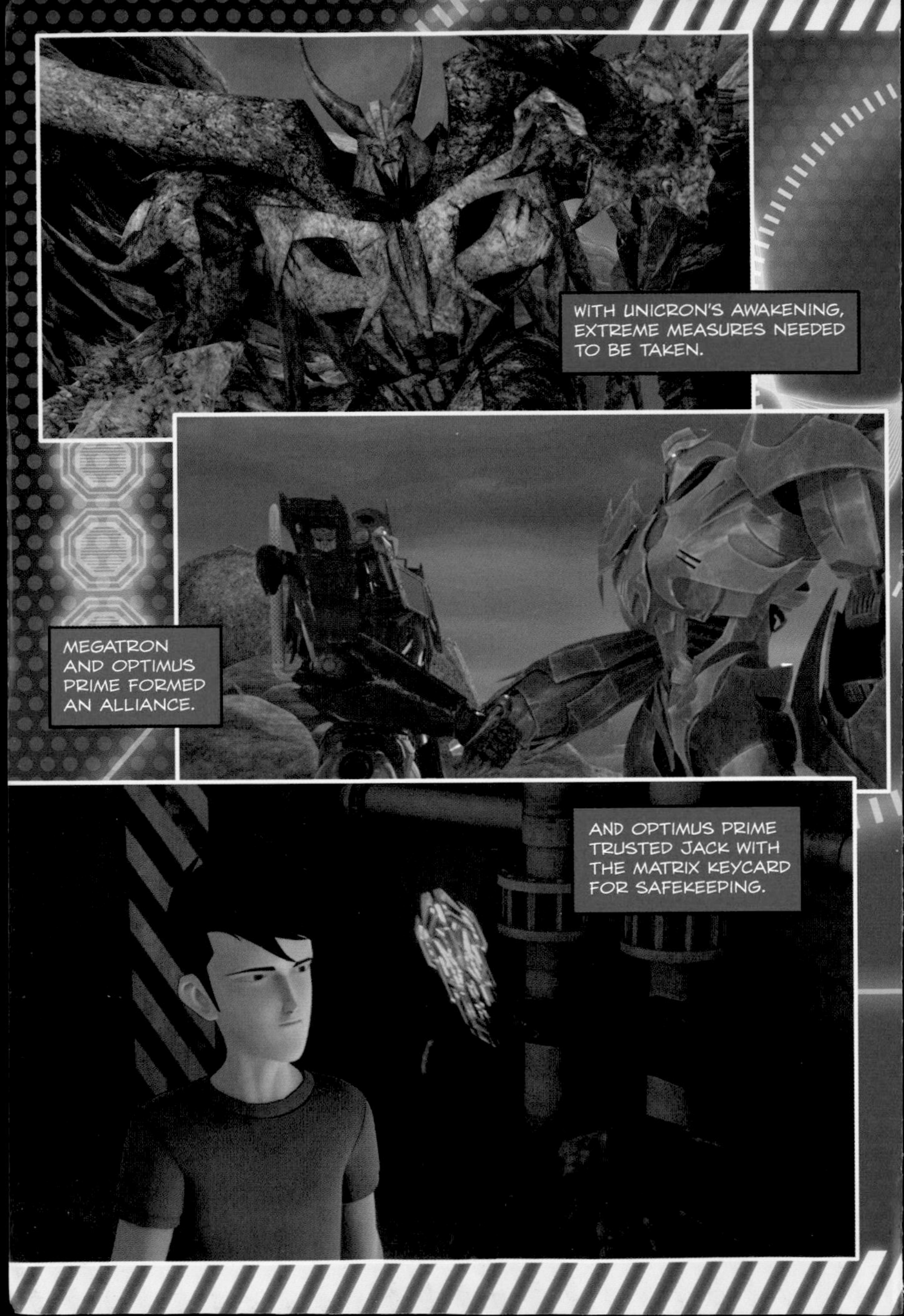
WITH UNICRON'S AWAKENING, EXTREME MEASURES NEEDED TO BE TAKEN.
MEGATRON AND OPTIMUS PRIME FORMED AN ALLIANCE.
AND OPTIMUS PRIME TRUSTED JACK WITH THE MATRIX KEYCARD FOR SAFEKEEPING.

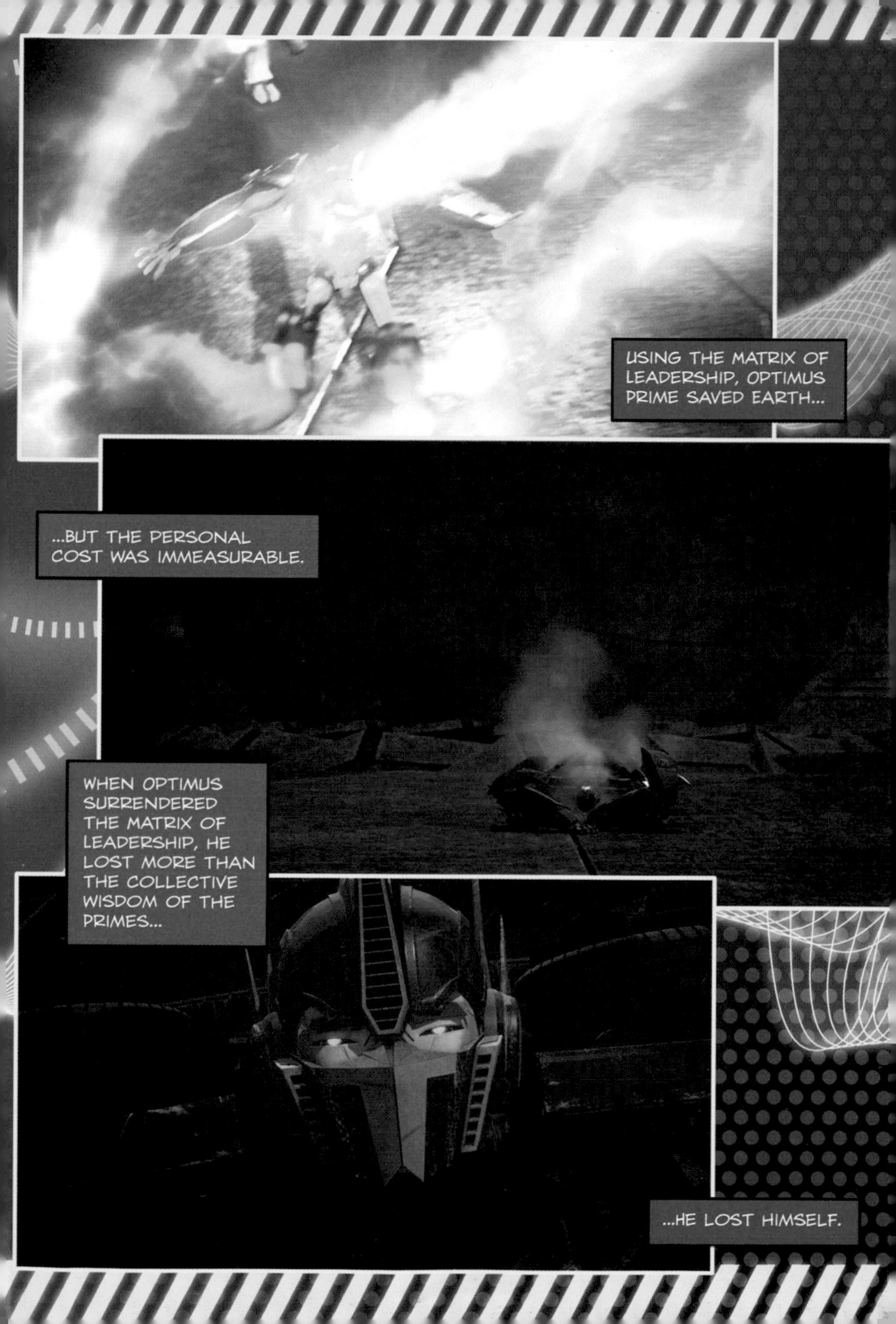
USING THE MATRIX OF LEADERSHIP, OPTIMUS PRIME SAVED EARTH...
...BUT THE PERSONAL COST WAS IMMEASURABLE.
WHEN OPTIMUS SURRENDERED THE MATRIX OF LEADERSHIP, HE LOST MORE THAN THE COLLECTIVE WISDOM OF THE PRIMES...
...HE LOST HIMSELF.

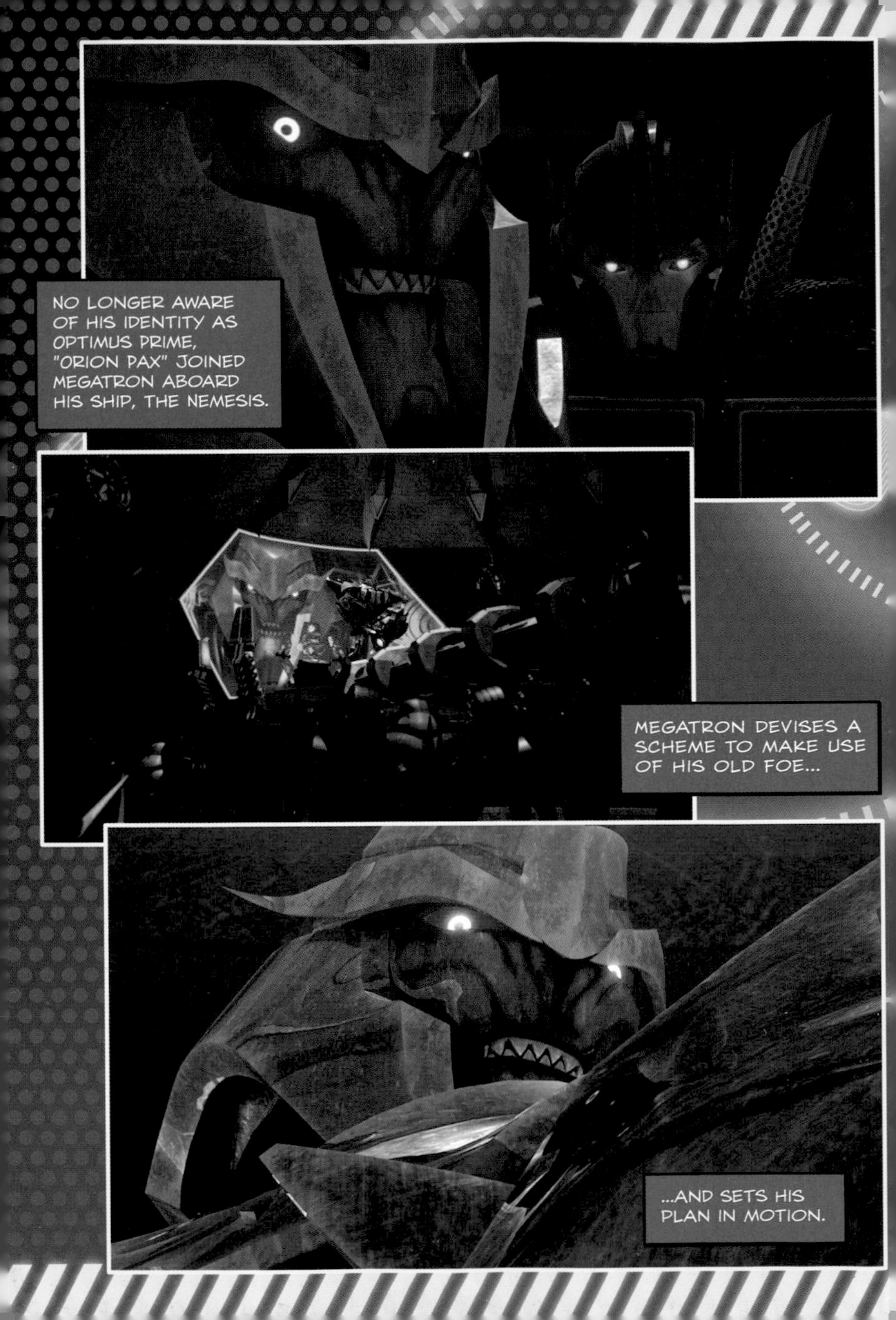
NO LONGER AWARE OF HIS IDENTITY AS OPTIMUS PRIME, "ORION PAX" JOINED MEGATRON ABOARD HIS SHIP, THE NEMESIS.
MEGATRON DEVISES A SCHEME TO MAKE USE OF HIS OLD FOE...
...AND SETS HIS PLAN IN MOTION.

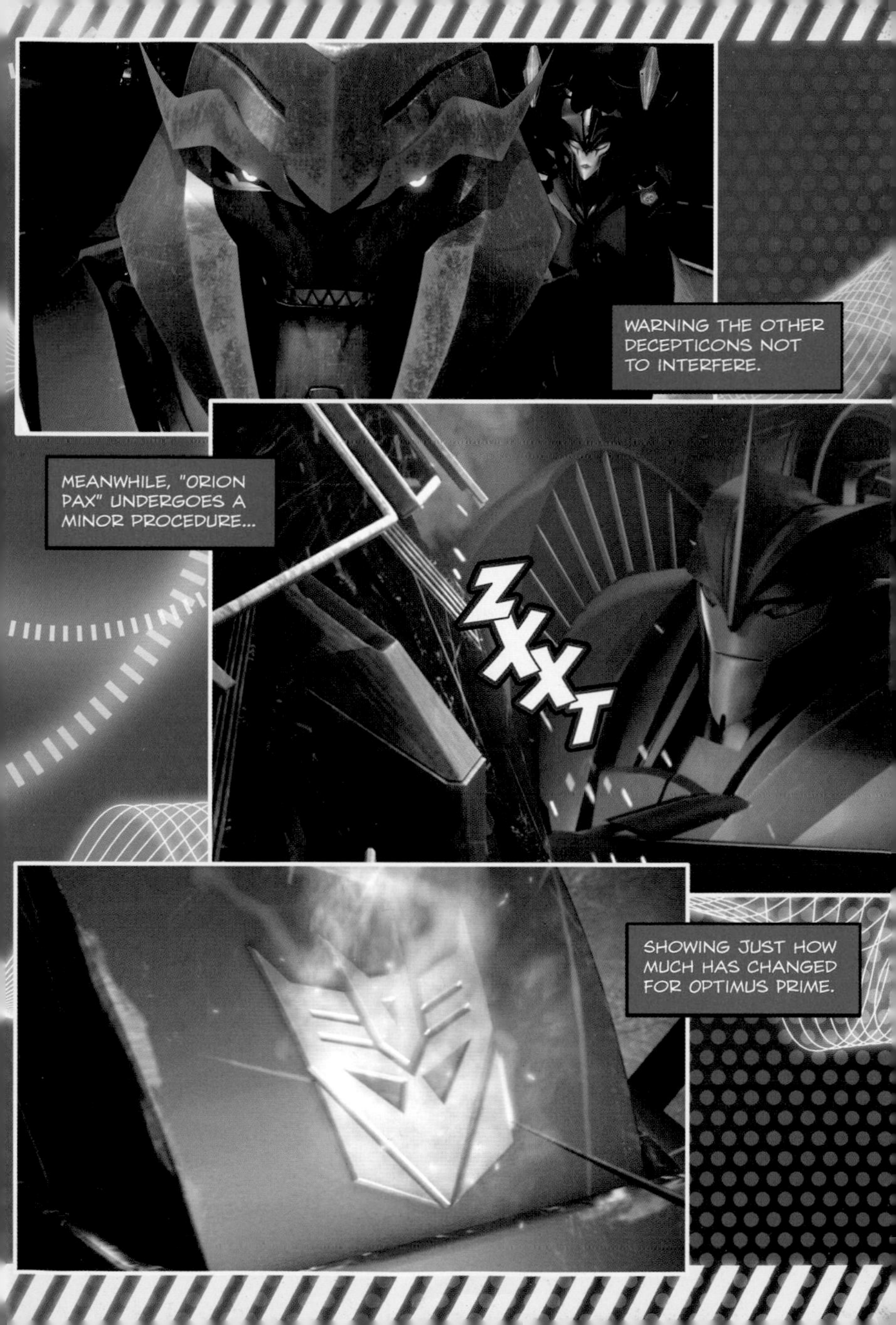
WARNING THE OTHER DECEPTICONS NOT TO INTERFERE.
MEANWHILE, "ORION PAX" UNDERGOES A MINOR PROCEDURE...
ZXXT
SHOWING JUST HOW MUCH HAS CHANGED FOR OPTIMUS PRIME.

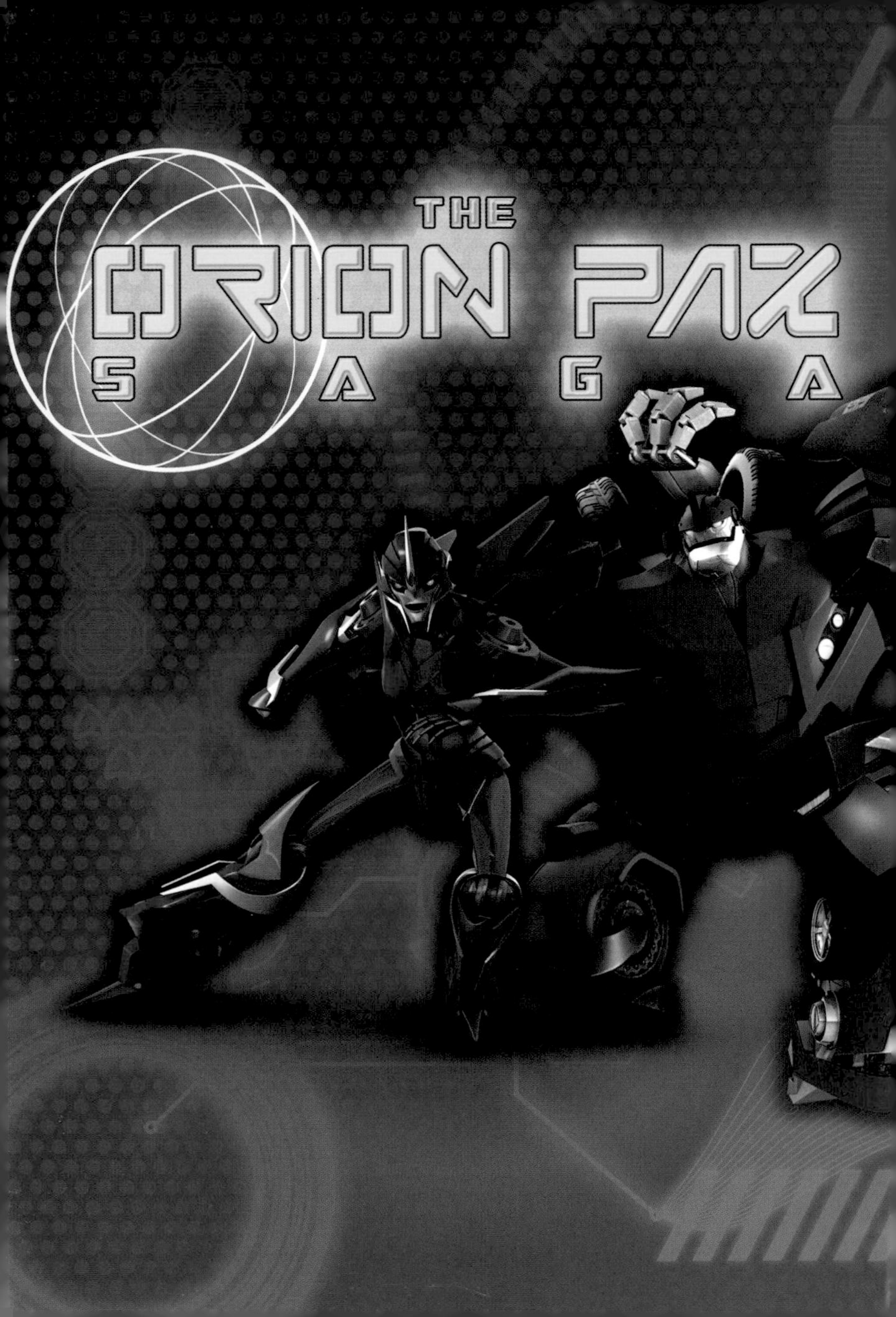
THE
ORION PAX
SAGA

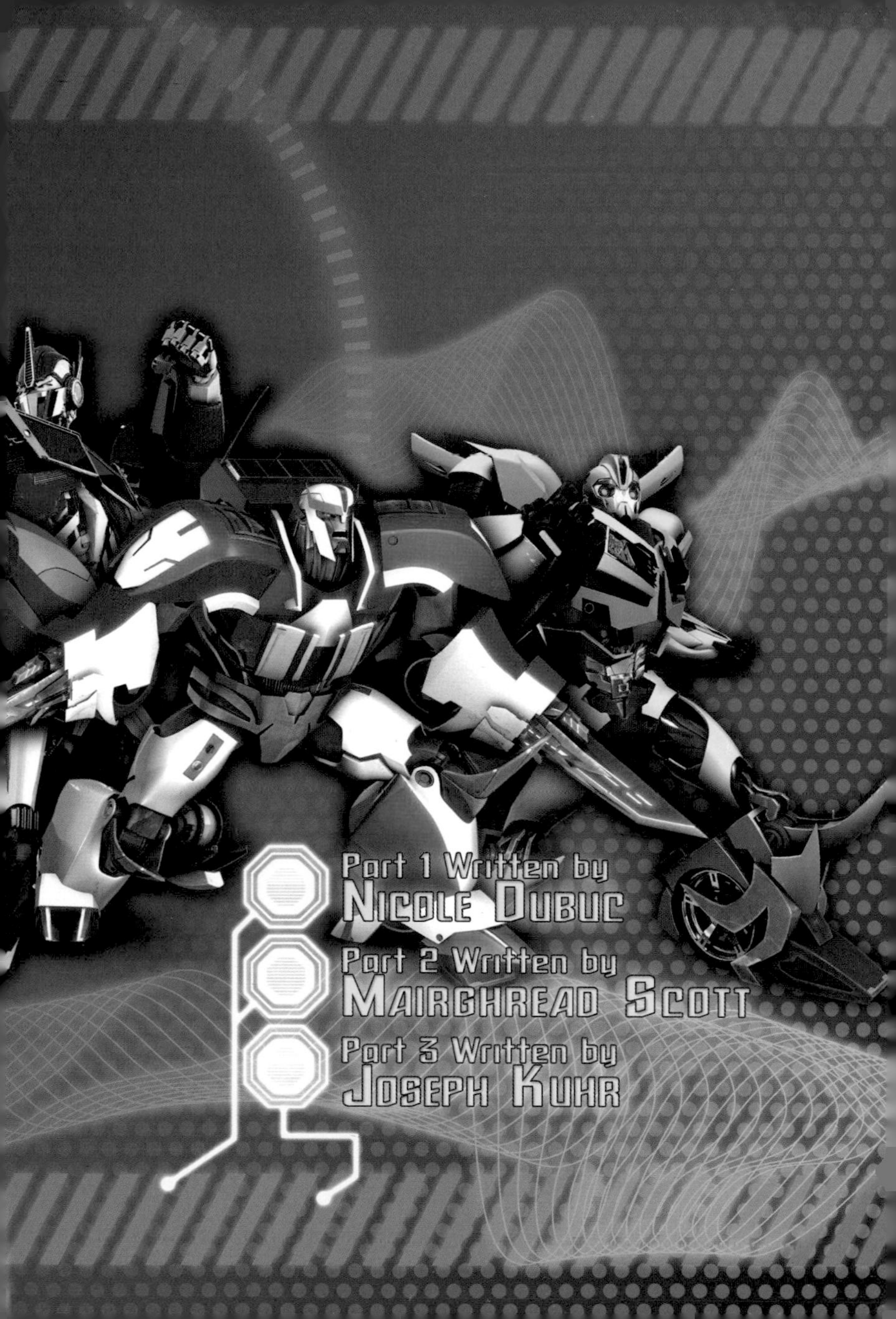

Part 1 Written by
NICOLE DUBUC

Part 2 Written by
MAIRGHREAD SCOTT

Part 3 Written by
JOSEPH KUHR

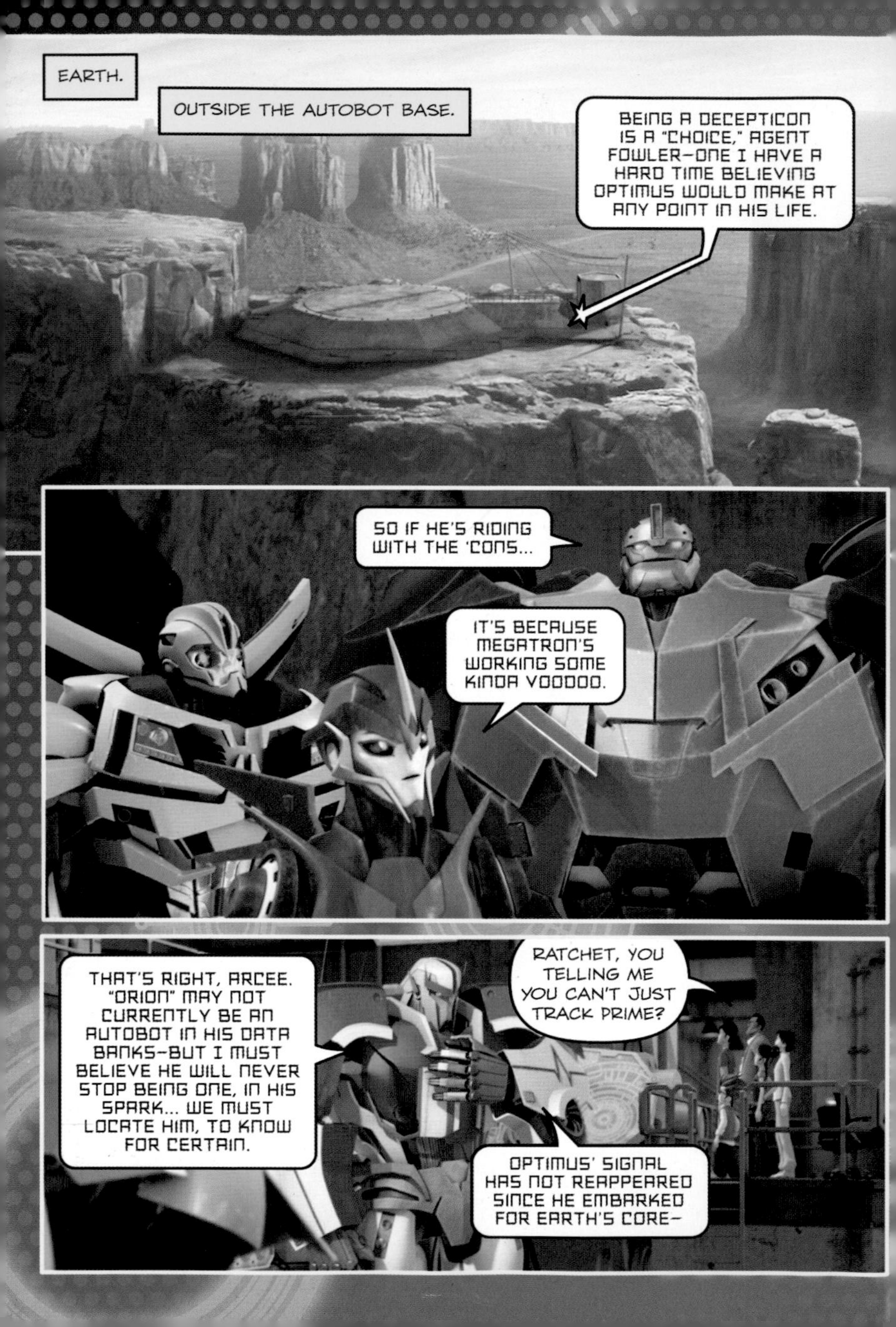
EARTH.
OUTSIDE THE AUTOBOT BASE.
BEING A DECEPTICON IS A "CHOICE," AGENT FOWLER—ONE I HAVE A HARD TIME BELIEVING OPTIMUS WOULD MAKE AT ANY POINT IN HIS LIFE.
SO IF HE'S RIDING WITH THE 'CONS...
IT'S BECAUSE MEGATRON'S WORKING SOME KINDA VOODOO.
THAT'S RIGHT, ARCEE. "ORION" MAY NOT CURRENTLY BE AN AUTOBOT IN HIS DATA BANKS—BUT I MUST BELIEVE HE WILL NEVER STOP BEING ONE, IN HIS SPARK... WE MUST LOCATE HIM, TO KNOW FOR CERTAIN.
RATCHET, YOU TELLING ME YOU CAN'T JUST TRACK PRIME?
OPTIMUS' SIGNAL HAS NOT REAPPEARED SINCE HE EMBARKED FOR EARTH'S CORE—

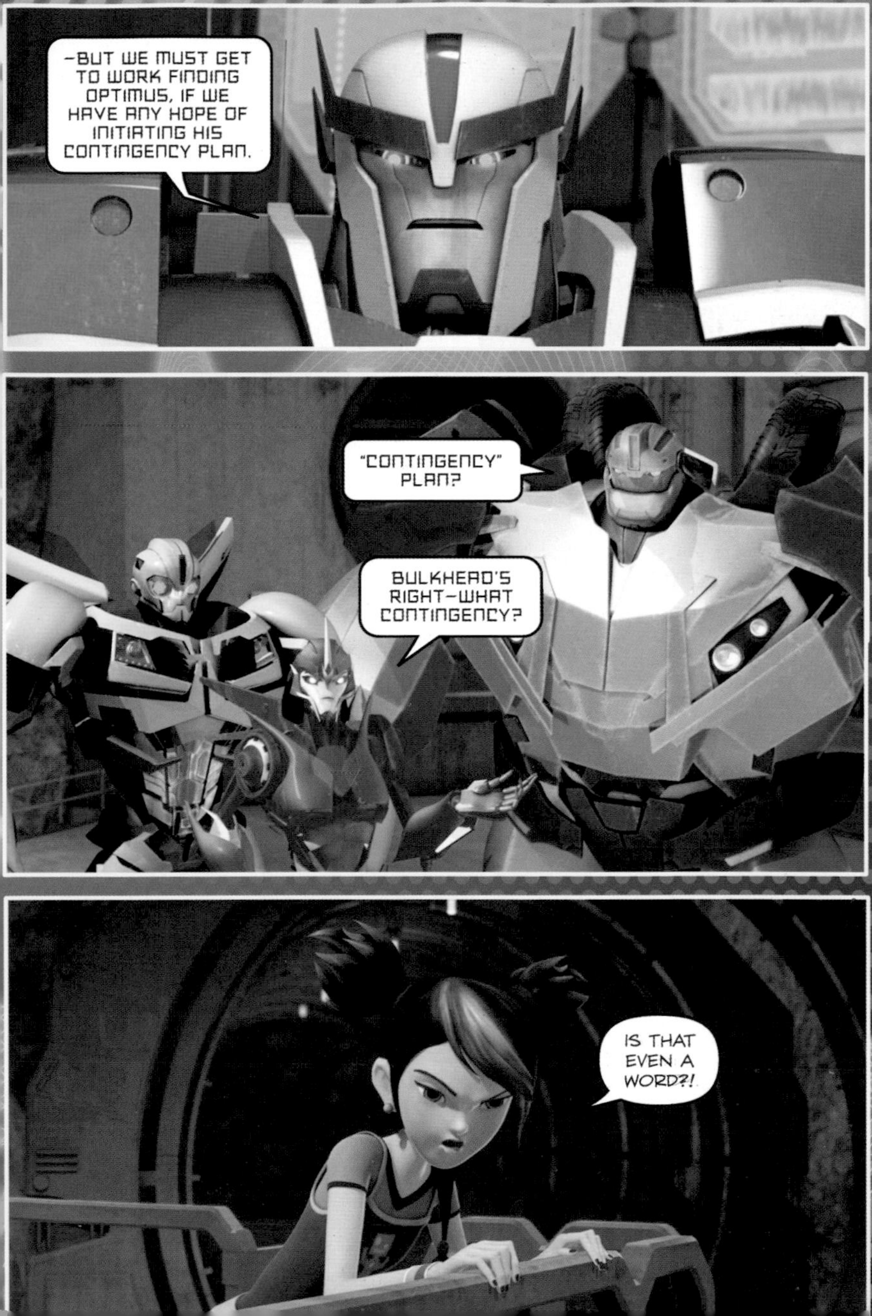
–BUT WE MUST GET TO WORK FINDING OPTIMUS, IF WE HAVE ANY HOPE OF INITIATING HIS CONTINGENCY PLAN.
"CONTINGENCY" PLAN?
BULKHEAD'S RIGHT–WHAT CONTINGENCY?
IS THAT EVEN A WORD?!

THE KEYCARD.

SO, WHAT'S IT DO?

IT GRANTS ACCESS TO VECTOR SIGMA, THE REPOSITORY OF THE WISDOM OF THE PRIMES.

IS THAT... SOME SORT OF SUPERCOMPUTER?

SO, WE CAN JUST DOWNLOAD OPTIMUS' MEMORIES BACK INTO HIM? GREAT!

WHICH ONE'S THE BIG V? OVER HERE?

VECTOR SIGMA IS MORE THAN A "SUPERCOMPUTER," RAF— MUCH MORE. IT IS AN ANCIENT SOURCE OF MYSTICAL POWER—

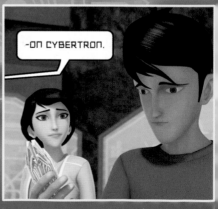

-ON CYBERTRON.

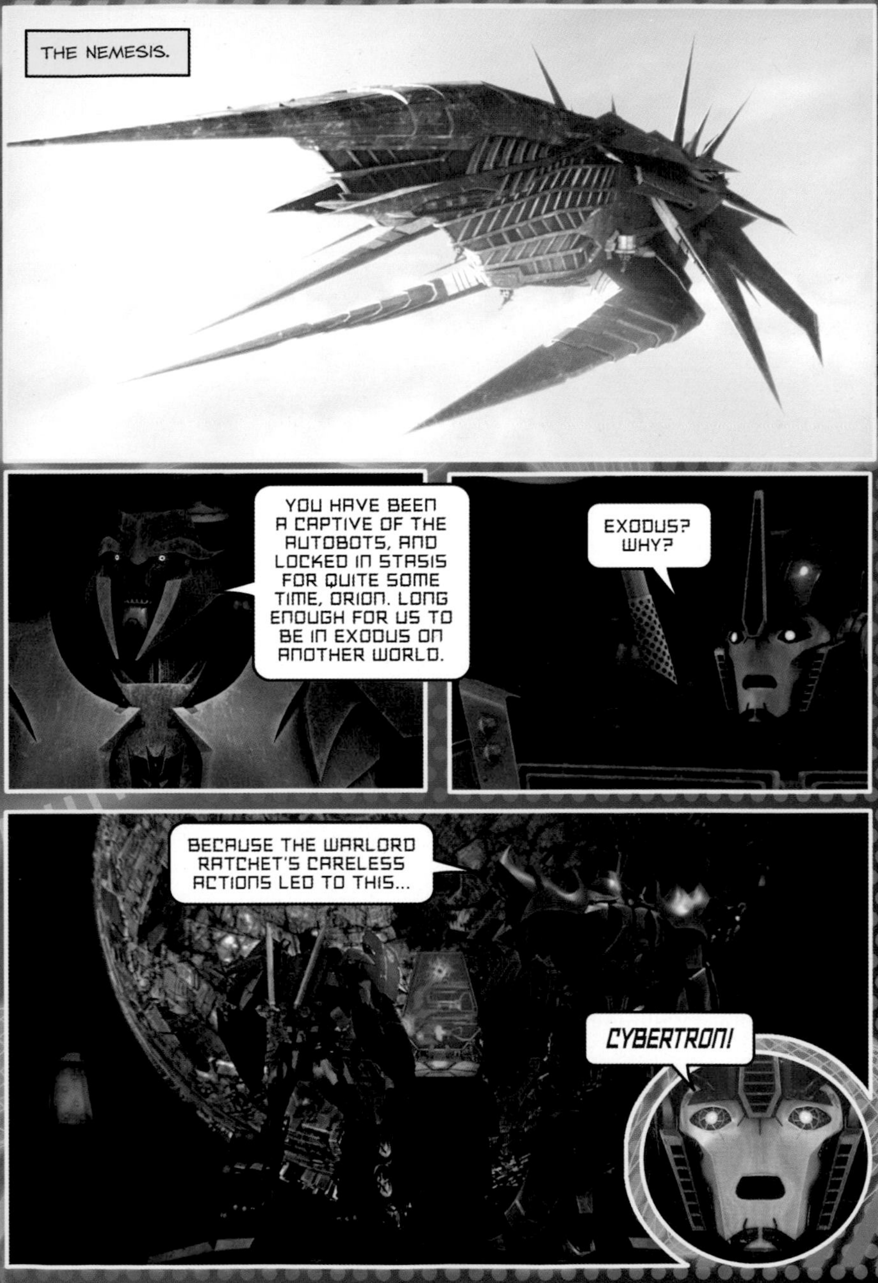
THE NEMESIS.
YOU HAVE BEEN A CAPTIVE OF THE AUTOBOTS, AND LOCKED IN STASIS FOR QUITE SOME TIME, ORION. LONG ENOUGH FOR US TO BE IN EXODUS ON ANOTHER WORLD.
EXODUS? WHY?
BECAUSE THE WARLORD RATCHET'S CARELESS ACTIONS LED TO THIS...
CYBERTRON!

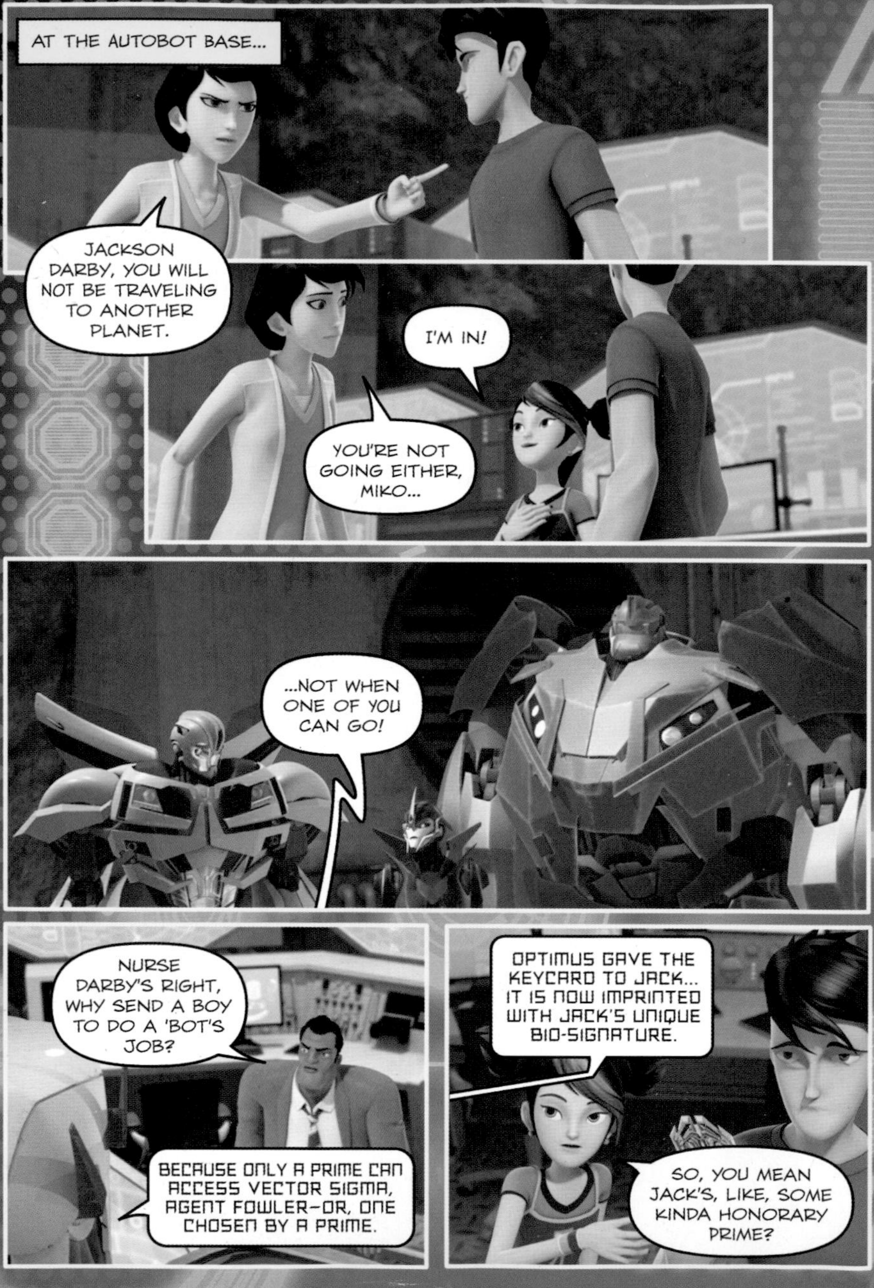
AT THE AUTOBOT BASE...
JACKSON DARBY, YOU WILL NOT BE TRAVELING TO ANOTHER PLANET.
I'M IN!
YOU'RE NOT GOING EITHER, MIKO...
...NOT WHEN ONE OF YOU CAN GO!
NURSE DARBY'S RIGHT, WHY SEND A BOY TO DO A 'BOT'S JOB?
BECAUSE ONLY A PRIME CAN ACCESS VECTOR SIGMA, AGENT FOWLER—OR, ONE CHOSEN BY A PRIME.
OPTIMUS GAVE THE KEYCARD TO JACK... IT IS NOW IMPRINTED WITH JACK'S UNIQUE BIO-SIGNATURE.
SO, YOU MEAN JACK'S, LIKE, SOME KINDA HONORARY PRIME?

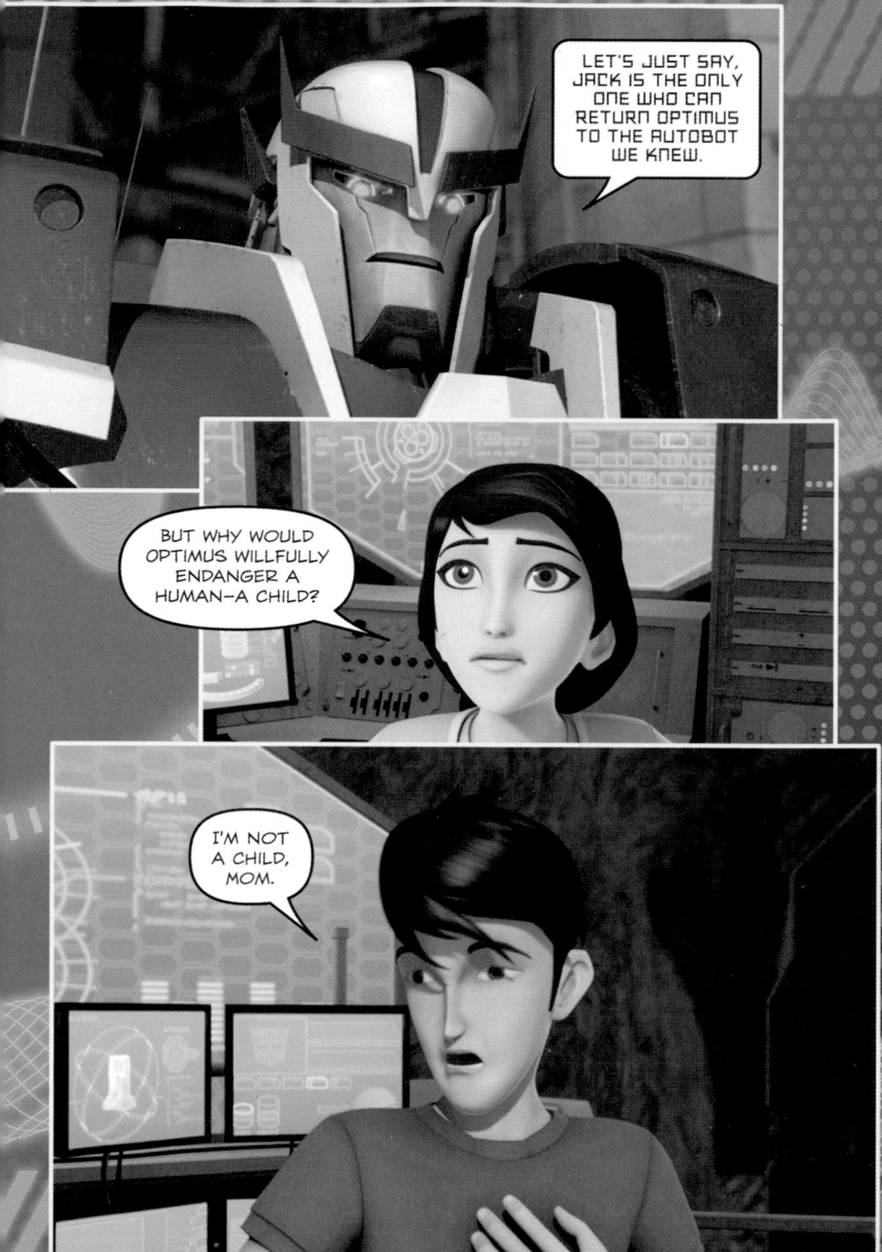
LET'S JUST SAY, JACK IS THE ONLY ONE WHO CAN RETURN OPTIMUS TO THE AUTOBOT WE KNEW.
BUT WHY WOULD OPTIMUS WILLFULLY ENDANGER A HUMAN–A CHILD?
I'M NOT A CHILD, MOM.

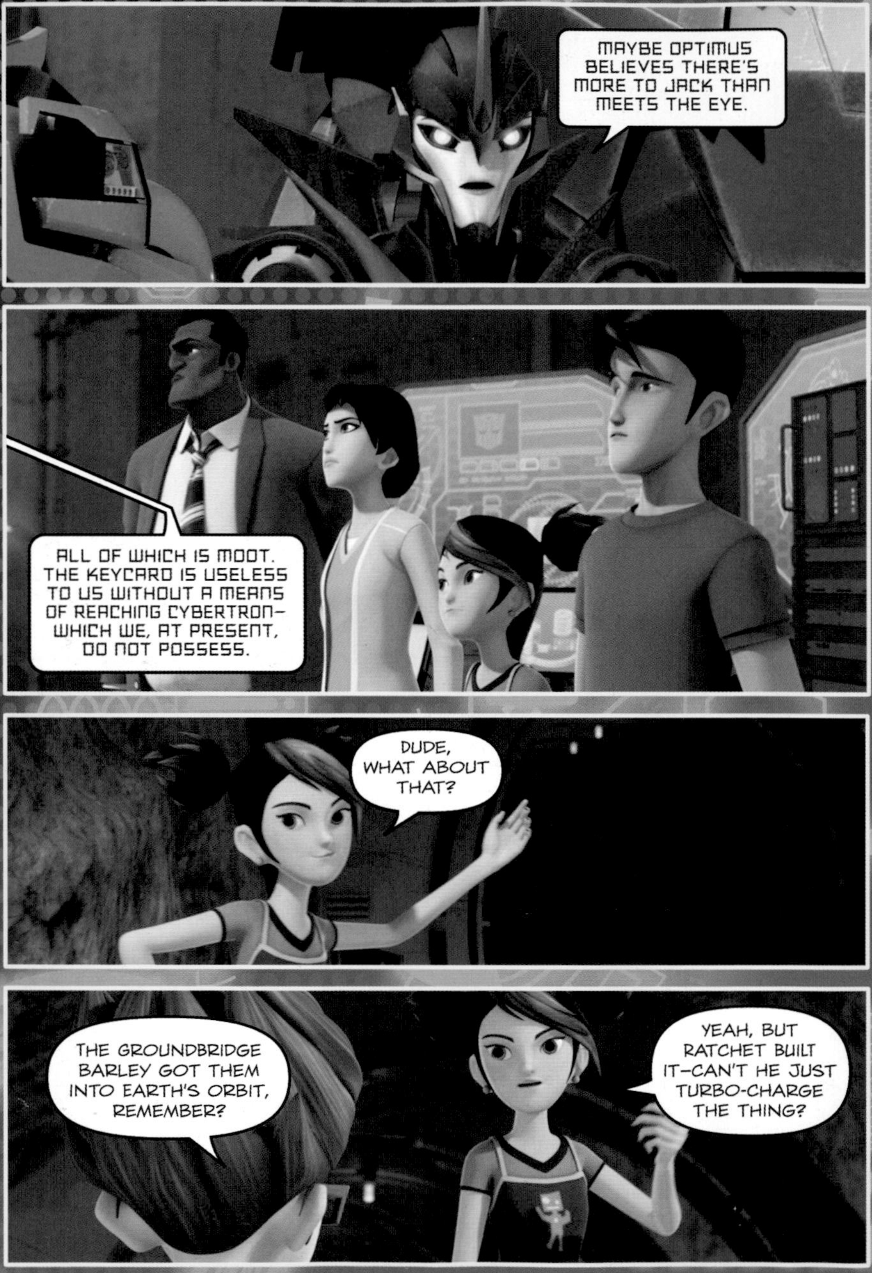
MAYBE OPTIMUS BELIEVES THERE'S MORE TO JACK THAN MEETS THE EYE.
ALL OF WHICH IS MOOT. THE KEYCARD IS USELESS TO US WITHOUT A MEANS OF REACHING CYBERTRON— WHICH WE, AT PRESENT, DO NOT POSSESS.
DUDE, WHAT ABOUT THAT?
THE GROUNDBRIDGE BARLEY GOT THEM INTO EARTH'S ORBIT, REMEMBER?
YEAH, BUT RATCHET BUILT IT—CAN'T HE JUST TURBO-CHARGE THE THING?

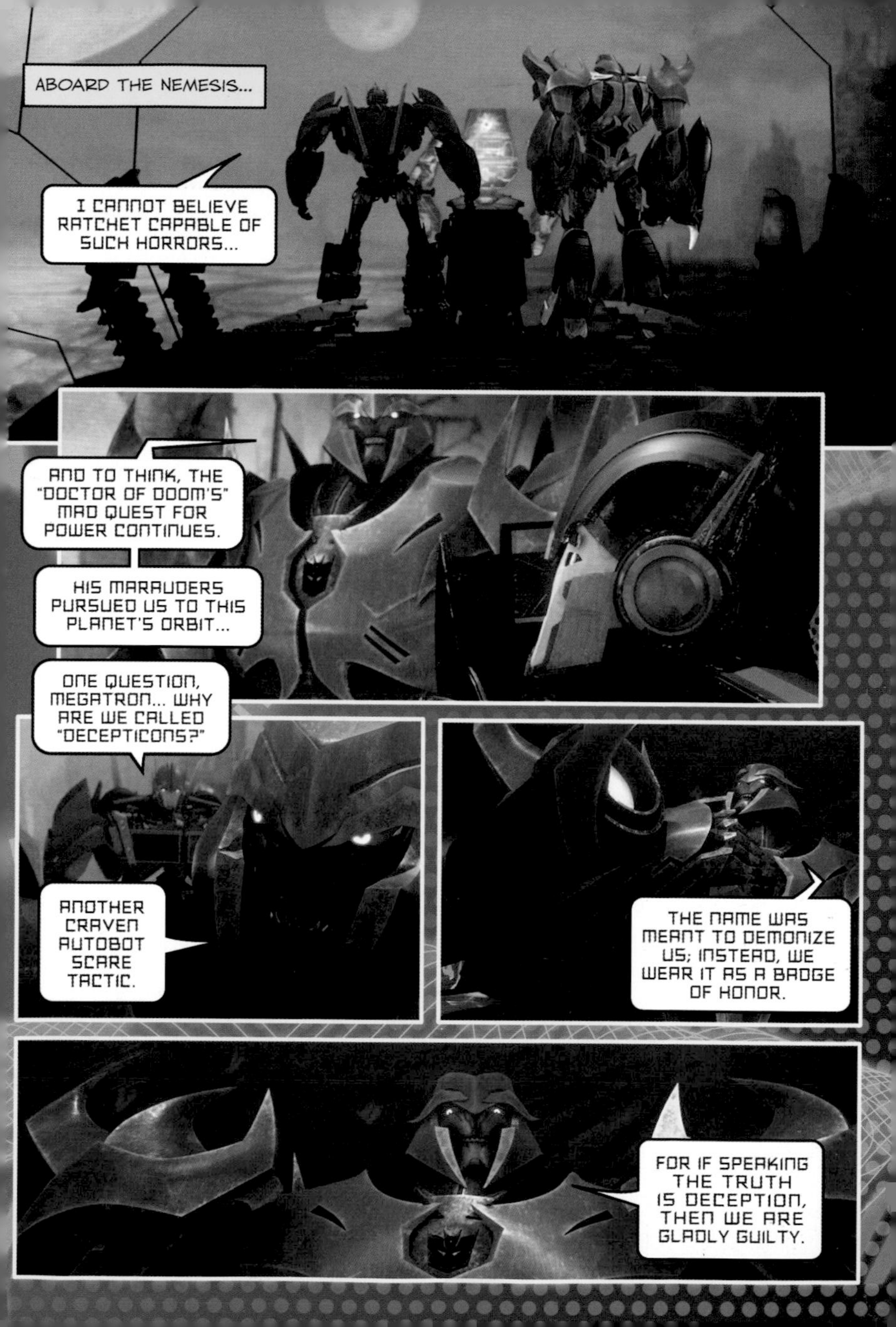
ABOARD THE NEMESIS...
I CANNOT BELIEVE RATCHET CAPABLE OF SUCH HORRORS...
AND TO THINK, THE "DOCTOR OF DOOM'S" MAD QUEST FOR POWER CONTINUES.
HIS MARAUDERS PURSUED US TO THIS PLANET'S ORBIT...
ONE QUESTION, MEGATRON... WHY ARE WE CALLED "DECEPTICONS?"
ANOTHER CRAVEN AUTOBOT SCARE TACTIC.
THE NAME WAS MEANT TO DEMONIZE US; INSTEAD, WE WEAR IT AS A BADGE OF HONOR.
FOR IF SPEAKING THE TRUTH IS DECEPTION, THEN WE ARE GLADLY GUILTY.

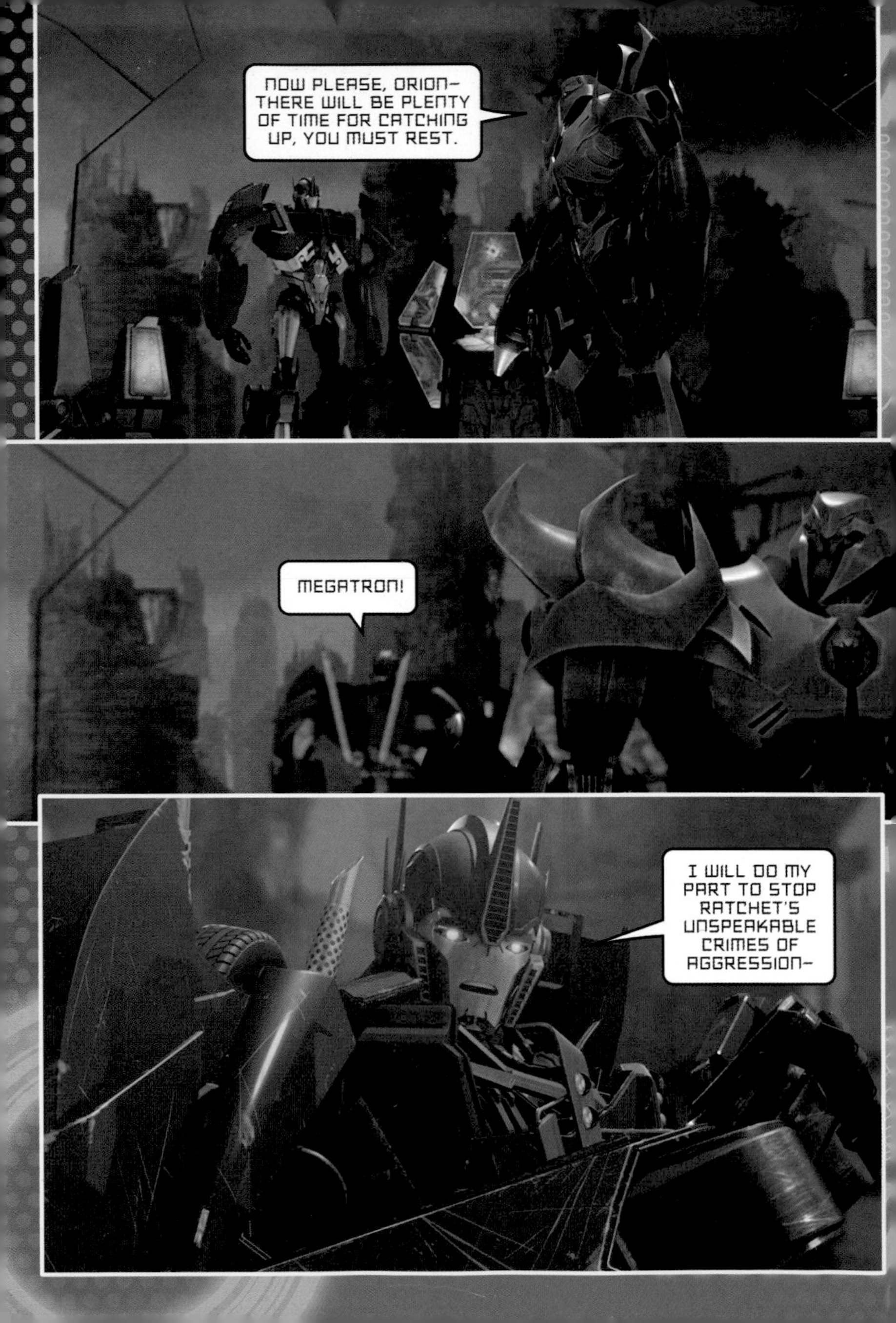
NOW PLEASE, ORION— THERE WILL BE PLENTY OF TIME FOR CATCHING UP, YOU MUST REST.
MEGATRON!
I WILL DO MY PART TO STOP RATCHET'S UNSPEAKABLE CRIMES OF AGGRESSION—

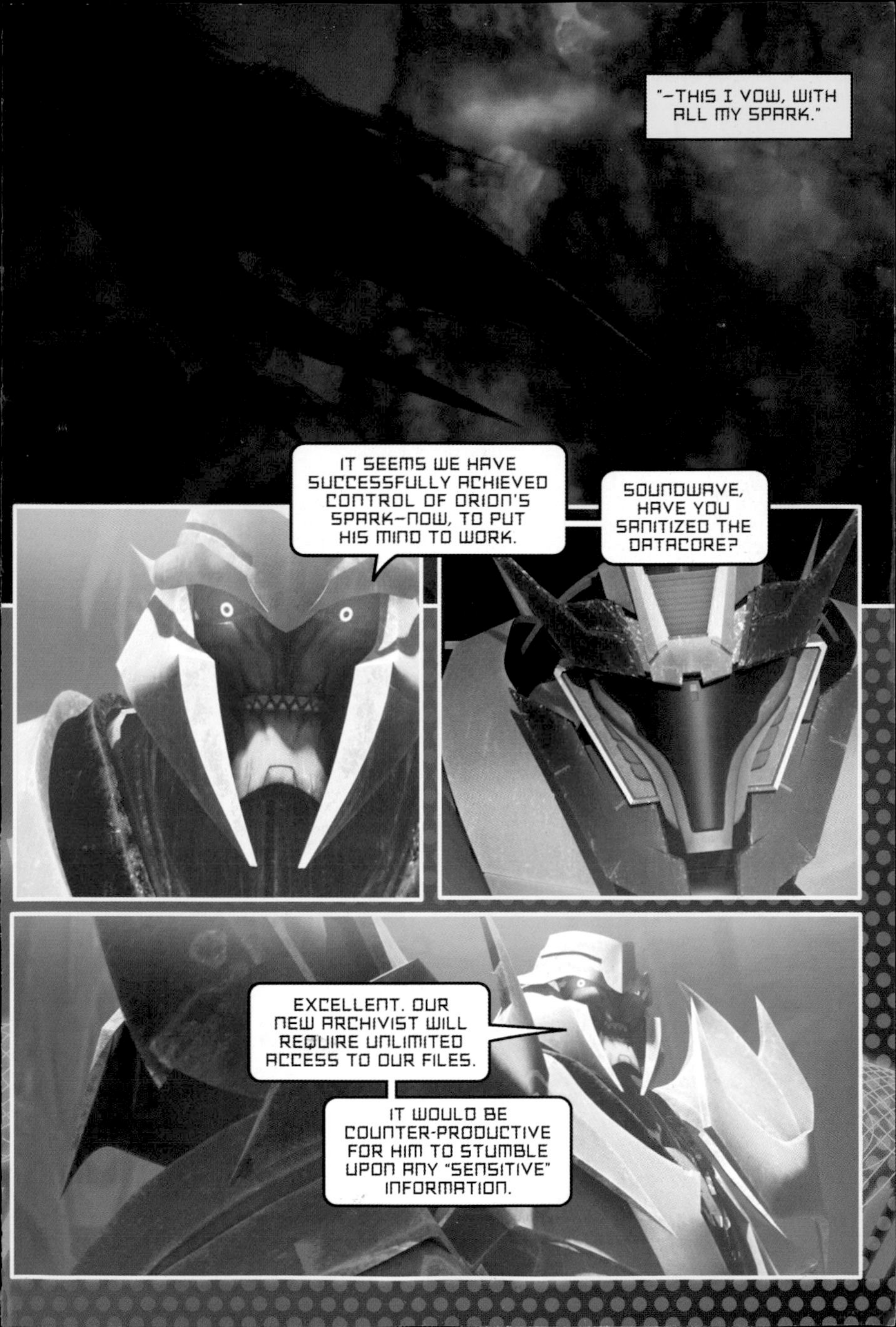
"–THIS I VOW, WITH ALL MY SPARK."
IT SEEMS WE HAVE SUCCESSFULLY ACHIEVED CONTROL OF ORION'S SPARK–NOW, TO PUT HIS MIND TO WORK.
SOUNDWAVE, HAVE YOU SANITIZED THE DATACORE?
EXCELLENT. OUR NEW ARCHIVIST WILL REQUIRE UNLIMITED ACCESS TO OUR FILES.
IT WOULD BE COUNTER-PRODUCTIVE FOR HIM TO STUMBLE UPON ANY "SENSITIVE" INFORMATION.

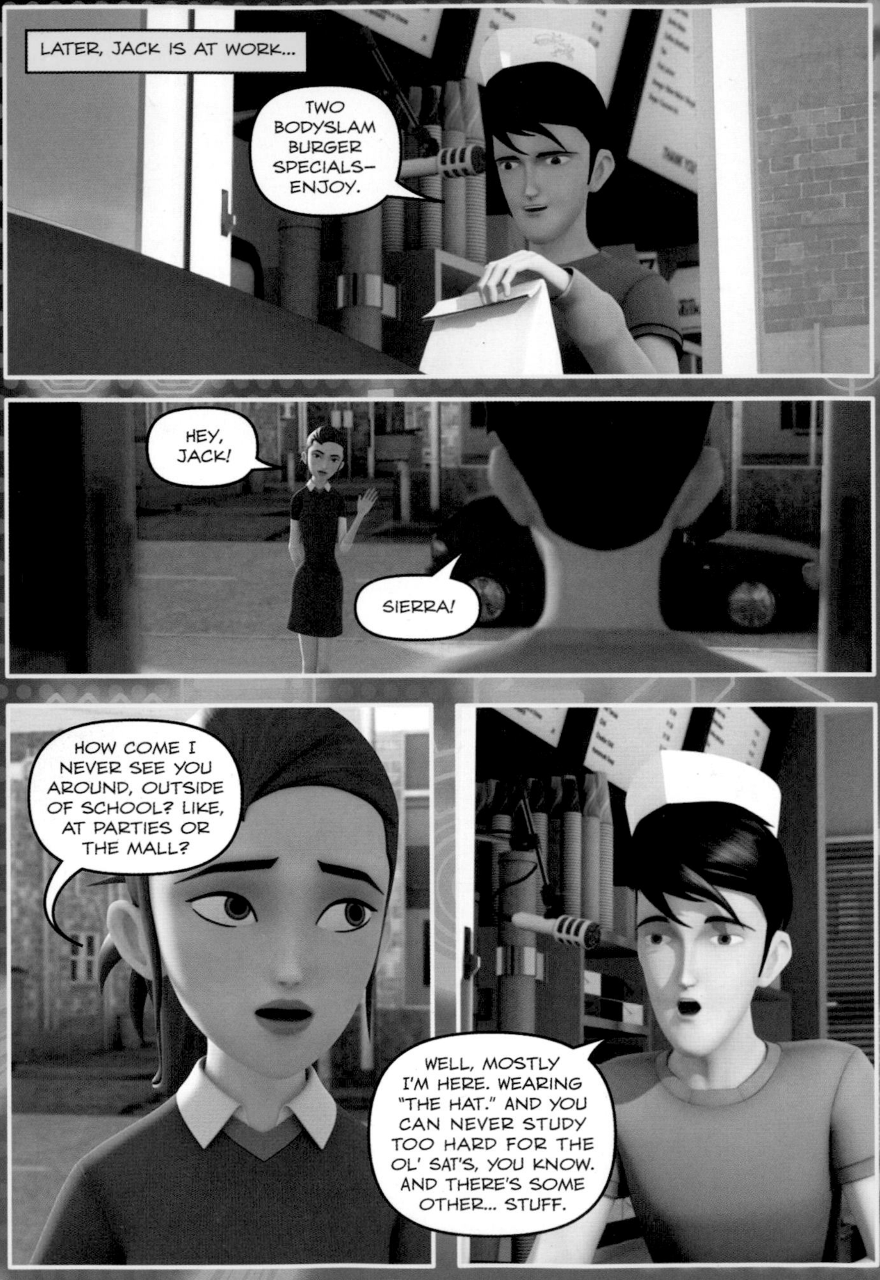
LATER, JACK IS AT WORK...
TWO BODYSLAM BURGER SPECIALS— ENJOY.
HEY, JACK!
SIERRA!
HOW COME I NEVER SEE YOU AROUND, OUTSIDE OF SCHOOL? LIKE, AT PARTIES OR THE MALL?
WELL, MOSTLY I'M HERE. WEARING "THE HAT." AND YOU CAN NEVER STUDY TOO HARD FOR THE OL' SAT'S, YOU KNOW. AND THERE'S SOME OTHER... STUFF.

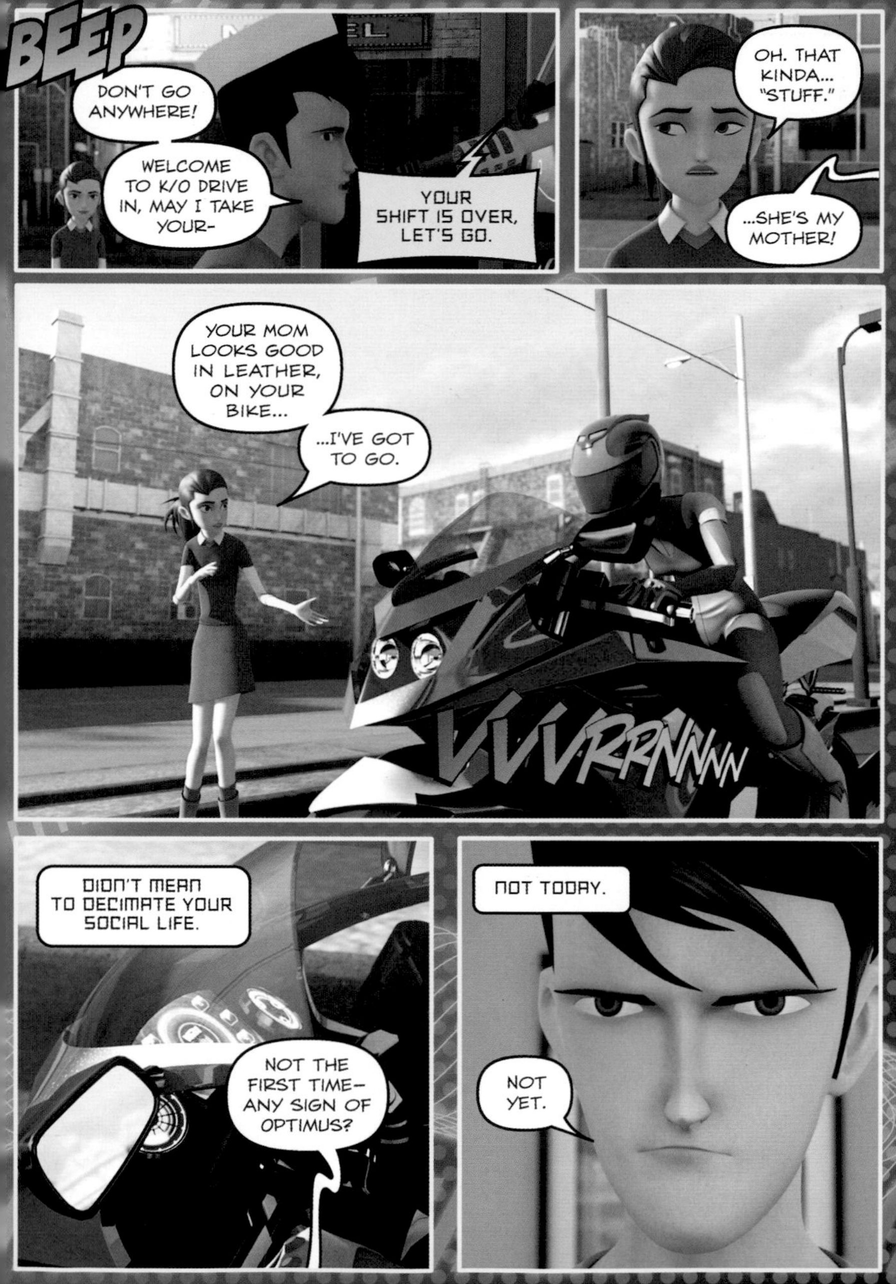
BEEP
DON'T GO ANYWHERE!
WELCOME TO K/O DRIVE IN, MAY I TAKE YOUR-
YOUR SHIFT IS OVER, LET'S GO.
OH. THAT KINDA... "STUFF."
...SHE'S MY MOTHER!
YOUR MOM LOOKS GOOD IN LEATHER, ON YOUR BIKE...
...I'VE GOT TO GO.
VVVRRNNNN
DIDN'T MEAN TO DECIMATE YOUR SOCIAL LIFE.
NOT THE FIRST TIME-ANY SIGN OF OPTIMUS?
NOT TODAY.
NOT YET.

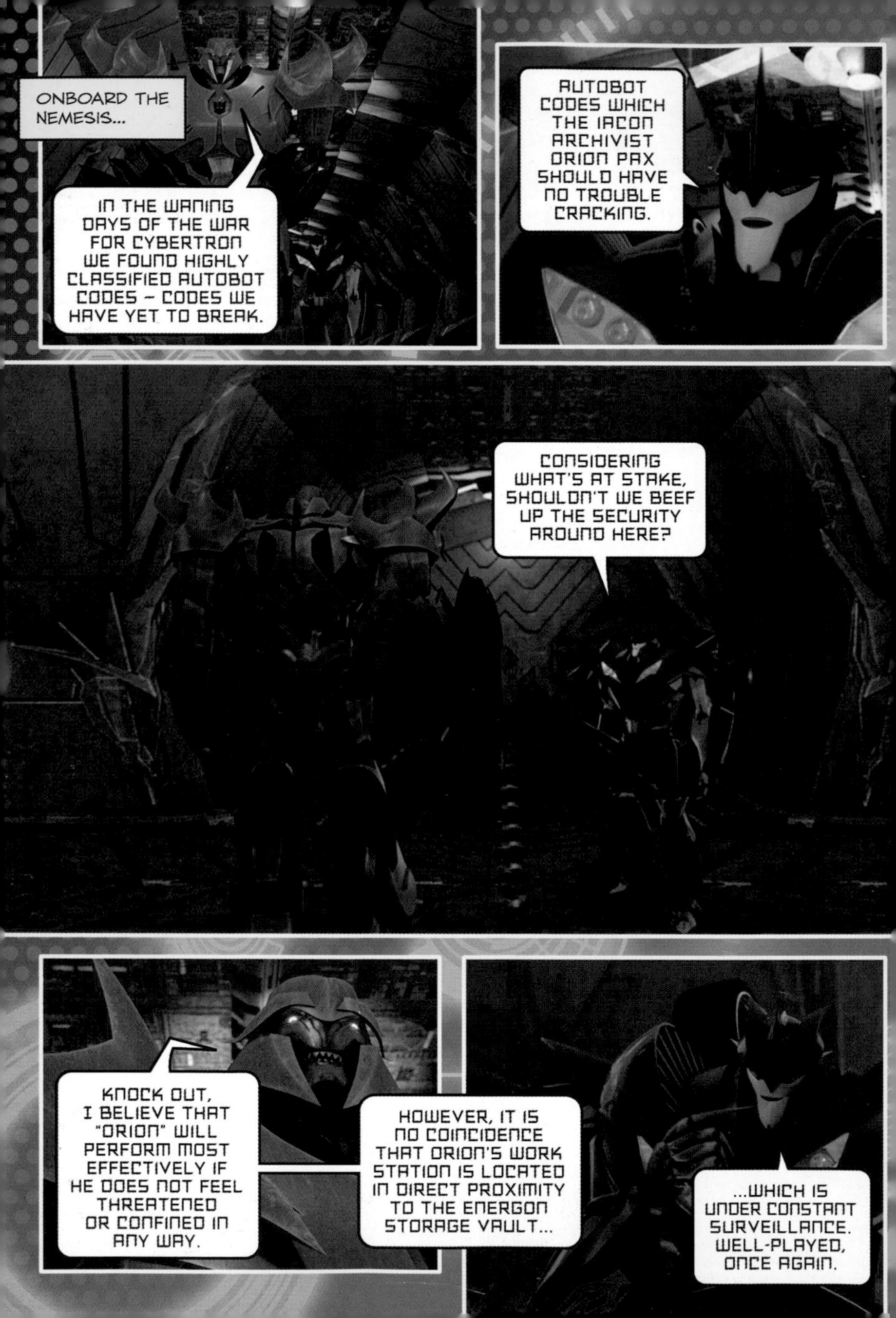
ONBOARD THE NEMESIS...
IN THE WANING DAYS OF THE WAR FOR CYBERTRON WE FOUND HIGHLY CLASSIFIED AUTOBOT CODES – CODES WE HAVE YET TO BREAK.
AUTOBOT CODES WHICH THE IACON ARCHIVIST ORION PAX SHOULD HAVE NO TROUBLE CRACKING.
CONSIDERING WHAT'S AT STAKE, SHOULDN'T WE BEEF UP THE SECURITY AROUND HERE?
KNOCK OUT, I BELIEVE THAT "ORION" WILL PERFORM MOST EFFECTIVELY IF HE DOES NOT FEEL THREATENED OR CONFINED IN ANY WAY.
HOWEVER, IT IS NO COINCIDENCE THAT ORION'S WORK STATION IS LOCATED IN DIRECT PROXIMITY TO THE ENERGON STORAGE VAULT...
...WHICH IS UNDER CONSTANT SURVEILLANCE. WELL-PLAYED, ONCE AGAIN.

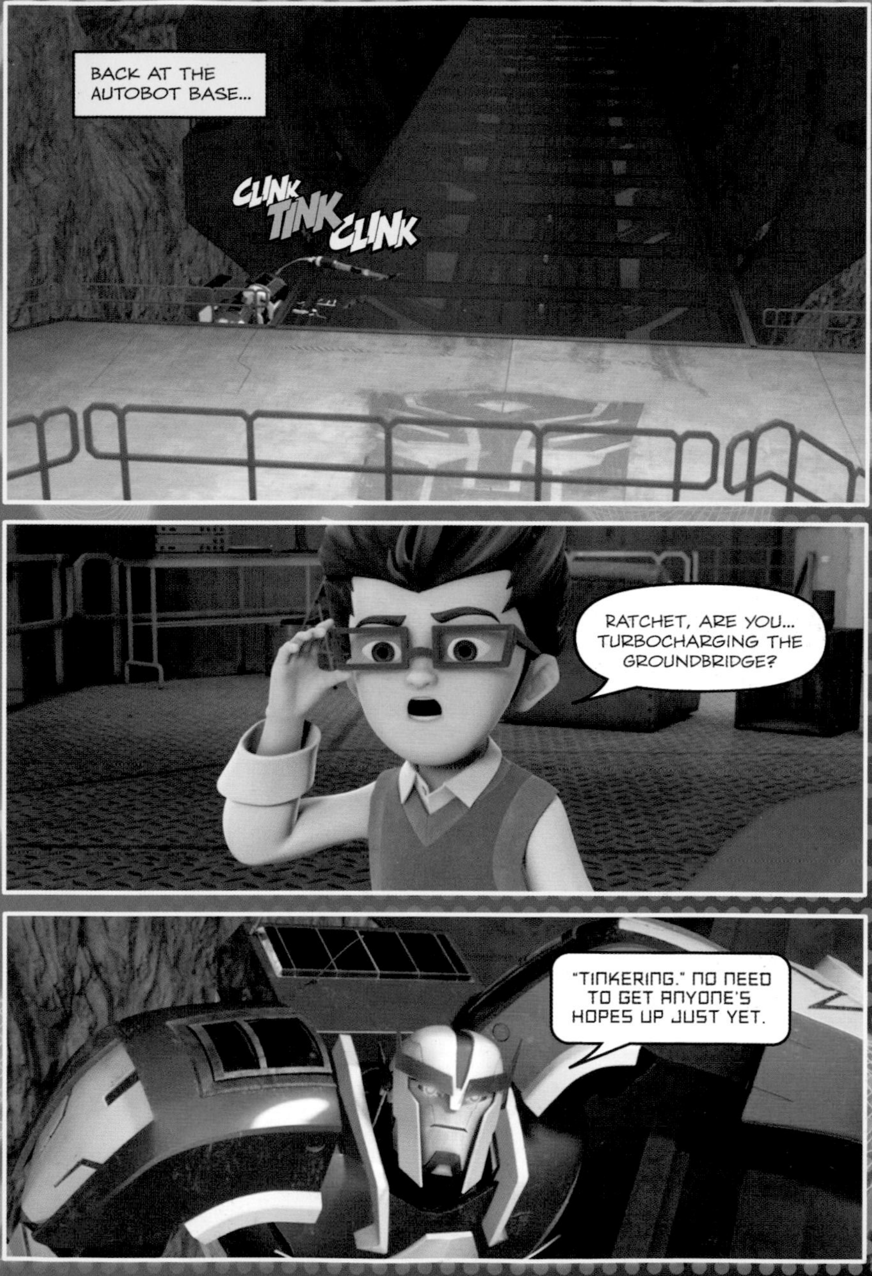
BACK AT THE AUTOBOT BASE...
CLINK TINK CLINK
RATCHET, ARE YOU... TURBOCHARGING THE GROUNDBRIDGE?
"TINKERING." NO NEED TO GET ANYONE'S HOPES UP JUST YET.

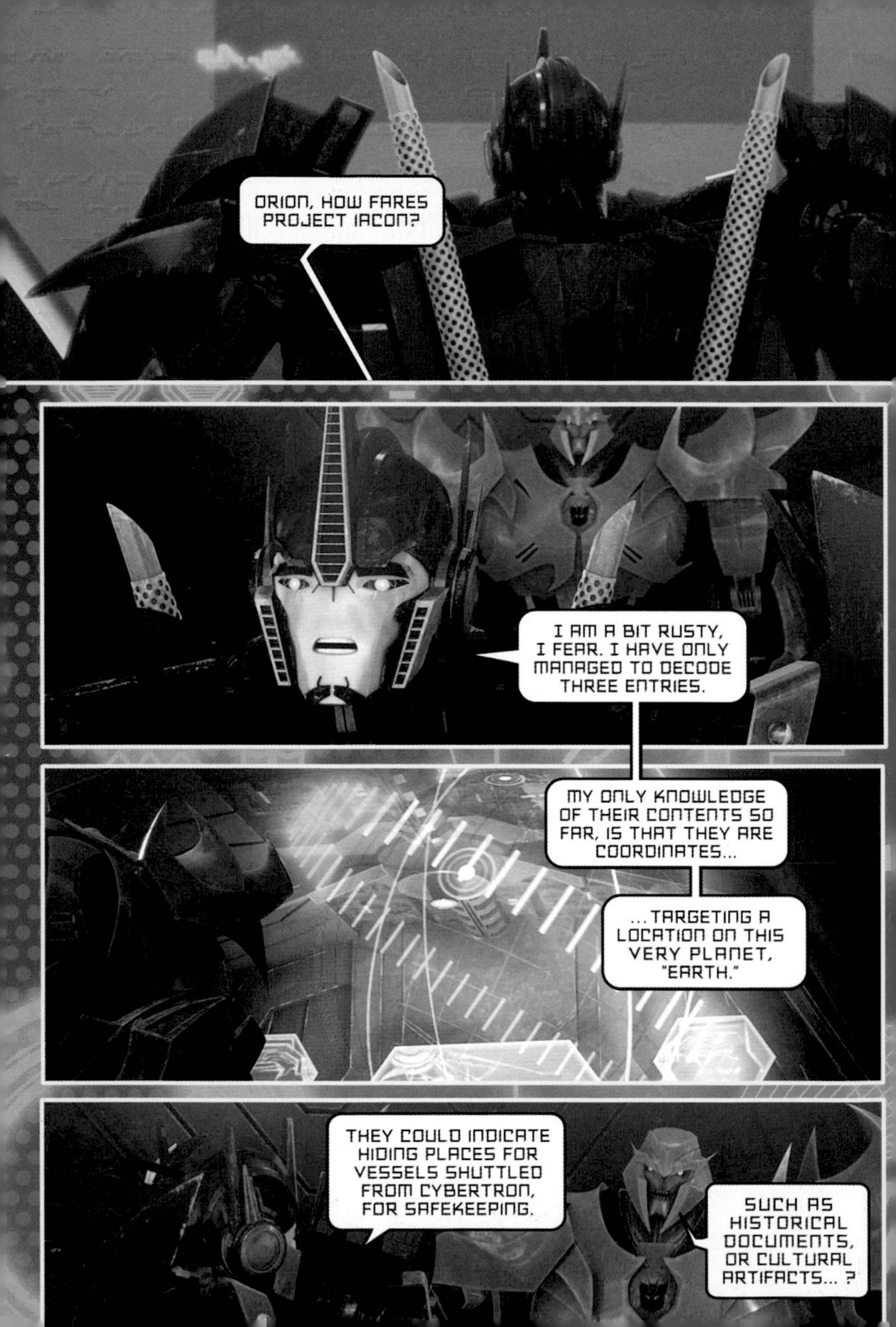
ORION, HOW FARES PROJECT IACON?
I AM A BIT RUSTY, I FEAR. I HAVE ONLY MANAGED TO DECODE THREE ENTRIES.
MY ONLY KNOWLEDGE OF THEIR CONTENTS SO FAR, IS THAT THEY ARE COORDINATES...
...TARGETING A LOCATION ON THIS VERY PLANET, "EARTH."
THEY COULD INDICATE HIDING PLACES FOR VESSELS SHUTTLED FROM CYBERTRON, FOR SAFEKEEPING.
SUCH AS HISTORICAL DOCUMENTS, OR CULTURAL ARTIFACTS... ?

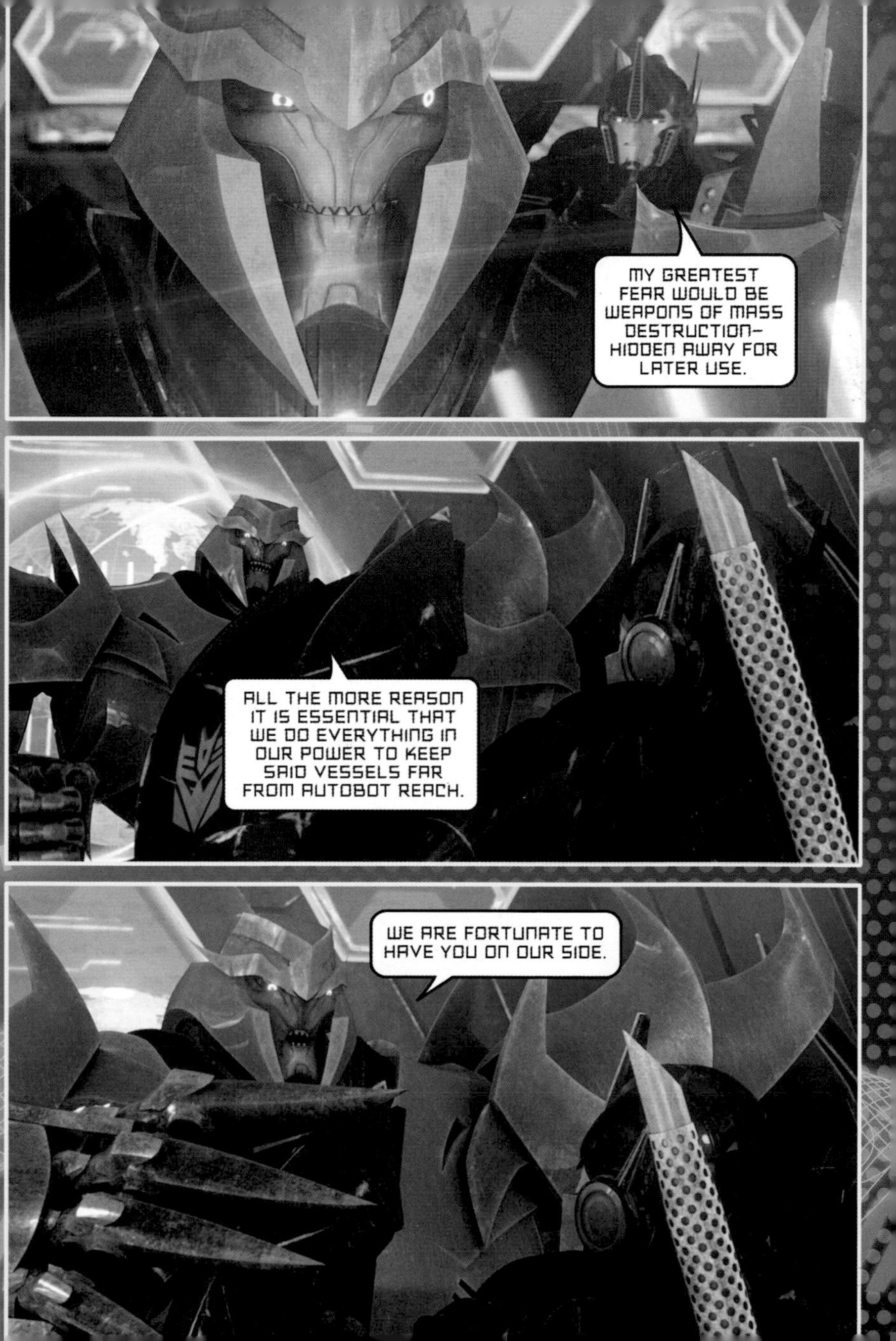
MY GREATEST FEAR WOULD BE WEAPONS OF MASS DESTRUCTION–HIDDEN AWAY FOR LATER USE.
ALL THE MORE REASON IT IS ESSENTIAL THAT WE DO EVERYTHING IN OUR POWER TO KEEP SAID VESSELS FAR FROM AUTOBOT REACH.
WE ARE FORTUNATE TO HAVE YOU ON OUR SIDE.

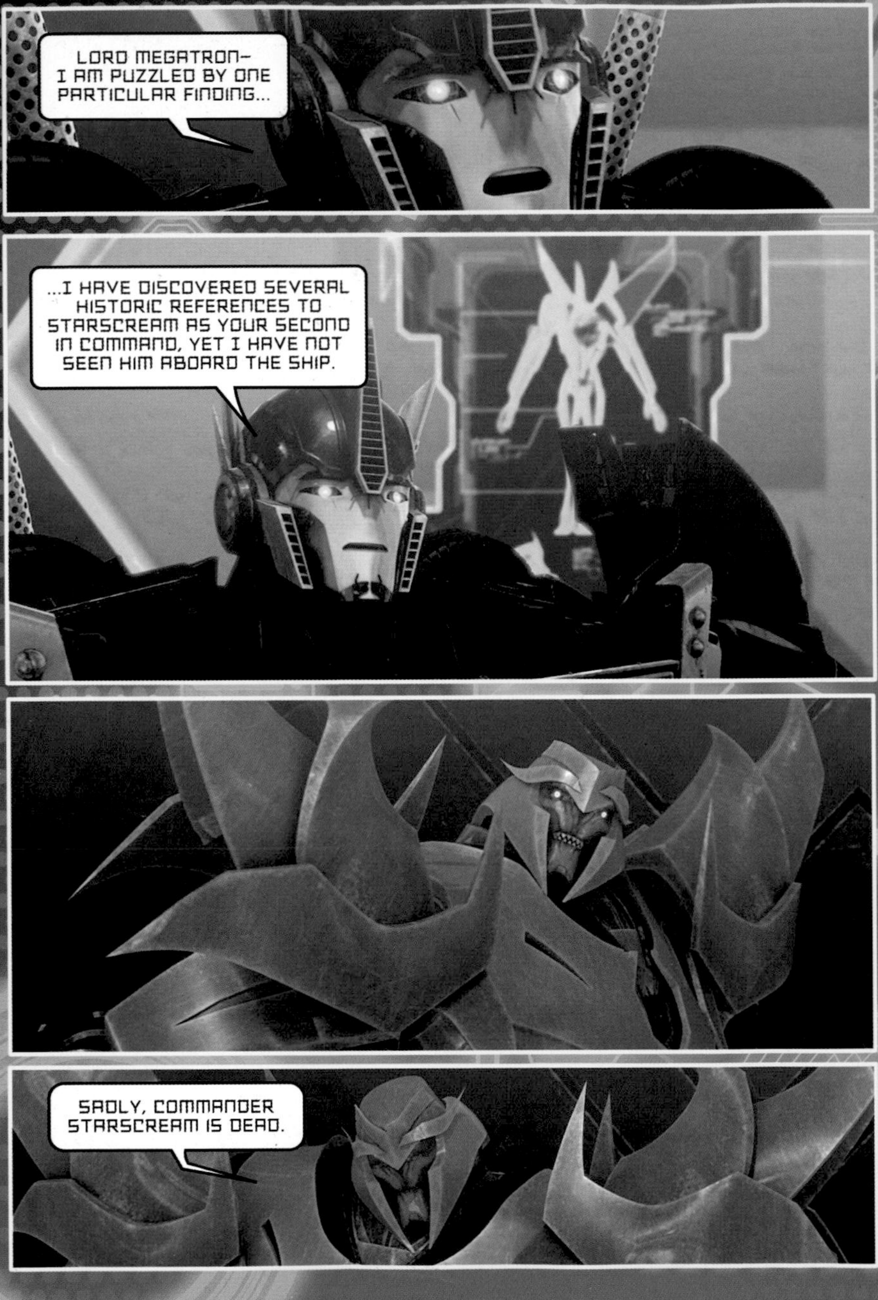
LORD MEGATRON– I AM PUZZLED BY ONE PARTICULAR FINDING...
...I HAVE DISCOVERED SEVERAL HISTORIC REFERENCES TO STARSCREAM AS YOUR SECOND IN COMMAND, YET I HAVE NOT SEEN HIM ABOARD THE SHIP.
SADLY, COMMANDER STARSCREAM IS DEAD.

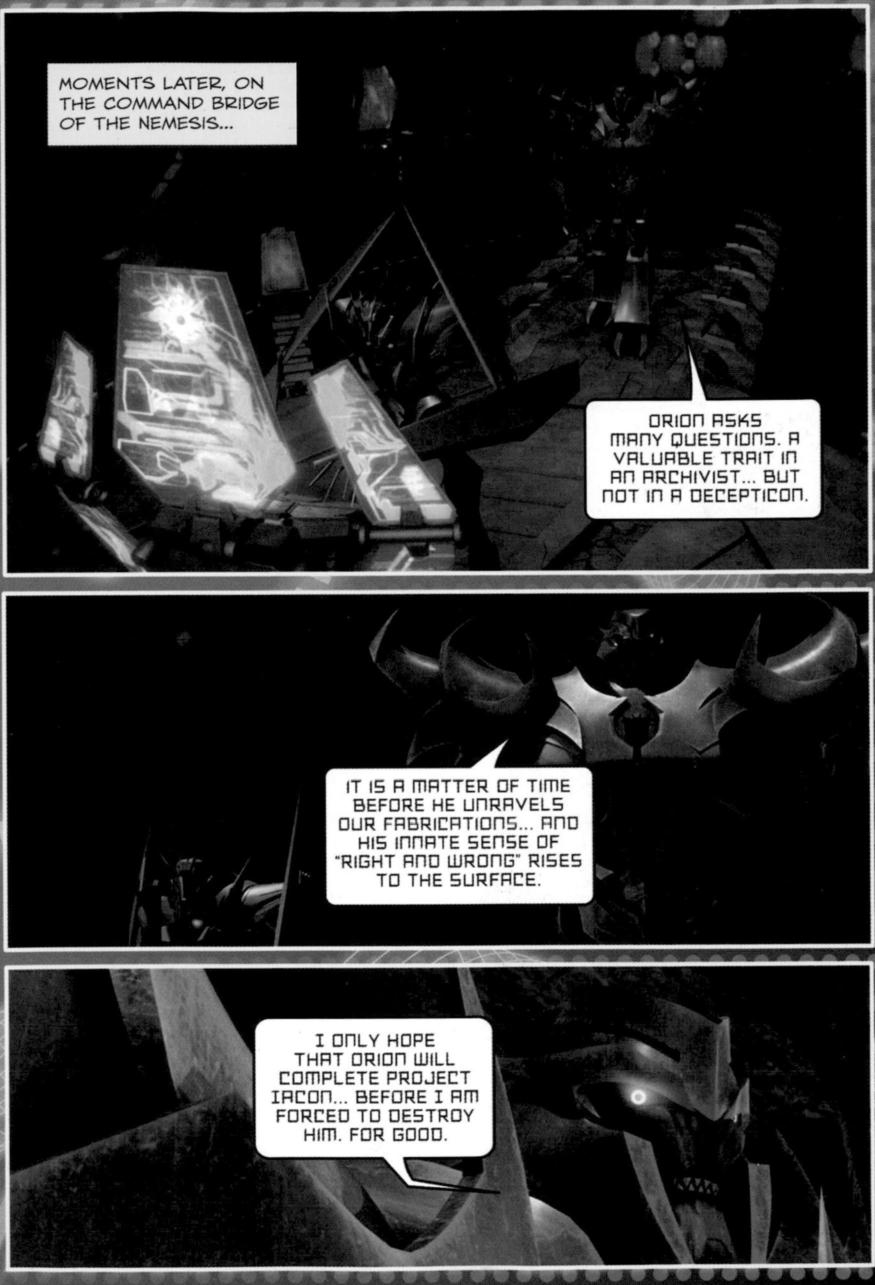
MOMENTS LATER, ON THE COMMAND BRIDGE OF THE NEMESIS...
ORION ASKS MANY QUESTIONS. A VALUABLE TRAIT IN AN ARCHIVIST... BUT NOT IN A DECEPTICON.
IT IS A MATTER OF TIME BEFORE HE UNRAVELS OUR FABRICATIONS... AND HIS INNATE SENSE OF "RIGHT AND WRONG" RISES TO THE SURFACE.
I ONLY HOPE THAT ORION WILL COMPLETE PROJECT IACON... BEFORE I AM FORCED TO DESTROY HIM. FOR GOOD.

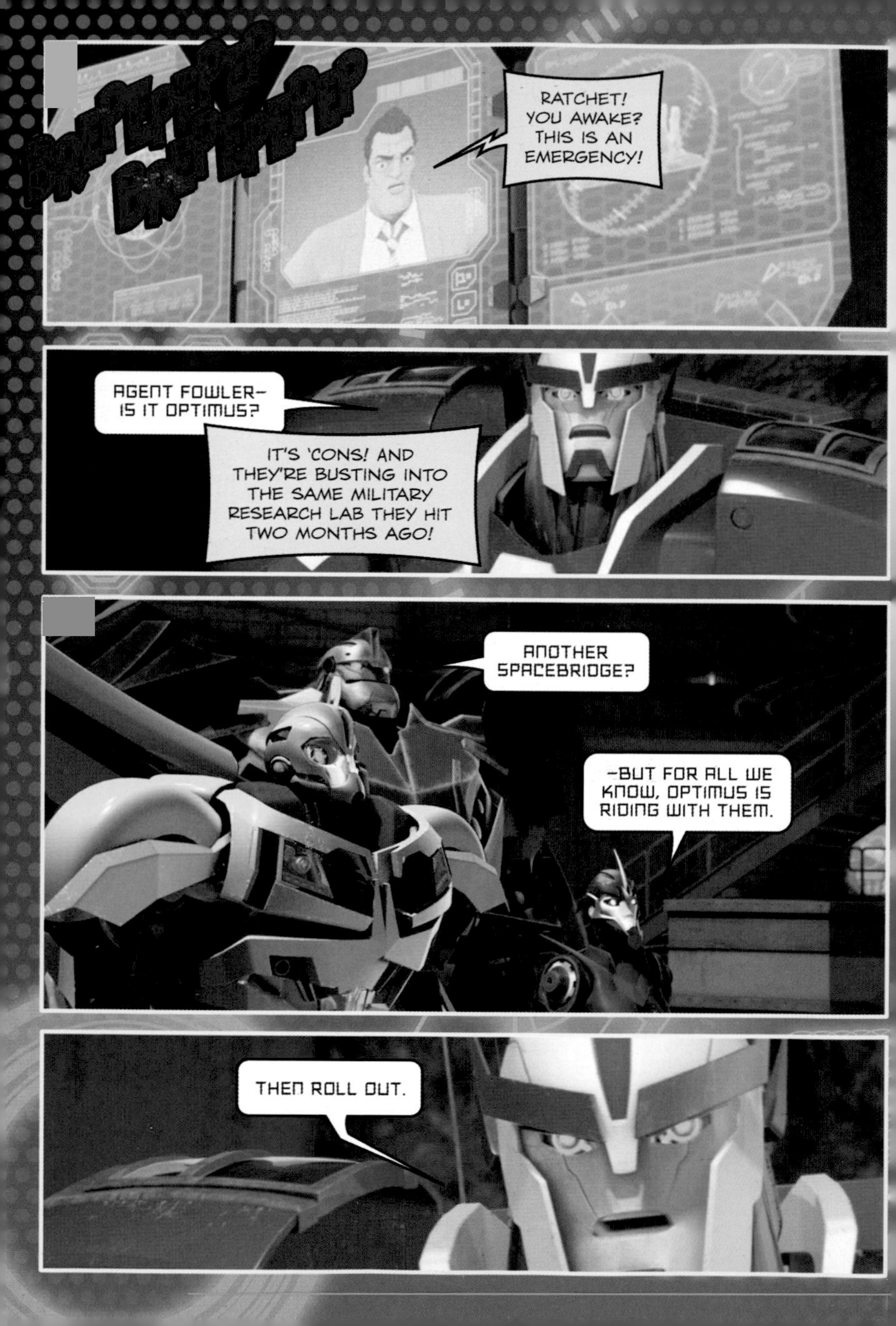

RATCHET! YOU AWAKE? THIS IS AN EMERGENCY!
AGENT FOWLER— IS IT OPTIMUS?
IT'S 'CONS! AND THEY'RE BUSTING INTO THE SAME MILITARY RESEARCH LAB THEY HIT TWO MONTHS AGO!
ANOTHER SPACEBRIDGE?
—BUT FOR ALL WE KNOW, OPTIMUS IS RIDING WITH THEM.
THEN ROLL OUT.

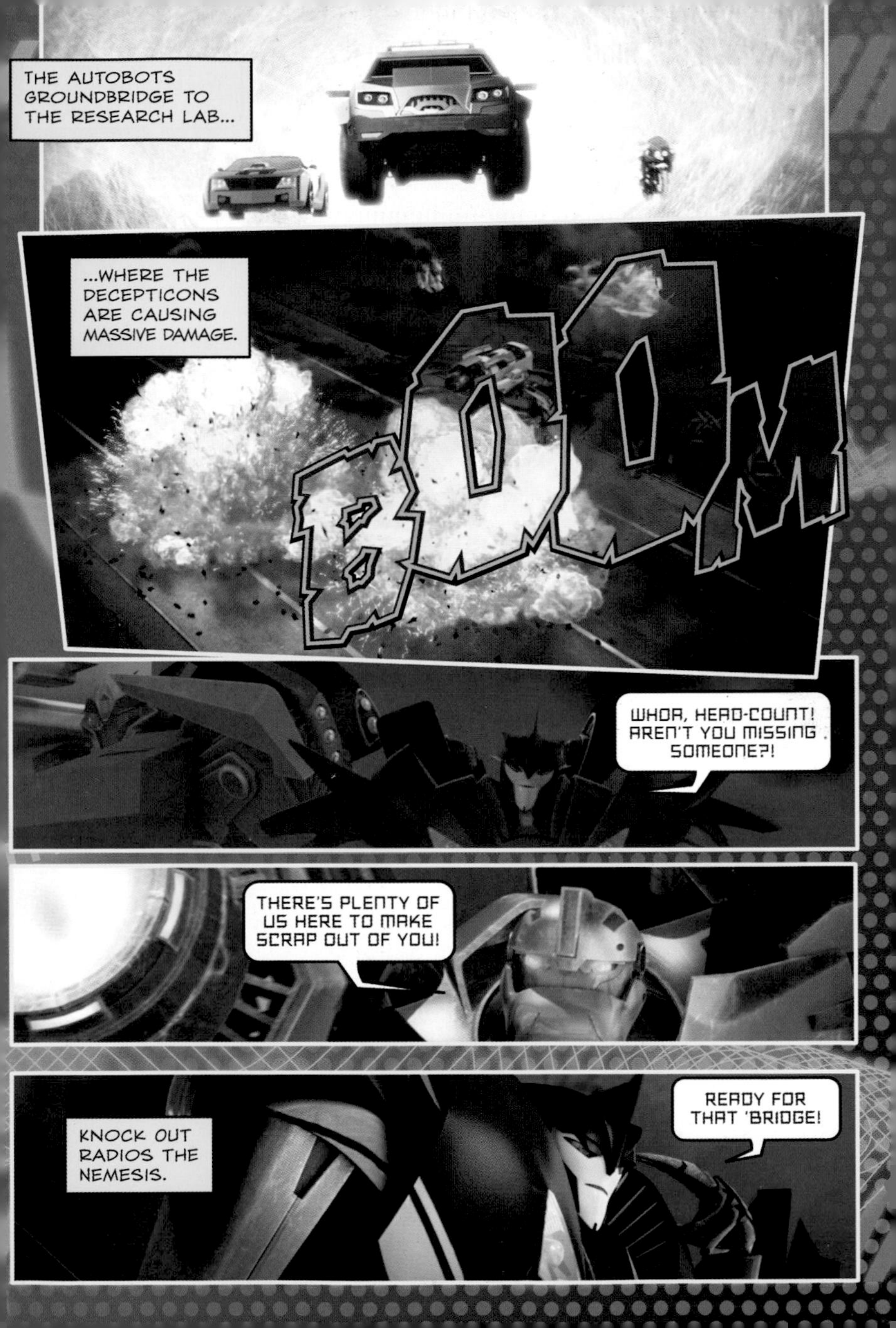
THE AUTOBOTS GROUNDBRIDGE TO THE RESEARCH LAB...
...WHERE THE DECEPTICONS ARE CAUSING MASSIVE DAMAGE.
BOOM
WHOA, HEAD-COUNT! AREN'T YOU MISSING SOMEONE?!
THERE'S PLENTY OF US HERE TO MAKE SCRAP OUT OF YOU!
KNOCK OUT RADIOS THE NEMESIS.
READY FOR THAT 'BRIDGE!

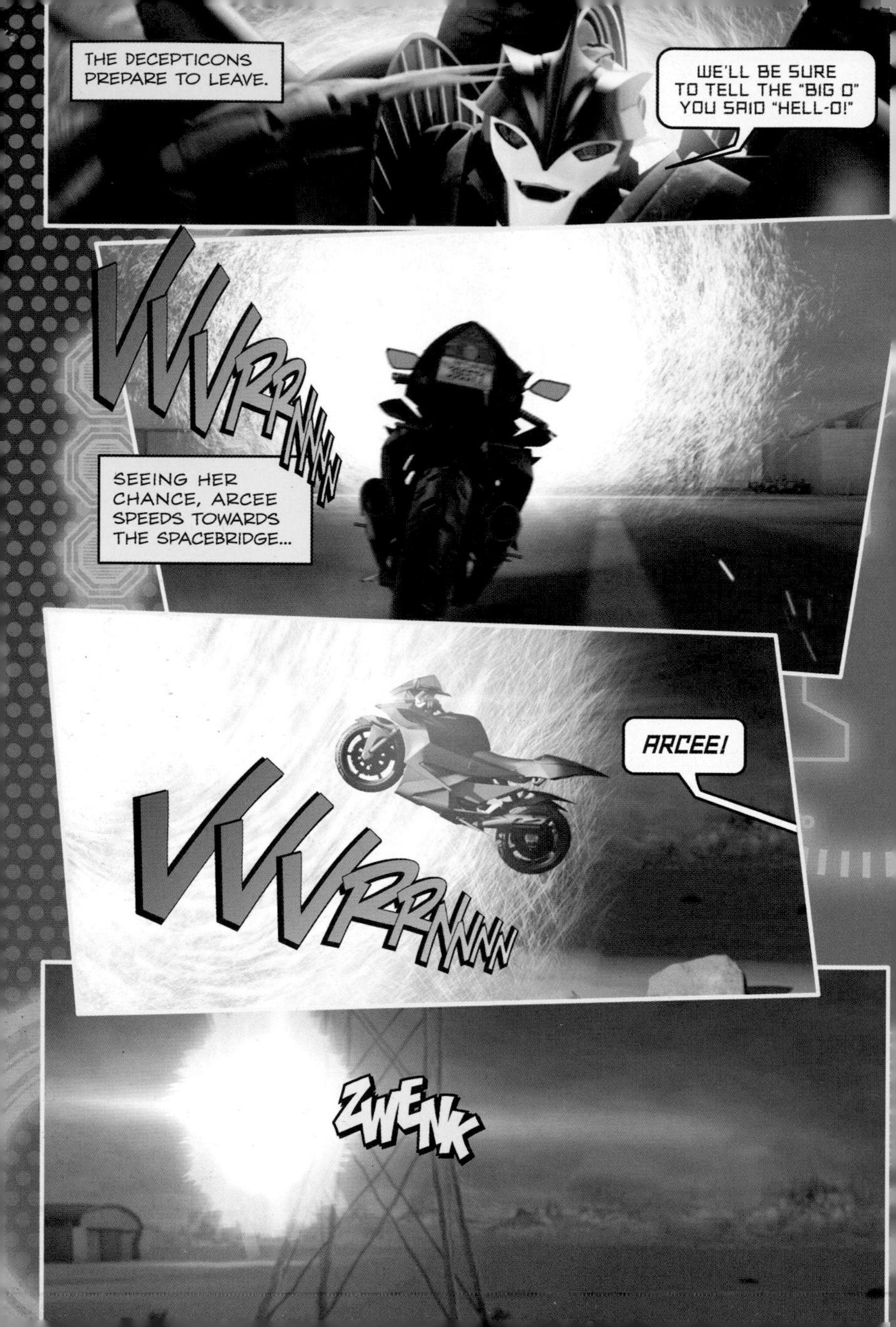
THE DECEPTICONS PREPARE TO LEAVE.
WE'LL BE SURE TO TELL THE "BIG O" YOU SAID "HELL-O!"
VVVRRRNNNN
SEEING HER CHANCE, ARCEE SPEEDS TOWARDS THE SPACEBRIDGE...
ARCEE!
VVVRRRNNNN
ZWENK

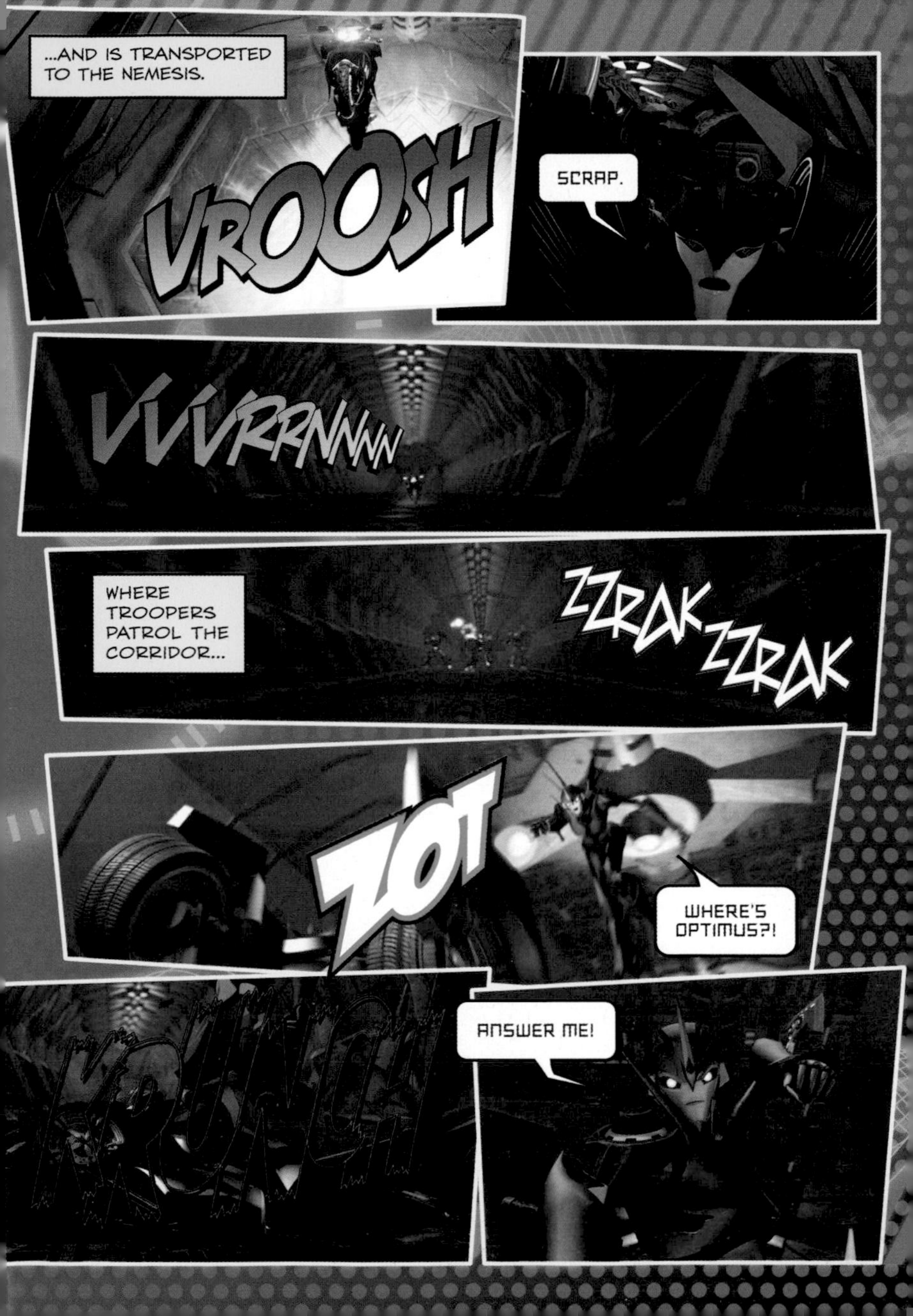
...AND IS TRANSPORTED TO THE NEMESIS.
VROOSH
SCRAP.
VVVRRNNNN
WHERE TROOPERS PATROL THE CORRIDOR...
ZZRAK ZZRAK
ZOT
WHERE'S OPTIMUS?!
ANSWER ME!

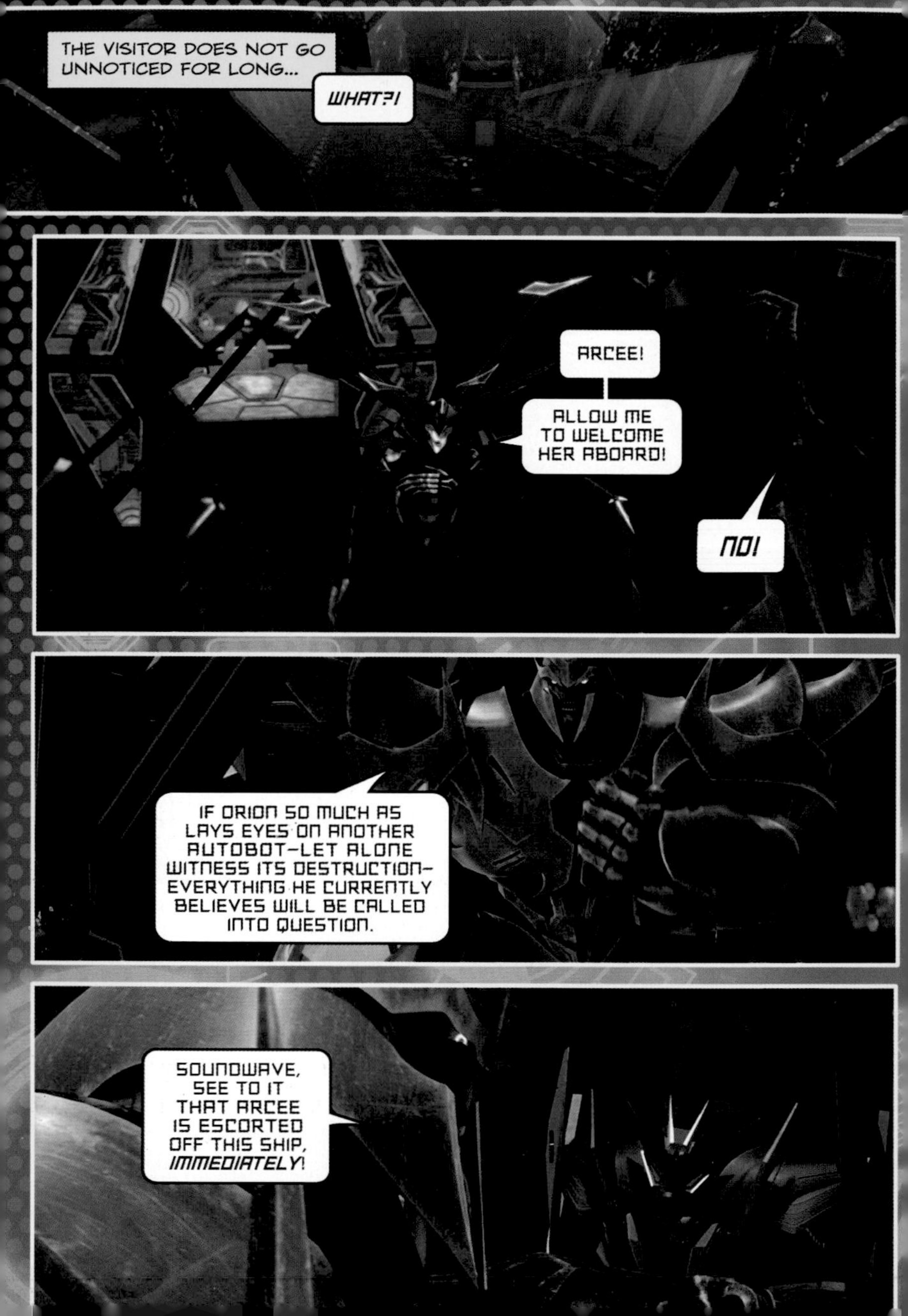
THE VISITOR DOES NOT GO UNNOTICED FOR LONG...
WHAT?!
ARCEE!
ALLOW ME TO WELCOME HER ABOARD!
NO!
IF ORION SO MUCH AS LAYS EYES ON ANOTHER AUTOBOT—LET ALONE WITNESS ITS DESTRUCTION—EVERYTHING HE CURRENTLY BELIEVES WILL BE CALLED INTO QUESTION.
SOUNDWAVE, SEE TO IT THAT ARCEE IS ESCORTED OFF THIS SHIP, *IMMEDIATELY*!

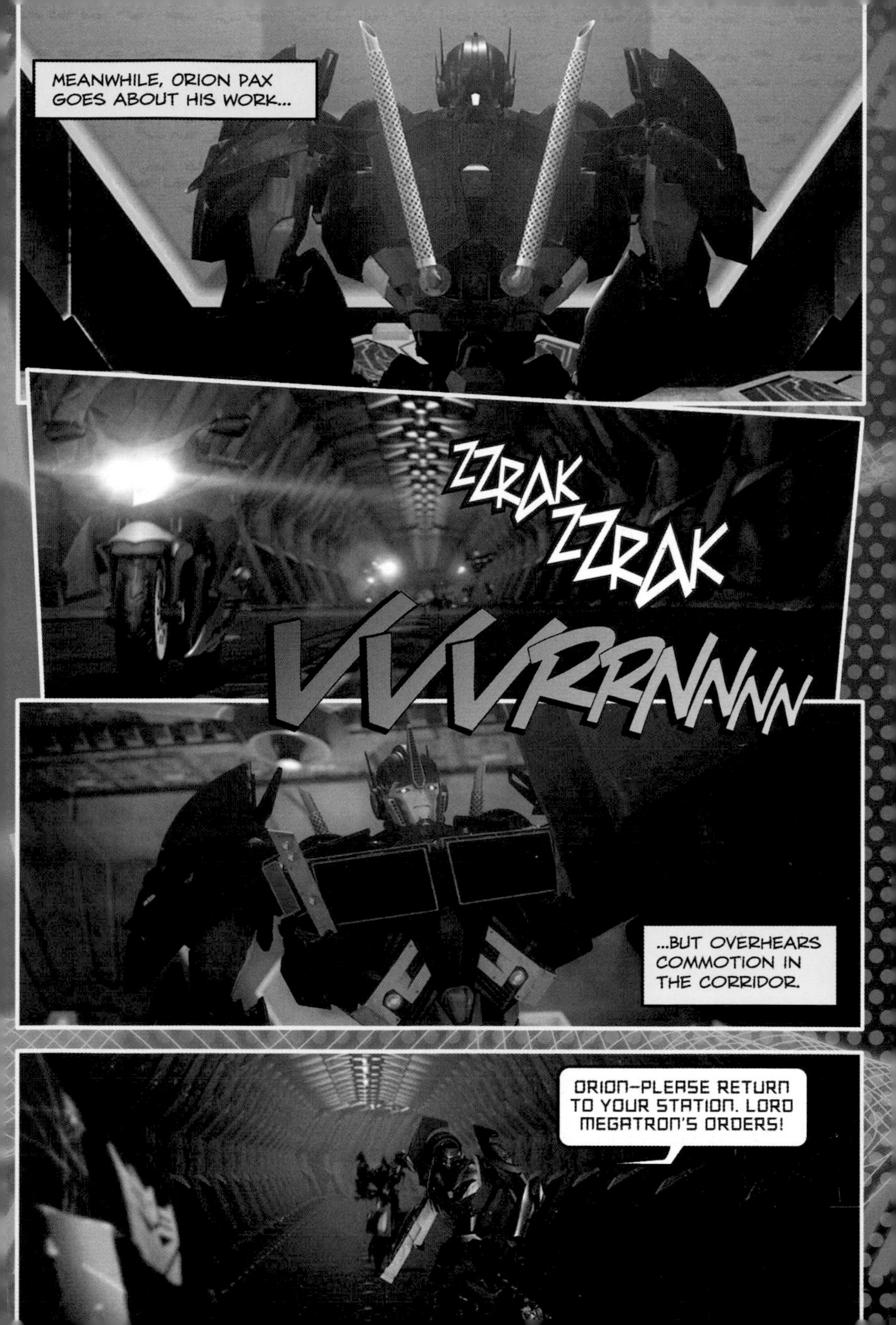
MEANWHILE, ORION PAX GOES ABOUT HIS WORK...
ZZRAK ZZRAK
VVVRRNNNN
...BUT OVERHEARS COMMOTION IN THE CORRIDOR.
ORION—PLEASE RETURN TO YOUR STATION. LORD MEGATRON'S ORDERS!

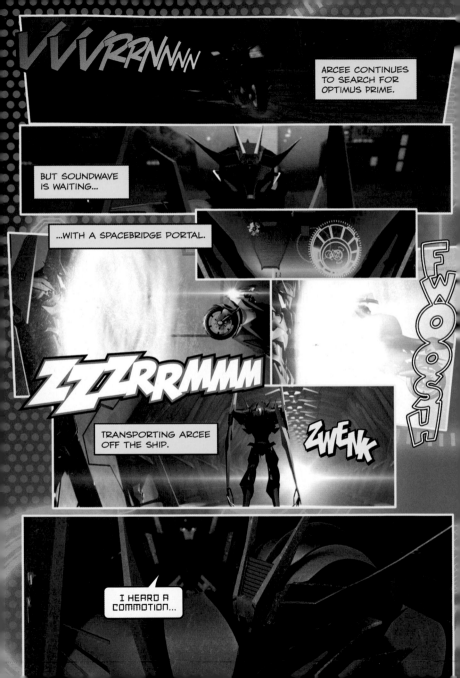

VVVRRNNnn

ARCEE CONTINUES TO SEARCH FOR OPTIMUS PRIME.

BUT SOUNDWAVE IS WAITING...

...WITH A SPACEBRIDGE PORTAL.

FWOOSH

ZZZRrMMM

TRANSPORTING ARCEE OFF THE SHIP.

ZWENK

I HEARD A COMMOTION...

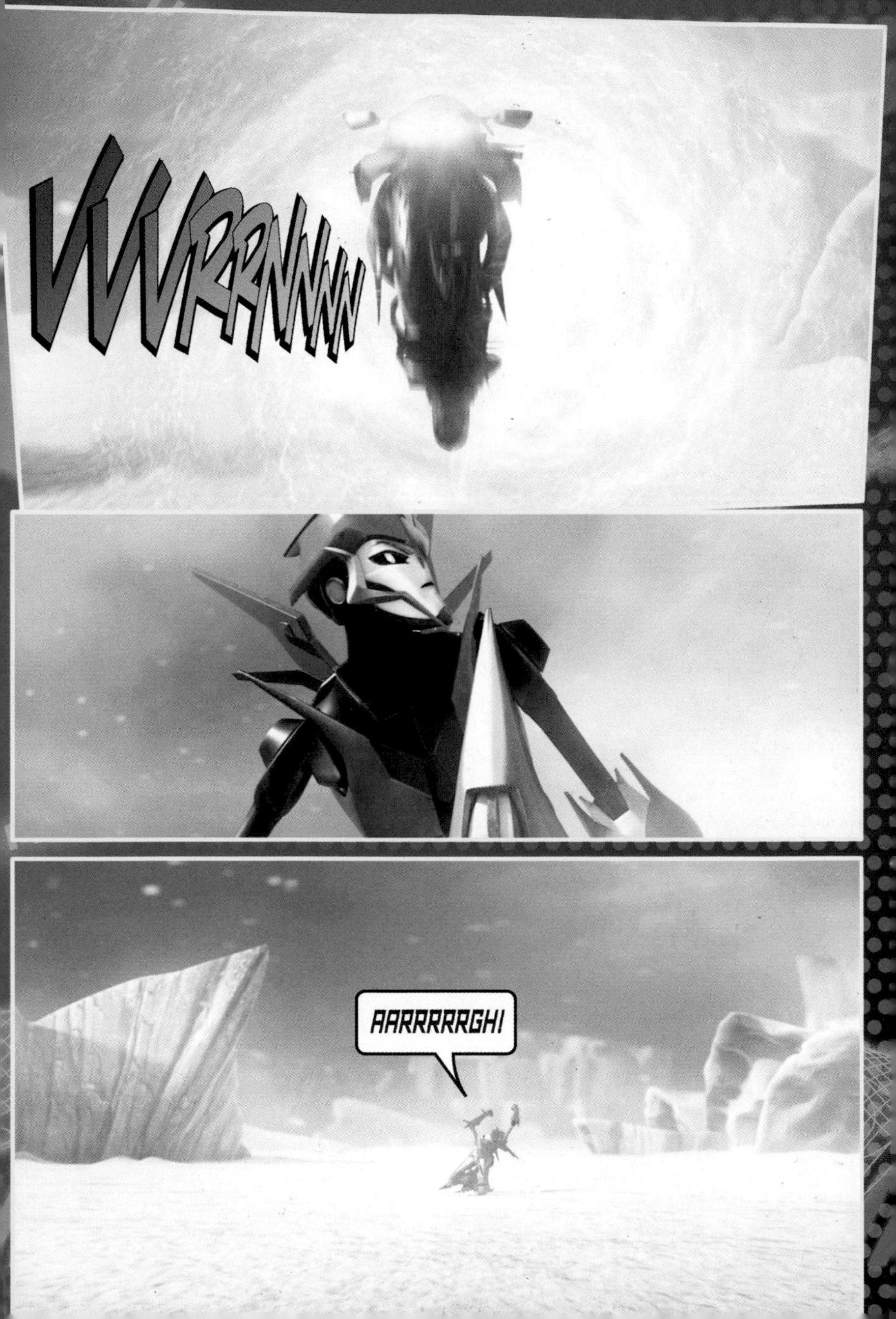

VVVRRNNNN
AARRRRRGH!

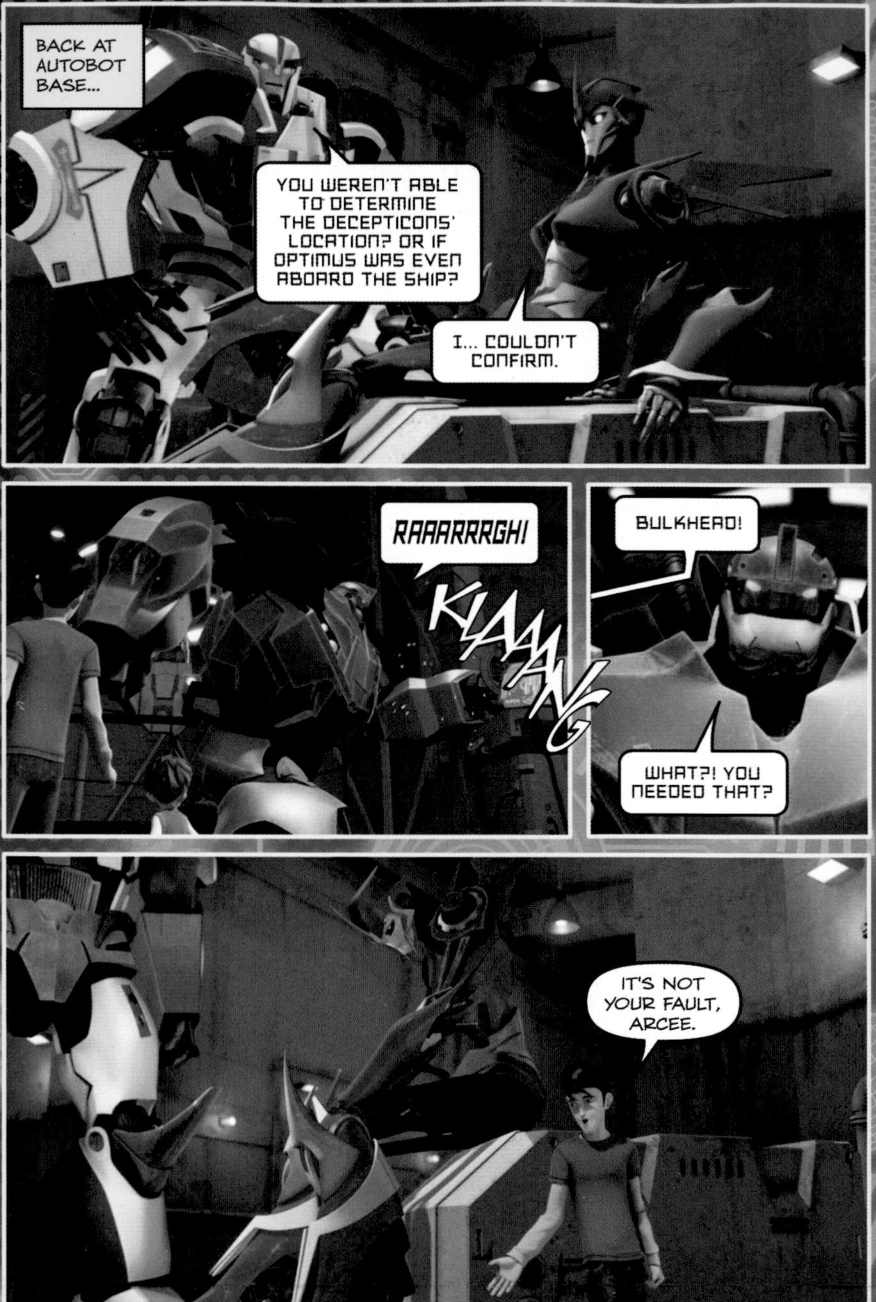
BACK AT AUTOBOT BASE...
YOU WEREN'T ABLE TO DETERMINE THE DECEPTICONS' LOCATION? OR IF OPTIMUS WAS EVEN ABOARD THE SHIP?
I... COULDN'T CONFIRM.
RAAARRRGH!
KLAAANG
BULKHEAD!
WHAT?! YOU NEEDED THAT?
IT'S NOT YOUR FAULT, ARCEE.

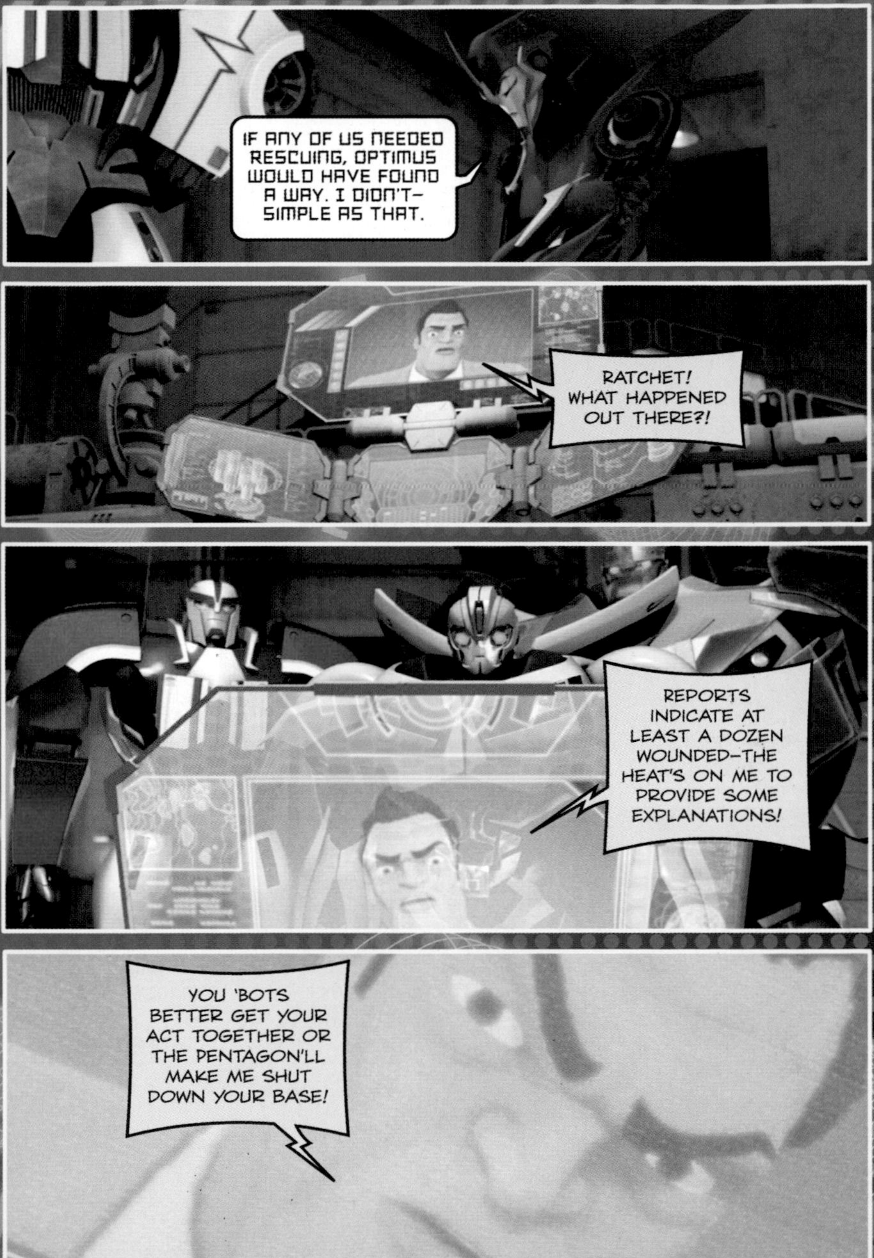
IF ANY OF US NEEDED RESCUING, OPTIMUS WOULD HAVE FOUND A WAY. I DIDN'T– SIMPLE AS THAT.
RATCHET! WHAT HAPPENED OUT THERE?!
REPORTS INDICATE AT LEAST A DOZEN WOUNDED–THE HEAT'S ON ME TO PROVIDE SOME EXPLANATIONS!
YOU 'BOTS BETTER GET YOUR ACT TOGETHER OR THE PENTAGON'LL MAKE ME SHUT DOWN YOUR BASE!

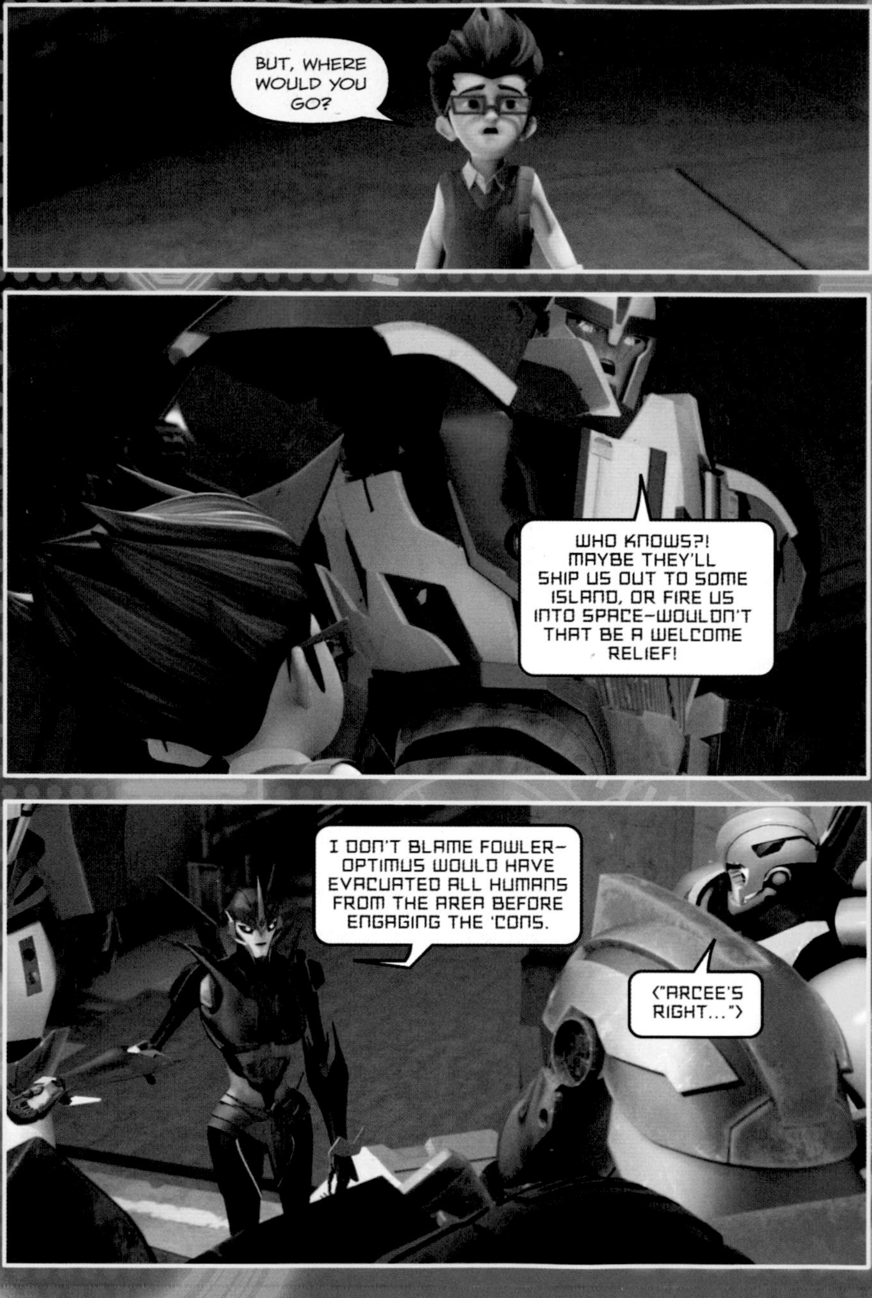
BUT, WHERE WOULD YOU GO?
WHO KNOWS?! MAYBE THEY'LL SHIP US OUT TO SOME ISLAND, OR FIRE US INTO SPACE—WOULDN'T THAT BE A WELCOME RELIEF!
I DON'T BLAME FOWLER—OPTIMUS WOULD HAVE EVACUATED ALL HUMANS FROM THE AREA BEFORE ENGAGING THE 'CONS.
<"ARCEE'S RIGHT...">

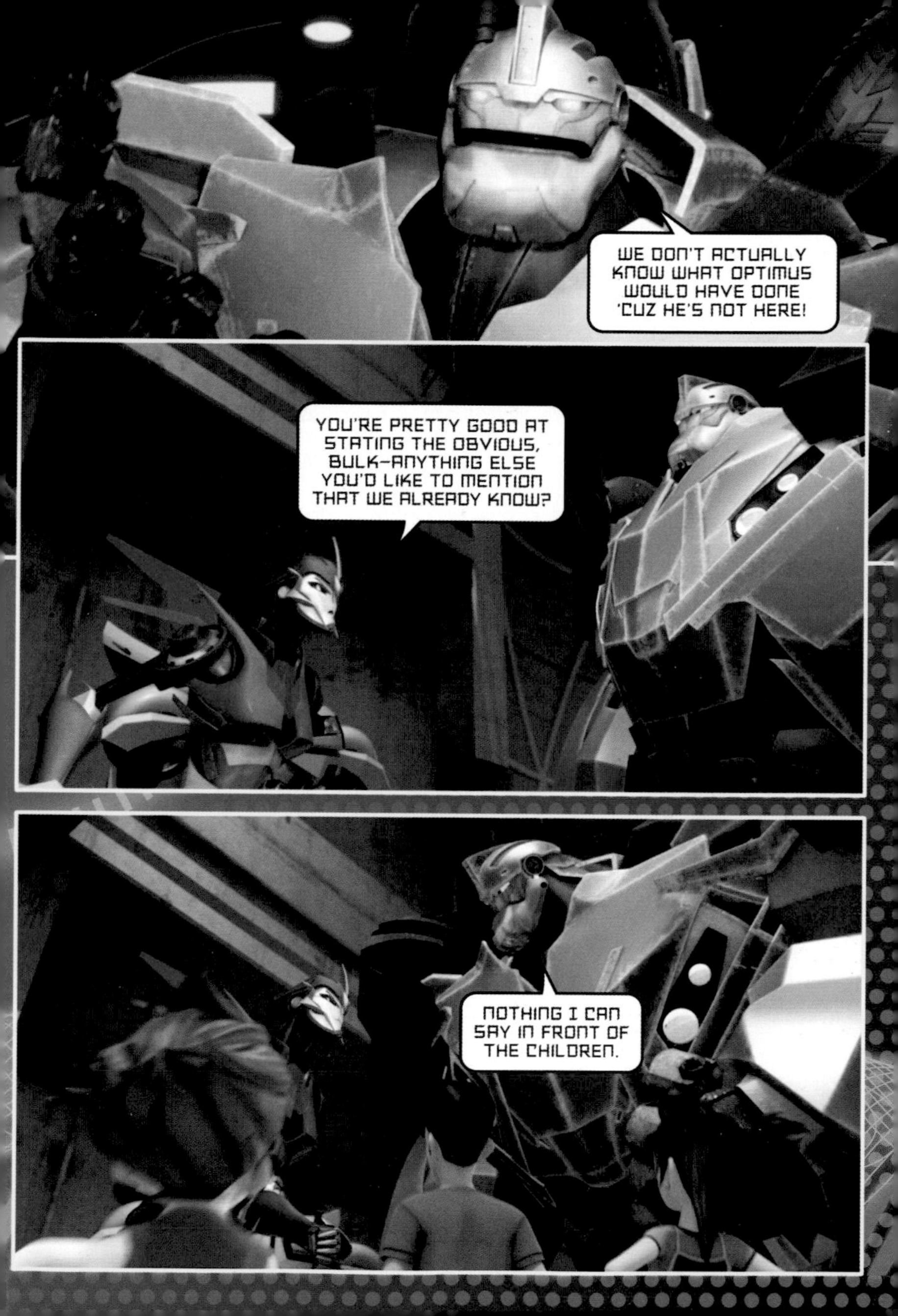
WE DON'T ACTUALLY KNOW WHAT OPTIMUS WOULD HAVE DONE 'CUZ HE'S NOT HERE!
YOU'RE PRETTY GOOD AT STATING THE OBVIOUS, BULK–ANYTHING ELSE YOU'D LIKE TO MENTION THAT WE ALREADY KNOW?
NOTHING I CAN SAY IN FRONT OF THE CHILDREN.

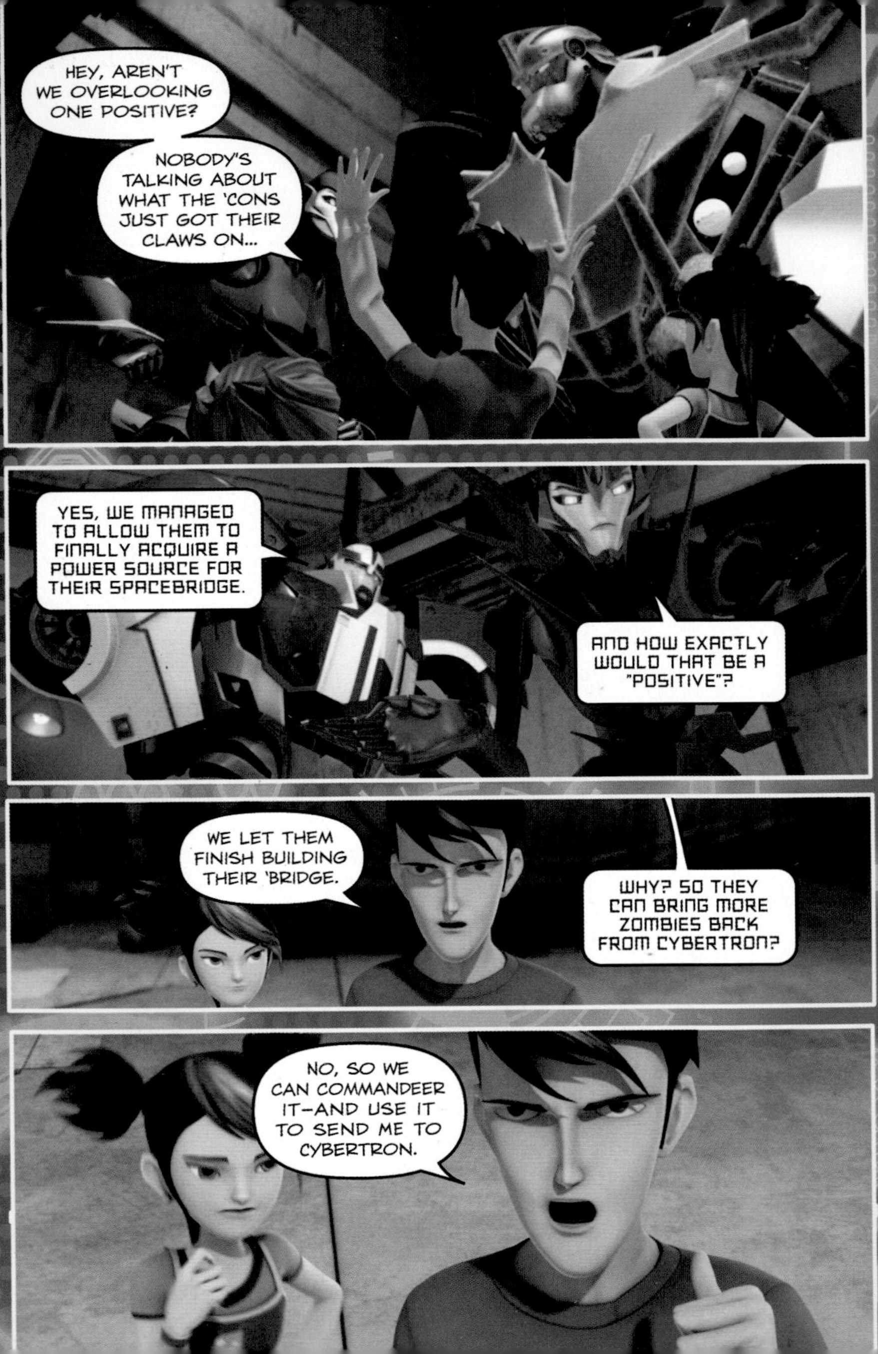
HEY, AREN'T WE OVERLOOKING ONE POSITIVE?
NOBODY'S TALKING ABOUT WHAT THE 'CONS JUST GOT THEIR CLAWS ON...
YES, WE MANAGED TO ALLOW THEM TO FINALLY ACQUIRE A POWER SOURCE FOR THEIR SPACEBRIDGE.
AND HOW EXACTLY WOULD THAT BE A "POSITIVE"?
WE LET THEM FINISH BUILDING THEIR 'BRIDGE.
WHY? SO THEY CAN BRING MORE ZOMBIES BACK FROM CYBERTRON?
NO, SO WE CAN COMMANDEER IT—AND USE IT TO SEND ME TO CYBERTRON.

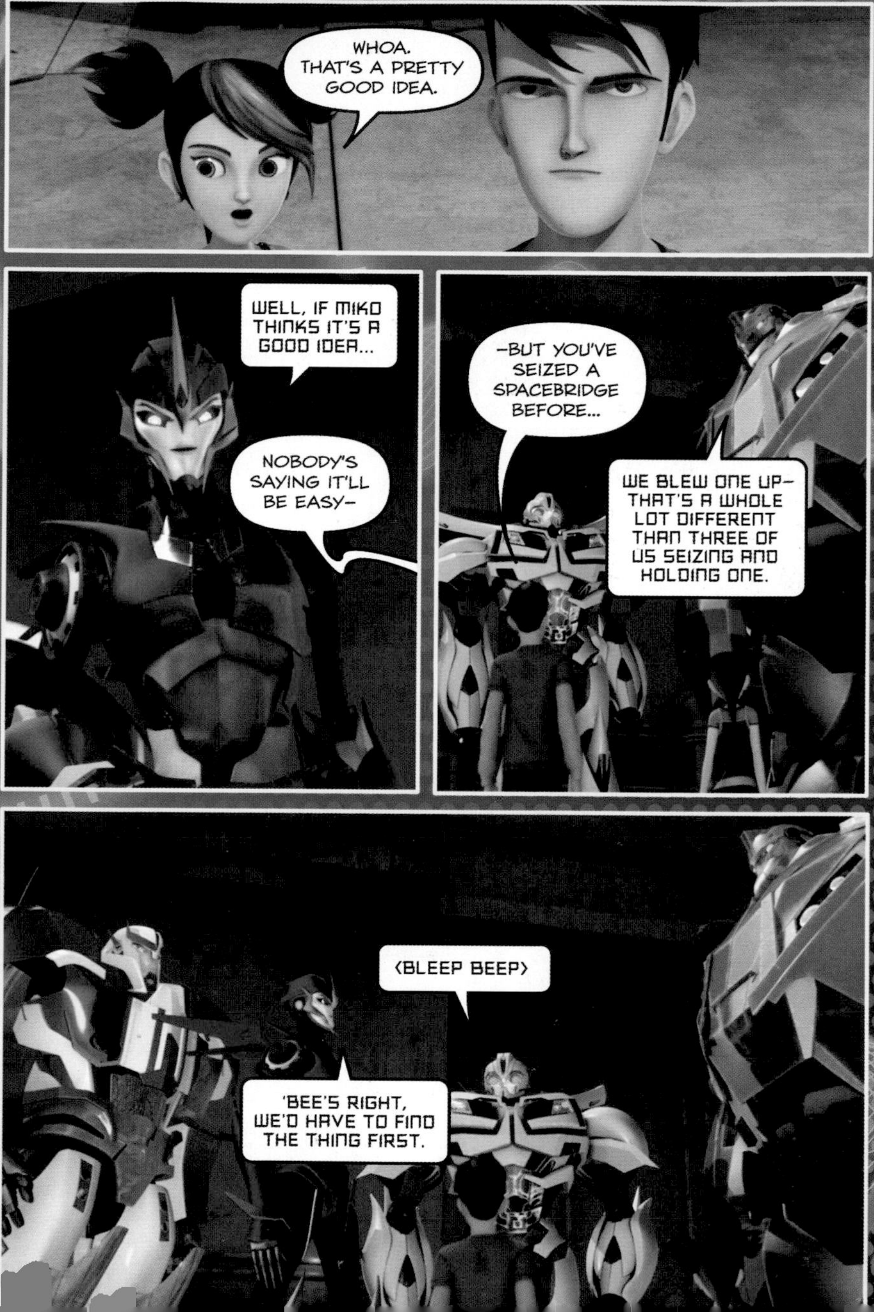
WHOA. THAT'S A PRETTY GOOD IDEA.
WELL, IF MIKO THINKS IT'S A GOOD IDEA...
NOBODY'S SAYING IT'LL BE EASY–
–BUT YOU'VE SEIZED A SPACEBRIDGE BEFORE...
WE BLEW ONE UP– THAT'S A WHOLE LOT DIFFERENT THAN THREE OF US SEIZING AND HOLDING ONE.
<BLEEP BEEP>
'BEE'S RIGHT, WE'D HAVE TO FIND THE THING FIRST.

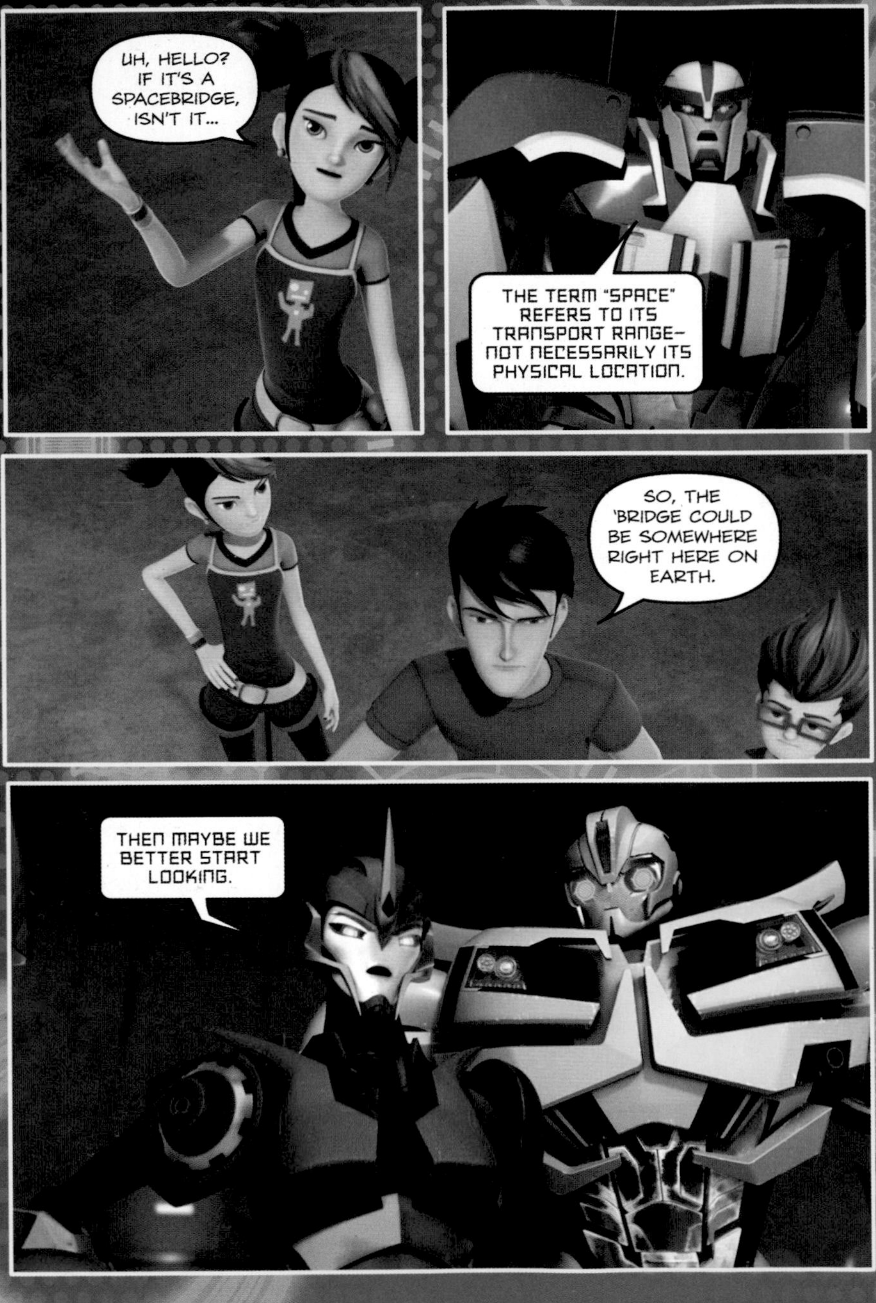
UH, HELLO? IF IT'S A SPACEBRIDGE, ISN'T IT...
THE TERM "SPACE" REFERS TO ITS TRANSPORT RANGE—NOT NECESSARILY ITS PHYSICAL LOCATION.
SO, THE 'BRIDGE COULD BE SOMEWHERE RIGHT HERE ON EARTH.
THEN MAYBE WE BETTER START LOOKING.

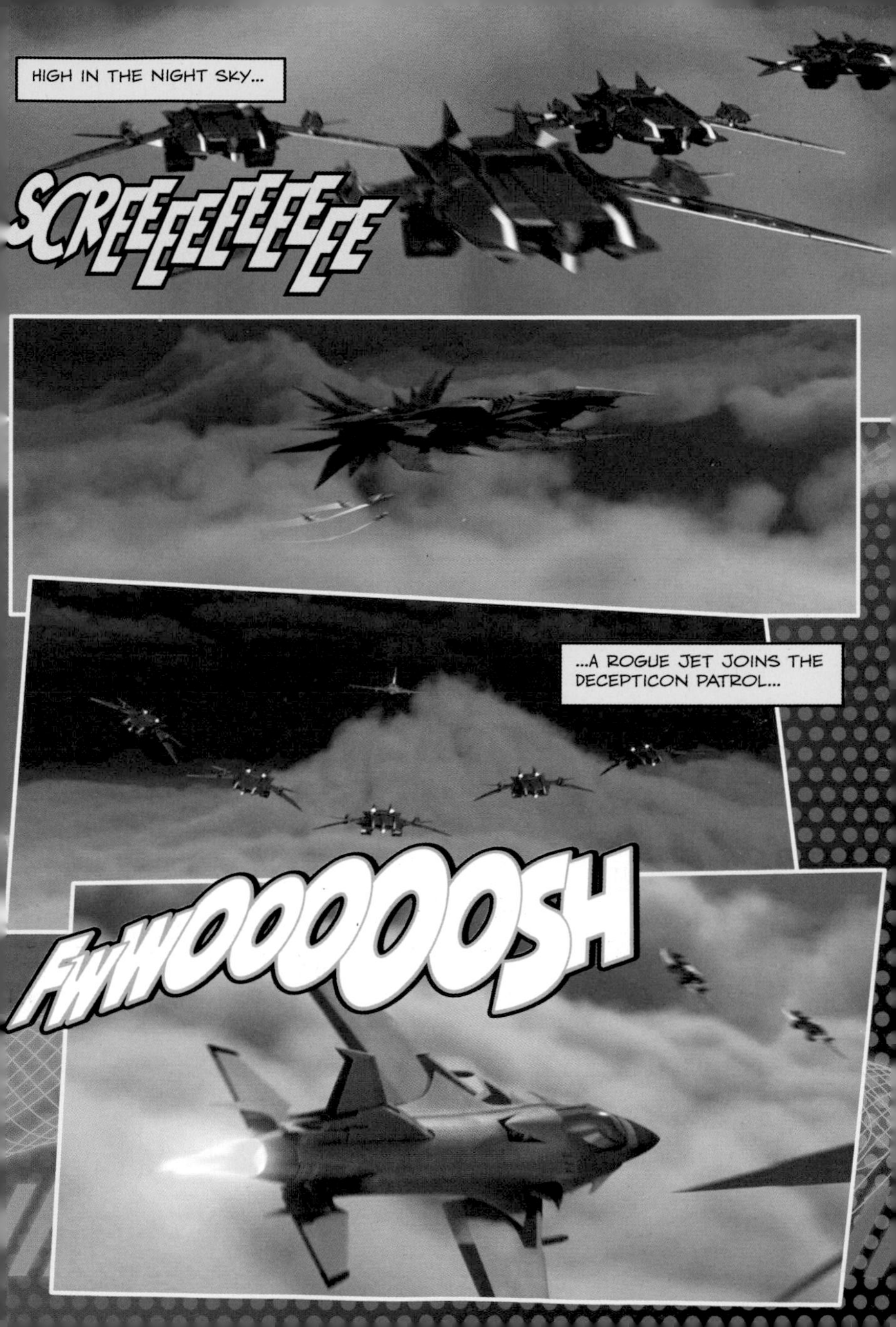
HIGH IN THE NIGHT SKY...
SCREEEEEEEEEEE
...A ROGUE JET JOINS THE DECEPTICON PATROL...
FWWOOOOOOSH

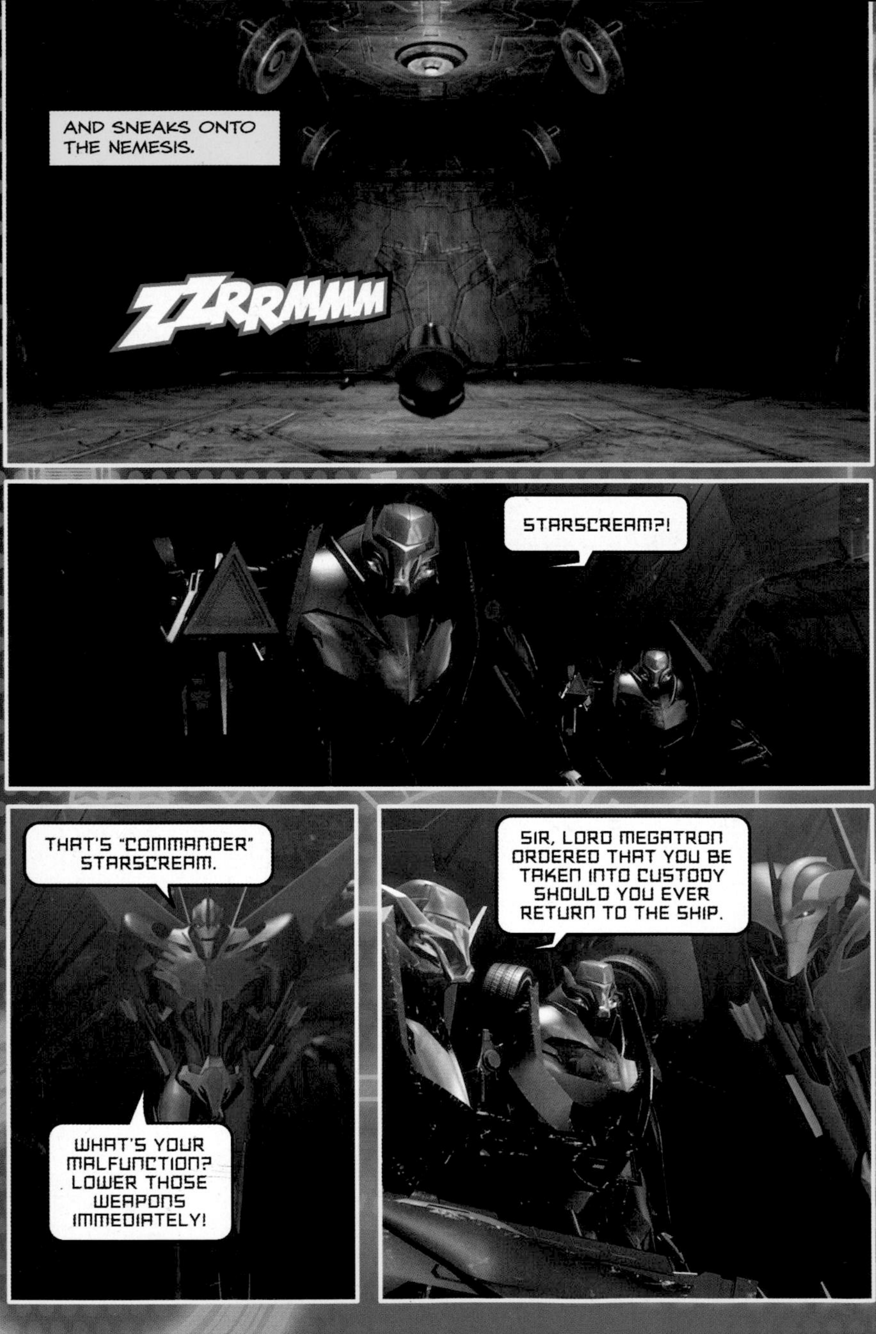
AND SNEAKS ONTO THE NEMESIS.
ZZRRMMM
STARSCREAM?!
THAT'S "COMMANDER" STARSCREAM.
WHAT'S YOUR MALFUNCTION? LOWER THOSE WEAPONS IMMEDIATELY!
SIR, LORD MEGATRON ORDERED THAT YOU BE TAKEN INTO CUSTODY SHOULD YOU EVER RETURN TO THE SHIP.

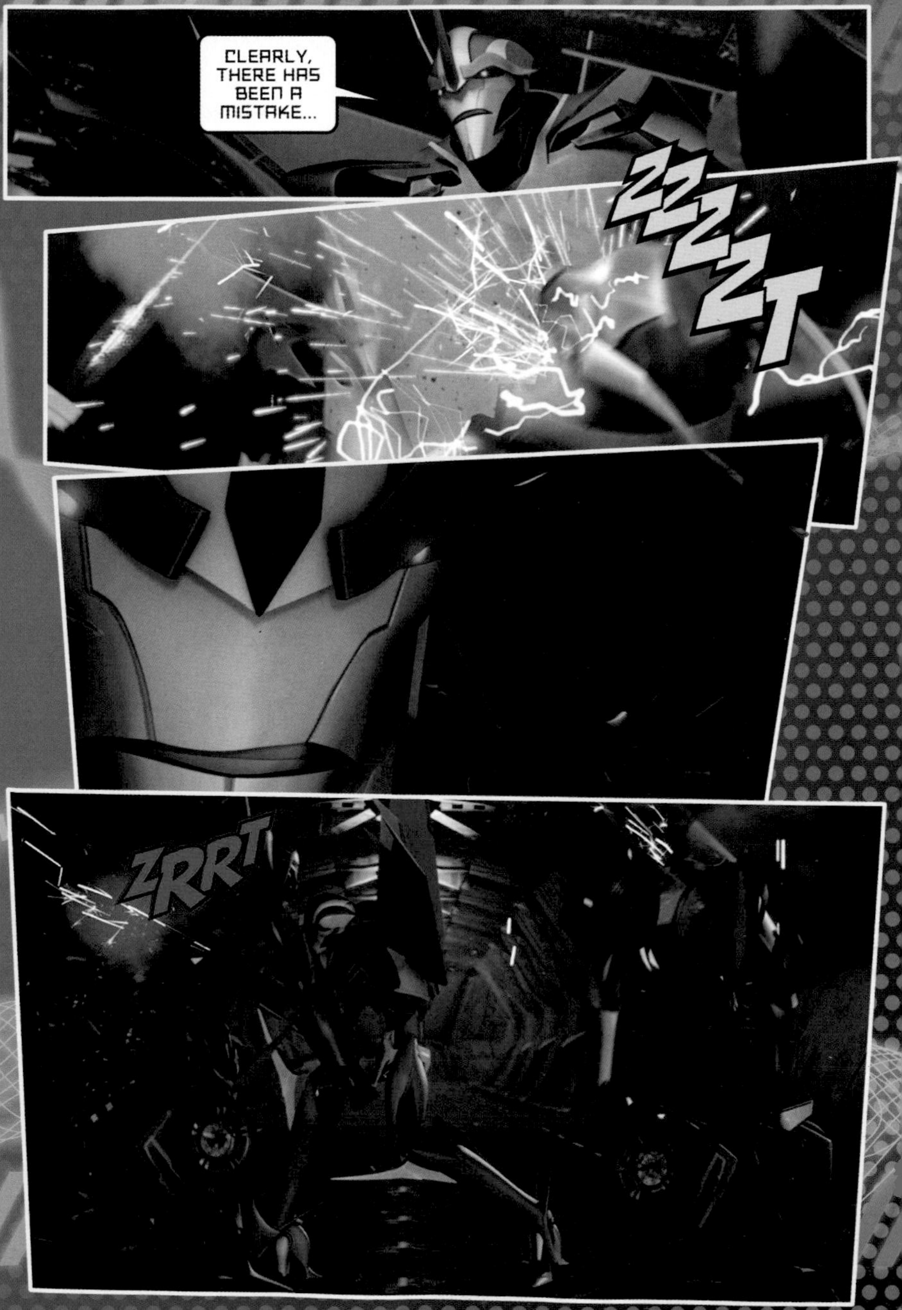
CLEARLY, THERE HAS BEEN A MISTAKE...
ZZZZT
ZRRT

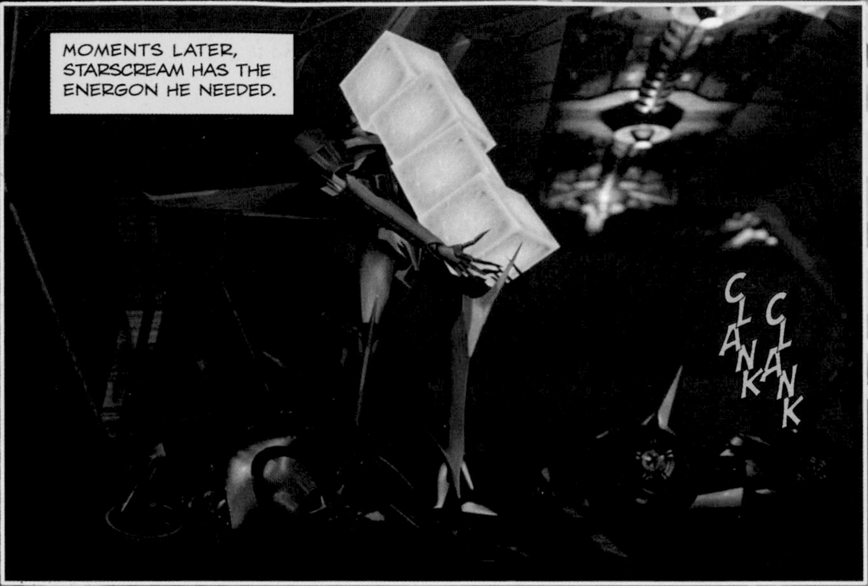
MOMENTS LATER, STARSCREAM HAS THE ENERGON HE NEEDED.
CLANK CLANK

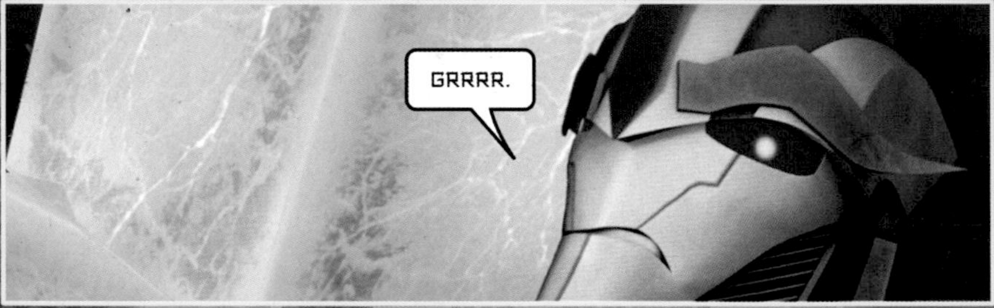
GRRRR.

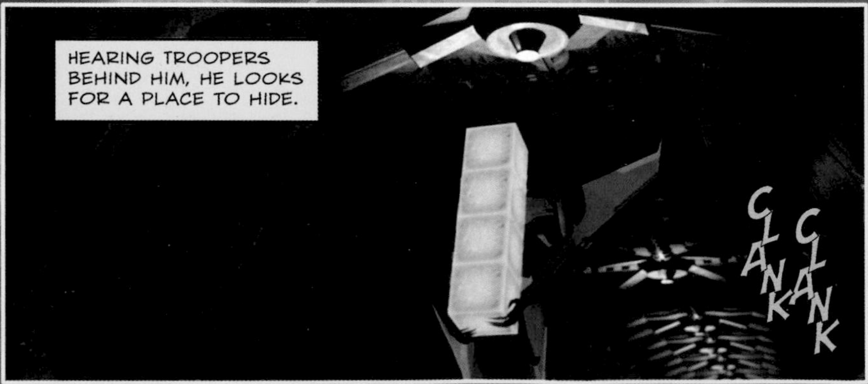
HEARING TROOPERS BEHIND HIM, HE LOOKS FOR A PLACE TO HIDE.
CLANK CLANK

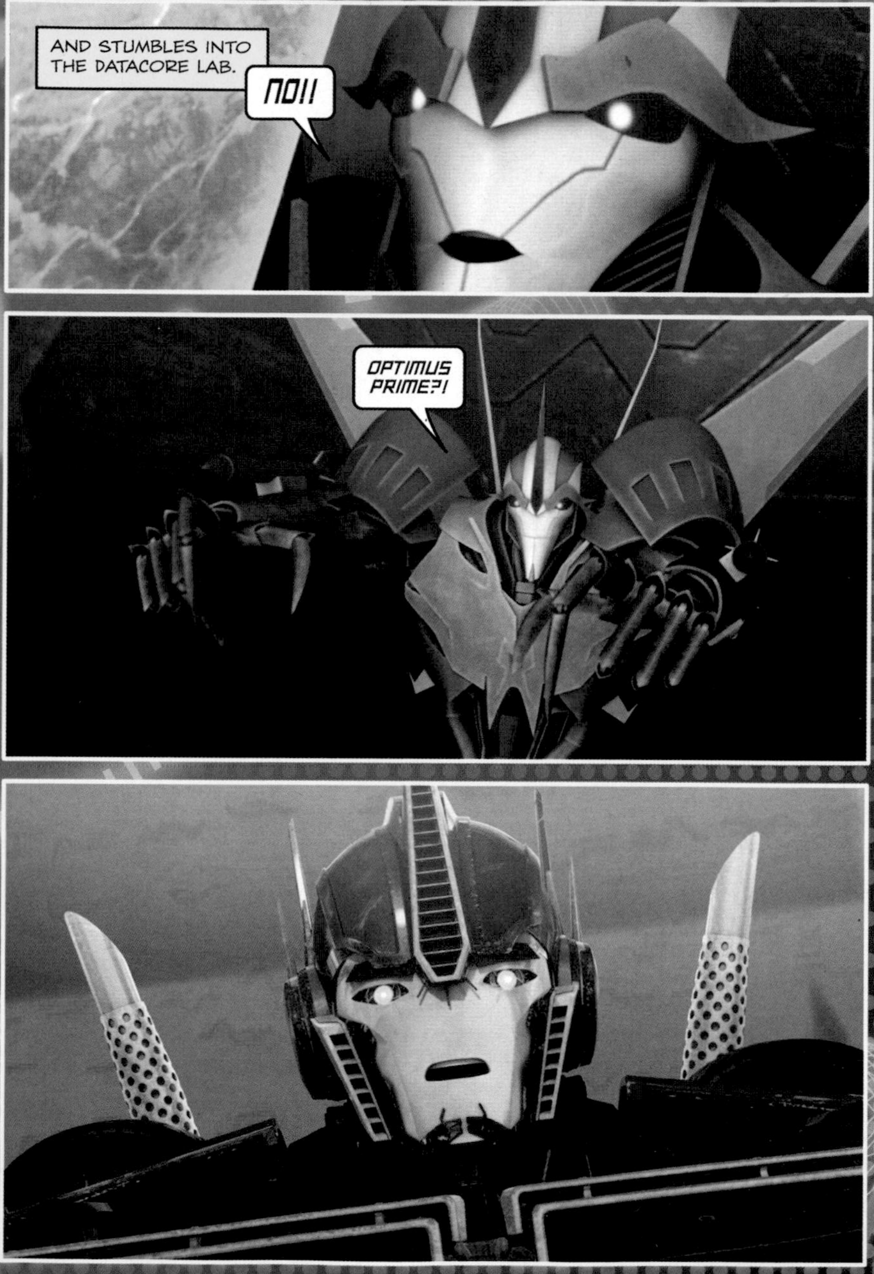
AND STUMBLES INTO THE DATACORE LAB.
NO!!
OPTIMUS PRIME?!

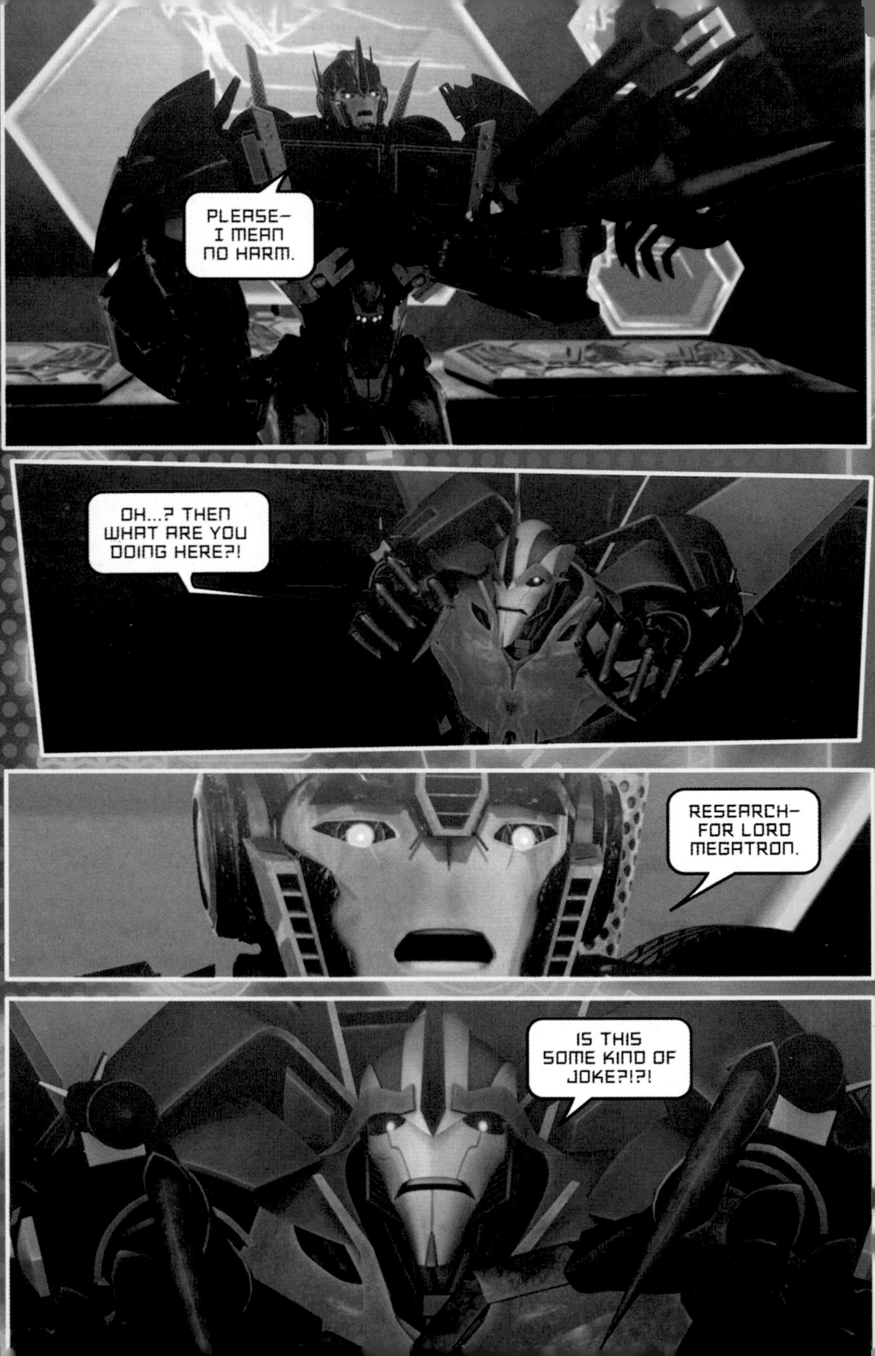
PLEASE—
I MEAN
NO HARM.
OH...? THEN
WHAT ARE YOU
DOING HERE?!
RESEARCH—
FOR LORD
MEGATRON.
IS THIS
SOME KIND OF
JOKE?!?!

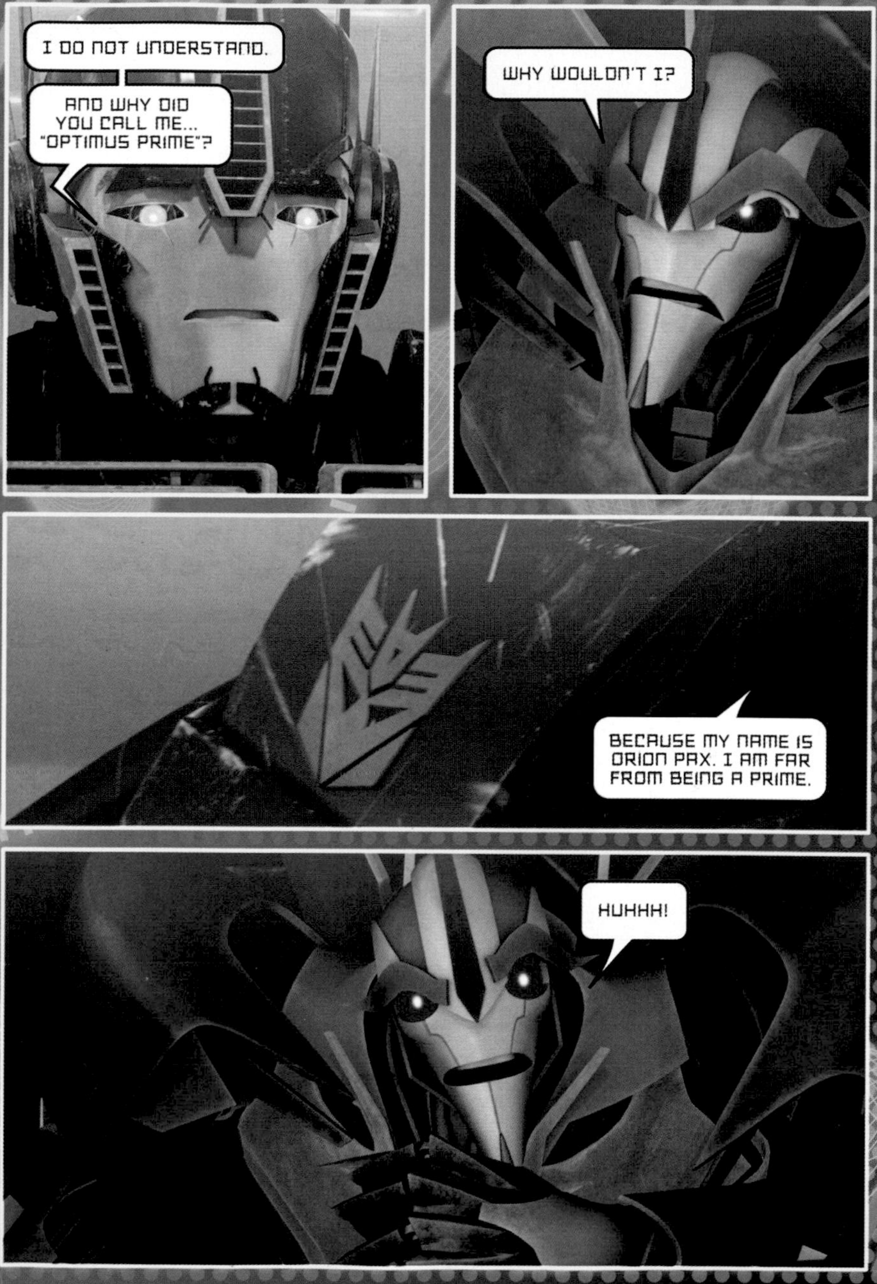
I DO NOT UNDERSTAND.
AND WHY DID YOU CALL ME... "OPTIMUS PRIME"?
WHY WOULDN'T I?
BECAUSE MY NAME IS ORION PAX. I AM FAR FROM BEING A PRIME.
HUHHH!

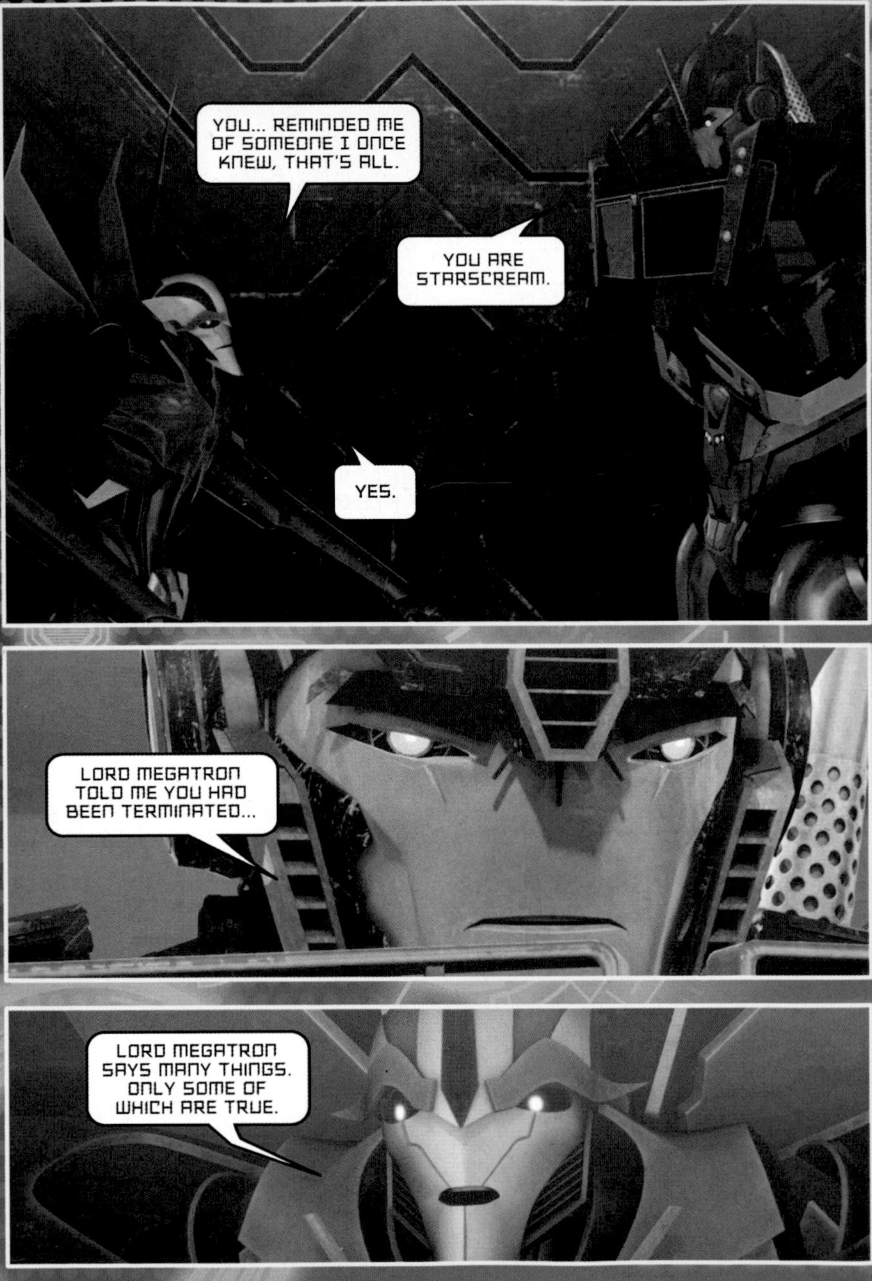
YOU... REMINDED ME OF SOMEONE I ONCE KNEW, THAT'S ALL.
YOU ARE STARSCREAM.
YES.
LORD MEGATRON TOLD ME YOU HAD BEEN TERMINATED...
LORD MEGATRON SAYS MANY THINGS. ONLY SOME OF WHICH ARE TRUE.

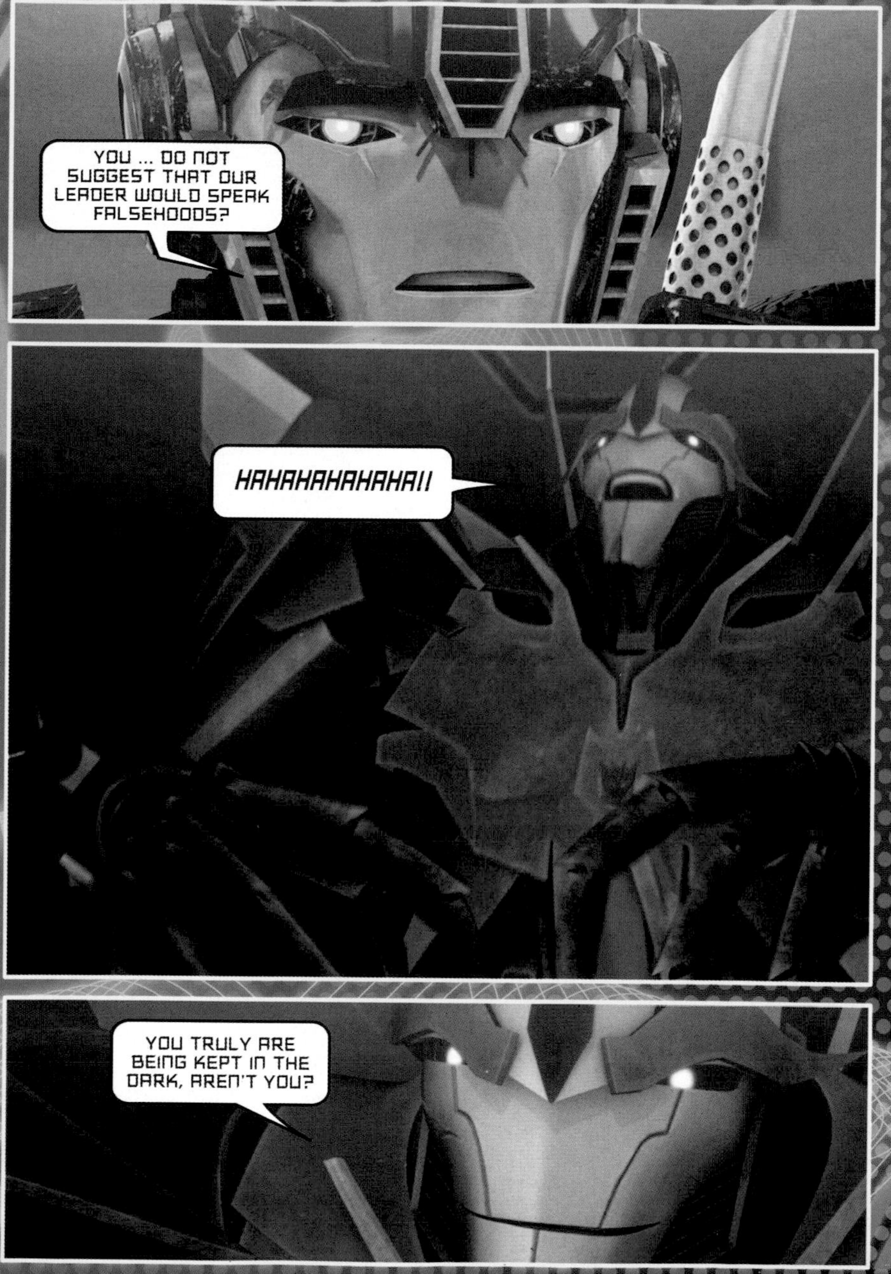
YOU ... DO NOT SUGGEST THAT OUR LEADER WOULD SPEAK FALSEHOODS?
HAHAHAHAHAHA!!
YOU TRULY ARE BEING KEPT IN THE DARK, AREN'T YOU?

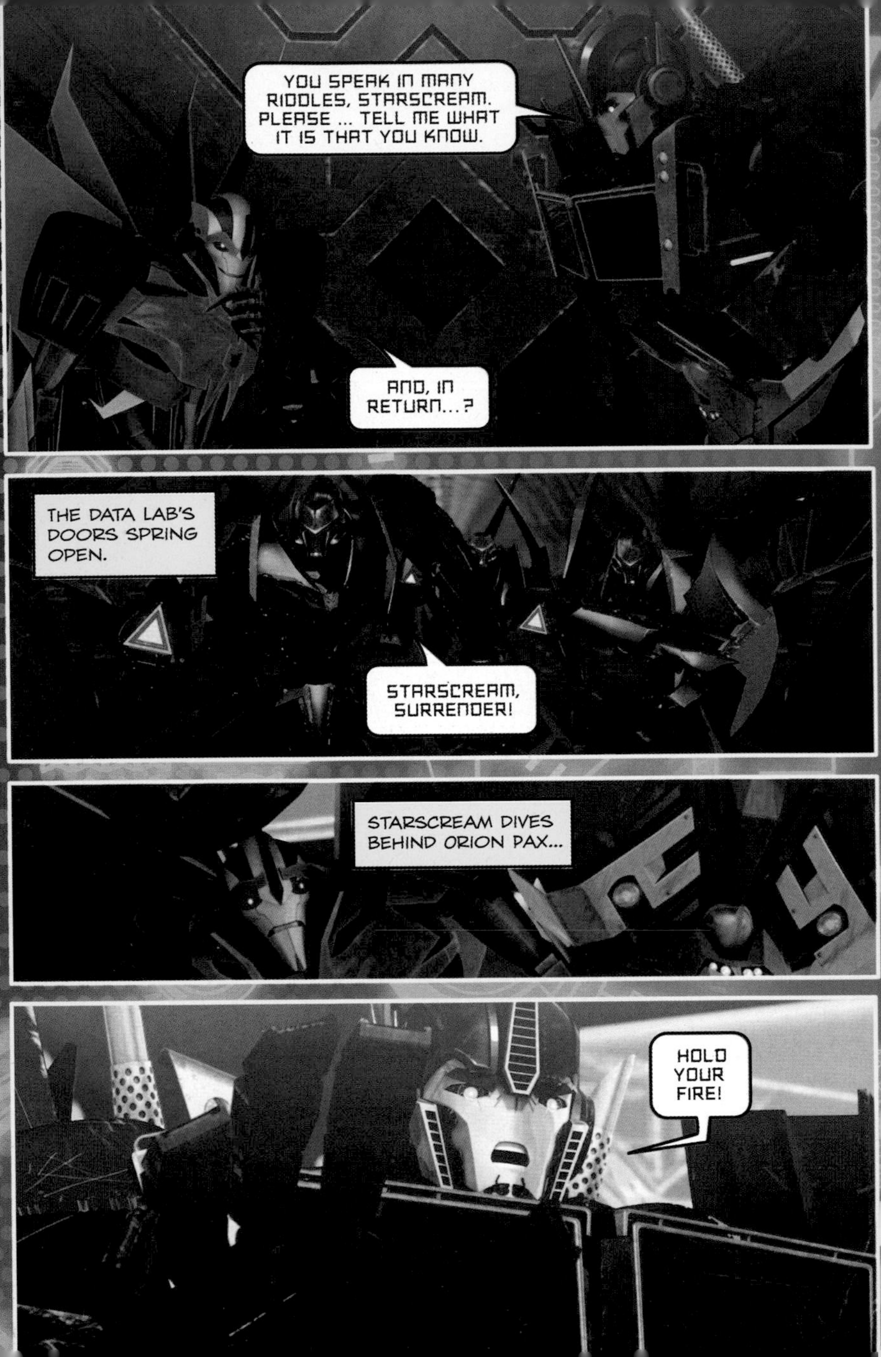
YOU SPEAK IN MANY RIDDLES, STARSCREAM. PLEASE ... TELL ME WHAT IT IS THAT YOU KNOW.
AND, IN RETURN...?
THE DATA LAB'S DOORS SPRING OPEN.
STARSCREAM, SURRENDER!
STARSCREAM DIVES BEHIND ORION PAX...
HOLD YOUR FIRE!

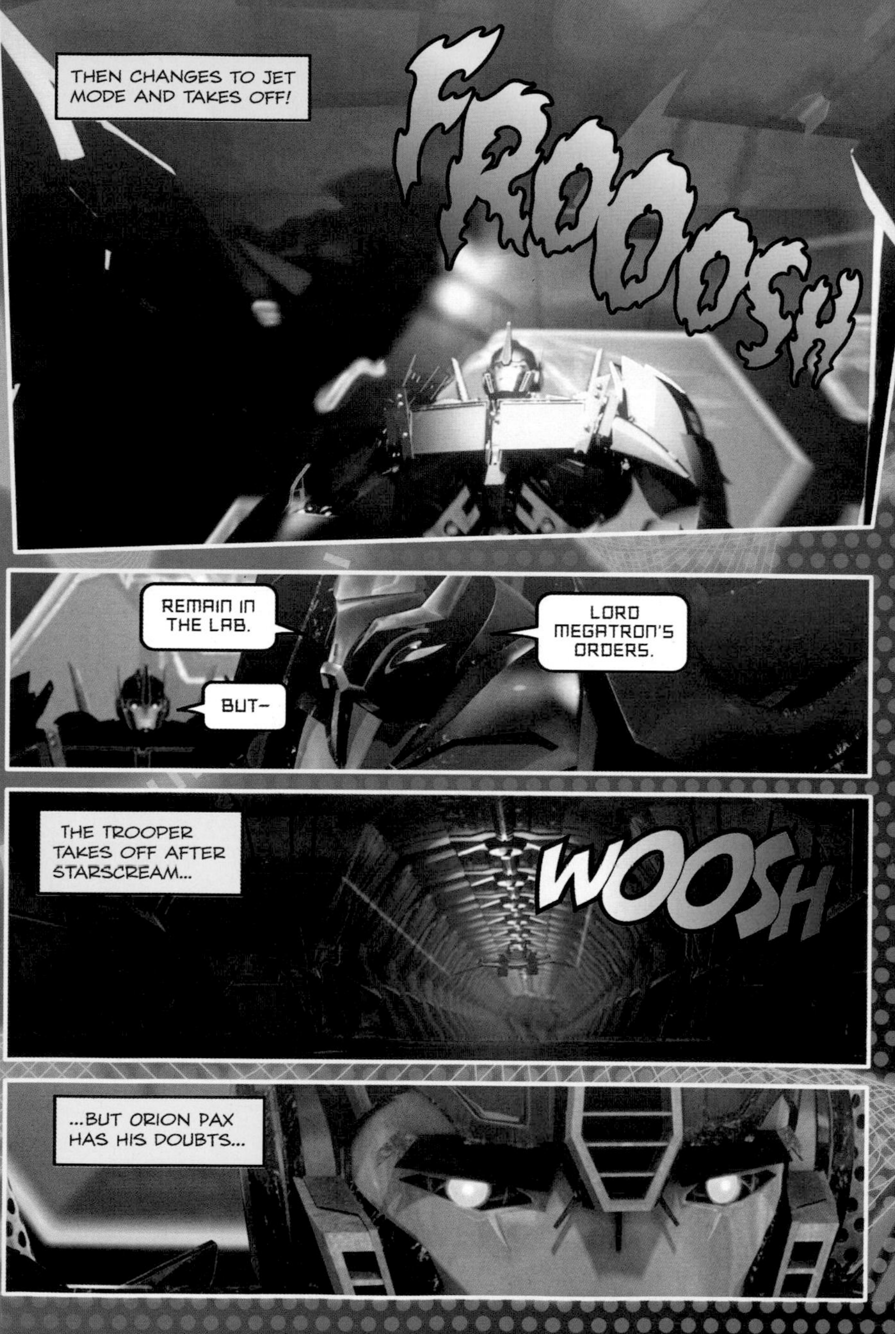
THEN CHANGES TO JET MODE AND TAKES OFF!
FROOOSH
REMAIN IN THE LAB.
LORD MEGATRON'S ORDERS.
BUT–
THE TROOPER TAKES OFF AFTER STARSCREAM...
WOOSH
...BUT ORION PAX HAS HIS DOUBTS...

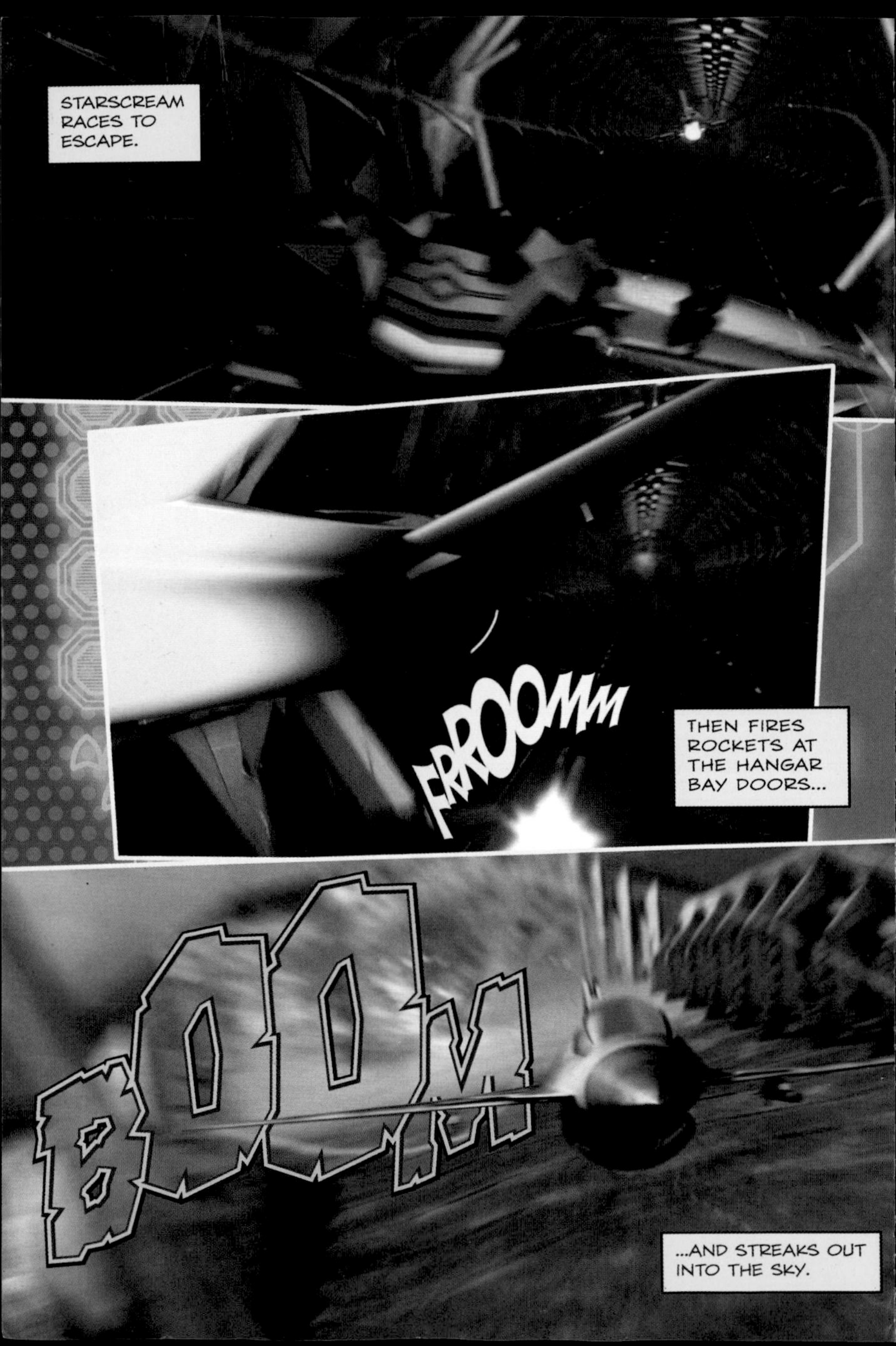
STARSCREAM RACES TO ESCAPE.
FRROOMMM
THEN FIRES ROCKETS AT THE HANGAR BAY DOORS...
BOOM
...AND STREAKS OUT INTO THE SKY.

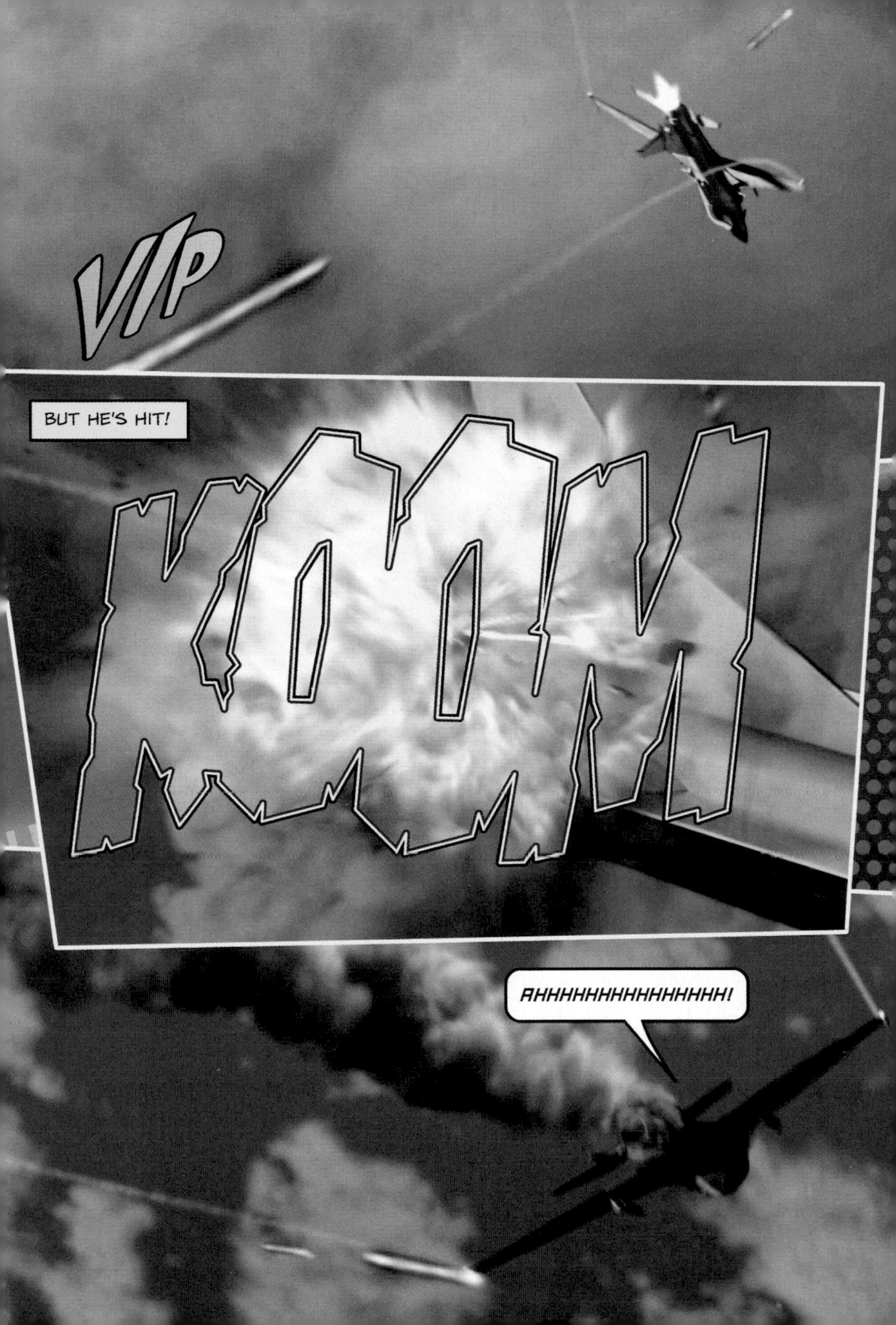
VIP
BUT HE'S HIT!
KOOM
AHHHHHHHHHHHHHHHH!

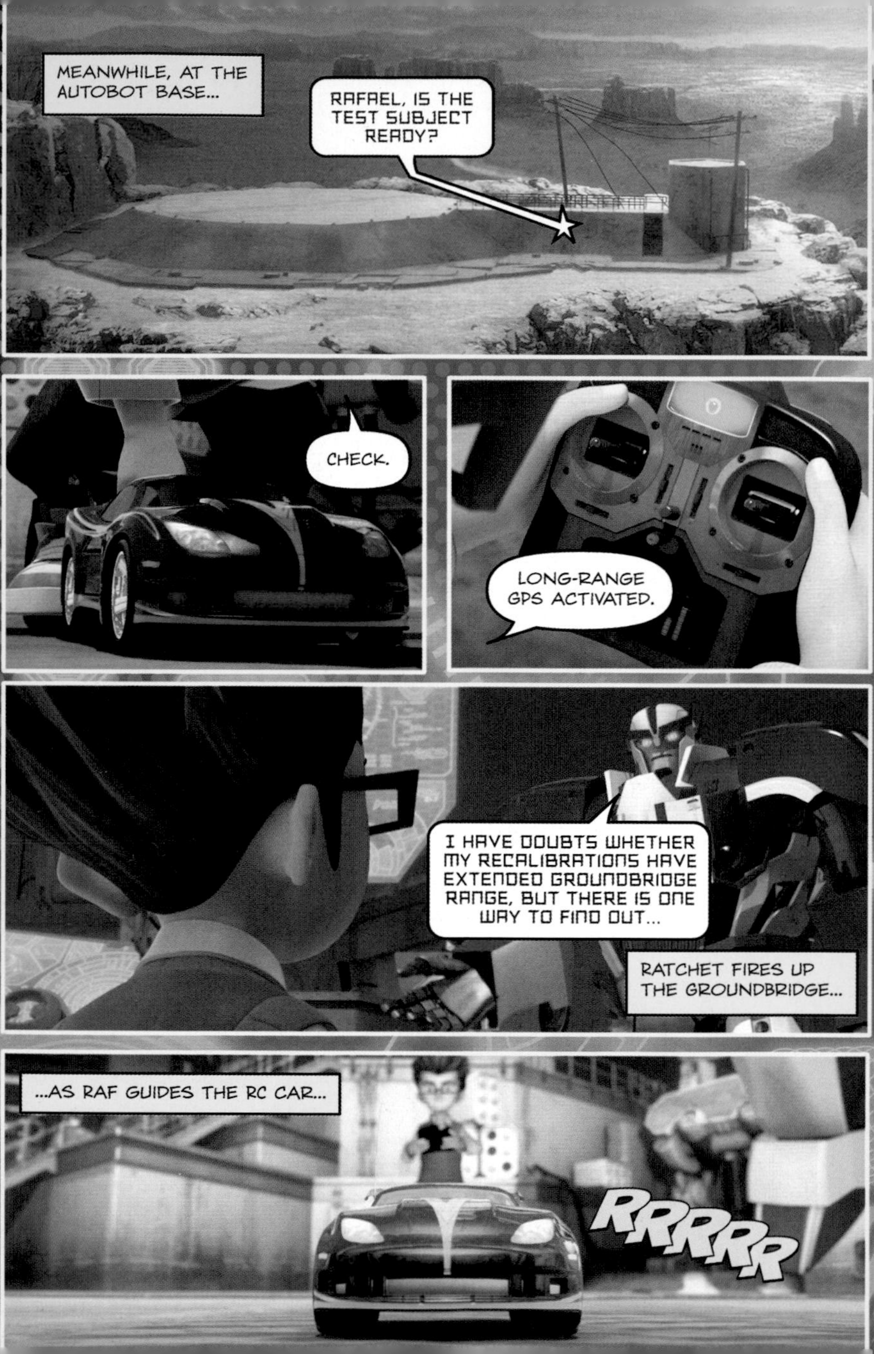
MEANWHILE, AT THE AUTOBOT BASE...
RAFAEL, IS THE TEST SUBJECT READY?
CHECK.
LONG-RANGE GPS ACTIVATED.
I HAVE DOUBTS WHETHER MY RECALIBRATIONS HAVE EXTENDED GROUNDBRIDGE RANGE, BUT THERE IS ONE WAY TO FIND OUT...
RATCHET FIRES UP THE GROUNDBRIDGE...
...AS RAF GUIDES THE RC CAR...
RRRRR

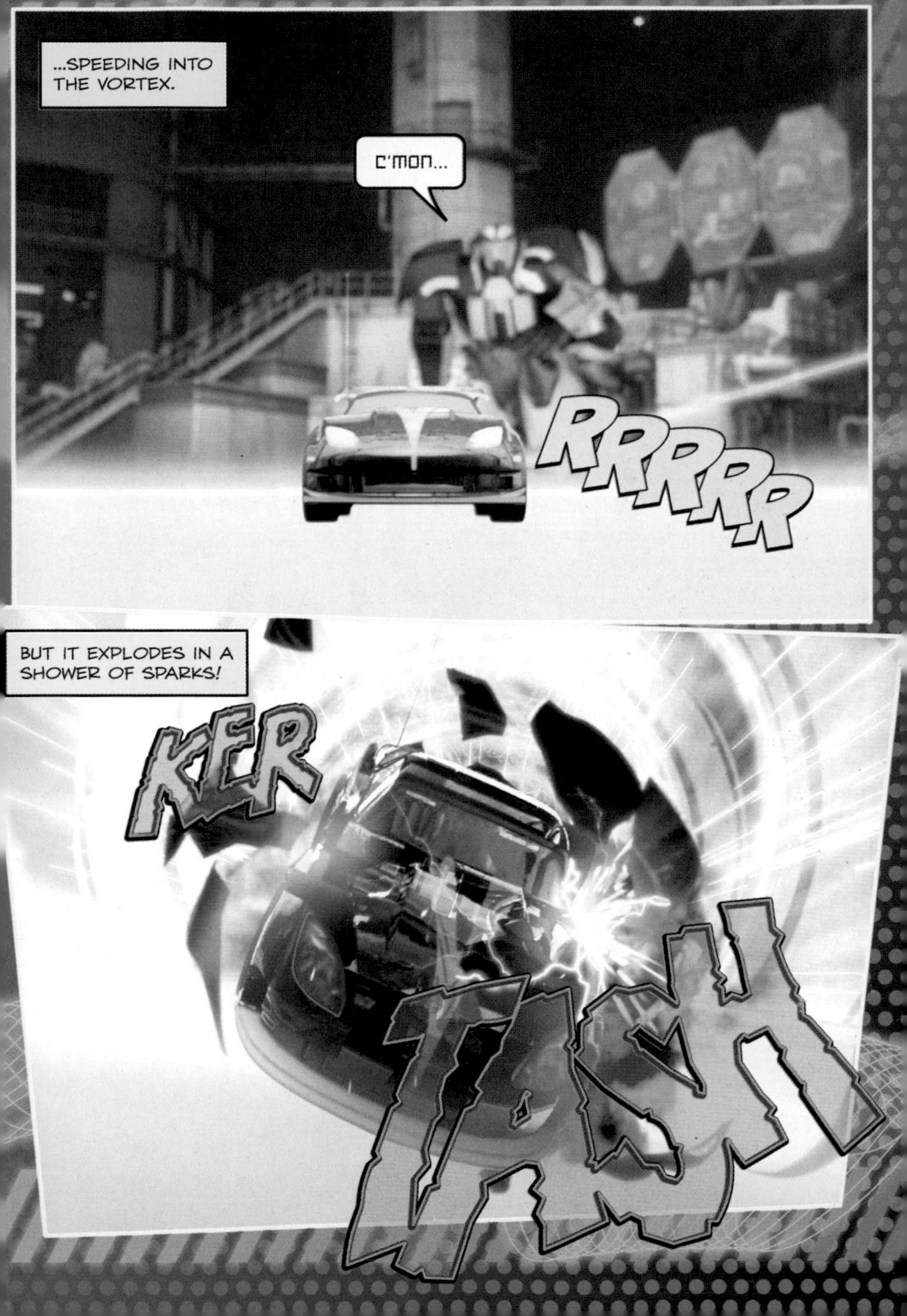
...SPEEDING INTO THE VORTEX.
C'MON...
RRRRR
BUT IT EXPLODES IN A SHOWER OF SPARKS!
KER
RASH

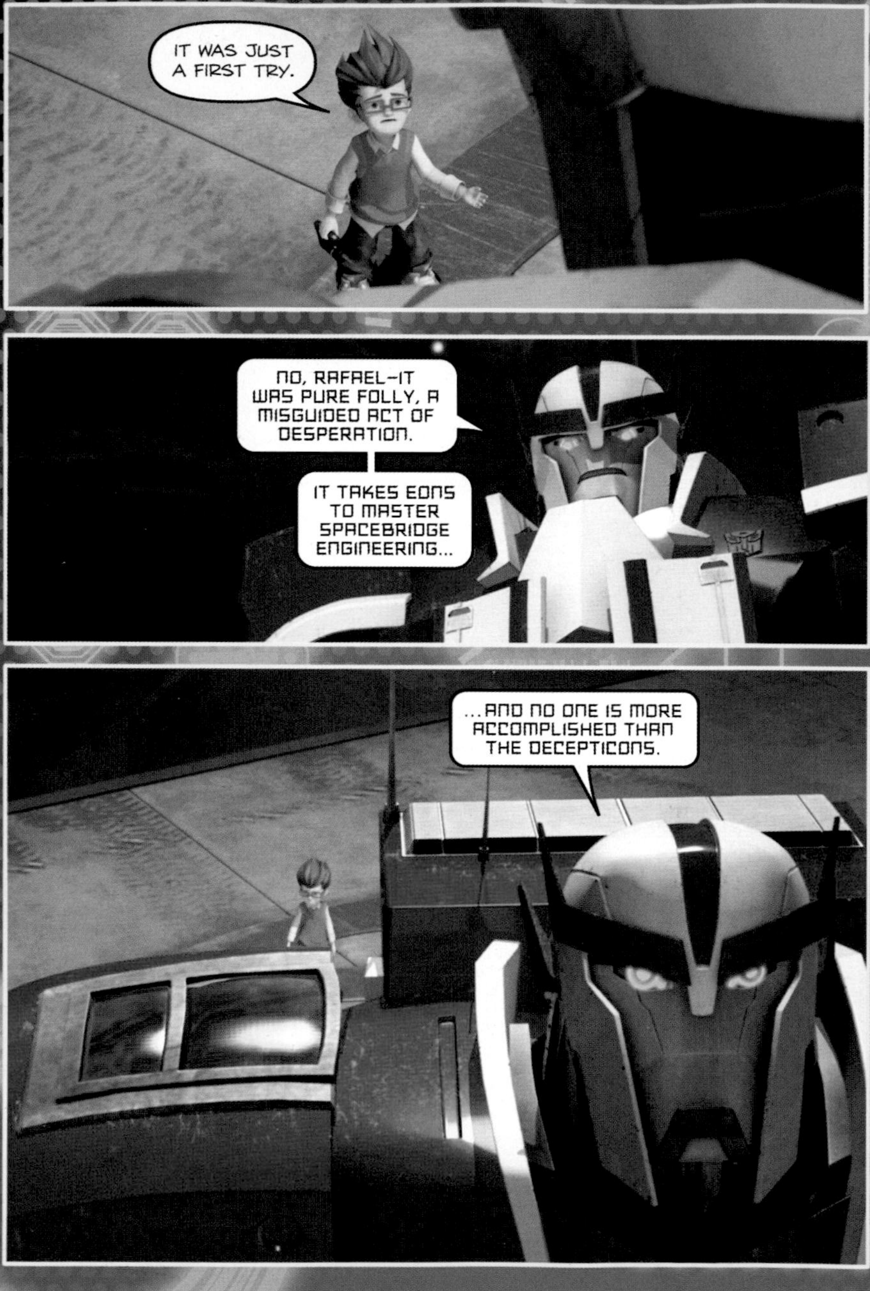
IT WAS JUST A FIRST TRY.
NO, RAFAEL—IT WAS PURE FOLLY, A MISGUIDED ACT OF DESPERATION.
IT TAKES EONS TO MASTER SPACEBRIDGE ENGINEERING...
...AND NO ONE IS MORE ACCOMPLISHED THAN THE DECEPTICONS.

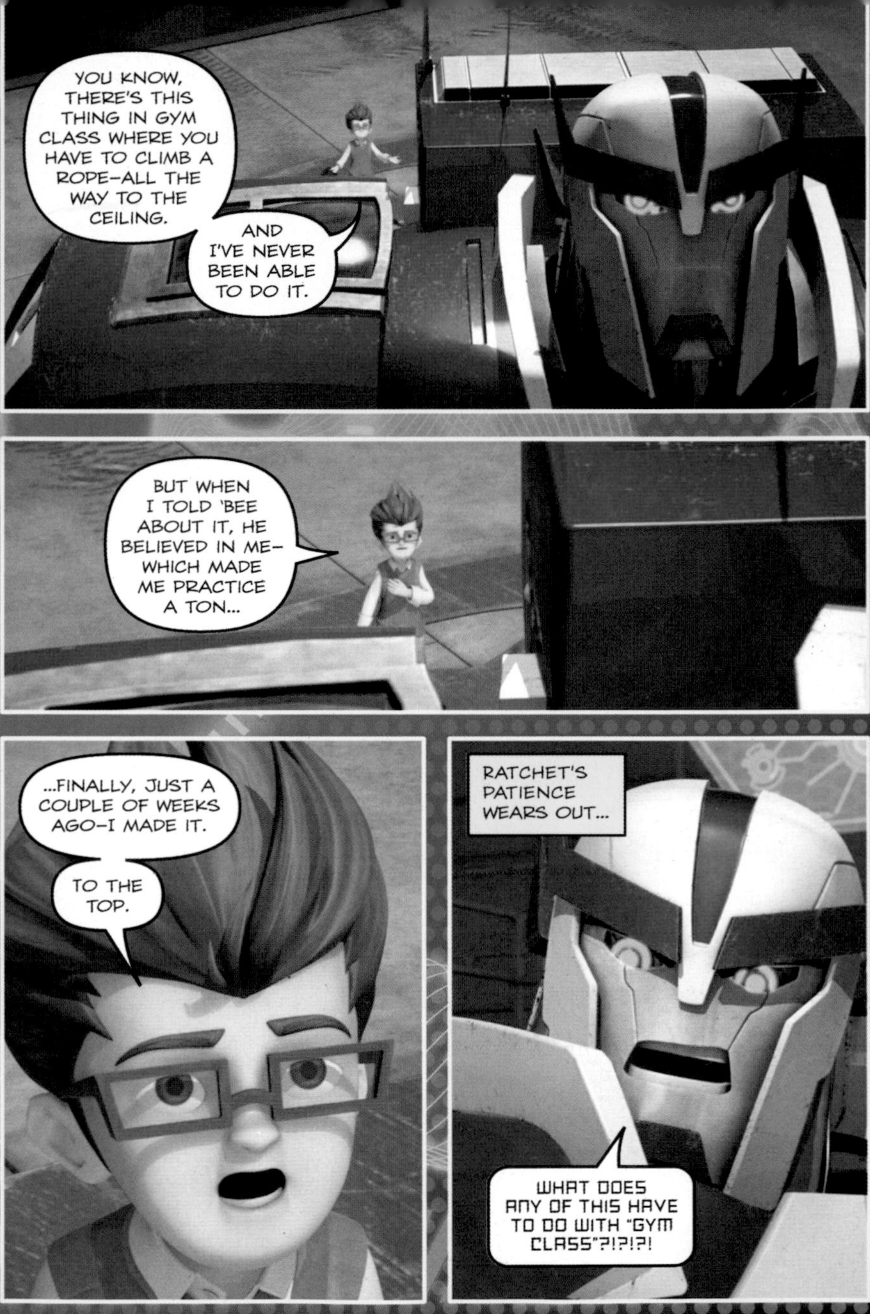
YOU KNOW, THERE'S THIS THING IN GYM CLASS WHERE YOU HAVE TO CLIMB A ROPE—ALL THE WAY TO THE CEILING.
AND I'VE NEVER BEEN ABLE TO DO IT.
BUT WHEN I TOLD 'BEE ABOUT IT, HE BELIEVED IN ME—WHICH MADE ME PRACTICE A TON...
...FINALLY, JUST A COUPLE OF WEEKS AGO—I MADE IT.
TO THE TOP.
RATCHET'S PATIENCE WEARS OUT...
WHAT DOES ANY OF THIS HAVE TO DO WITH "GYM CLASS"?!?!?!

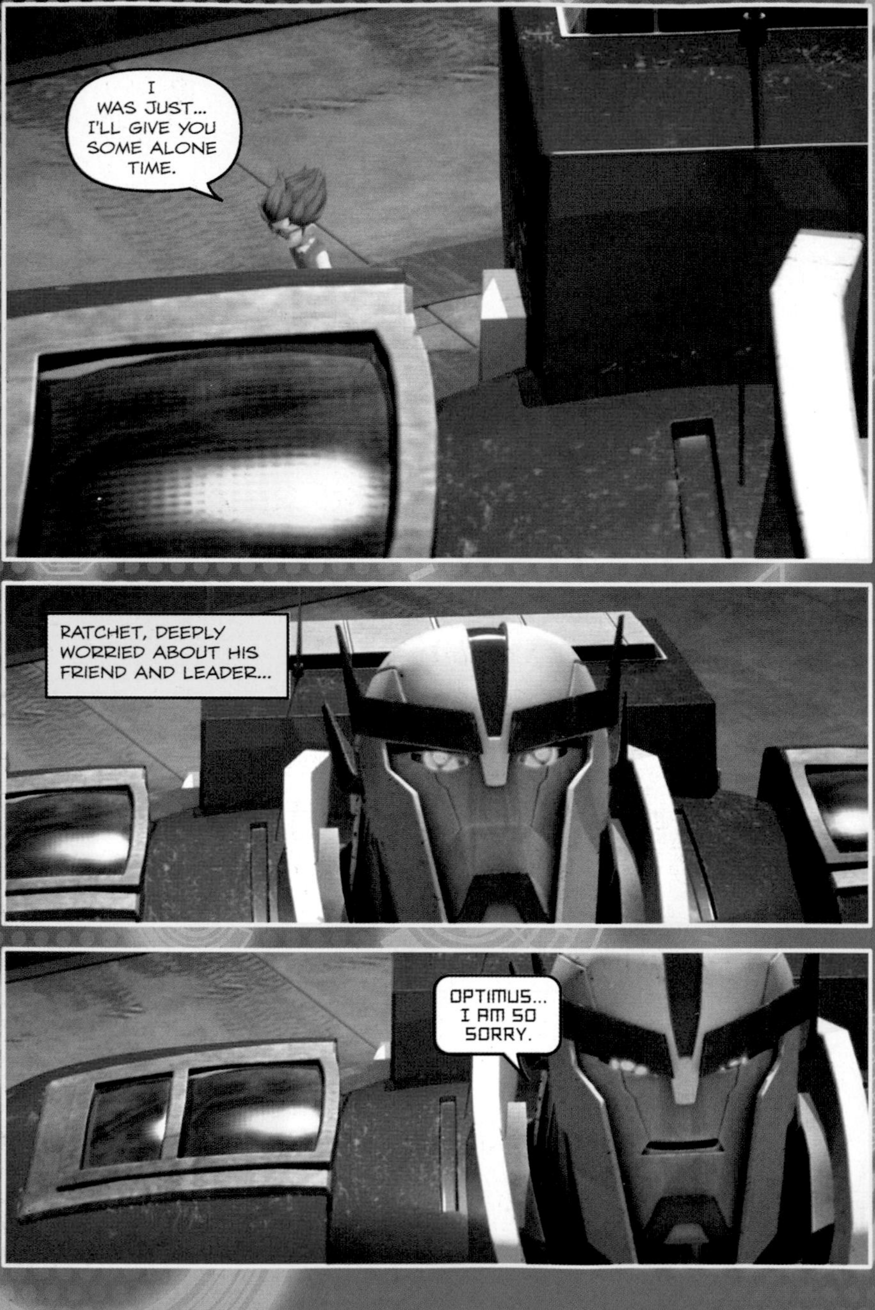
I WAS JUST... I'LL GIVE YOU SOME ALONE TIME.
RATCHET, DEEPLY WORRIED ABOUT HIS FRIEND AND LEADER...
OPTIMUS... I AM SO SORRY.

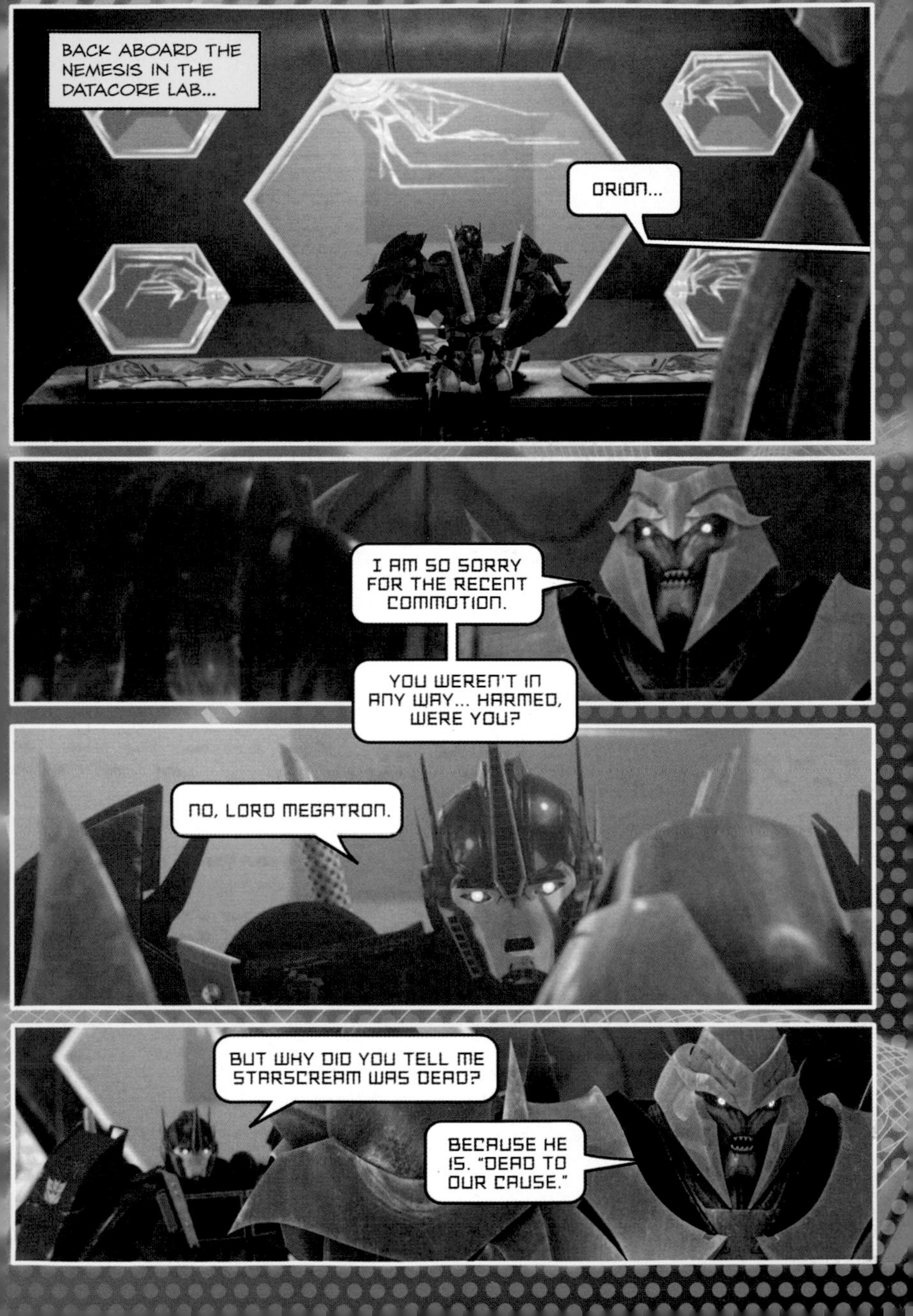
BACK ABOARD THE NEMESIS IN THE DATACORE LAB...
ORION...
I AM SO SORRY FOR THE RECENT COMMOTION.
YOU WEREN'T IN ANY WAY... HARMED, WERE YOU?
NO, LORD MEGATRON.
BUT WHY DID YOU TELL ME STARSCREAM WAS DEAD?
BECAUSE HE IS. "DEAD TO OUR CAUSE."

STARSCREAM WAS MY MOST TRUSTED LIEUTENANT... UNTIL HE TURNED TRAITOR, AND JOINED THE AUTOBOTS.
HE DID NOT... DO OR SAY ANYTHING TROUBLING TO YOU?
NO.
GOOD. PERHAPS IT IS BEST TO FORGET THE ENTIRE INCIDENT, AND RETURN TO YOUR PROJECT.
AS YOU WISH, MY LORD.

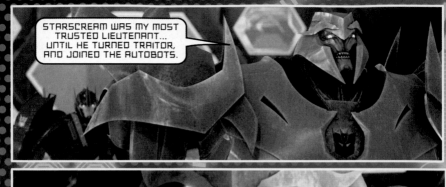

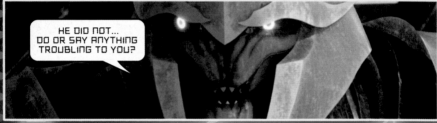

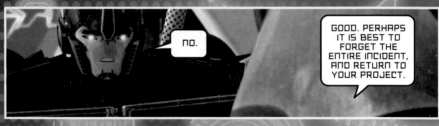

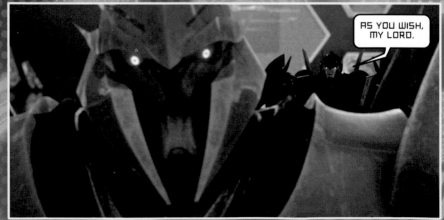

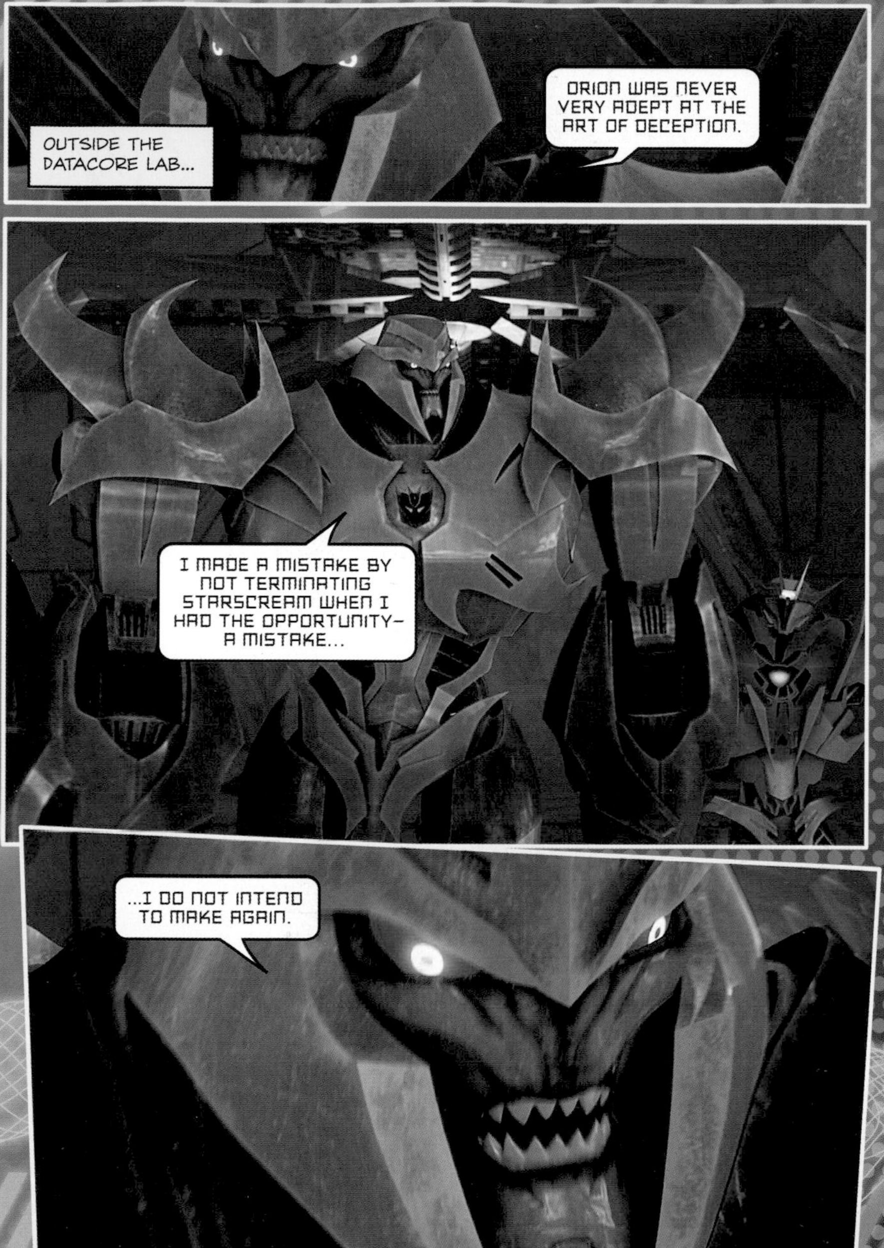
OUTSIDE THE DATACORE LAB...
ORION WAS NEVER VERY ADEPT AT THE ART OF DECEPTION.
I MADE A MISTAKE BY NOT TERMINATING STARSCREAM WHEN I HAD THE OPPORTUNITY— A MISTAKE...
...I DO NOT INTEND TO MAKE AGAIN.

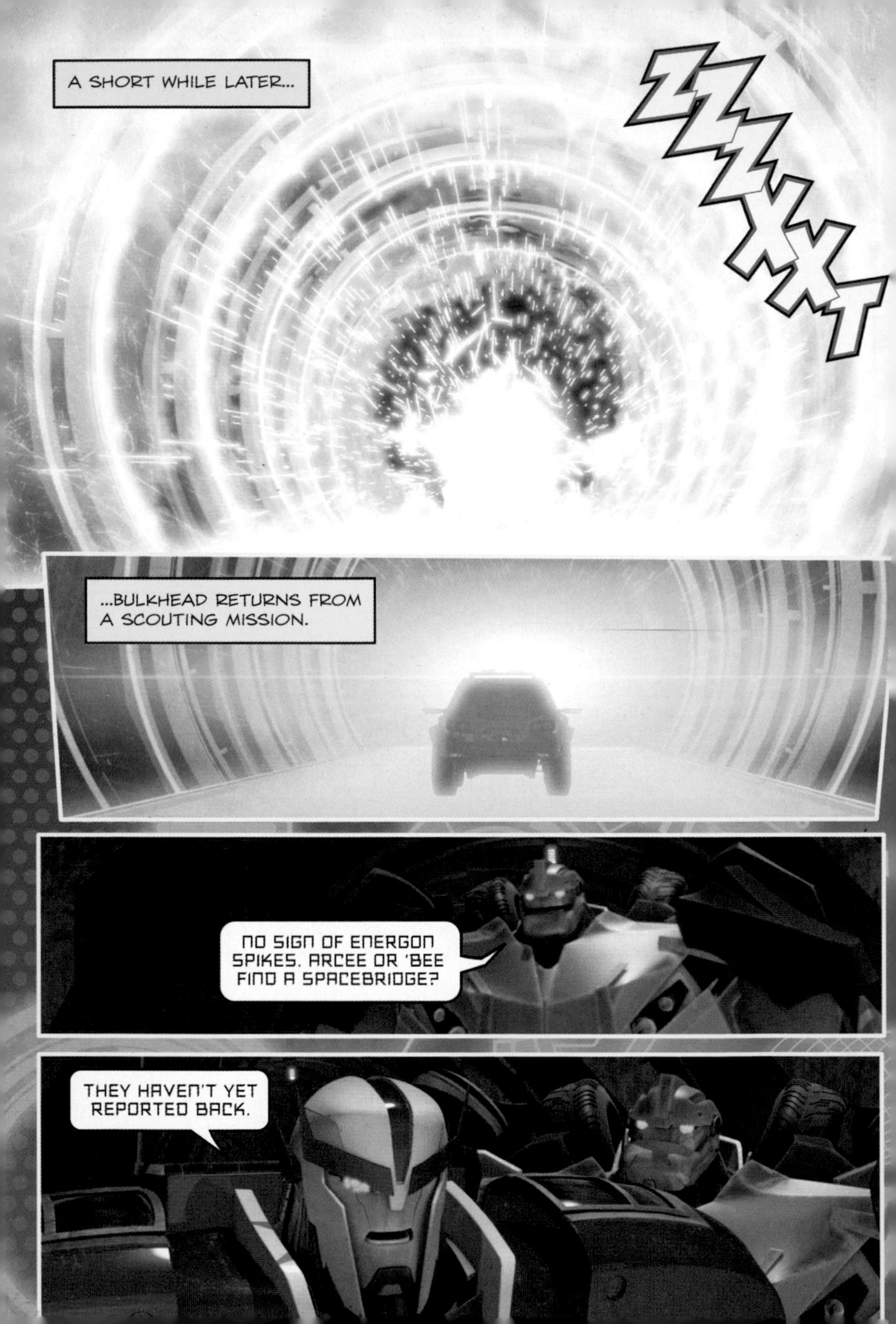
A SHORT WHILE LATER...
ZZZXXT
...BULKHEAD RETURNS FROM A SCOUTING MISSION.
NO SIGN OF ENERGON SPIKES. ARCEE OR 'BEE FIND A SPACEBRIDGE?
THEY HAVEN'T YET REPORTED BACK.

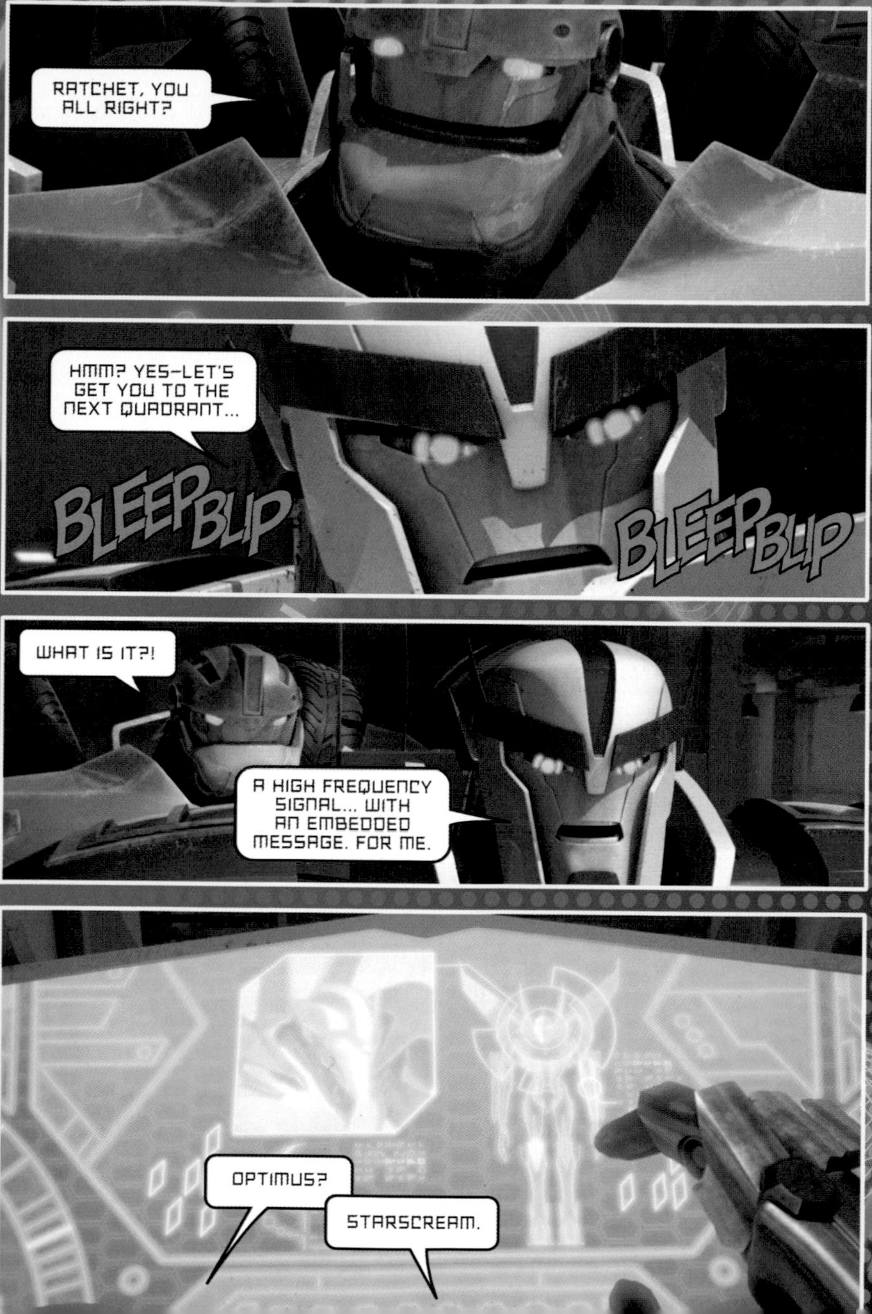
RATCHET, YOU ALL RIGHT?
HMM? YES–LET'S GET YOU TO THE NEXT QUADRANT...
BLEEP BLIP
BLEEP BLIP
WHAT IS IT?!
A HIGH FREQUENCY SIGNAL... WITH AN EMBEDDED MESSAGE. FOR ME.
OPTIMUS?
STARSCREAM.

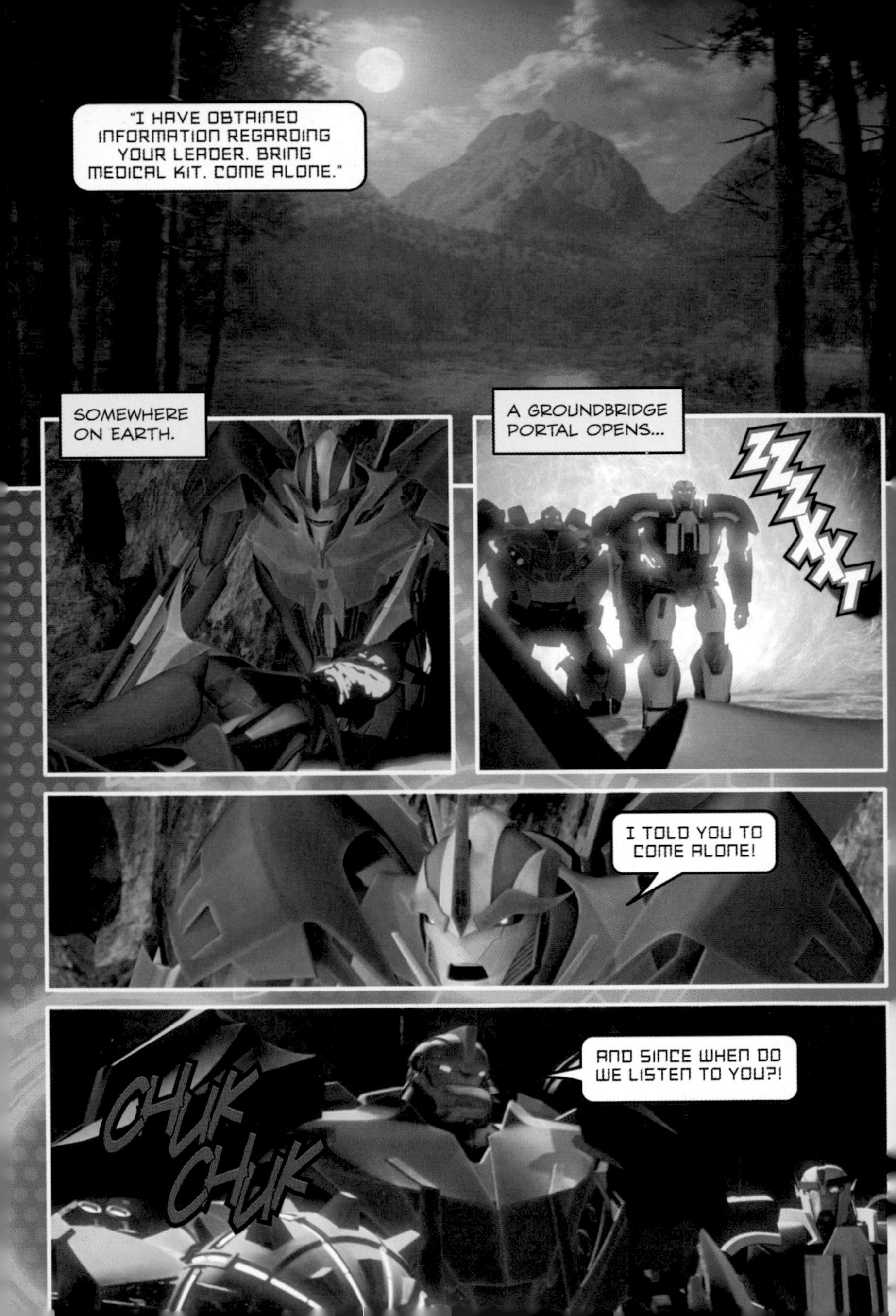
"I HAVE OBTAINED INFORMATION REGARDING YOUR LEADER. BRING MEDICAL KIT. COME ALONE."
SOMEWHERE ON EARTH.
A GROUNDBRIDGE PORTAL OPENS...
ZZZZXXT
I TOLD YOU TO COME ALONE!
CHUK CHUK
AND SINCE WHEN DO WE LISTEN TO YOU?!

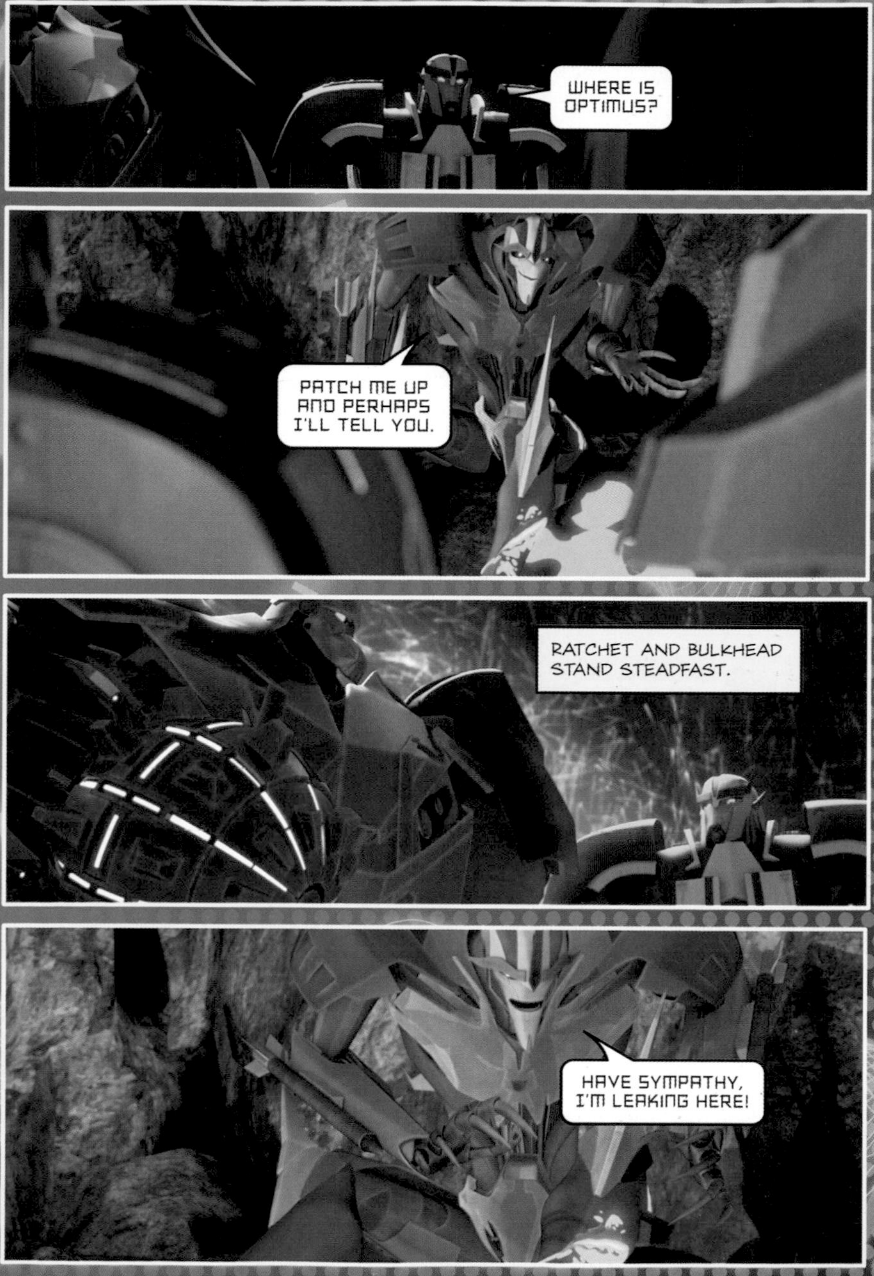
WHERE IS OPTIMUS?
PATCH ME UP AND PERHAPS I'LL TELL YOU.
RATCHET AND BULKHEAD STAND STEADFAST.
HAVE SYMPATHY, I'M LEAKING HERE!

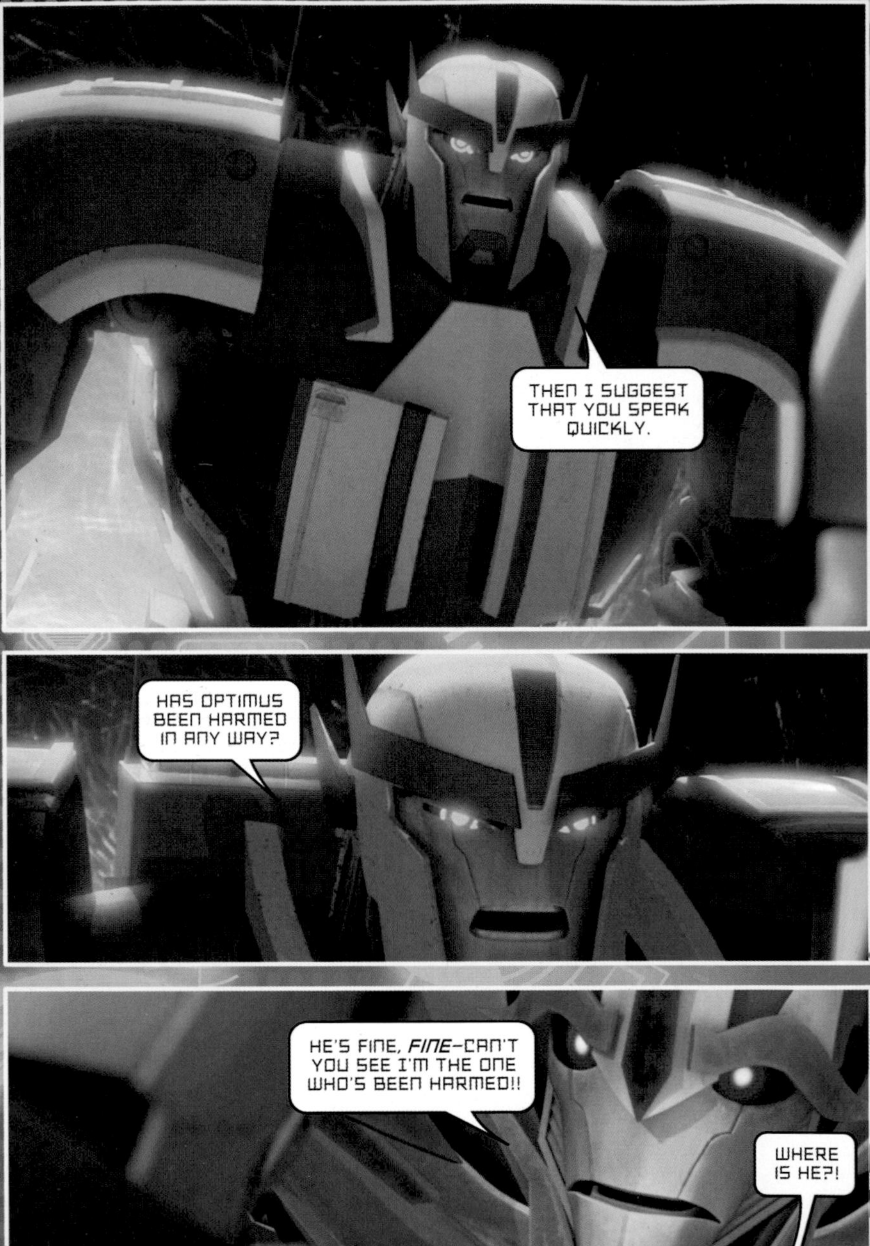
THEN I SUGGEST THAT YOU SPEAK QUICKLY.
HAS OPTIMUS BEEN HARMED IN ANY WAY?
HE'S FINE, *FINE*—CAN'T YOU SEE I'M THE ONE WHO'S BEEN HARMED!!
WHERE IS HE?!

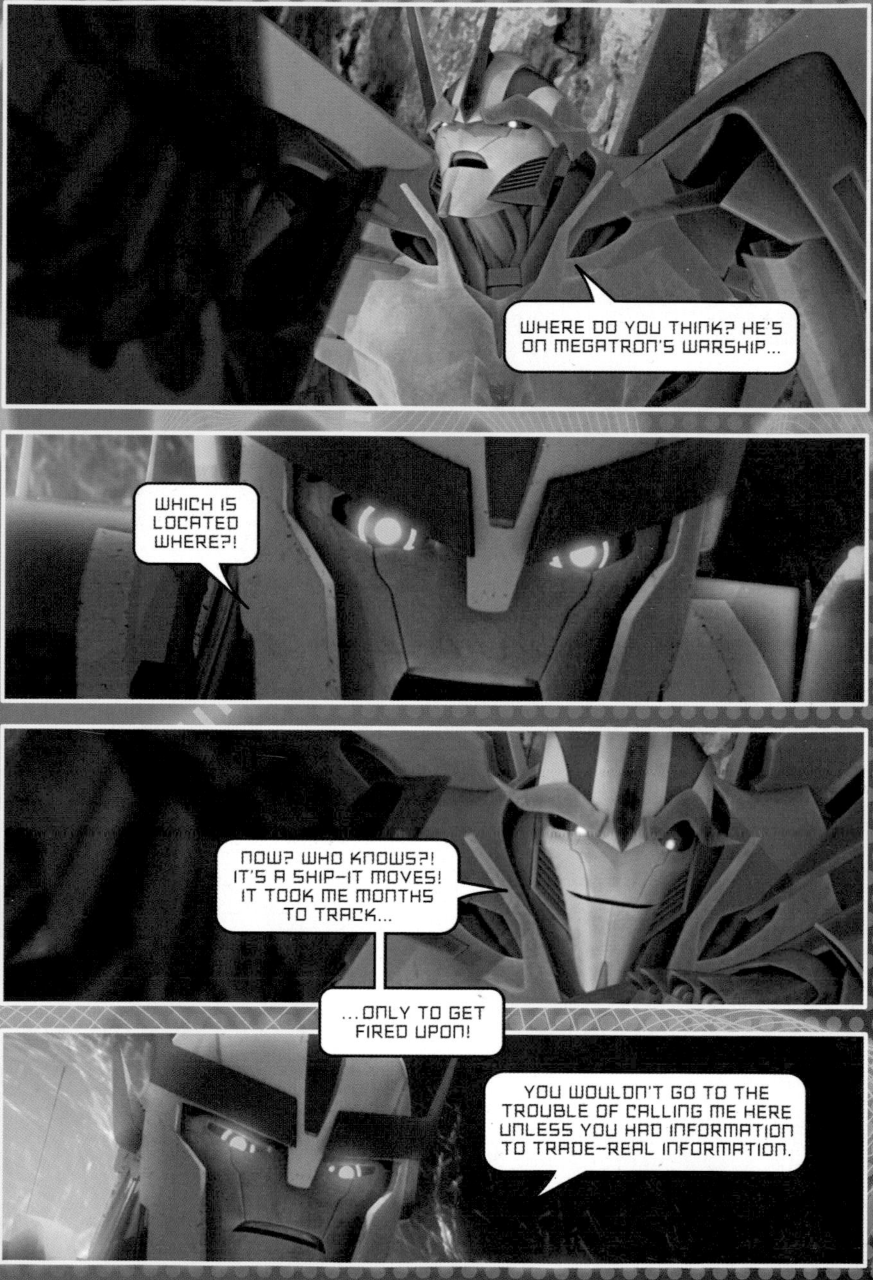
WHERE DO YOU THINK? HE'S ON MEGATRON'S WARSHIP...
WHICH IS LOCATED WHERE?!
NOW? WHO KNOWS?! IT'S A SHIP–IT MOVES! IT TOOK ME MONTHS TO TRACK...
...ONLY TO GET FIRED UPON!
YOU WOULDN'T GO TO THE TROUBLE OF CALLING ME HERE UNLESS YOU HAD INFORMATION TO TRADE–REAL INFORMATION.

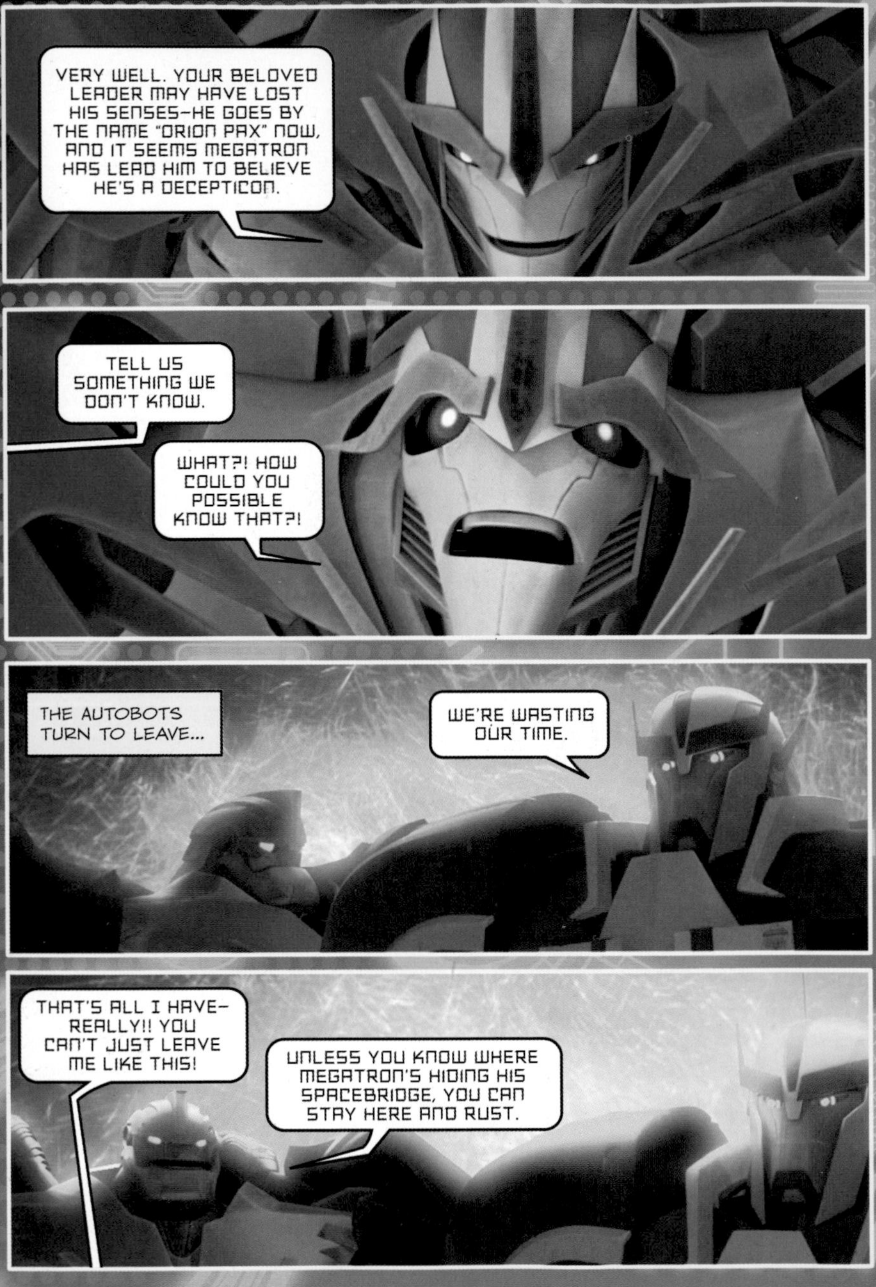
VERY WELL. YOUR BELOVED LEADER MAY HAVE LOST HIS SENSES—HE GOES BY THE NAME "ORION PAX" NOW, AND IT SEEMS MEGATRON HAS LEAD HIM TO BELIEVE HE'S A DECEPTICON.
TELL US SOMETHING WE DON'T KNOW.
WHAT?! HOW COULD YOU POSSIBLE KNOW THAT?!
THE AUTOBOTS TURN TO LEAVE...
WE'RE WASTING OUR TIME.
THAT'S ALL I HAVE—REALLY!! YOU CAN'T JUST LEAVE ME LIKE THIS!
UNLESS YOU KNOW WHERE MEGATRON'S HIDING HIS SPACEBRIDGE, YOU CAN STAY HERE AND RUST.

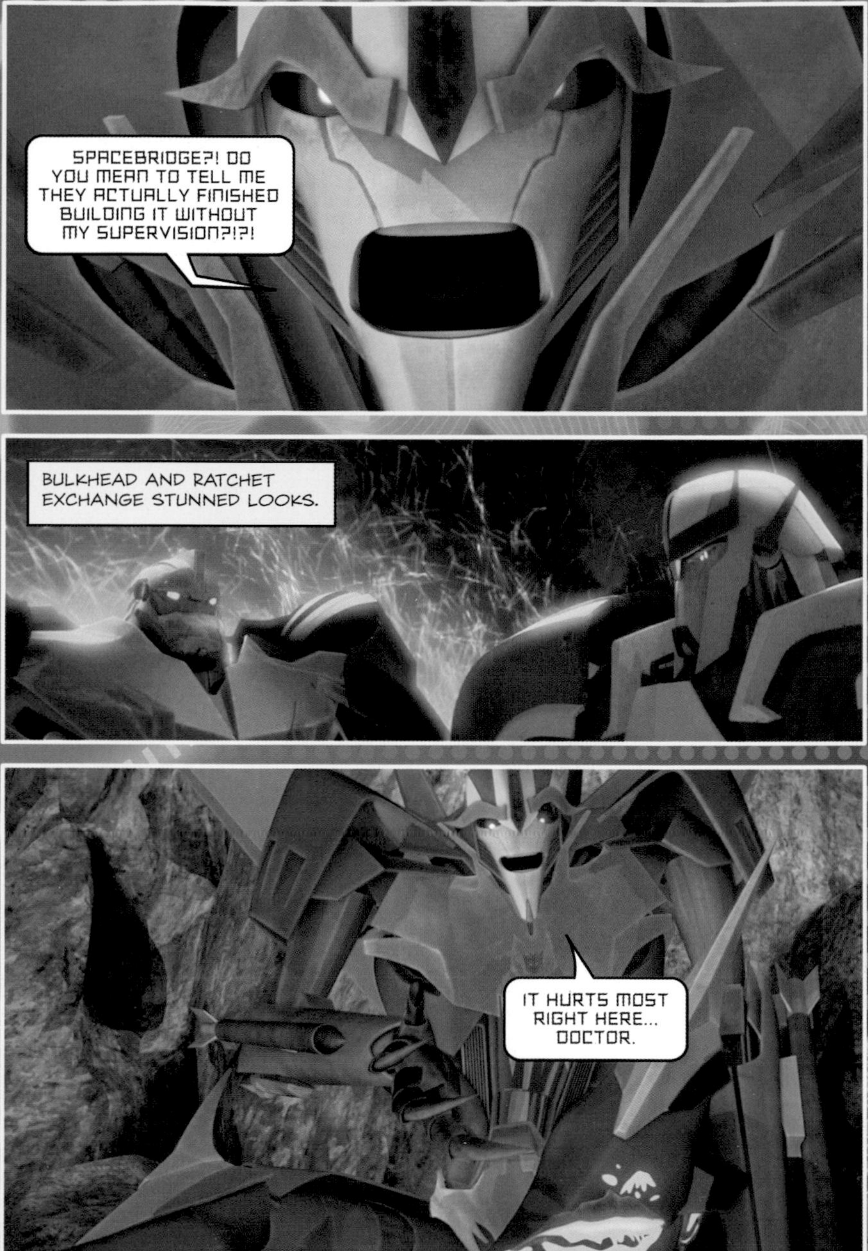
SPACEBRIDGE?! DO YOU MEAN TO TELL ME THEY ACTUALLY FINISHED BUILDING IT WITHOUT MY SUPERVISION?!?!
BULKHEAD AND RATCHET EXCHANGE STUNNED LOOKS.
IT HURTS MOST RIGHT HERE... DOCTOR.

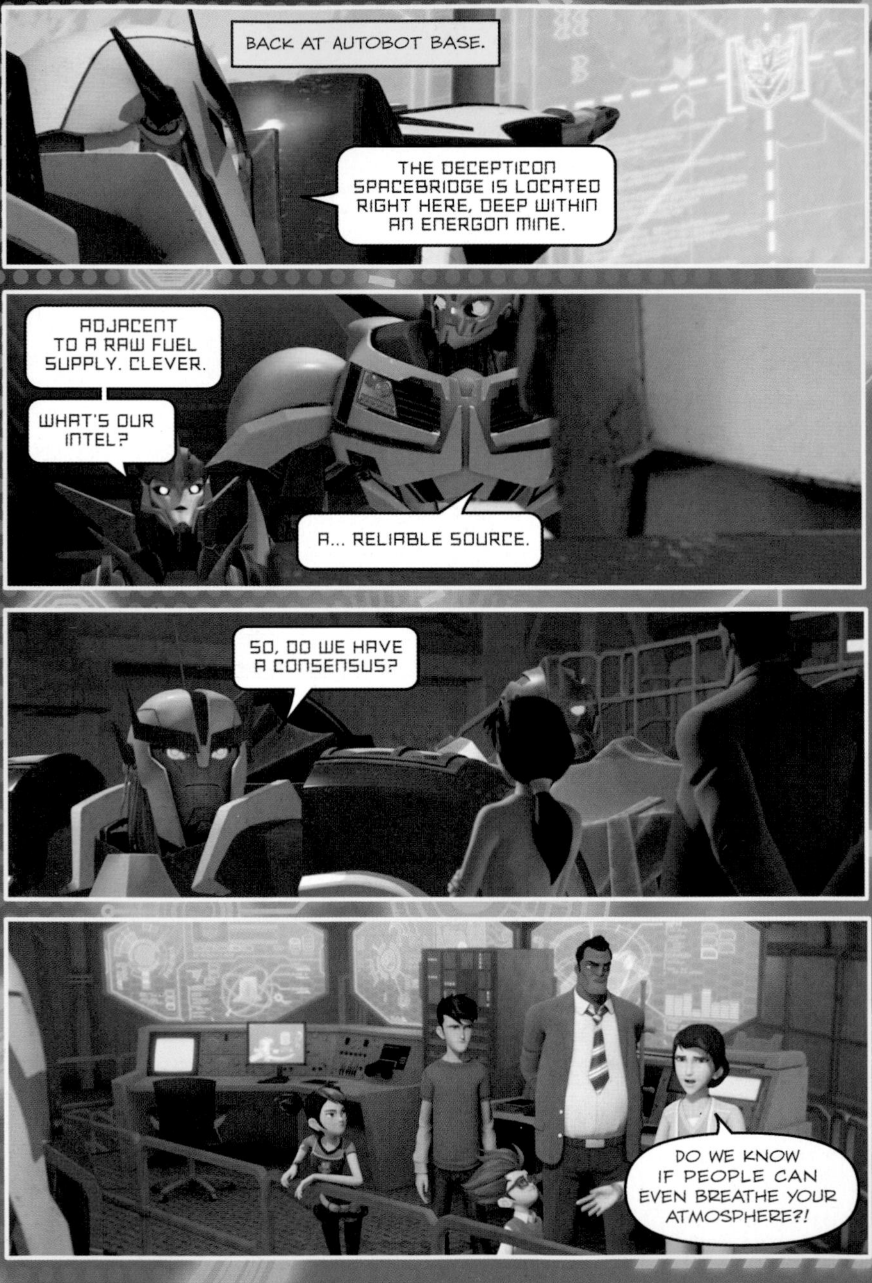
BACK AT AUTOBOT BASE.
THE DECEPTICON SPACEBRIDGE IS LOCATED RIGHT HERE, DEEP WITHIN AN ENERGON MINE.
ADJACENT TO A RAW FUEL SUPPLY. CLEVER.
WHAT'S OUR INTEL?
A... RELIABLE SOURCE.
SO, DO WE HAVE A CONSENSUS?
DO WE KNOW IF PEOPLE CAN EVEN BREATHE YOUR ATMOSPHERE?!

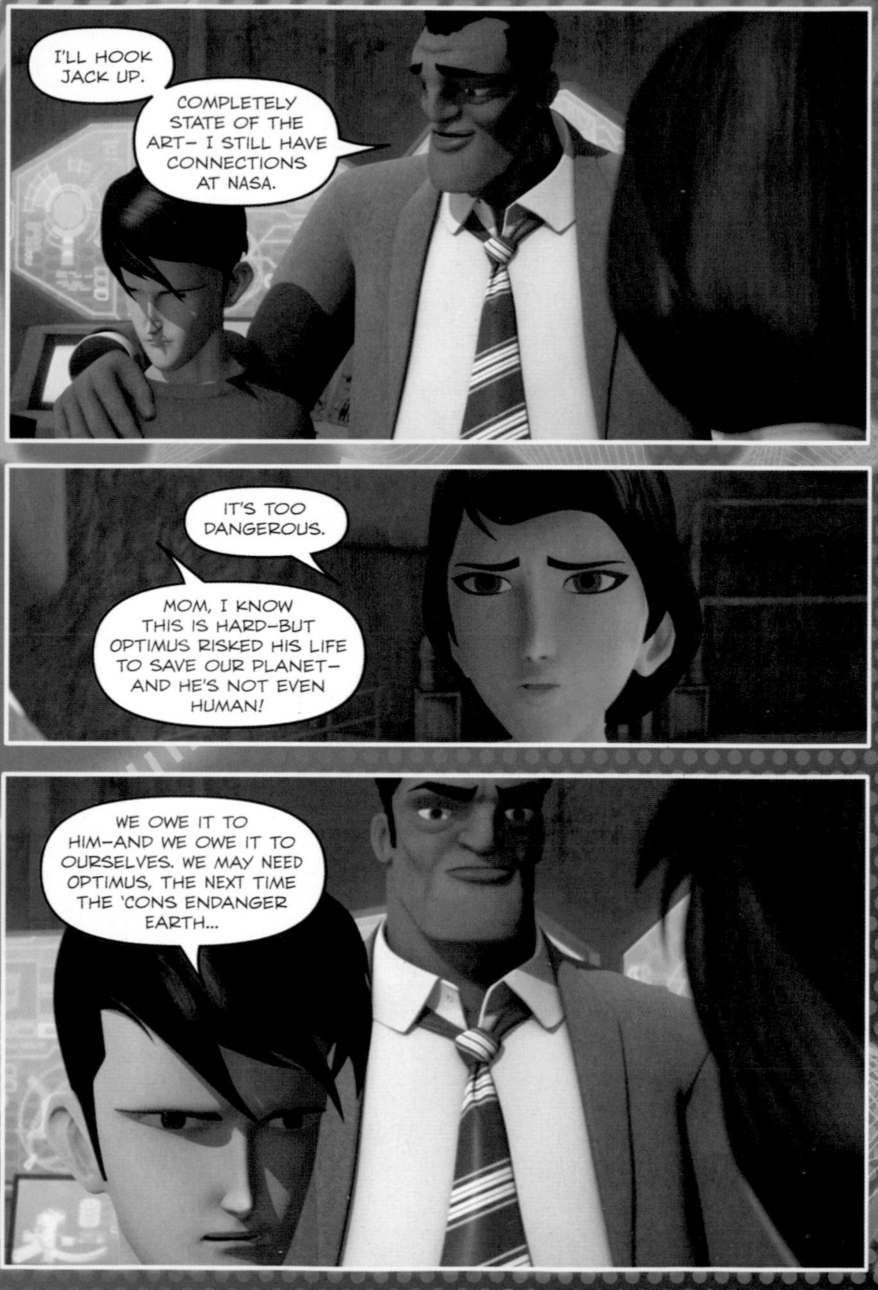
I'LL HOOK JACK UP.
COMPLETELY STATE OF THE ART– I STILL HAVE CONNECTIONS AT NASA.
IT'S TOO DANGEROUS.
MOM, I KNOW THIS IS HARD–BUT OPTIMUS RISKED HIS LIFE TO SAVE OUR PLANET– AND HE'S NOT EVEN HUMAN!
WE OWE IT TO HIM–AND WE OWE IT TO OURSELVES. WE MAY NEED OPTIMUS, THE NEXT TIME THE 'CONS ENDANGER EARTH...

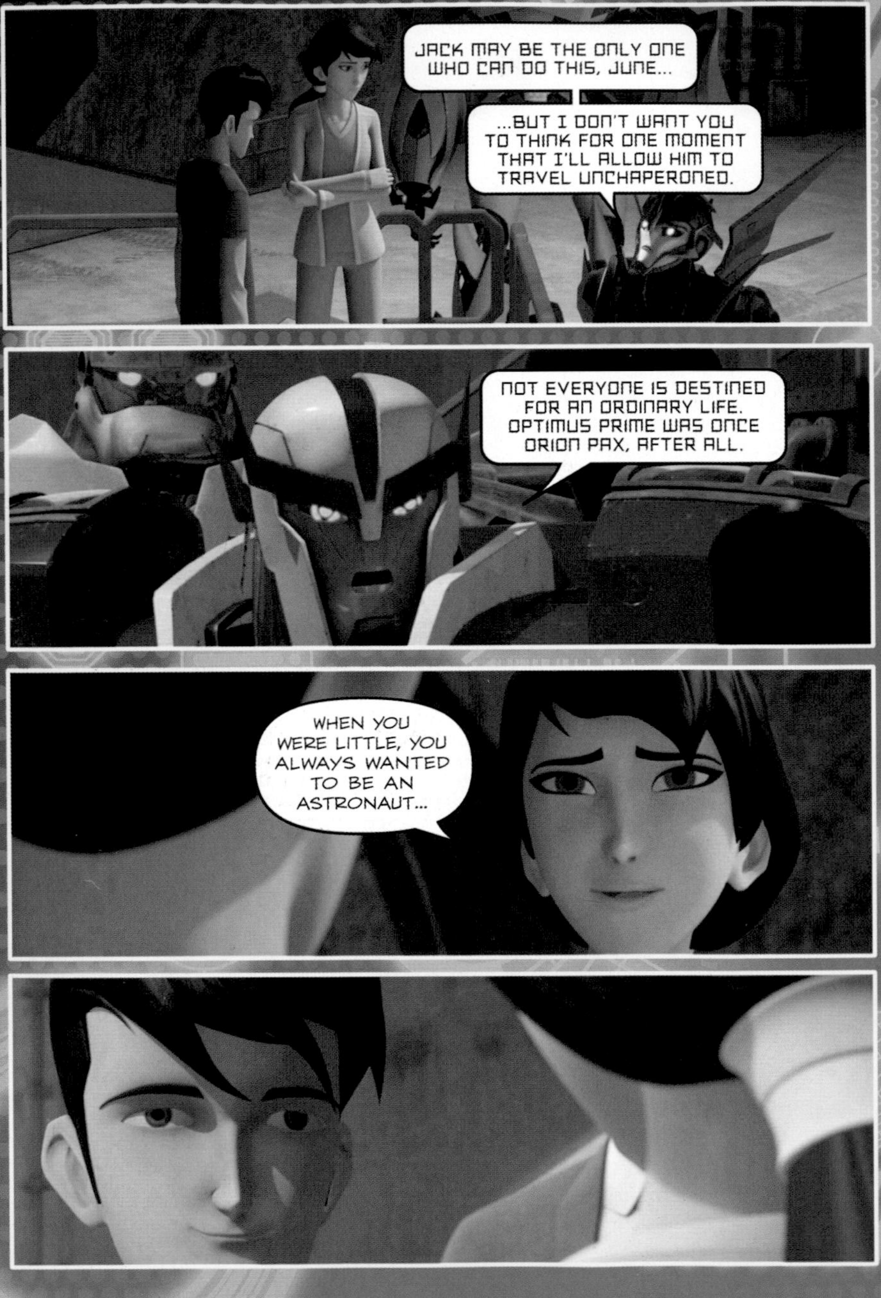
JACK MAY BE THE ONLY ONE WHO CAN DO THIS, JUNE...
...BUT I DON'T WANT YOU TO THINK FOR ONE MOMENT THAT I'LL ALLOW HIM TO TRAVEL UNCHAPERONED.
NOT EVERYONE IS DESTINED FOR AN ORDINARY LIFE. OPTIMUS PRIME WAS ONCE ORION PAX, AFTER ALL.
WHEN YOU WERE LITTLE, YOU ALWAYS WANTED TO BE AN ASTRONAUT...

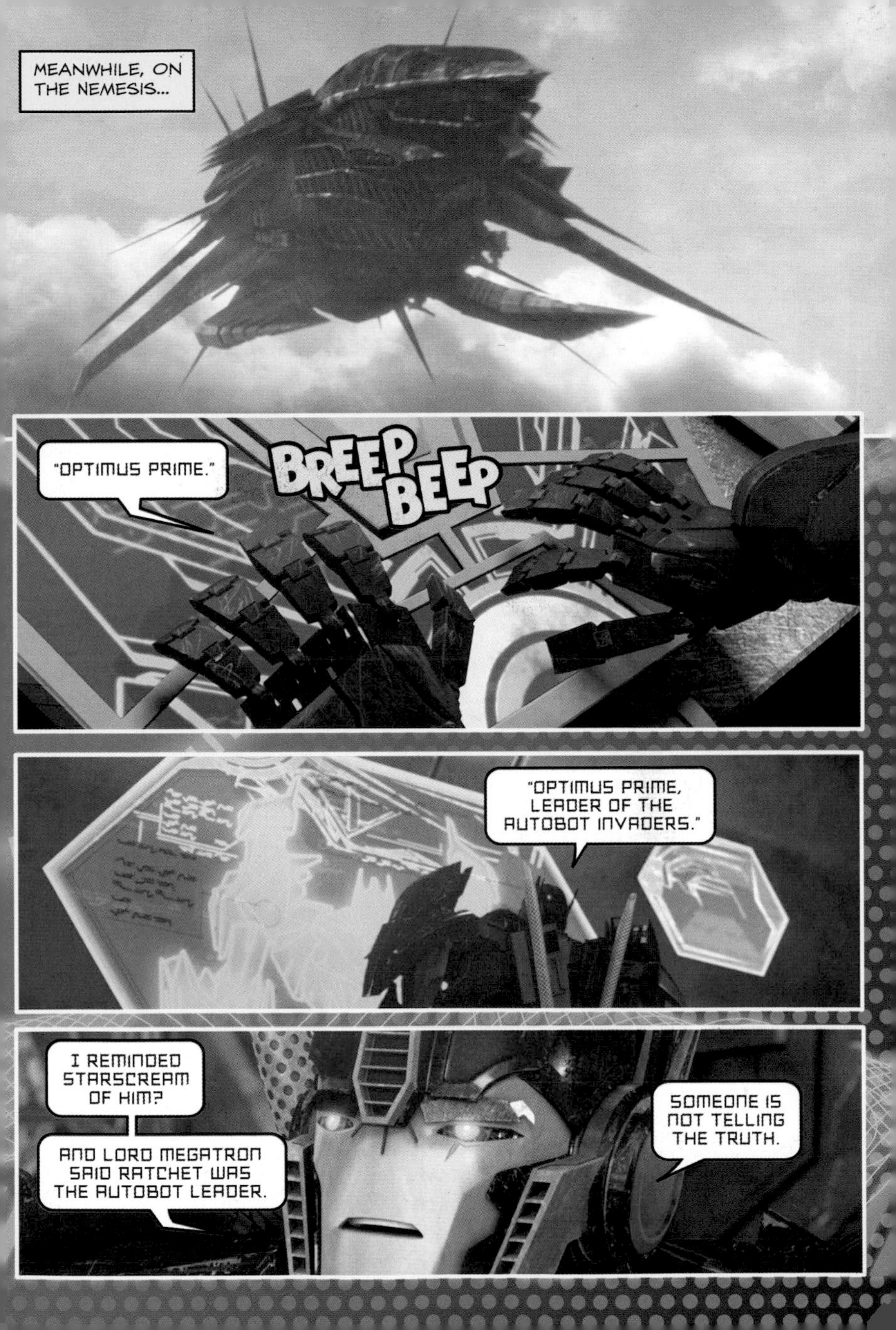
MEANWHILE, ON THE NEMESIS...
"OPTIMUS PRIME."
BREEP BEEP
"OPTIMUS PRIME, LEADER OF THE AUTOBOT INVADERS."
I REMINDED STARSCREAM OF HIM?
AND LORD MEGATRON SAID RATCHET WAS THE AUTOBOT LEADER.
SOMEONE IS NOT TELLING THE TRUTH.

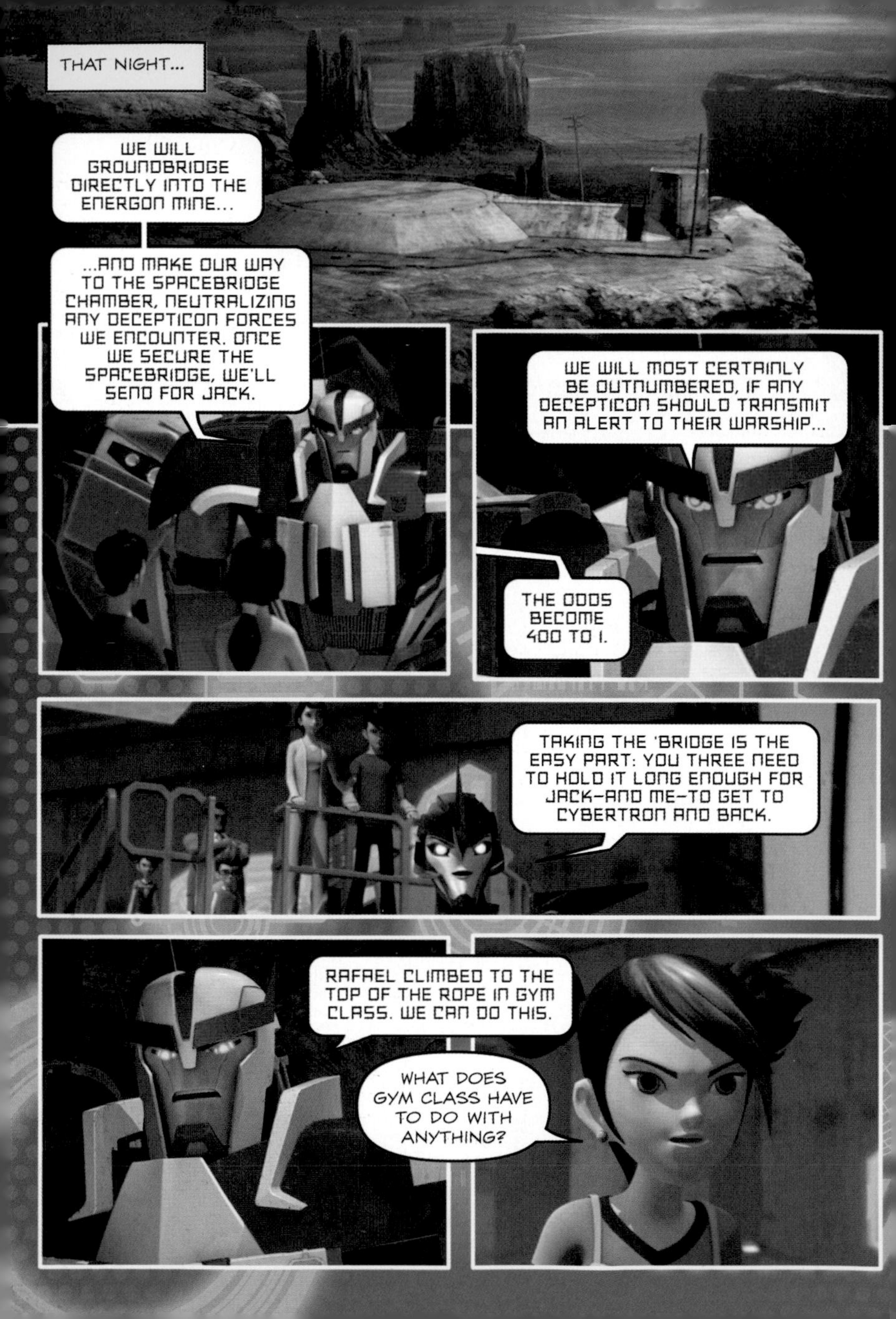
THAT NIGHT...
WE WILL GROUNDBRIDGE DIRECTLY INTO THE ENERGON MINE...
...AND MAKE OUR WAY TO THE SPACEBRIDGE CHAMBER, NEUTRALIZING ANY DECEPTICON FORCES WE ENCOUNTER. ONCE WE SECURE THE SPACEBRIDGE, WE'LL SEND FOR JACK.
WE WILL MOST CERTAINLY BE OUTNUMBERED, IF ANY DECEPTICON SHOULD TRANSMIT AN ALERT TO THEIR WARSHIP...
THE ODDS BECOME 400 TO 1.
TAKING THE 'BRIDGE IS THE EASY PART: YOU THREE NEED TO HOLD IT LONG ENOUGH FOR JACK—AND ME—TO GET TO CYBERTRON AND BACK.
RAFAEL CLIMBED TO THE TOP OF THE ROPE IN GYM CLASS. WE CAN DO THIS.
WHAT DOES GYM CLASS HAVE TO DO WITH ANYTHING?

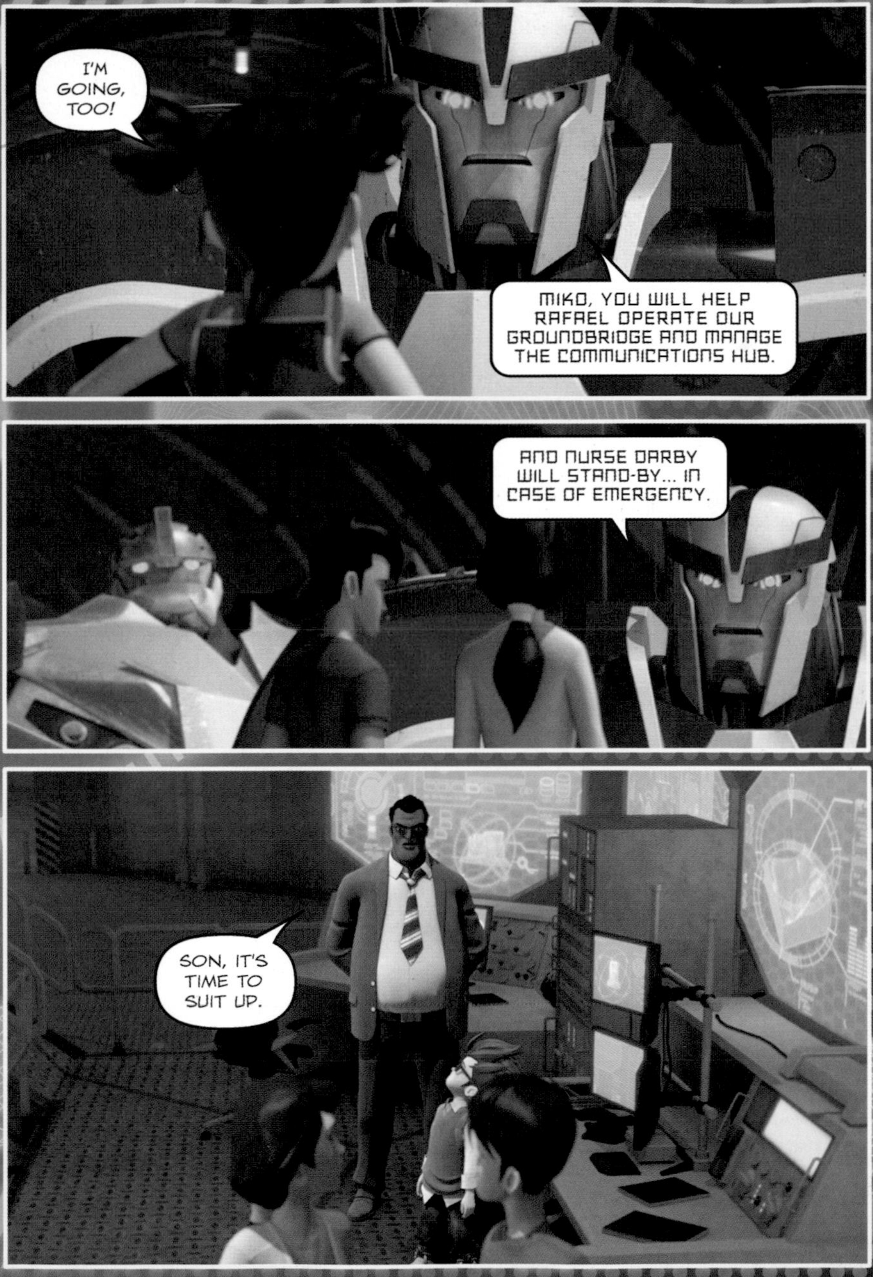
I'M GOING, TOO!
MIKO, YOU WILL HELP RAFAEL OPERATE OUR GROUNDBRIDGE AND MANAGE THE COMMUNICATIONS HUB.
AND NURSE DARBY WILL STAND-BY... IN CASE OF EMERGENCY.
SON, IT'S TIME TO SUIT UP.

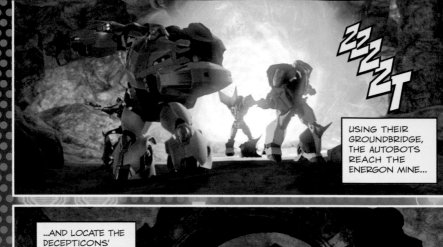

ZZZZT

USING THEIR GROUNDBRIDGE, THE AUTOBOTS REACH THE ENERGON MINE...

...AND LOCATE THE DECEPTICONS' SPACEBRIDGE.

THANK YOU, STARSCREAM.

HUH?

WHO ELSE WOULD IT BE?

THEN PRESS TOWARDS THE CONTROL PLATFORM.

ZZRAK

ZZRAK

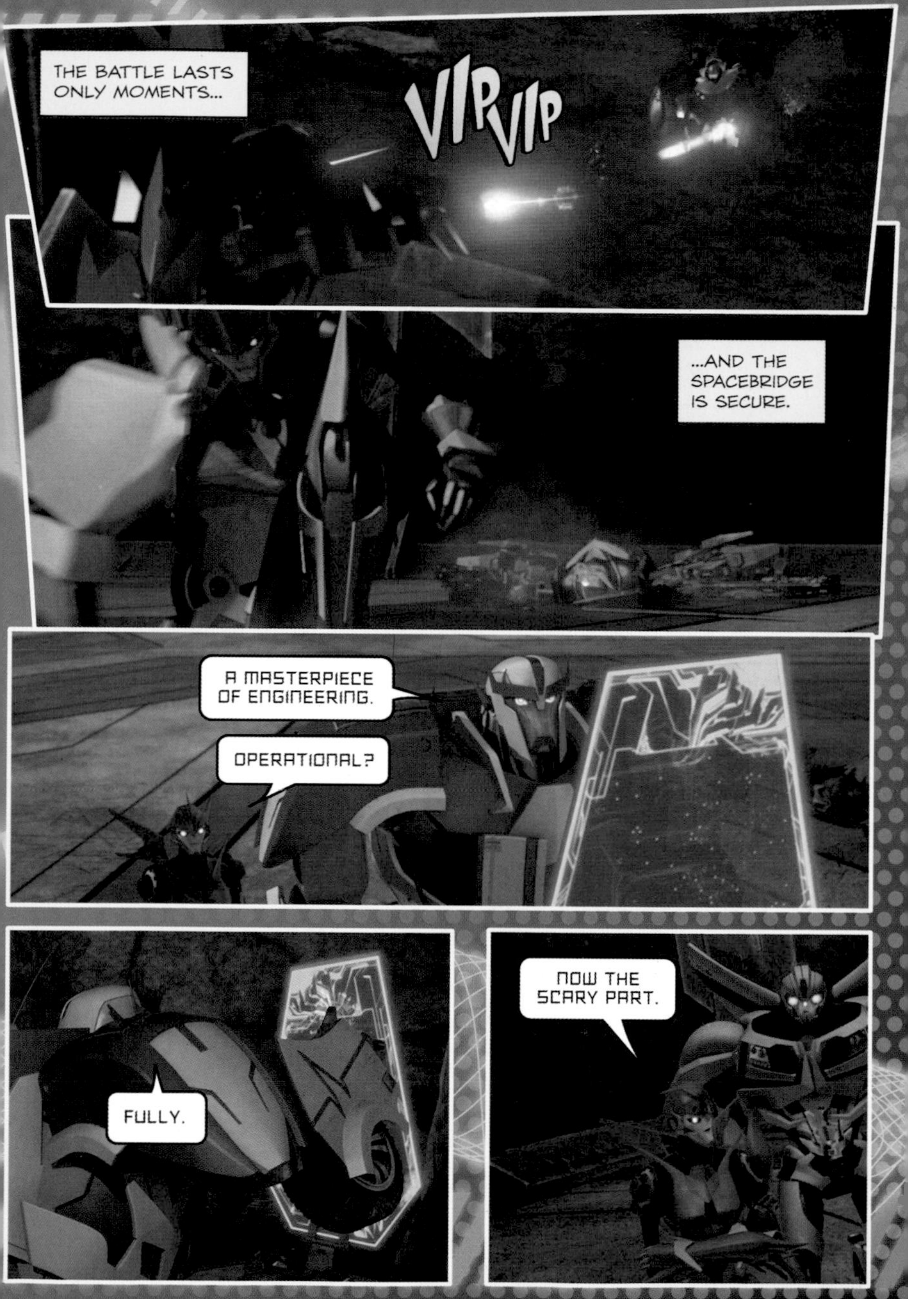
THE BATTLE LASTS ONLY MOMENTS...
VIP VIP
...AND THE SPACEBRIDGE IS SECURE.
A MASTERPIECE OF ENGINEERING.
OPERATIONAL?
FULLY.
NOW THE SCARY PART.

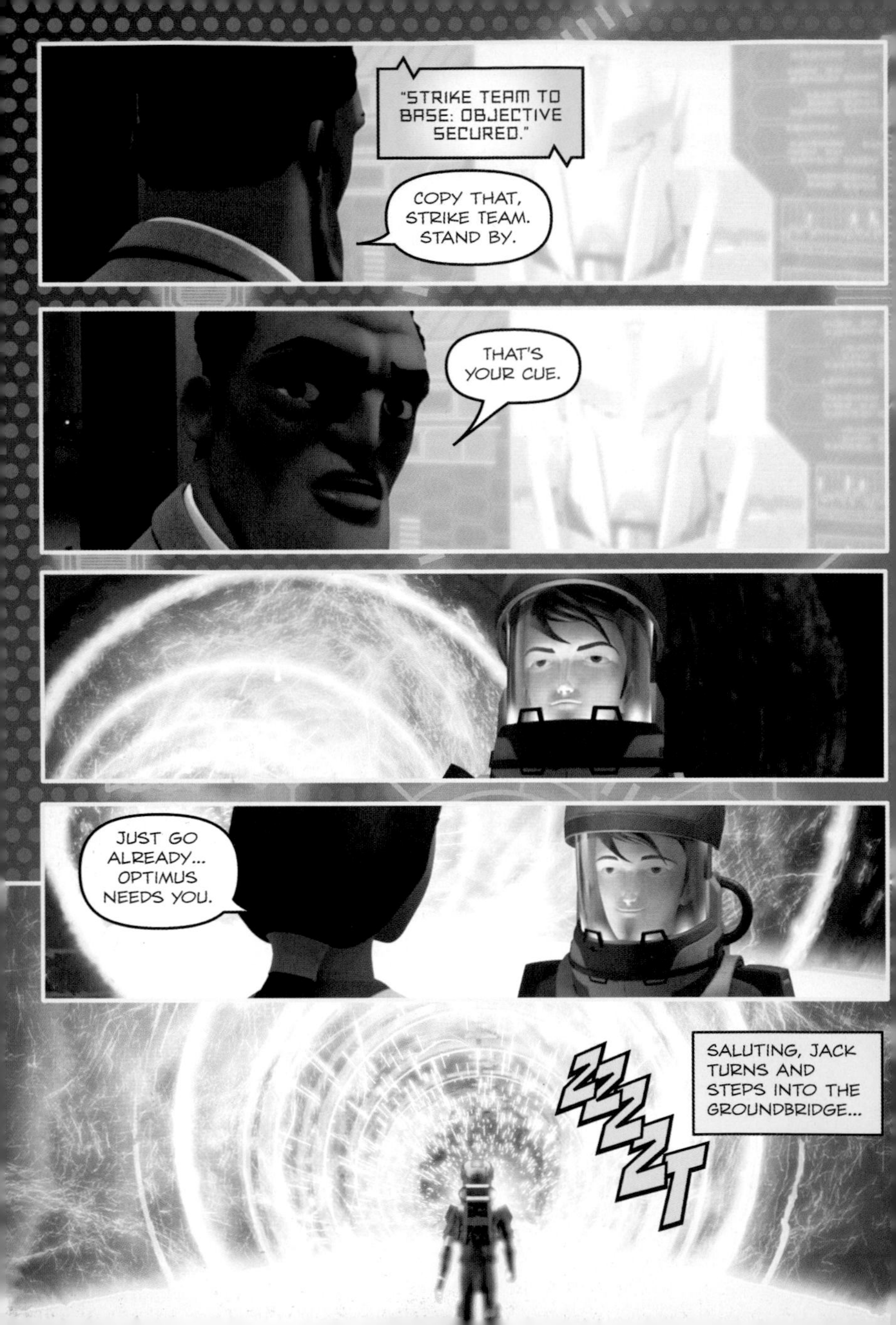
"STRIKE TEAM TO BASE: OBJECTIVE SECURED."
COPY THAT, STRIKE TEAM. STAND BY.
THAT'S YOUR CUE.
JUST GO ALREADY... OPTIMUS NEEDS YOU.
ZZZZT
SALUTING, JACK TURNS AND STEPS INTO THE GROUNDBRIDGE...

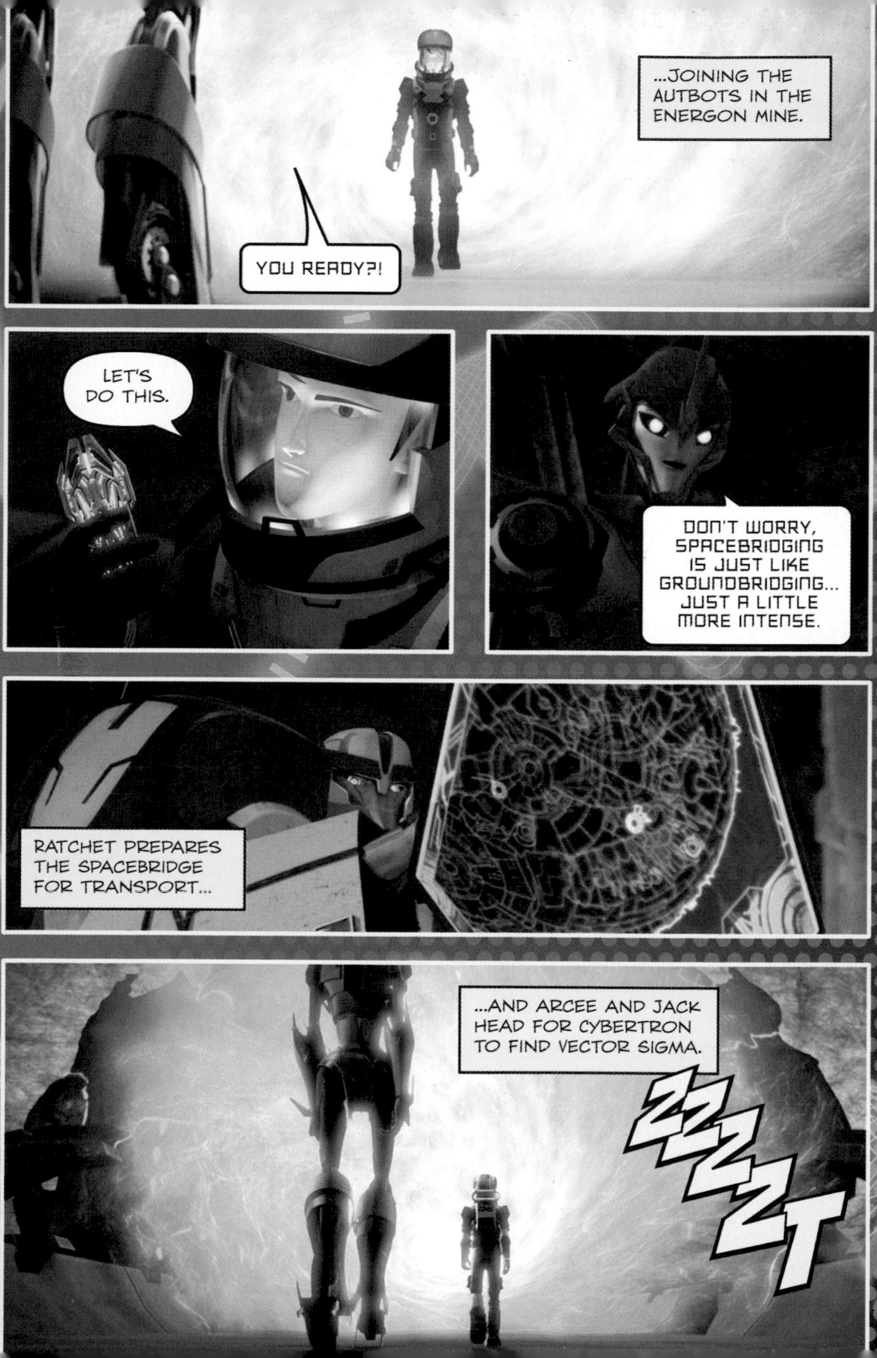
...JOINING THE AUTBOTS IN THE ENERGON MINE.
YOU READY?!
LET'S DO THIS.
DON'T WORRY, SPACEBRIDGING IS JUST LIKE GROUNDBRIDGING... JUST A LITTLE MORE INTENSE.
RATCHET PREPARES THE SPACEBRIDGE FOR TRANSPORT...
...AND ARCEE AND JACK HEAD FOR CYBERTRON TO FIND VECTOR SIGMA.
ZZZZT

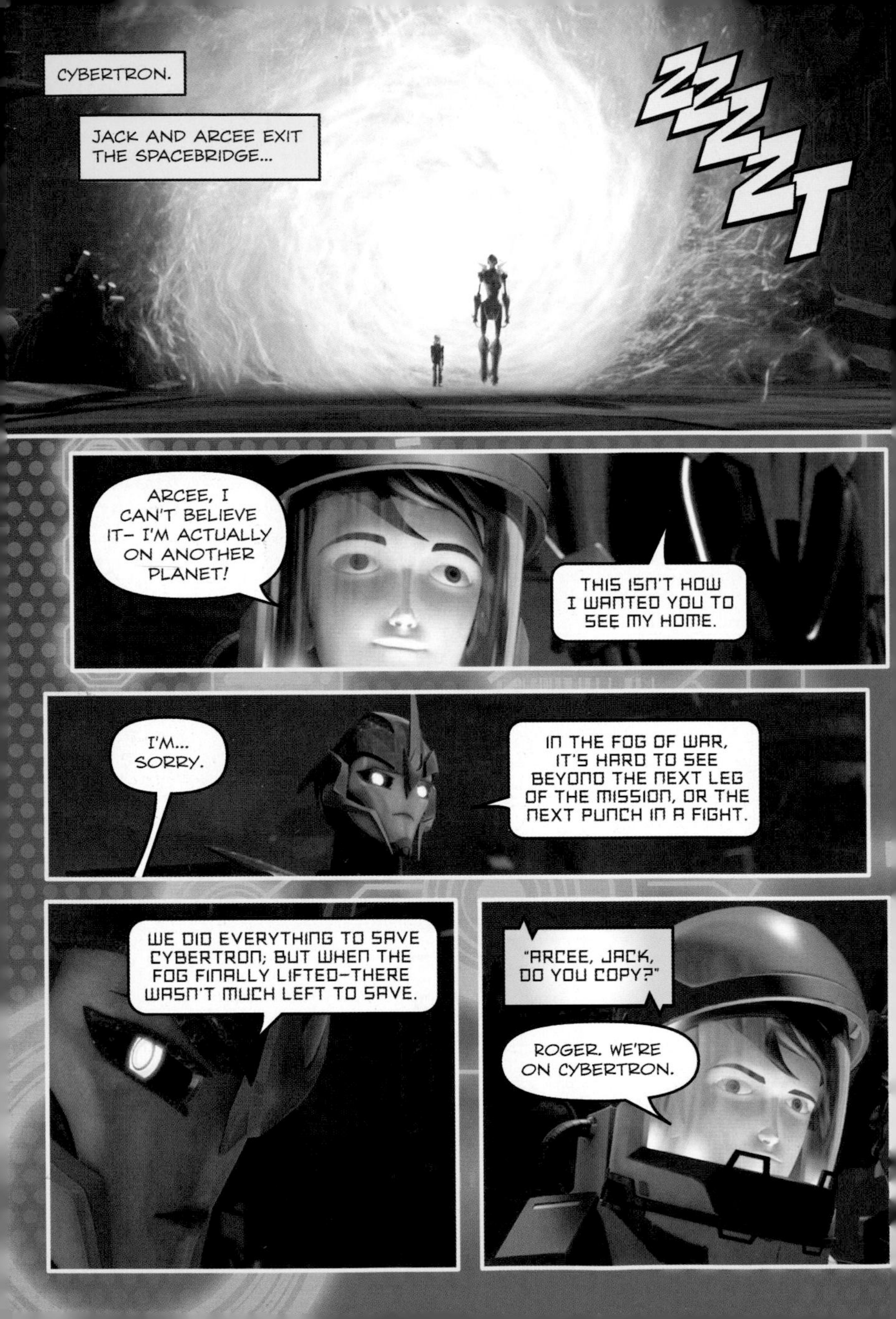
CYBERTRON.
JACK AND ARCEE EXIT THE SPACEBRIDGE...
ZZZZT
ARCEE, I CAN'T BELIEVE IT– I'M ACTUALLY ON ANOTHER PLANET!
THIS ISN'T HOW I WANTED YOU TO SEE MY HOME.
I'M... SORRY.
IN THE FOG OF WAR, IT'S HARD TO SEE BEYOND THE NEXT LEG OF THE MISSION, OR THE NEXT PUNCH IN A FIGHT.
WE DID EVERYTHING TO SAVE CYBERTRON; BUT WHEN THE FOG FINALLY LIFTED–THERE WASN'T MUCH LEFT TO SAVE.
"ARCEE, JACK, DO YOU COPY?"
ROGER. WE'RE ON CYBERTRON.

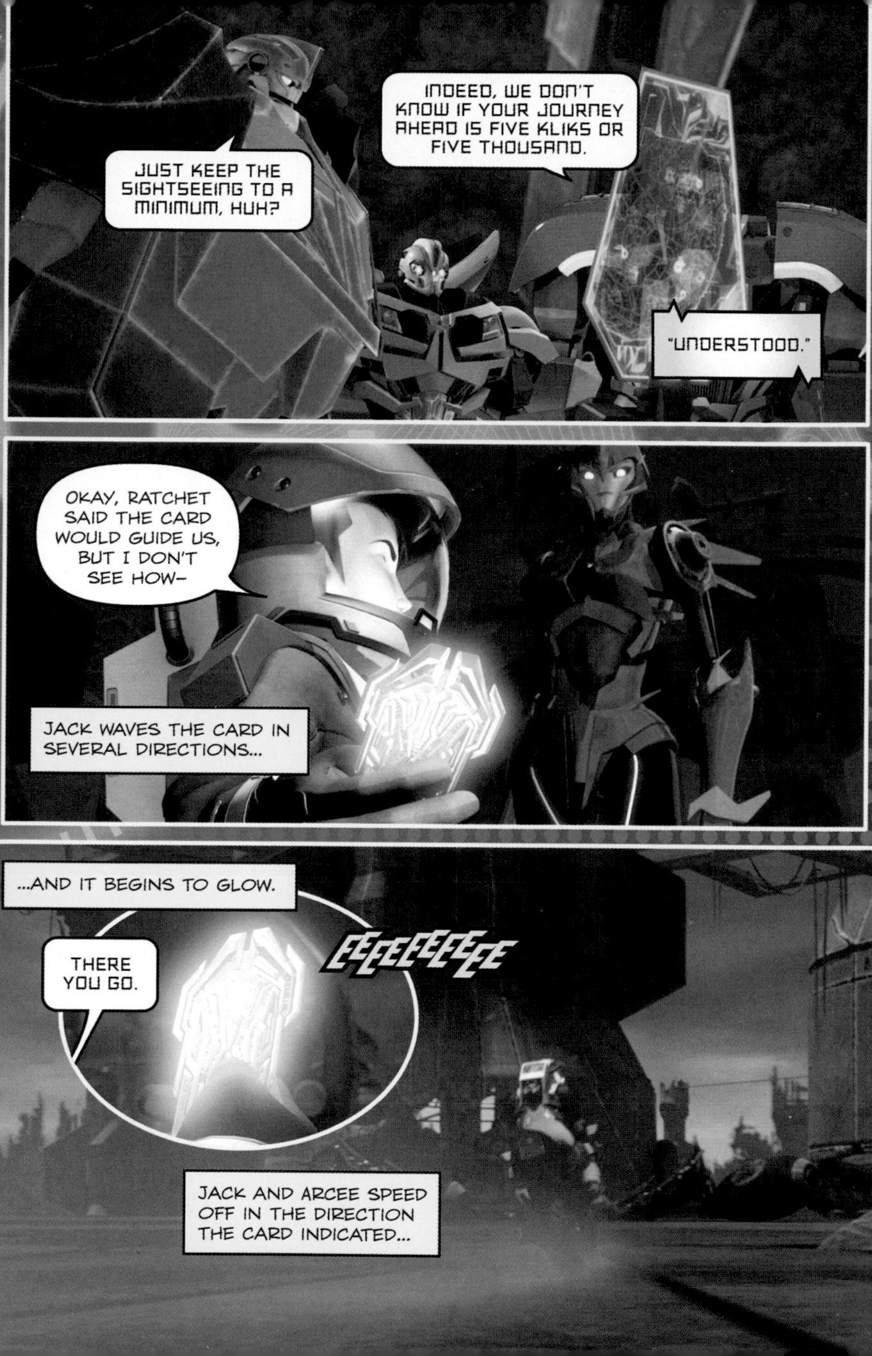
JUST KEEP THE SIGHTSEEING TO A MINIMUM, HUH?
INDEED, WE DON'T KNOW IF YOUR JOURNEY AHEAD IS FIVE KLIKS OR FIVE THOUSAND.
"UNDERSTOOD."
OKAY, RATCHET SAID THE CARD WOULD GUIDE US, BUT I DON'T SEE HOW–
JACK WAVES THE CARD IN SEVERAL DIRECTIONS...
...AND IT BEGINS TO GLOW.
THERE YOU GO.
EEEEEEEEEE
JACK AND ARCEE SPEED OFF IN THE DIRECTION THE CARD INDICATED...

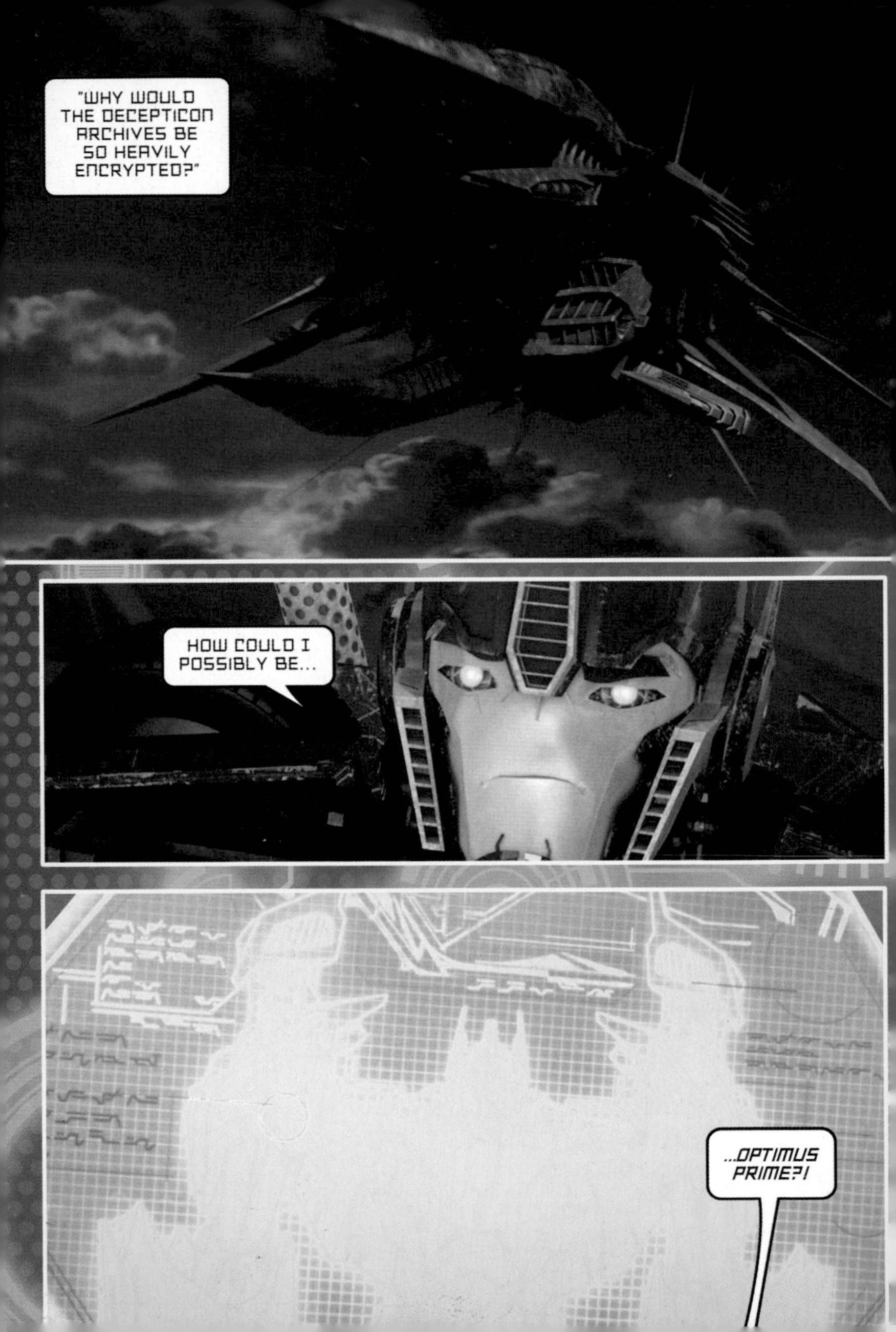
"WHY WOULD THE DECEPTICON ARCHIVES BE SO HEAVILY ENCRYPTED?"
HOW COULD I POSSIBLY BE...
...OPTIMUS PRIME?!

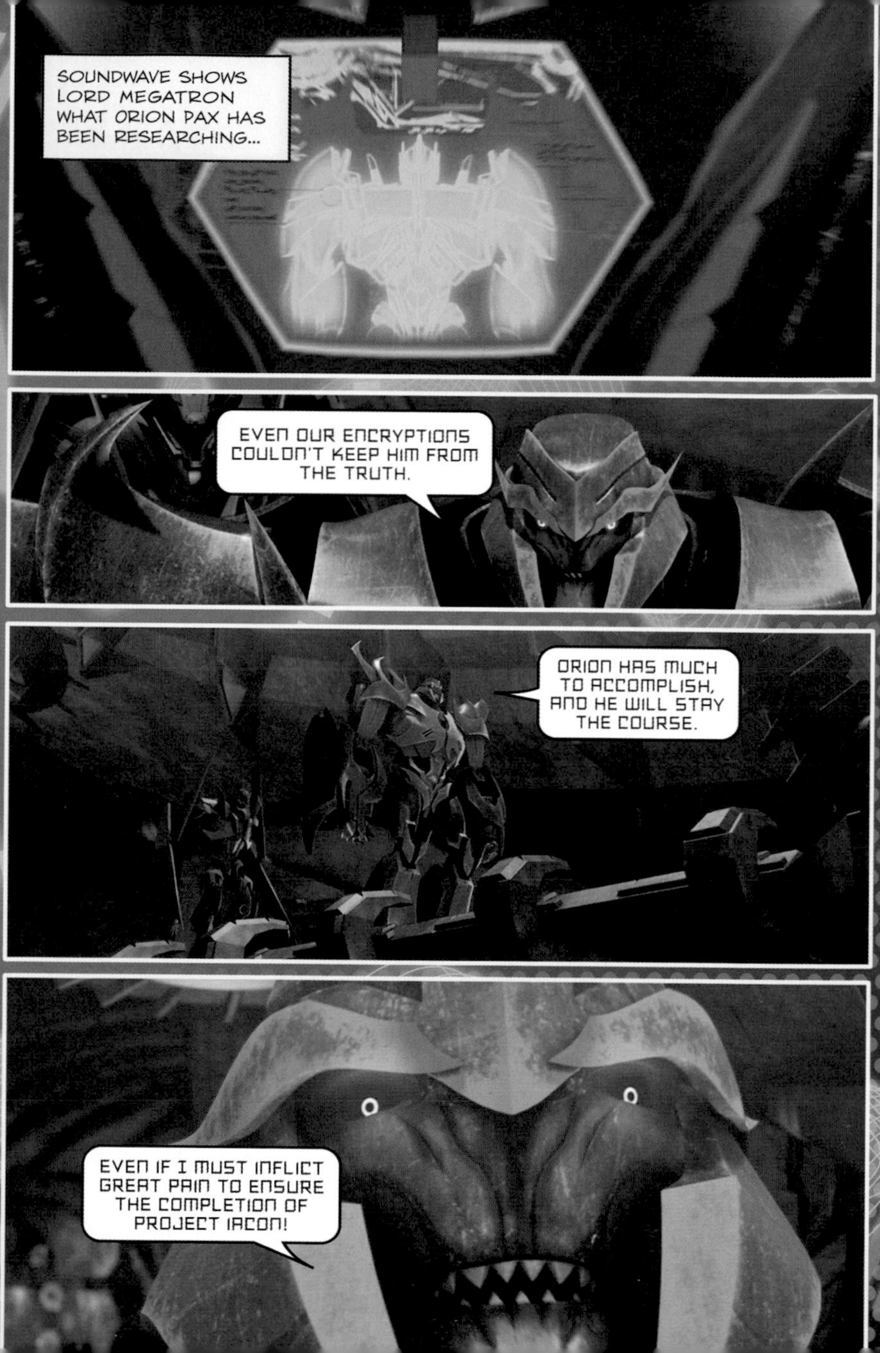
SOUNDWAVE SHOWS LORD MEGATRON WHAT ORION PAX HAS BEEN RESEARCHING...
EVEN OUR ENCRYPTIONS COULDN'T KEEP HIM FROM THE TRUTH.
ORION HAS MUCH TO ACCOMPLISH, AND HE WILL STAY THE COURSE.
EVEN IF I MUST INFLICT GREAT PAIN TO ENSURE THE COMPLETION OF PROJECT IACON!

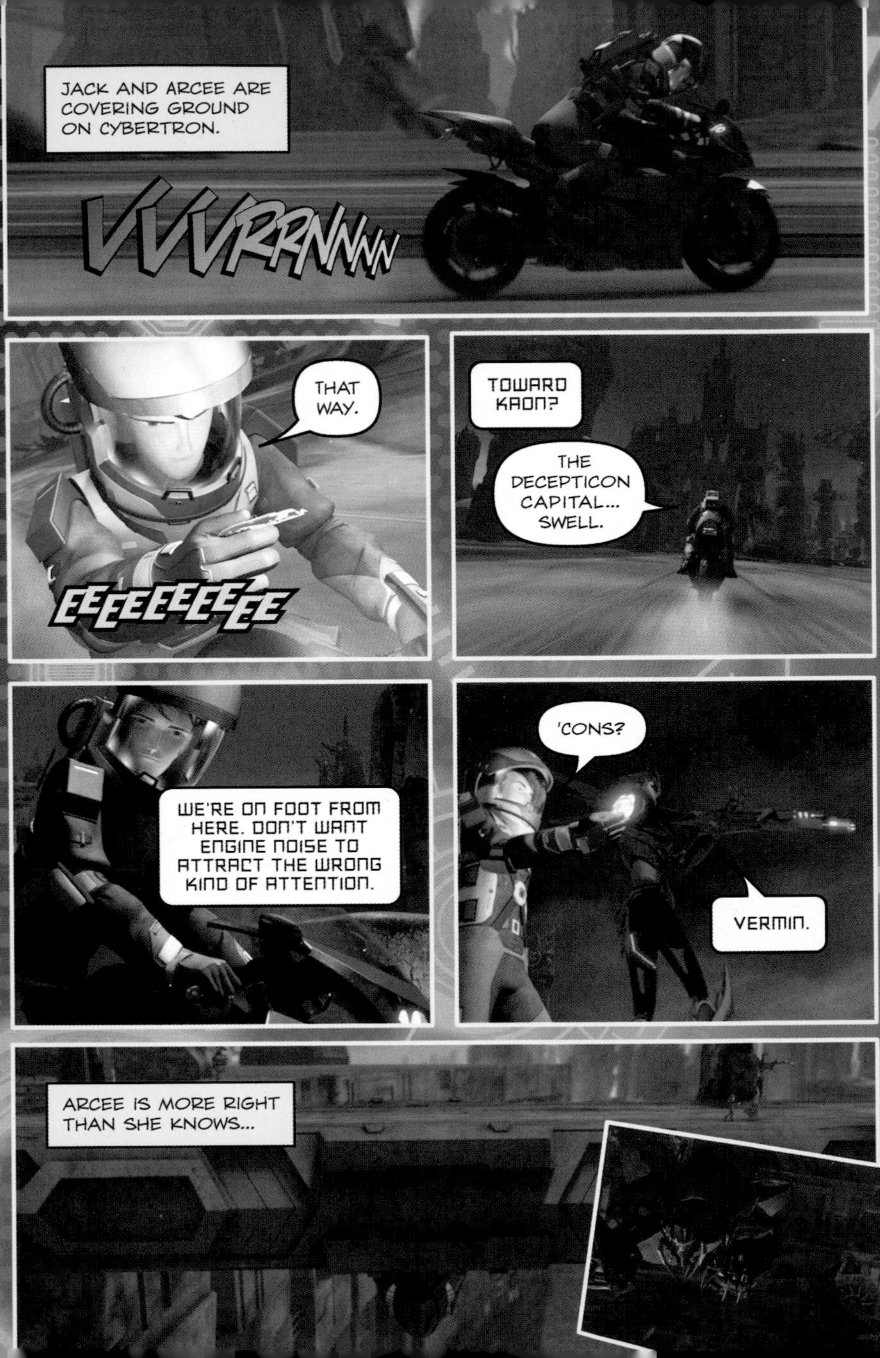
JACK AND ARCEE ARE COVERING GROUND ON CYBERTRON.
VVVRRNNNN
THAT WAY.
EEEEEEEEEE
TOWARD KAON?
THE DECEPTICON CAPITAL... SWELL.
WE'RE ON FOOT FROM HERE. DON'T WANT ENGINE NOISE TO ATTRACT THE WRONG KIND OF ATTENTION.
'CONS?
VERMIN.
ARCEE IS MORE RIGHT THAN SHE KNOWS...

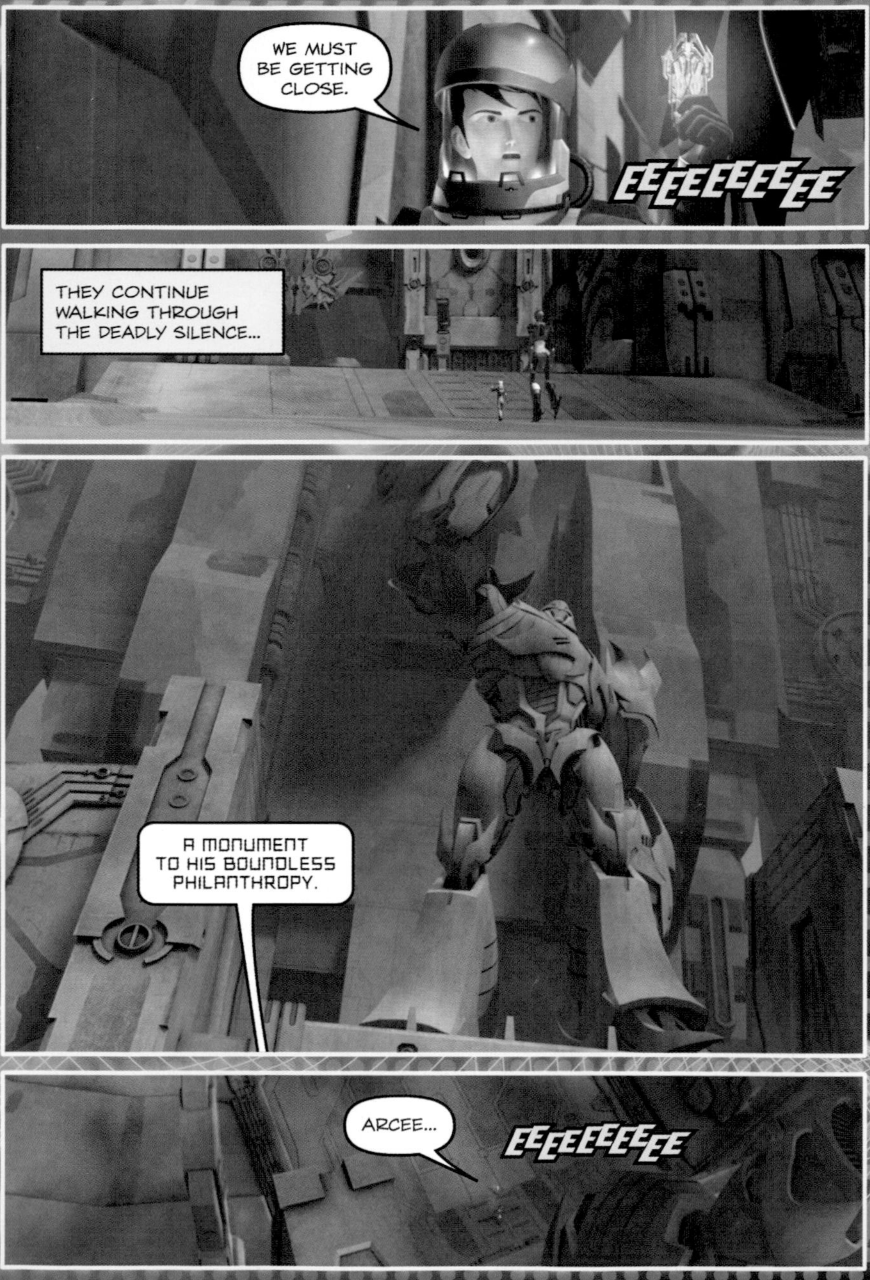

WE MUST BE GETTING CLOSE.
EEEEEEEEEEE
THEY CONTINUE WALKING THROUGH THE DEADLY SILENCE...
A MONUMENT TO HIS BOUNDLESS PHILANTHROPY.
ARCEE...
EEEEEEEEEE

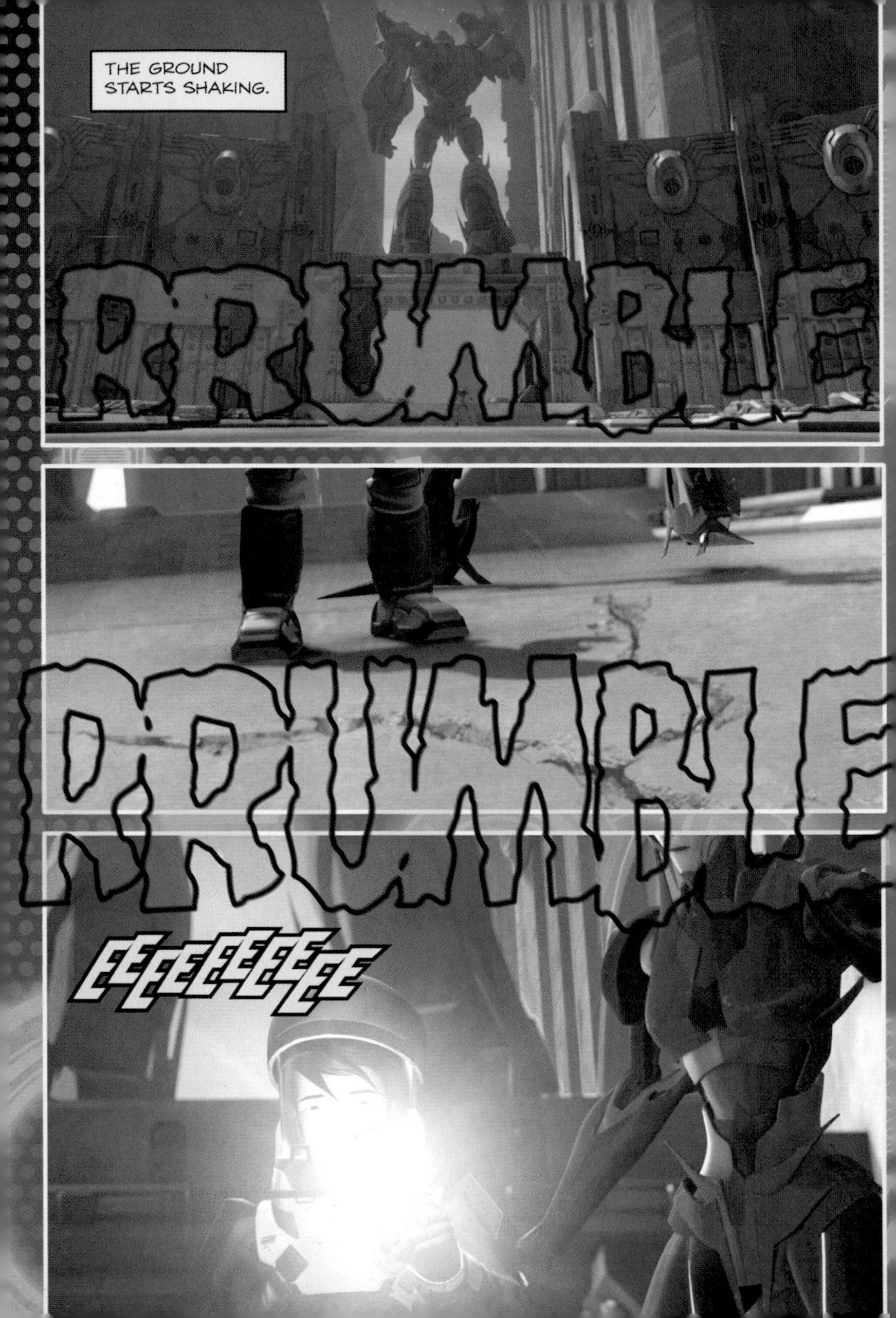
THE GROUND STARTS SHAKING.
RRUMBLE
RRUMBLE
EEEEEEEEEE

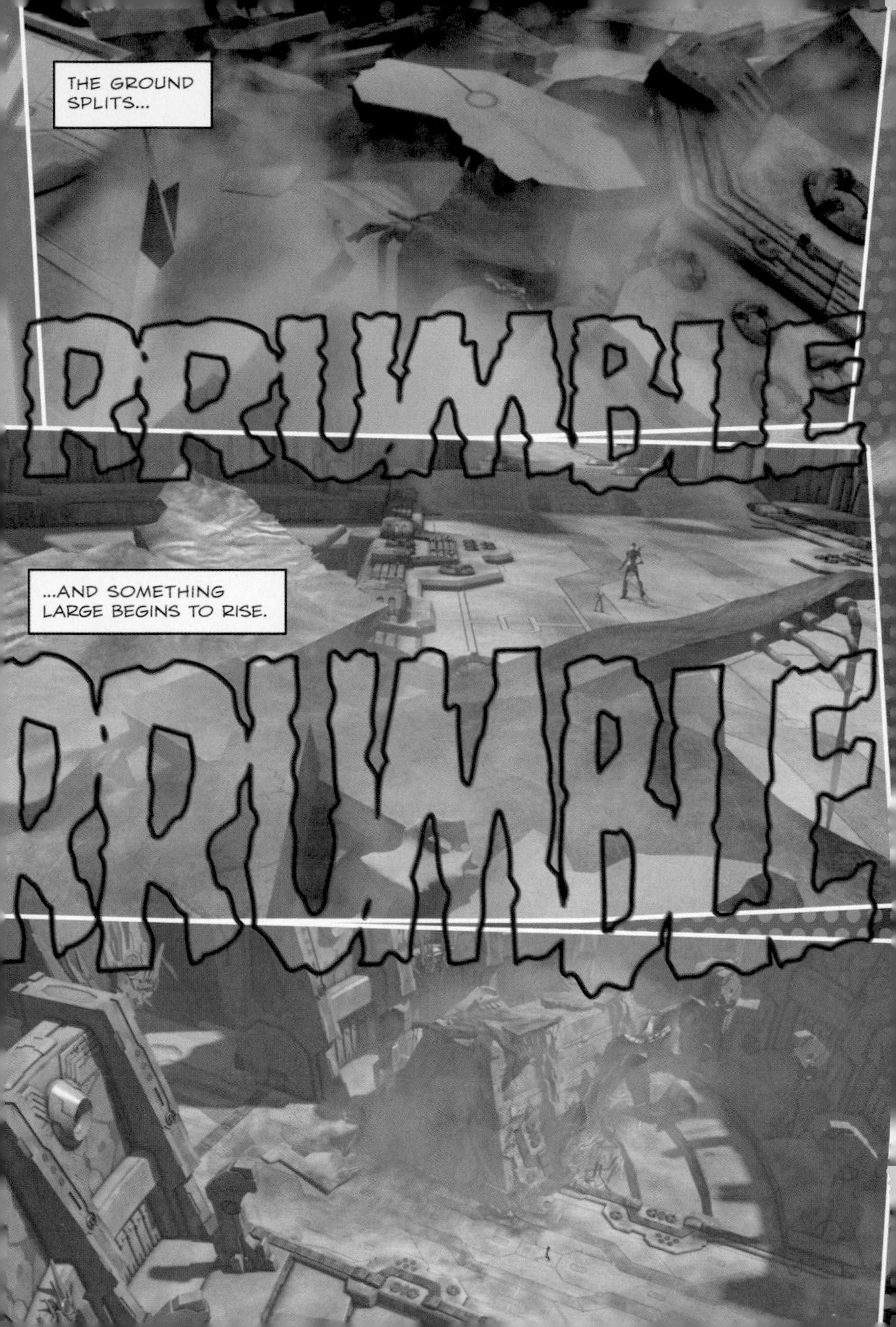
THE GROUND SPLITS...
RRUMBLE
...AND SOMETHING LARGE BEGINS TO RISE.
RRUMBLE

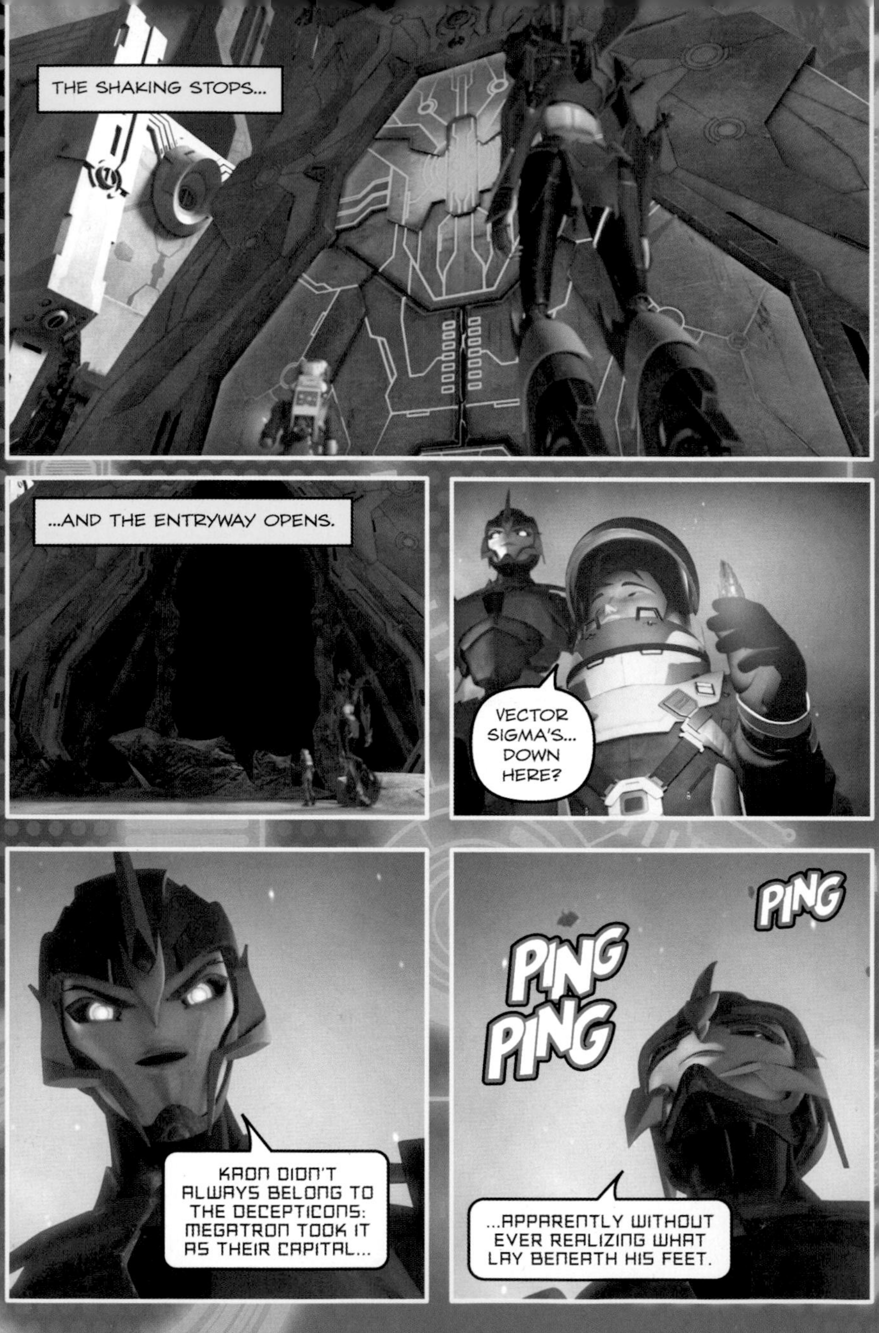
THE SHAKING STOPS...
...AND THE ENTRYWAY OPENS.
VECTOR SIGMA'S... DOWN HERE?
KAON DIDN'T ALWAYS BELONG TO THE DECEPTICONS: MEGATRON TOOK IT AS THEIR CAPITAL...
PING
PING
PING
...APPARENTLY WITHOUT EVER REALIZING WHAT LAY BENEATH HIS FEET.

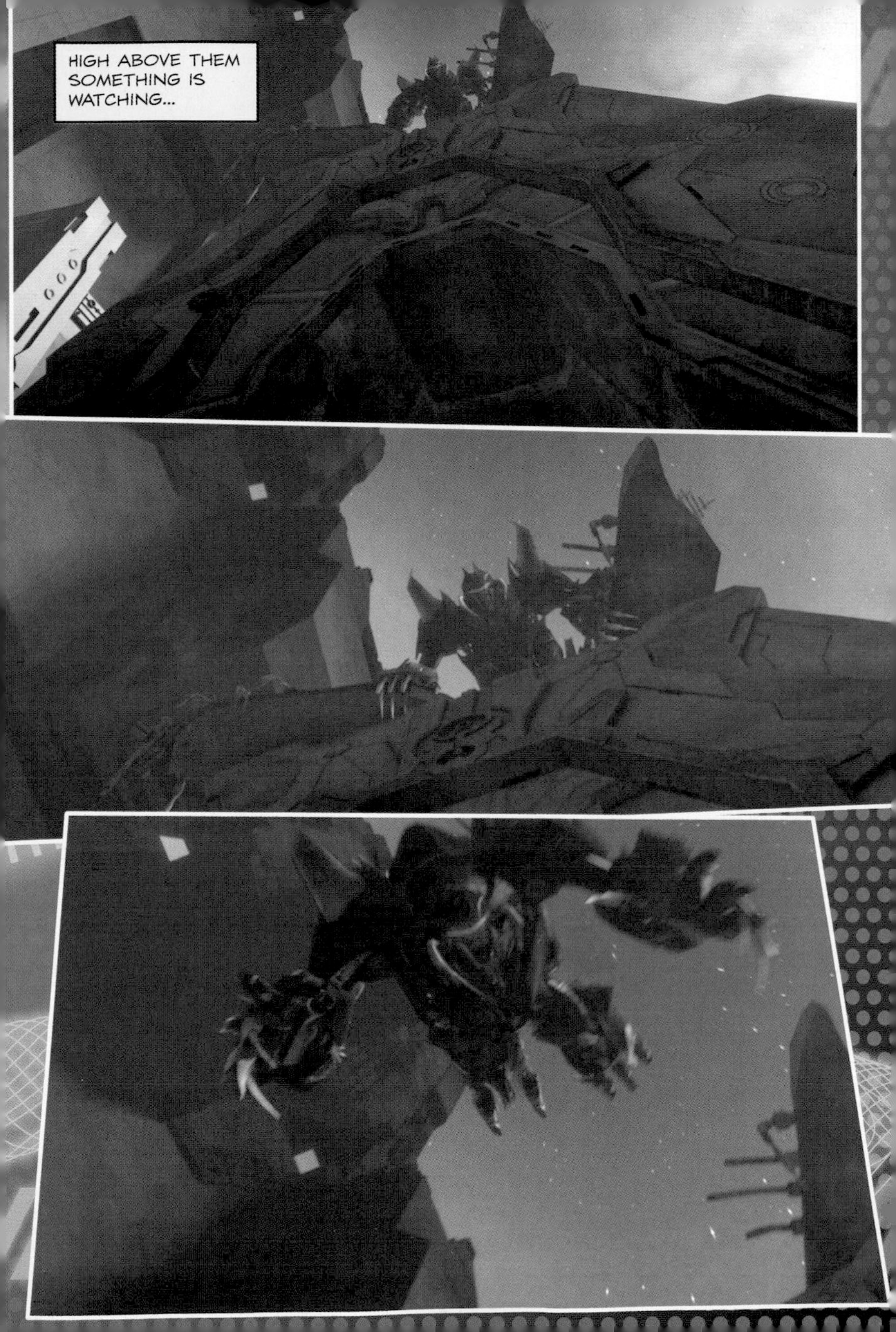
HIGH ABOVE THEM SOMETHING IS WATCHING...

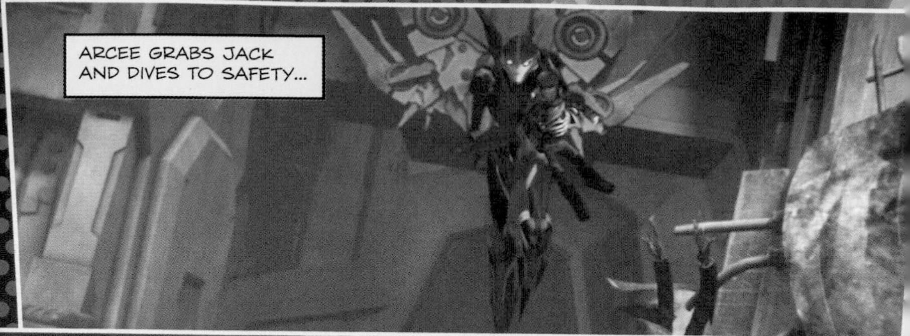
ARCEE GRABS JACK AND DIVES TO SAFETY...

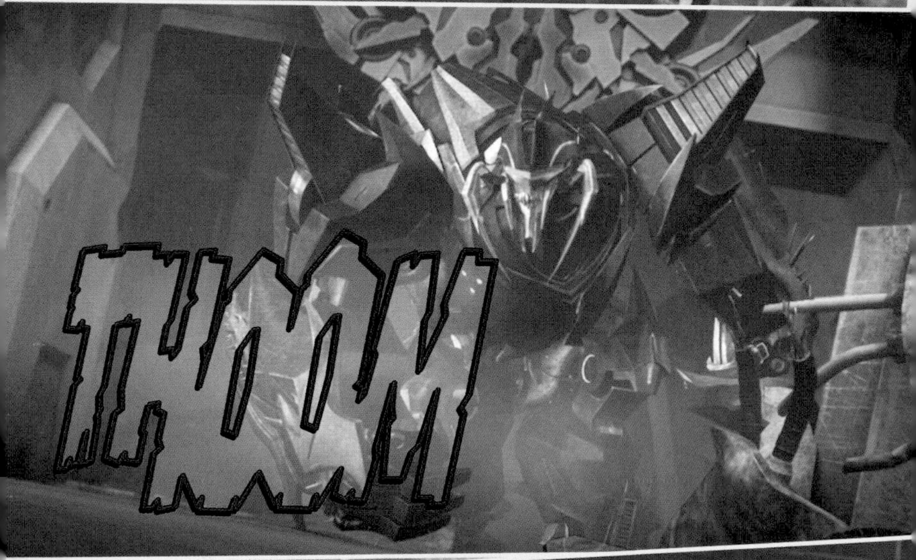
THOOM

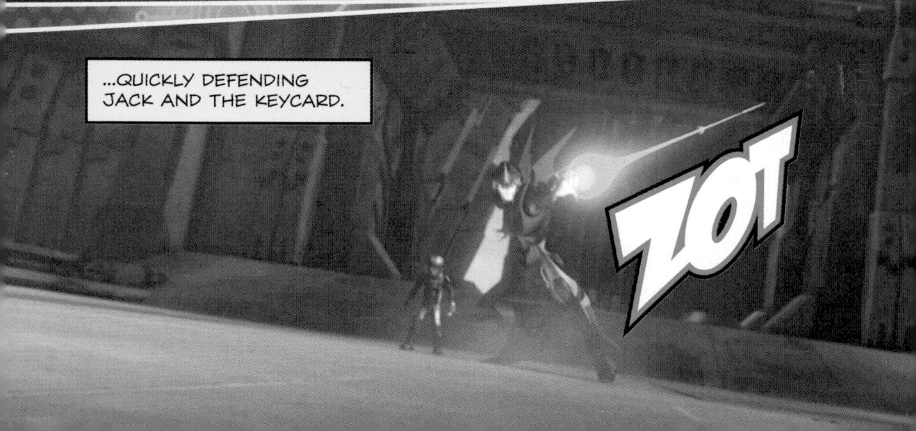
...QUICKLY DEFENDING JACK AND THE KEYCARD.
ZOT

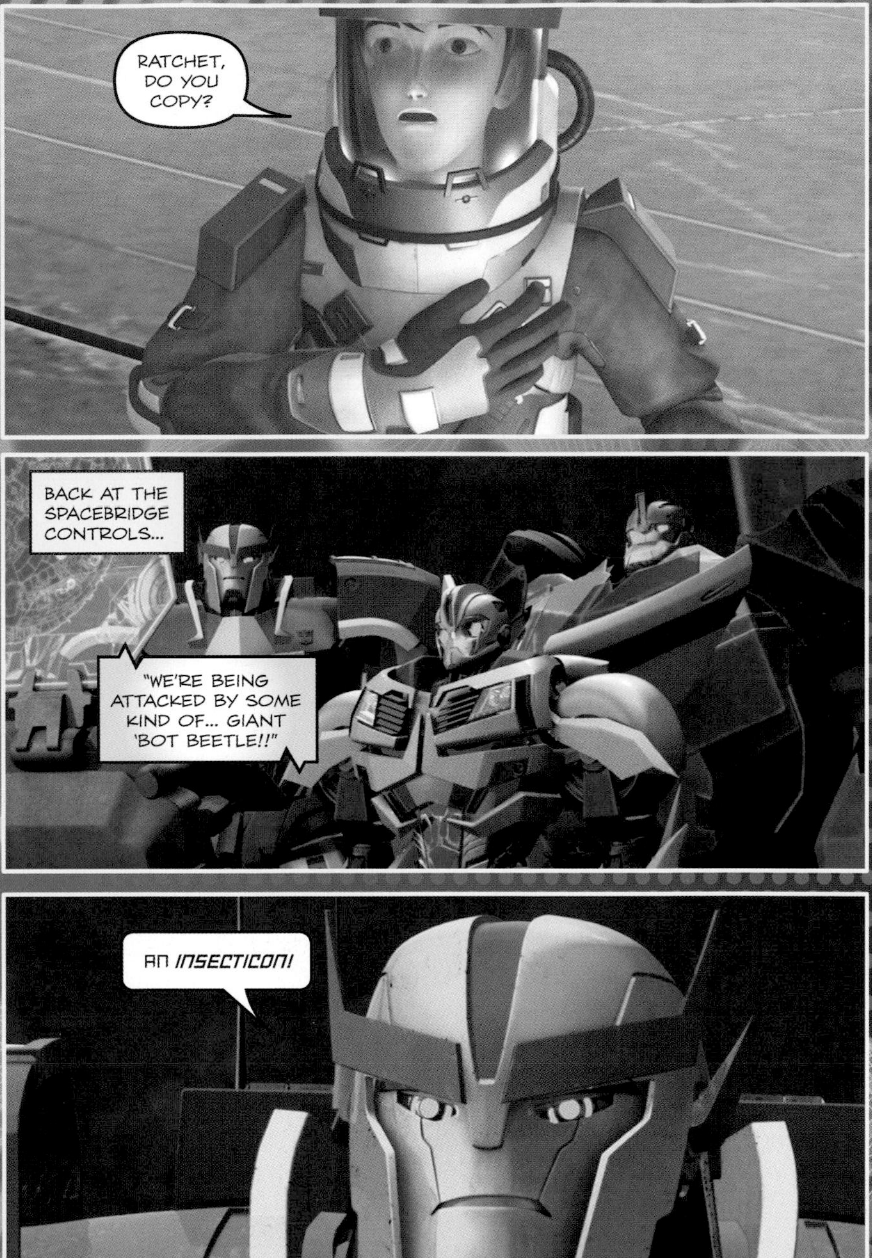
RATCHET, DO YOU COPY?
BACK AT THE SPACEBRIDGE CONTROLS...
"WE'RE BEING ATTACKED BY SOME KIND OF... GIANT 'BOT BEETLE!!"
AN *INSECTICON!*

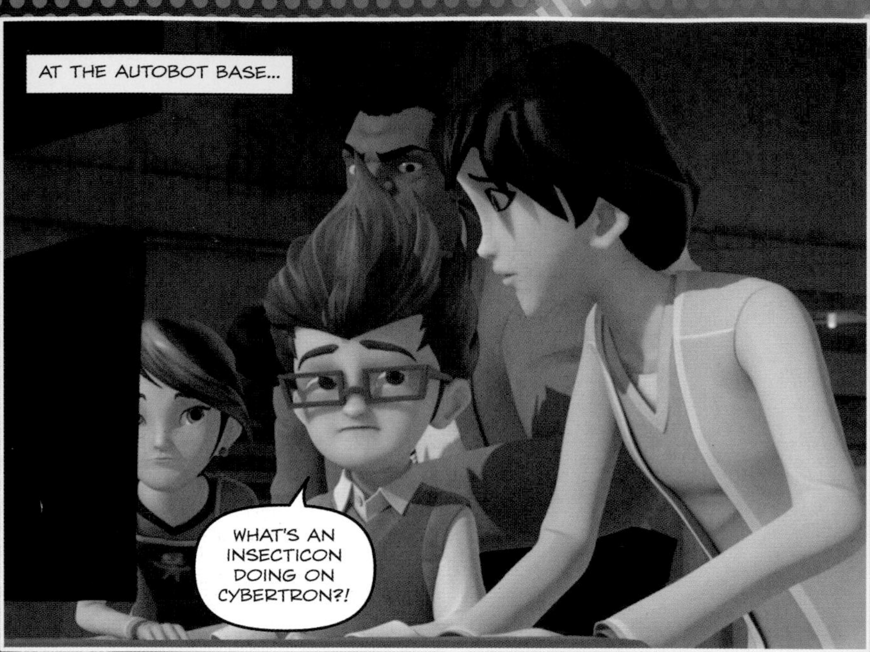
AT THE AUTOBOT BASE...
WHAT'S AN INSECTICON DOING ON CYBERTRON?!

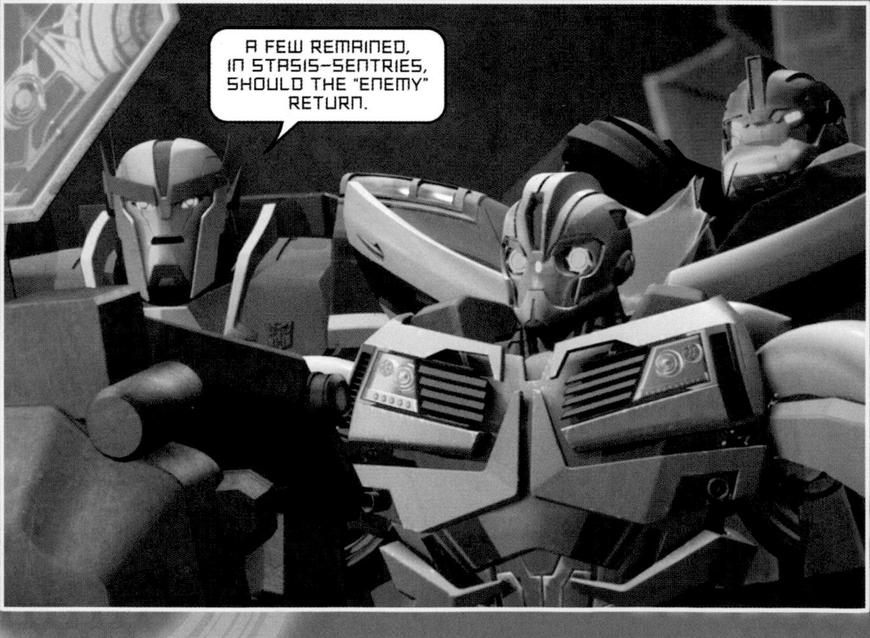
A FEW REMAINED, IN STASIS-SENTRIES, SHOULD THE "ENEMY" RETURN.

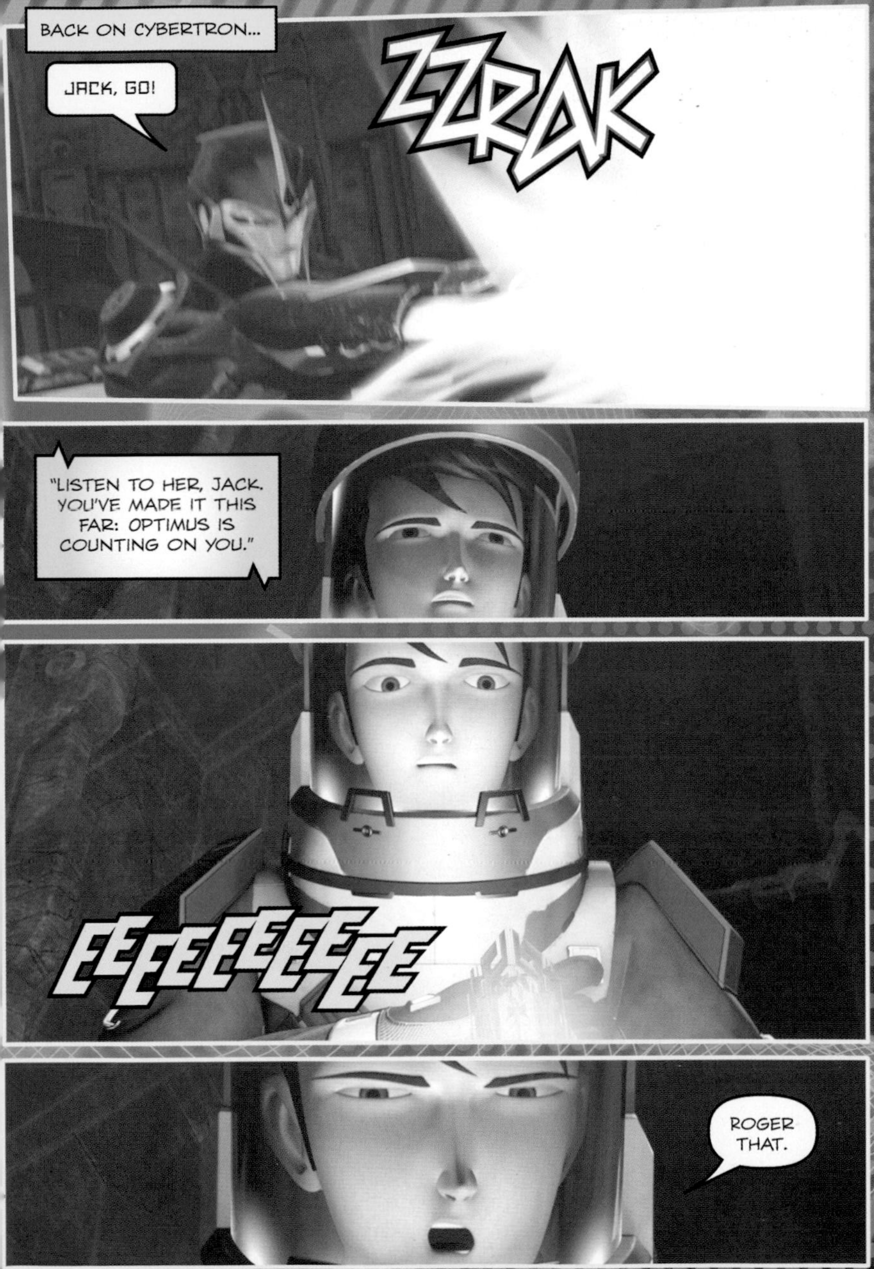
BACK ON CYBERTRON...
JACK, GO!
ZZRAK
"LISTEN TO HER, JACK. YOU'VE MADE IT THIS FAR: OPTIMUS IS COUNTING ON YOU."
EEEEEEEEEEE
ROGER THAT.

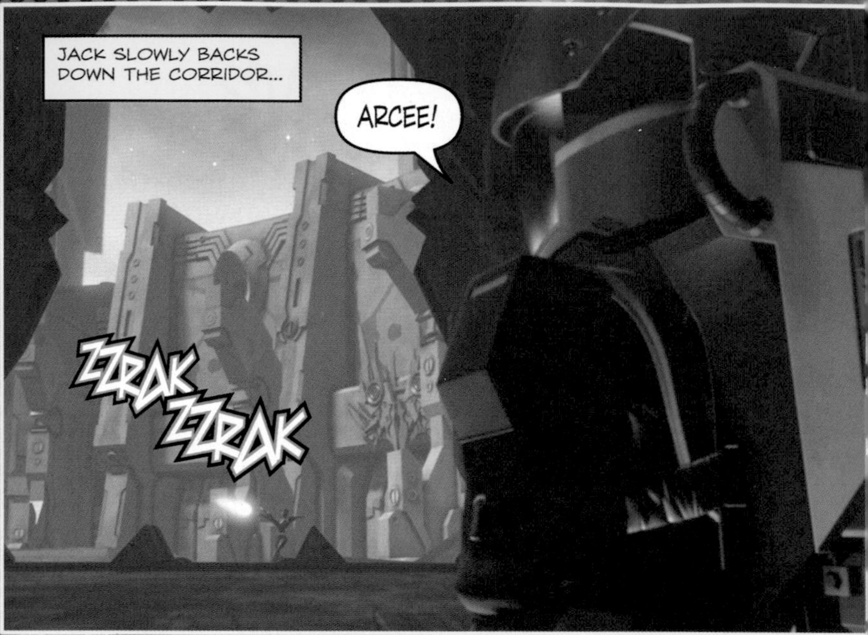
JACK SLOWLY BACKS DOWN THE CORRIDOR...
ARCEE!
ZZRAK
ZZRAK

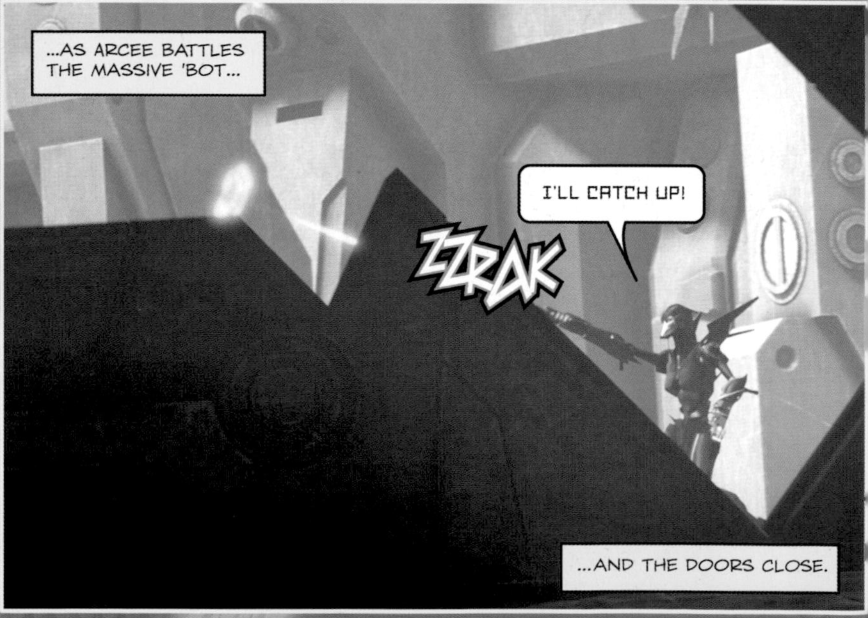
...AS ARCEE BATTLES THE MASSIVE 'BOT...
I'LL CATCH UP!
ZZRAK
...AND THE DOORS CLOSE.

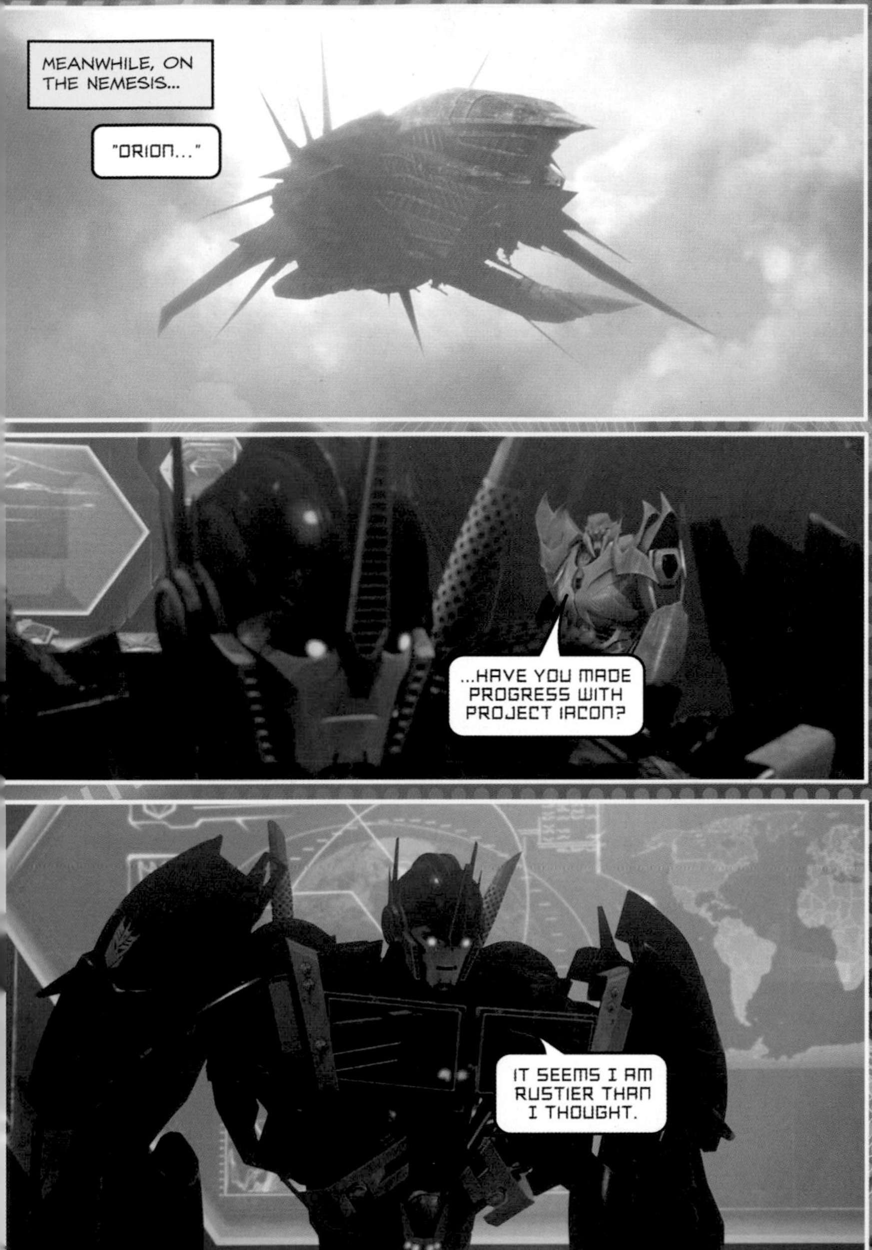
MEANWHILE, ON THE NEMESIS...
"ORION..."
...HAVE YOU MADE PROGRESS WITH PROJECT IACON?
IT SEEMS I AM RUSTIER THAN I THOUGHT.

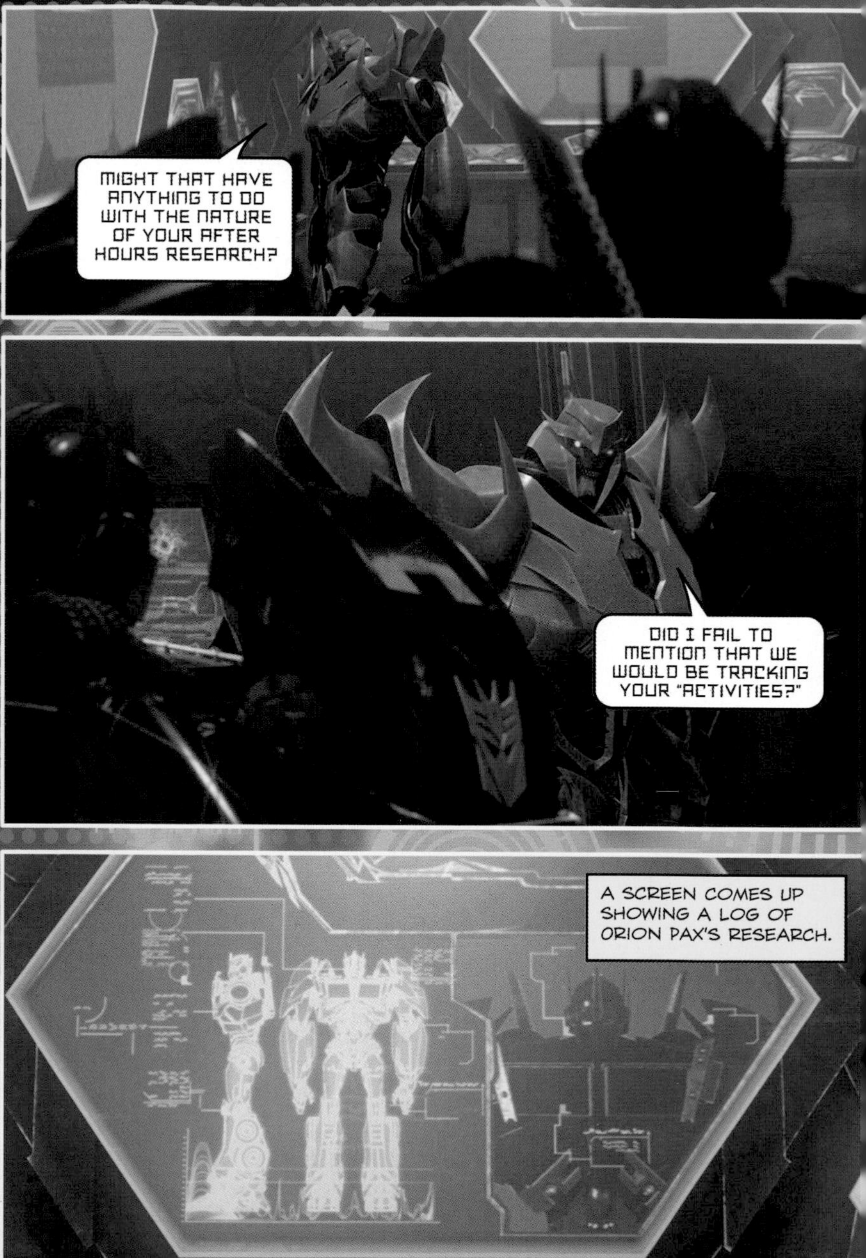
MIGHT THAT HAVE ANYTHING TO DO WITH THE NATURE OF YOUR AFTER HOURS RESEARCH?
DID I FAIL TO MENTION THAT WE WOULD BE TRACKING YOUR "ACTIVITIES?"
A SCREEN COMES UP SHOWING A LOG OF ORION PAX'S RESEARCH.

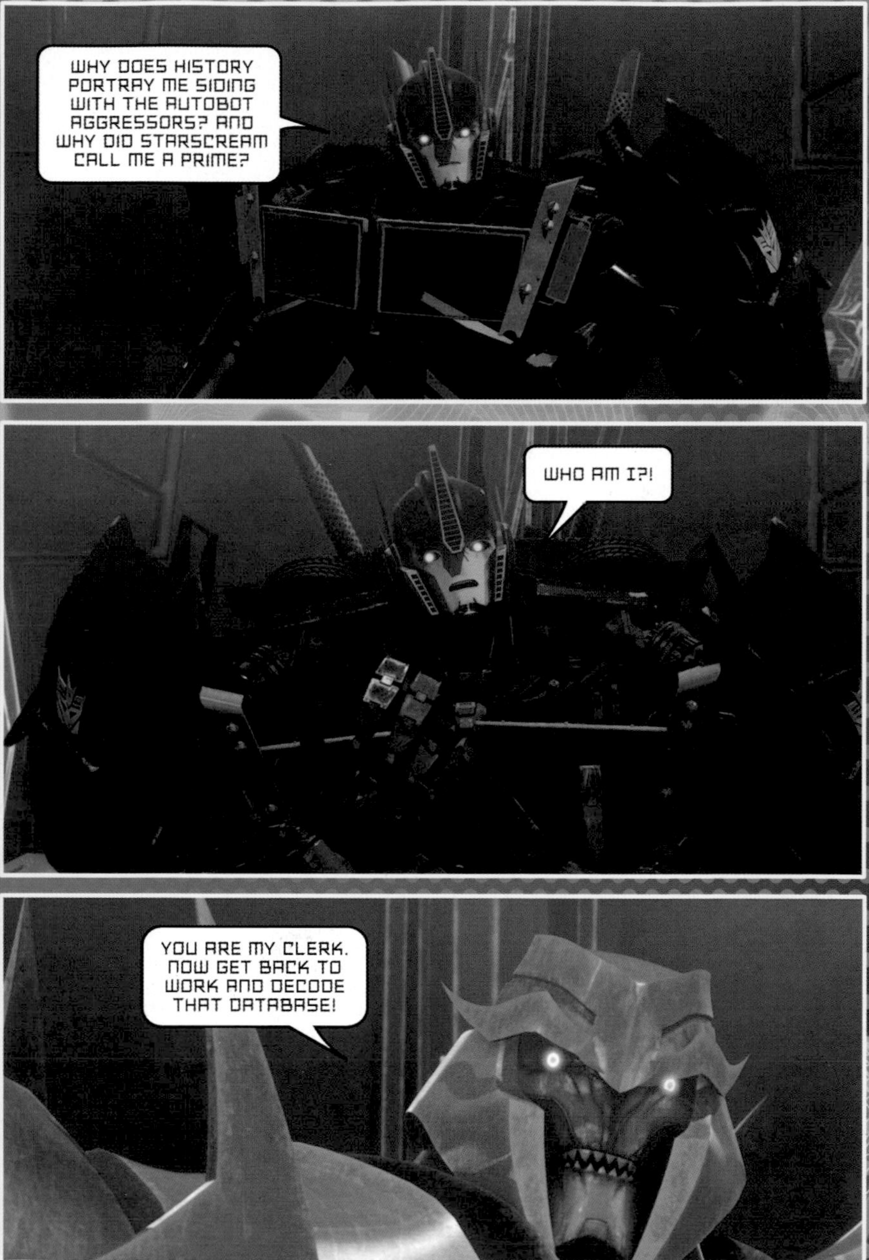
WHY DOES HISTORY PORTRAY ME SIDING WITH THE AUTOBOT AGGRESSORS? AND WHY DID STARSCREAM CALL ME A PRIME?
WHO AM I?!
YOU ARE MY CLERK. NOW GET BACK TO WORK AND DECODE THAT DATABASE!

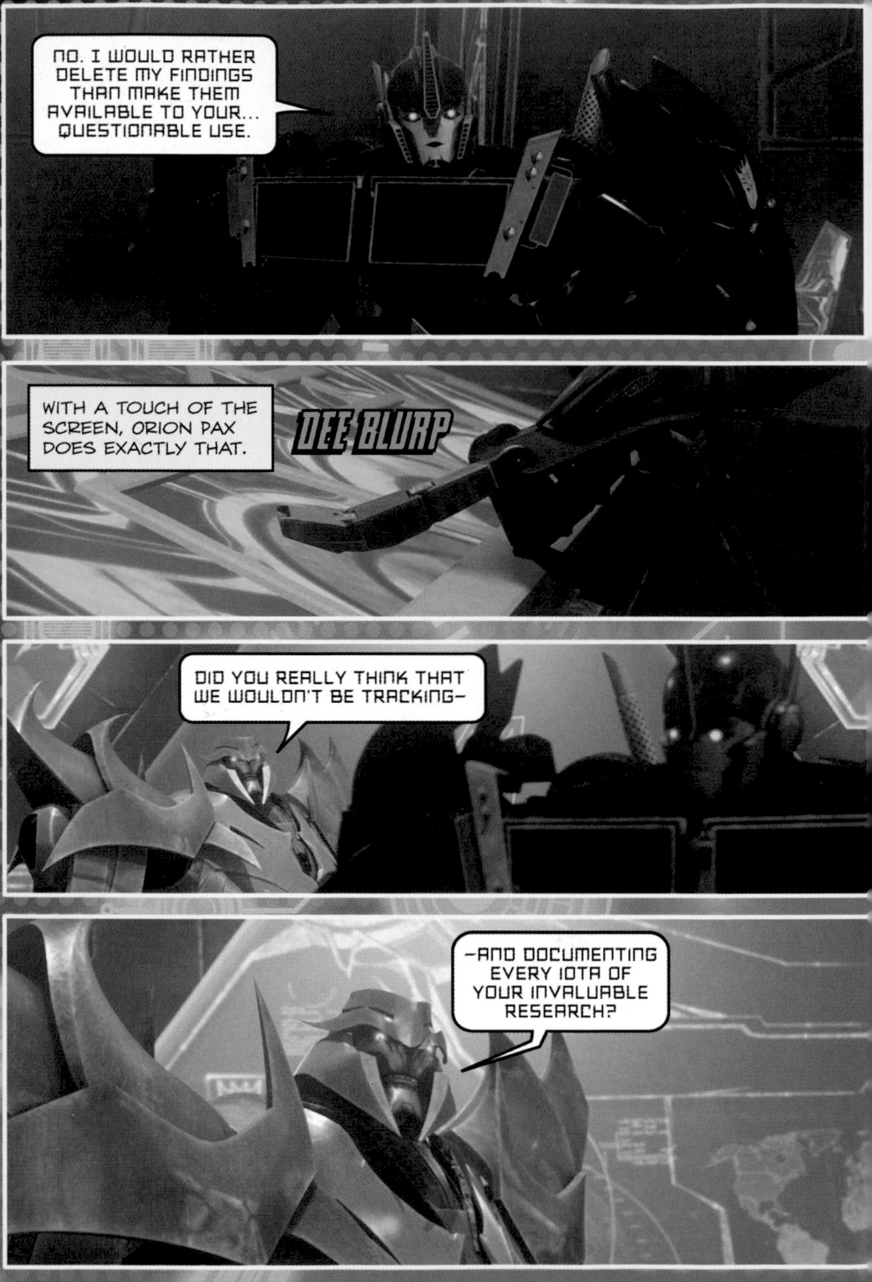
NO. I WOULD RATHER DELETE MY FINDINGS THAN MAKE THEM AVAILABLE TO YOUR... QUESTIONABLE USE.
WITH A TOUCH OF THE SCREEN, ORION PAX DOES EXACTLY THAT.
DEE BLURP
DID YOU REALLY THINK THAT WE WOULDN'T BE TRACKING—
—AND DOCUMENTING EVERY IOTA OF YOUR INVALUABLE RESEARCH?

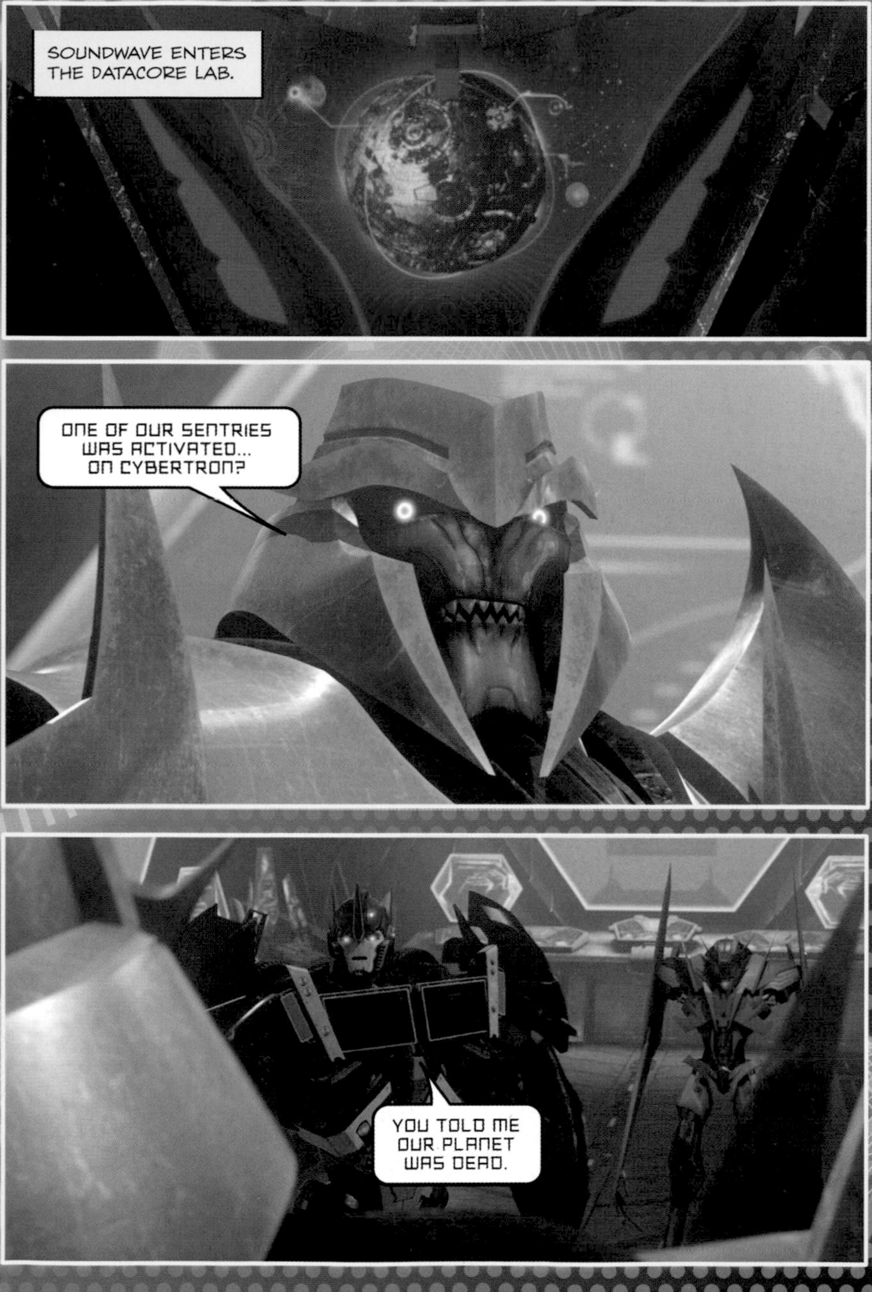
SOUNDWAVE ENTERS THE DATACORE LAB.
ONE OF OUR SENTRIES WAS ACTIVATED... ON CYBERTRON?
YOU TOLD ME OUR PLANET WAS DEAD.

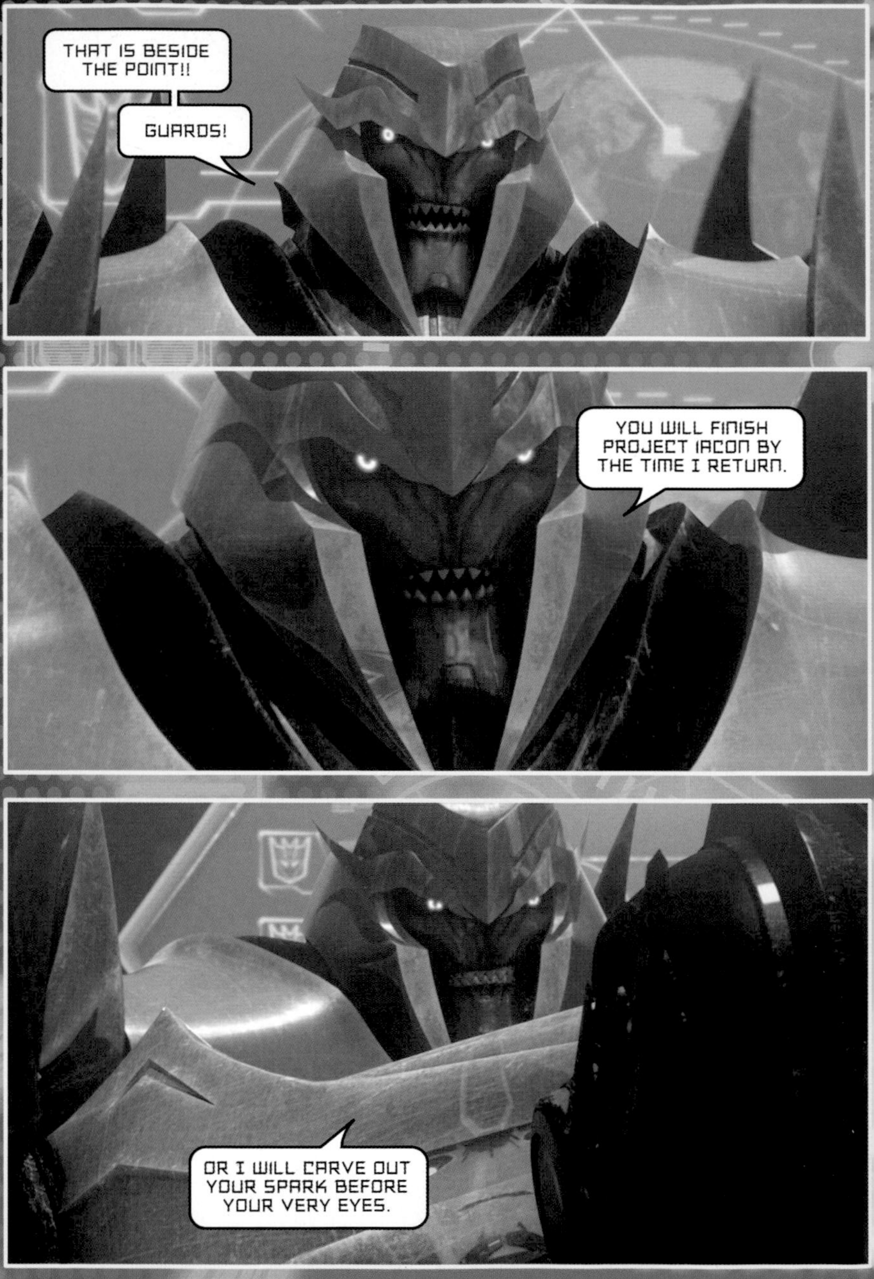
THAT IS BESIDE THE POINT!!
GUARDS!
YOU WILL FINISH PROJECT IACON BY THE TIME I RETURN.
OR I WILL CARVE OUT YOUR SPARK BEFORE YOUR VERY EYES.

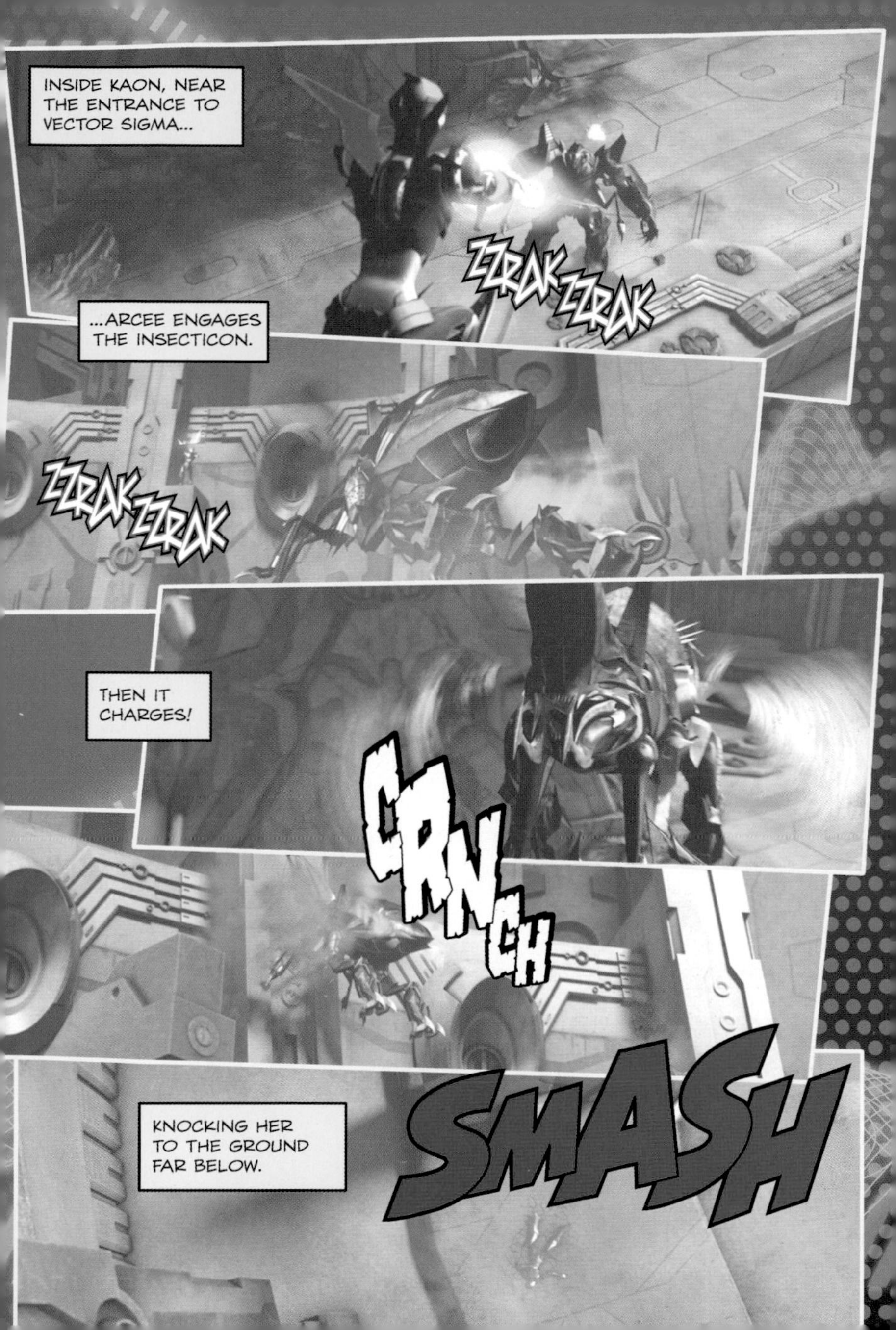
INSIDE KAON, NEAR THE ENTRANCE TO VECTOR SIGMA...
ZZRAK ZZRAK
...ARCEE ENGAGES THE INSECTICON.
ZZRAK ZZRAK
THEN IT CHARGES!
CRNCH
KNOCKING HER TO THE GROUND FAR BELOW.
SMASH

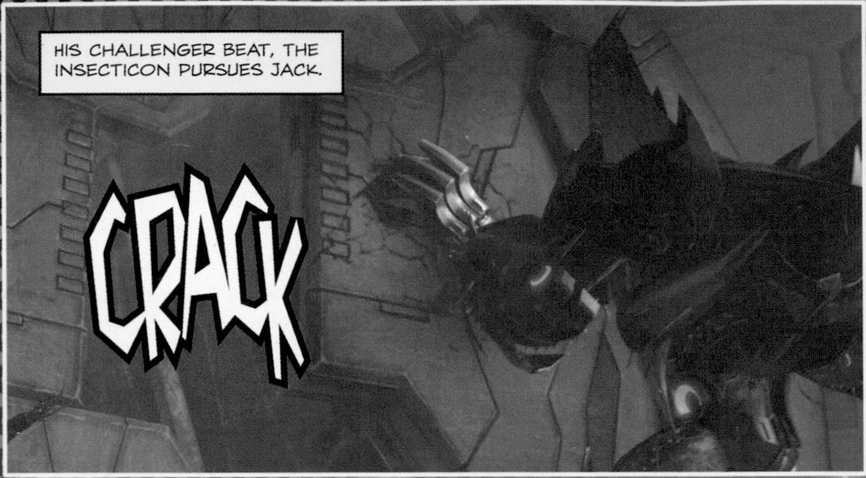
HIS CHALLENGER BEAT, THE INSECTICON PURSUES JACK.
CRACK

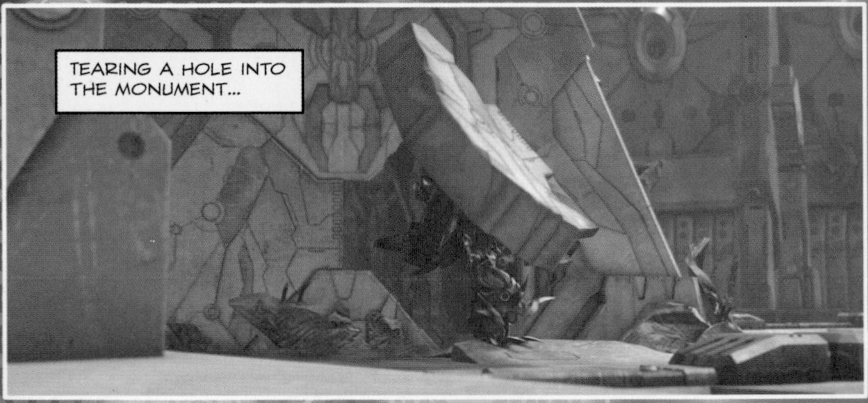
TEARING A HOLE INTO THE MONUMENT...

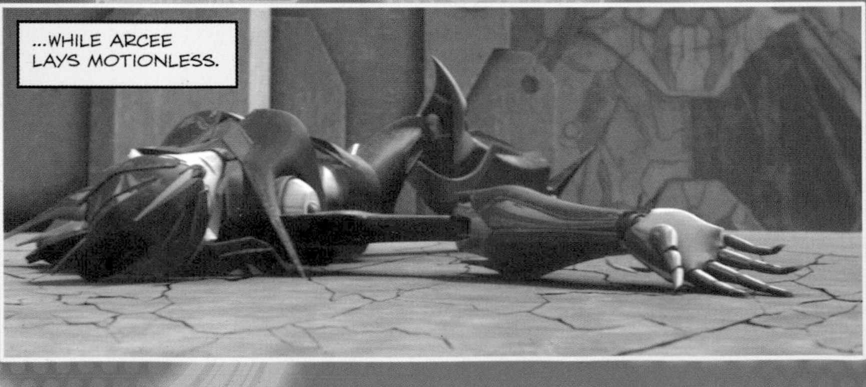
...WHILE ARCEE LAYS MOTIONLESS.

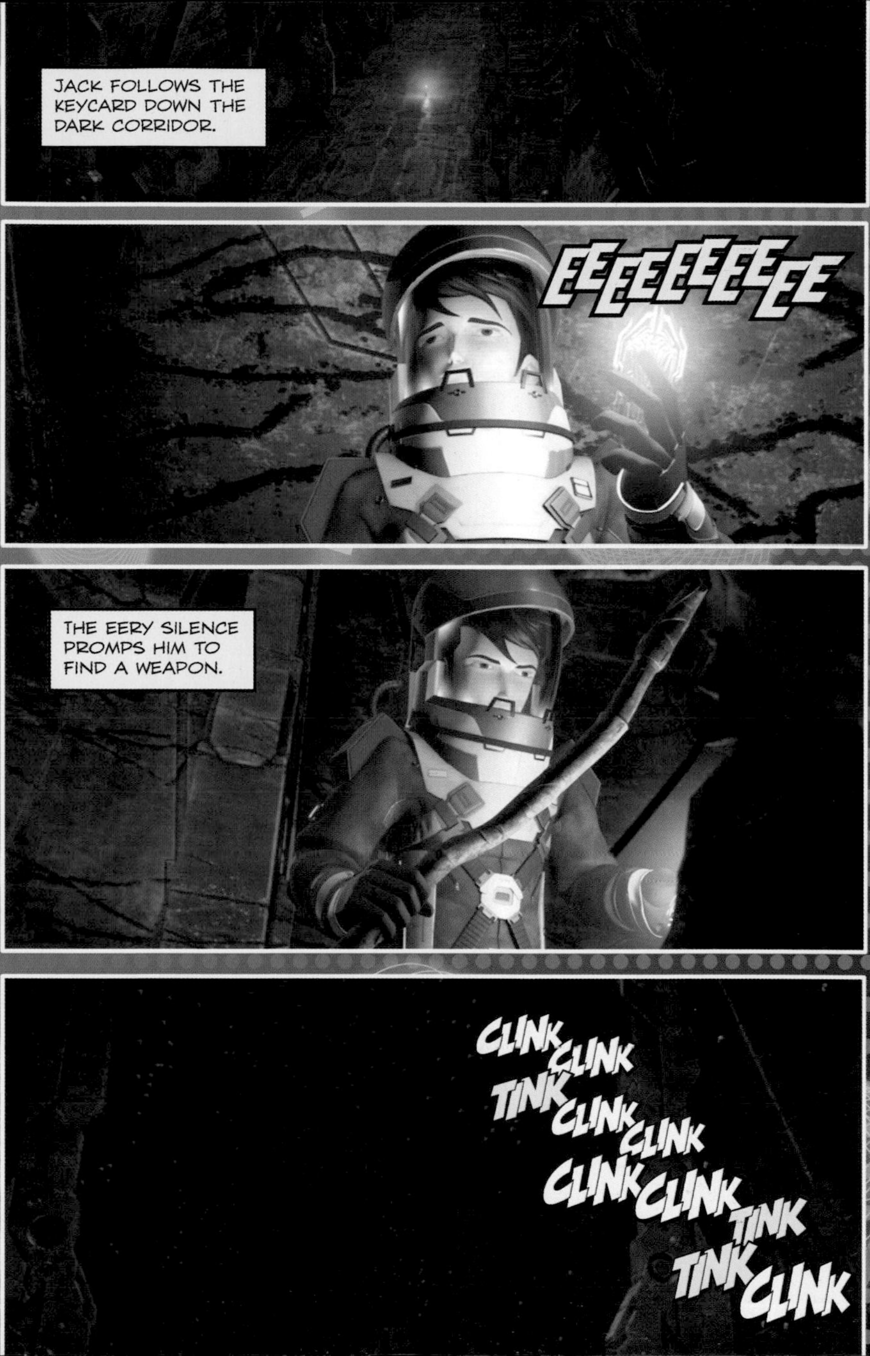
JACK FOLLOWS THE KEYCARD DOWN THE DARK CORRIDOR.
EEEEEEEEEEE
THE EERY SILENCE PROMPS HIM TO FIND A WEAPON.
CLINK CLINK
TINK CLINK CLINK
CLINK CLINK TINK
TINK CLINK

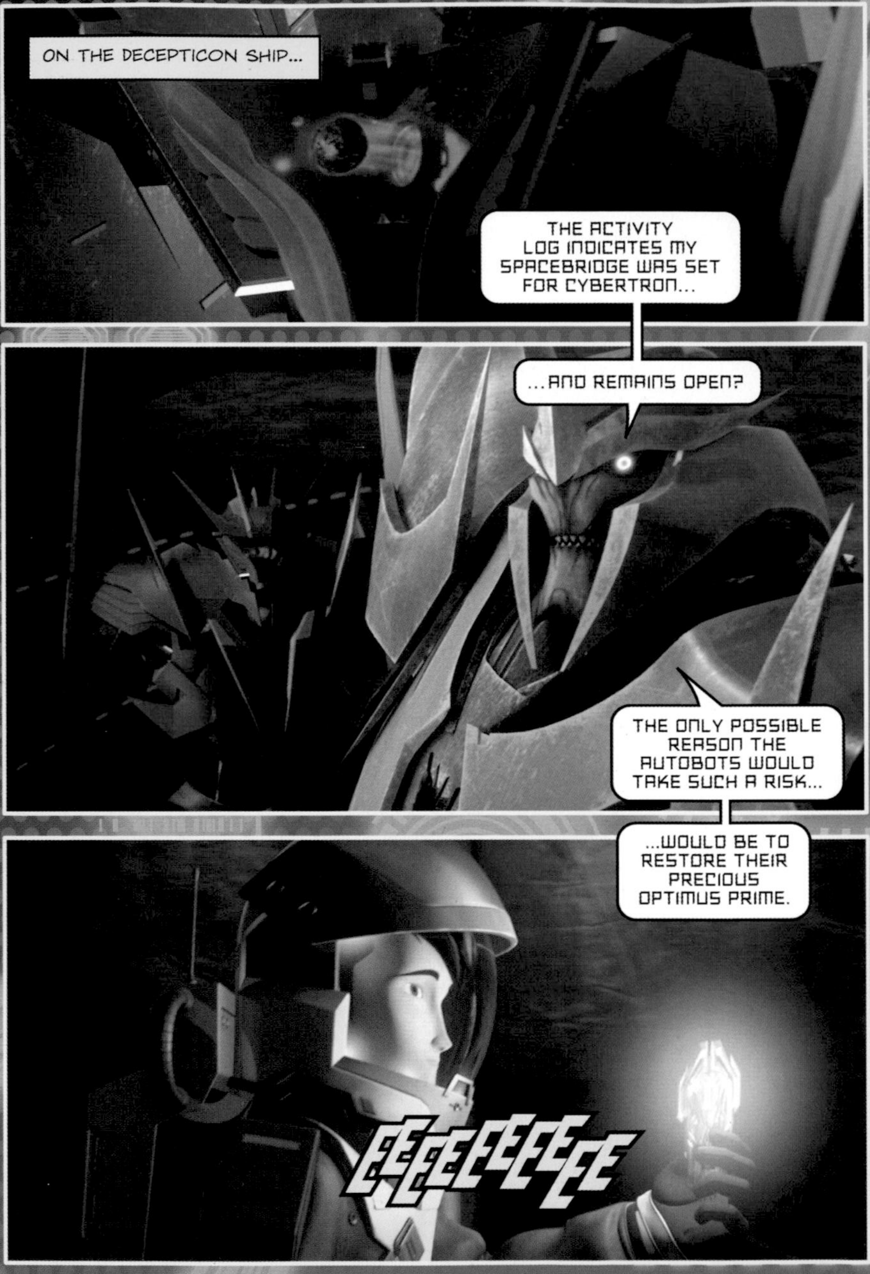

ON THE DECEPTICON SHIP...
THE ACTIVITY LOG INDICATES MY SPACEBRIDGE WAS SET FOR CYBERTRON...
...AND REMAINS OPEN?
THE ONLY POSSIBLE REASON THE AUTOBOTS WOULD TAKE SUCH A RISK...
...WOULD BE TO RESTORE THEIR PRECIOUS OPTIMUS PRIME.
EEEEEEEEEEE

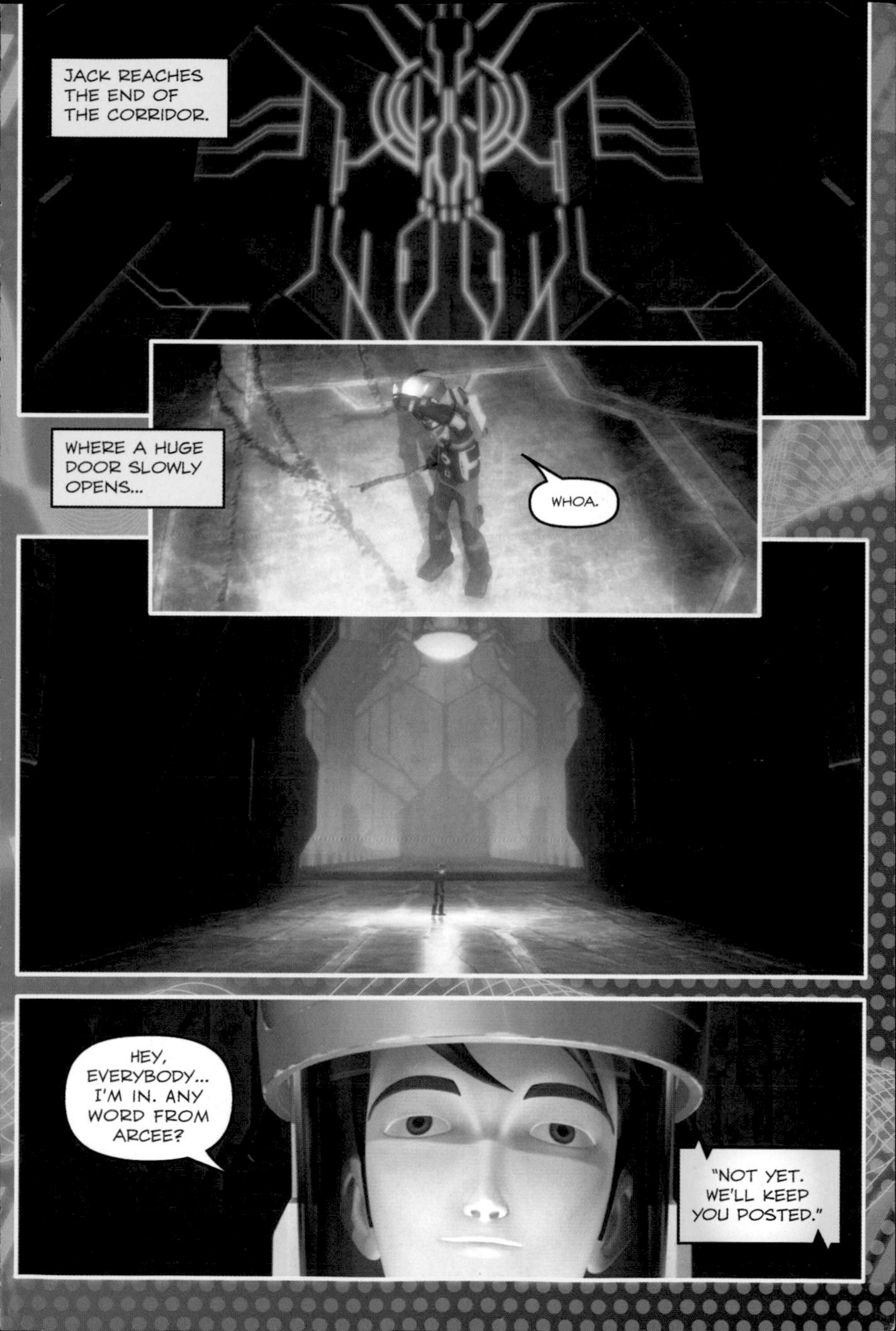
JACK REACHES THE END OF THE CORRIDOR.
WHERE A HUGE DOOR SLOWLY OPENS...
WHOA.
HEY, EVERYBODY... I'M IN. ANY WORD FROM ARCEE?
"NOT YET. WE'LL KEEP YOU POSTED."

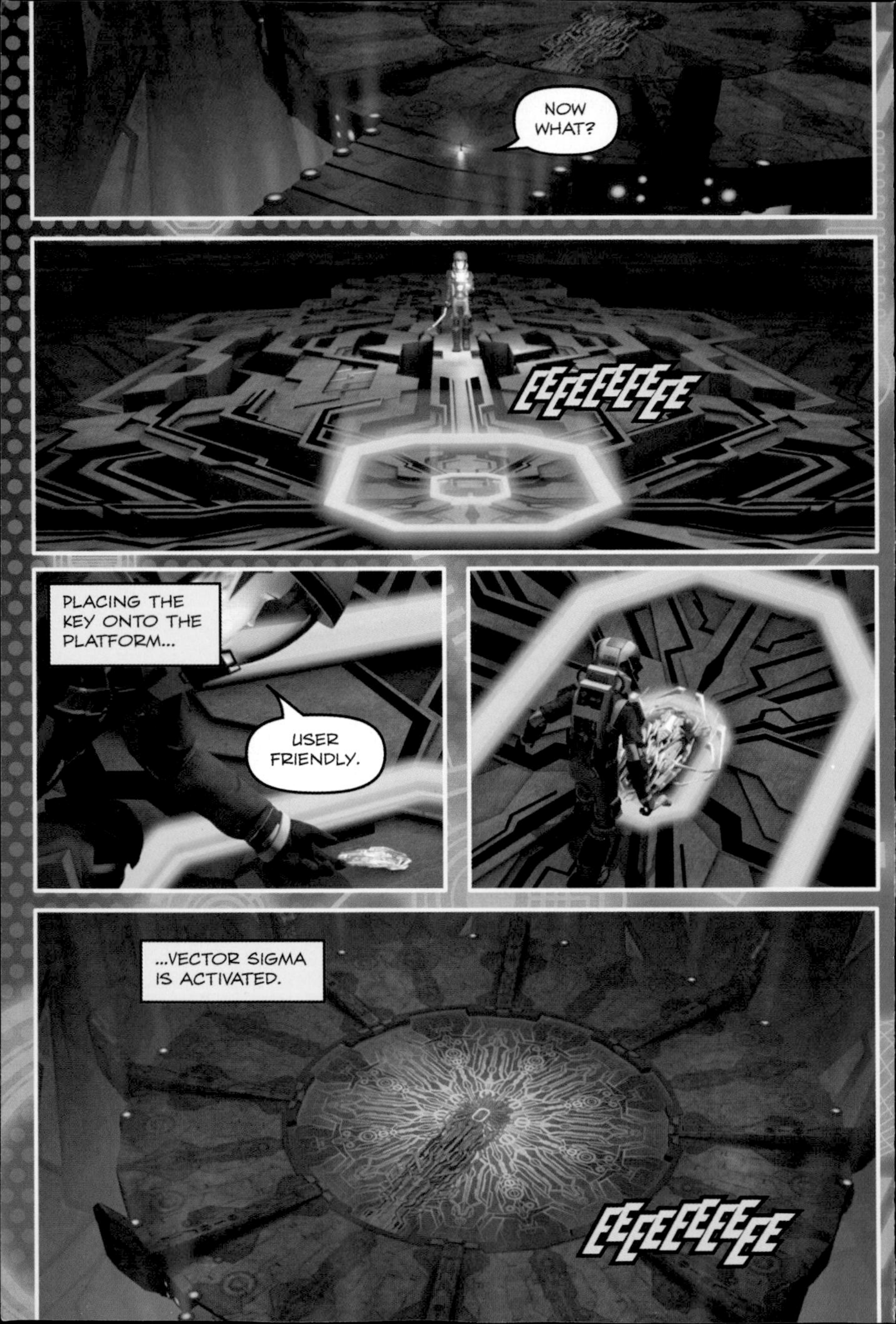
NOW WHAT?
EEEEEEEEEE
PLACING THE KEY ONTO THE PLATFORM...
USER FRIENDLY.
...VECTOR SIGMA IS ACTIVATED.
EEEEEEEEEE

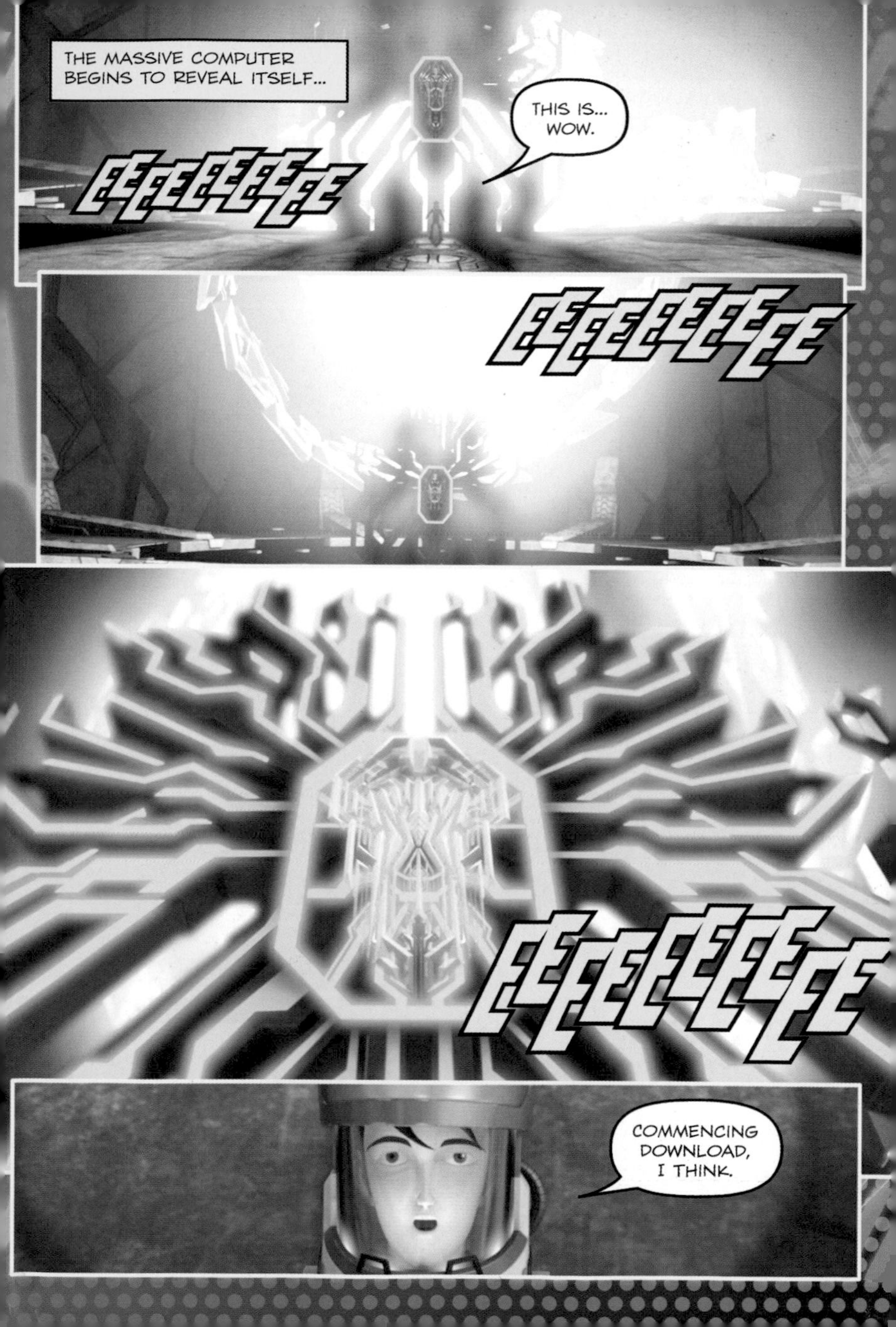
THE MASSIVE COMPUTER BEGINS TO REVEAL ITSELF...
EEEEEEEEEEE
THIS IS... WOW.
EEEEEEEEEEEE
EEEEEEEEEEEE
COMMENCING DOWNLOAD, I THINK.

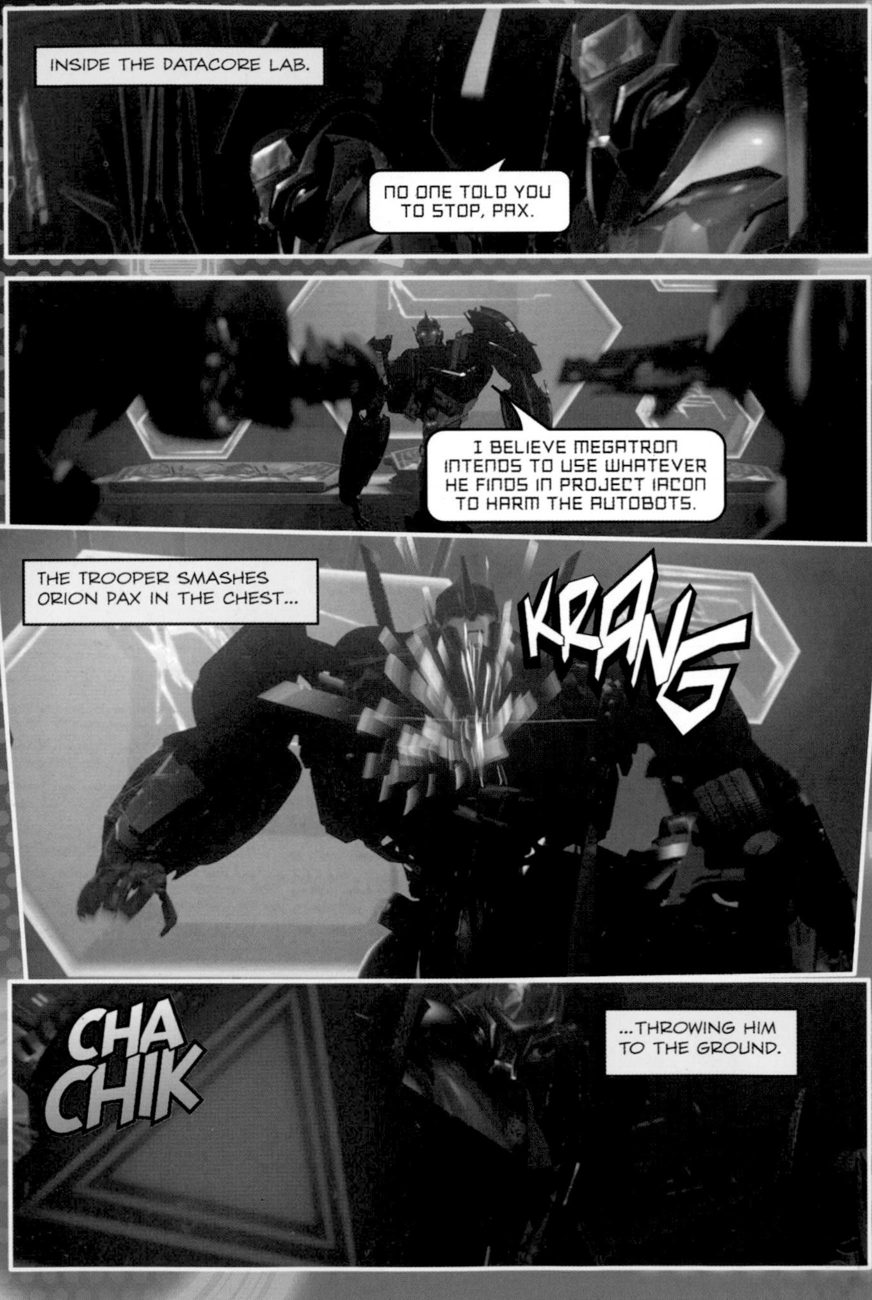
INSIDE THE DATACORE LAB.
NO ONE TOLD YOU TO STOP, PAX.
I BELIEVE MEGATRON INTENDS TO USE WHATEVER HE FINDS IN PROJECT IACON TO HARM THE AUTOBOTS.
THE TROOPER SMASHES ORION PAX IN THE CHEST...
KRANG
CHA CHIK
...THROWING HIM TO THE GROUND.

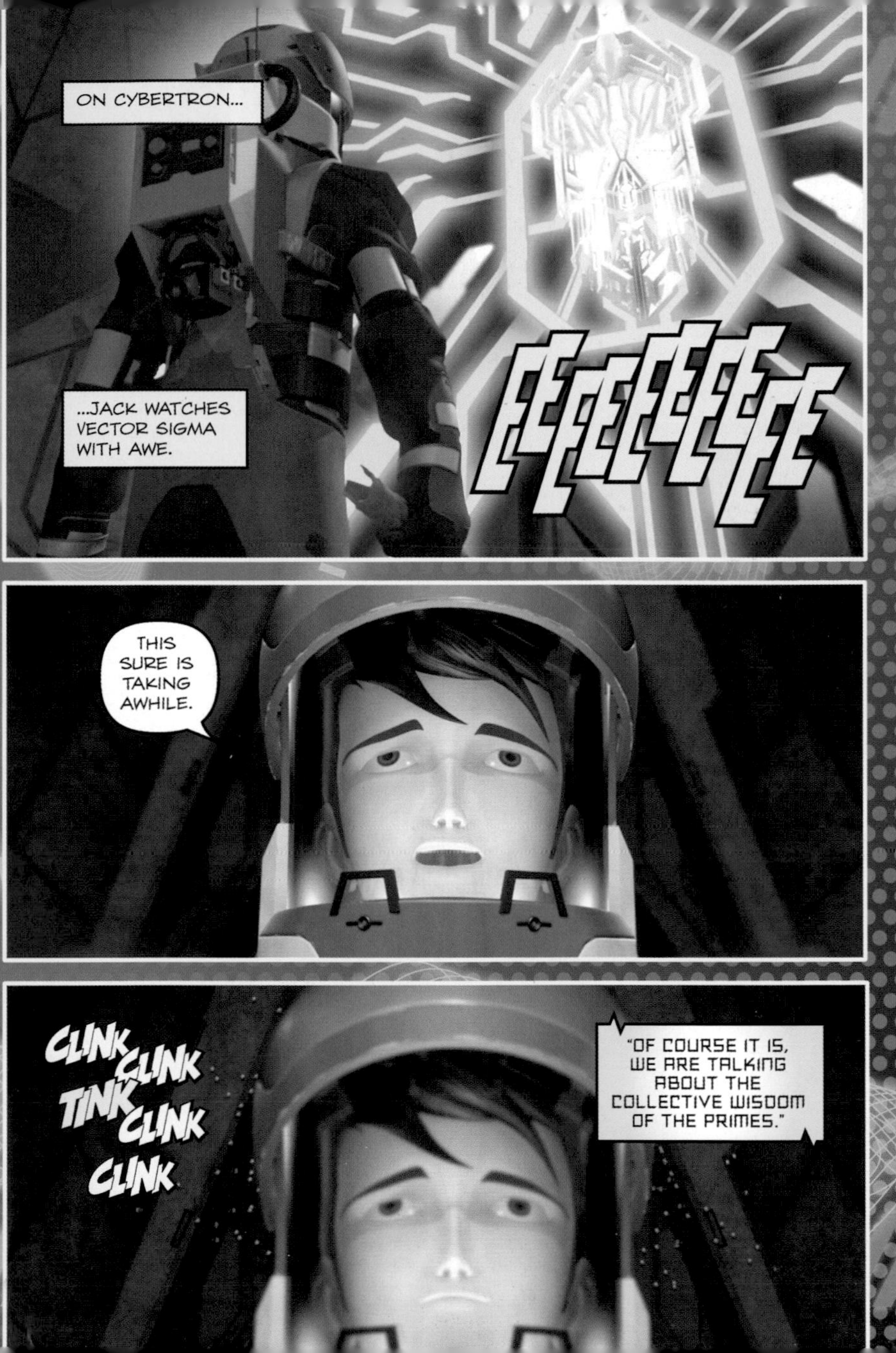

ON CYBERTRON...
...JACK WATCHES VECTOR SIGMA WITH AWE.
EEEEEEEEEEEE
THIS SURE IS TAKING AWHILE.
CLINK CLINK TINK CLINK CLINK
"OF COURSE IT IS, WE ARE TALKING ABOUT THE COLLECTIVE WISDOM OF THE PRIMES."

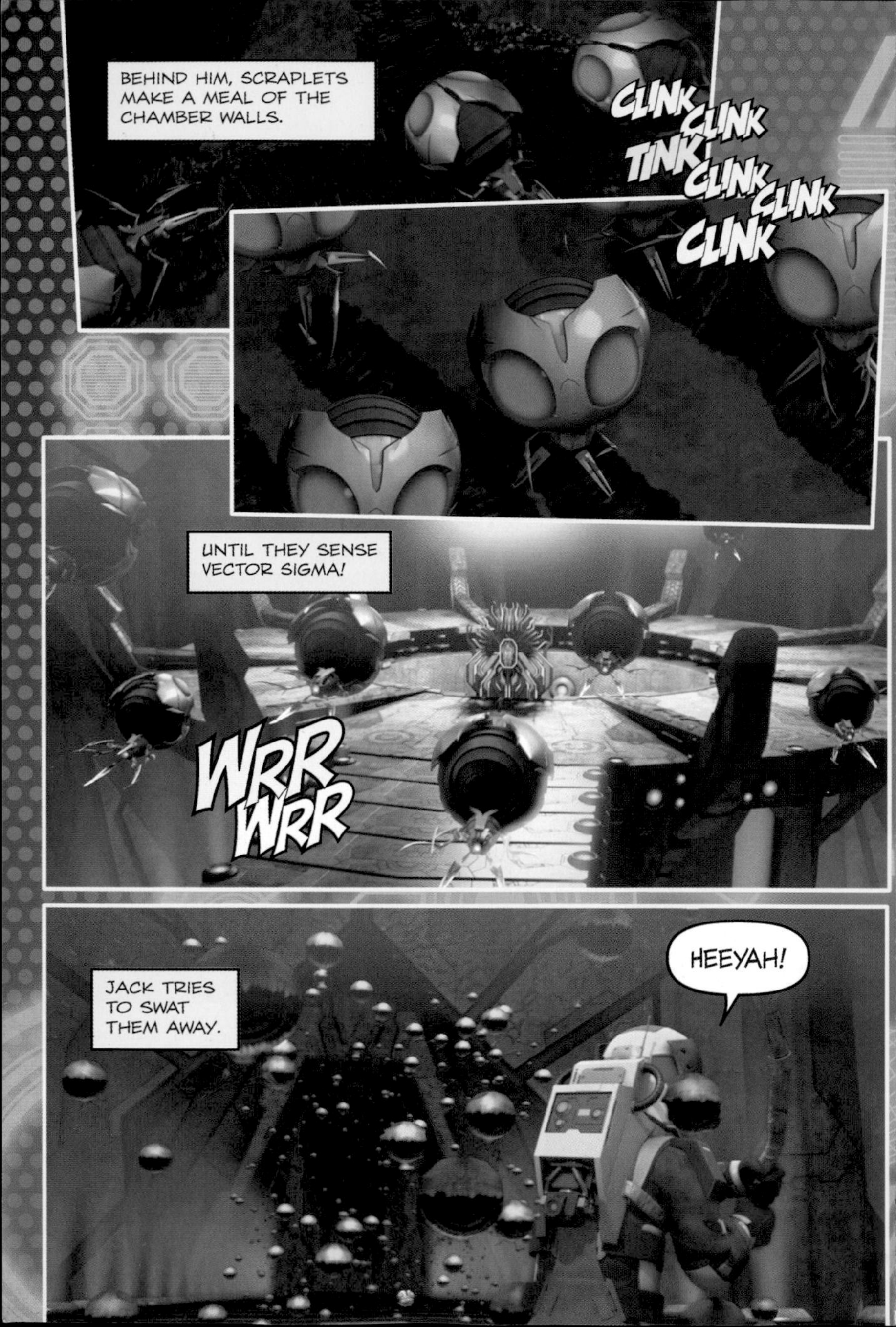
BEHIND HIM, SCRAPLETS MAKE A MEAL OF THE CHAMBER WALLS.
CLINK CLINK
TINK CLINK CLINK
CLINK
UNTIL THEY SENSE VECTOR SIGMA!
WRR WRR
JACK TRIES TO SWAT THEM AWAY.
HEEYAH!

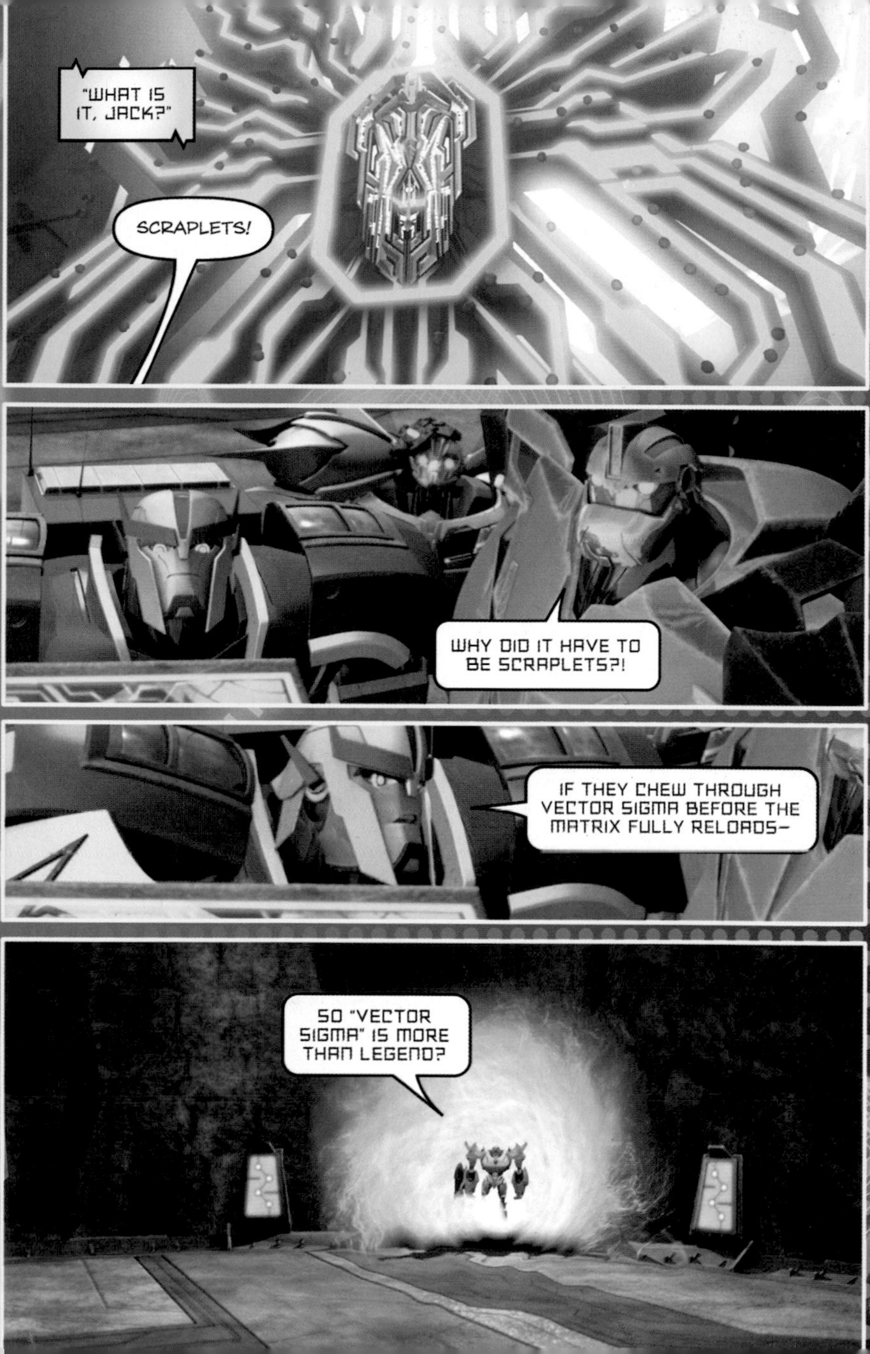
"WHAT IS IT, JACK?"
SCRAPLETS!
WHY DID IT HAVE TO BE SCRAPLETS?!
IF THEY CHEW THROUGH VECTOR SIGMA BEFORE THE MATRIX FULLY RELOADS—
SO "VECTOR SIGMA" IS MORE THAN LEGEND?

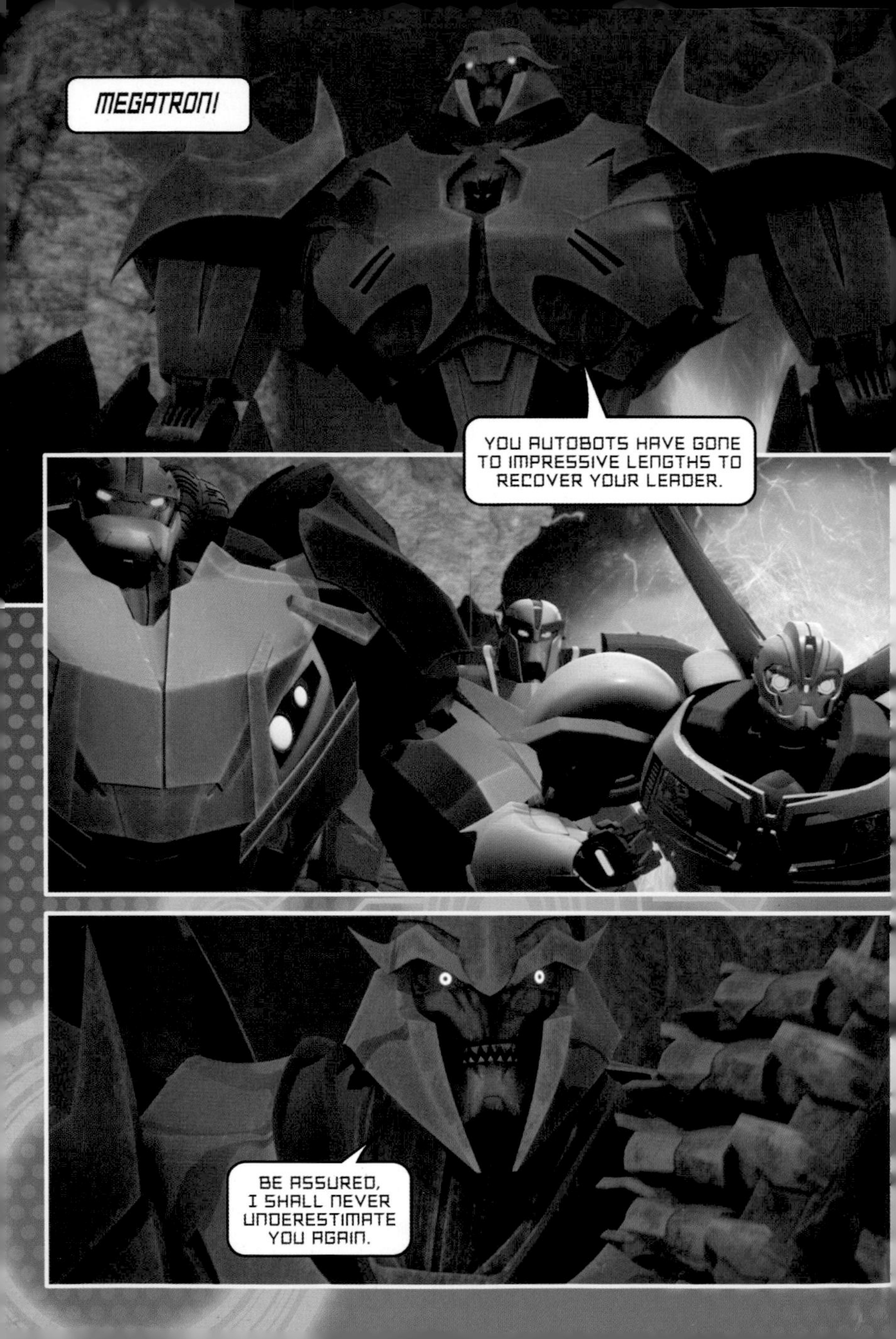
MEGATRON!
YOU AUTOBOTS HAVE GONE TO IMPRESSIVE LENGTHS TO RECOVER YOUR LEADER.
BE ASSURED, I SHALL NEVER UNDERESTIMATE YOU AGAIN.

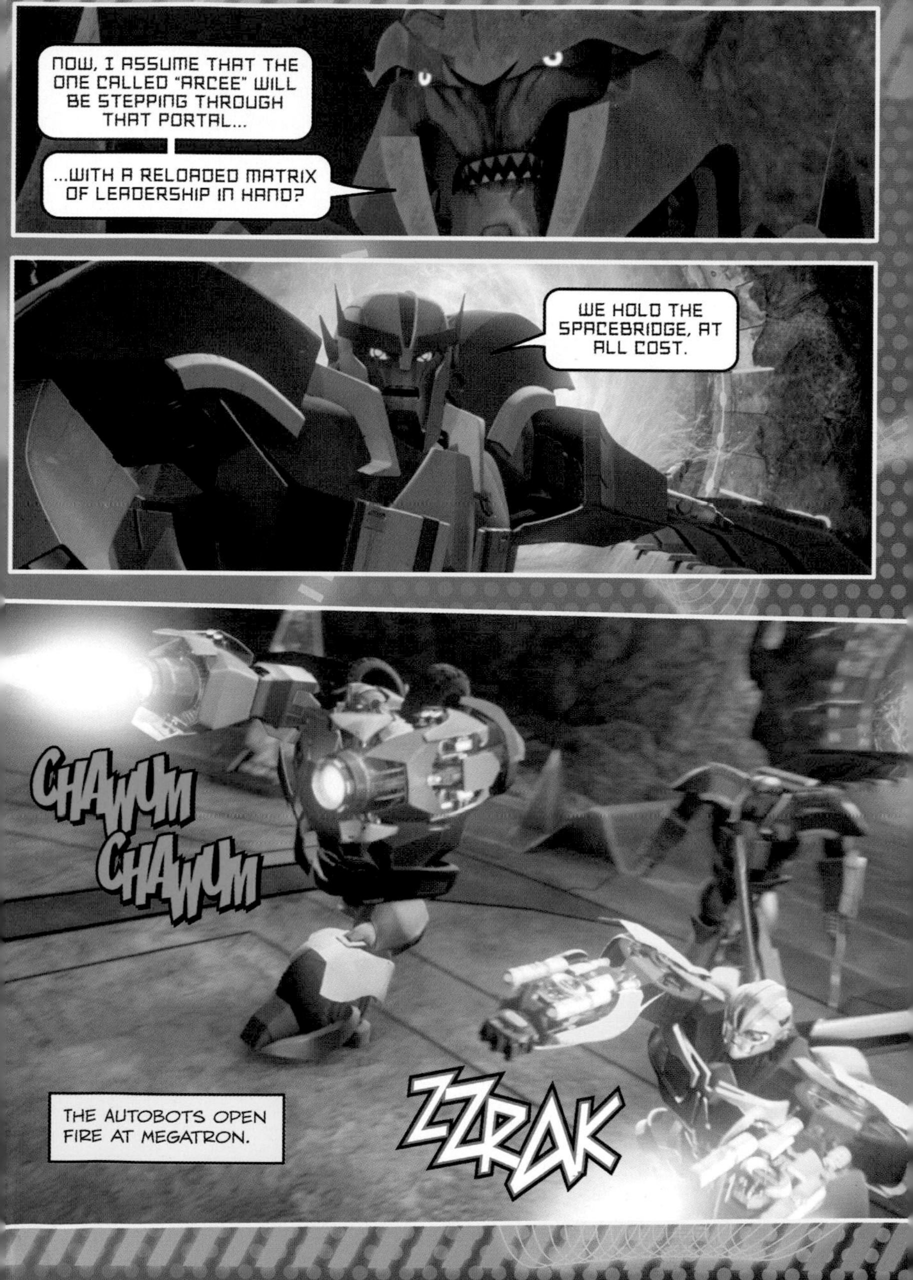
NOW, I ASSUME THAT THE ONE CALLED "ARCEE" WILL BE STEPPING THROUGH THAT PORTAL...
...WITH A RELOADED MATRIX OF LEADERSHIP IN HAND?
WE HOLD THE SPACEBRIDGE, AT ALL COST.
CHAWUM CHAWUM
THE AUTOBOTS OPEN FIRE AT MEGATRON.
ZZRAK

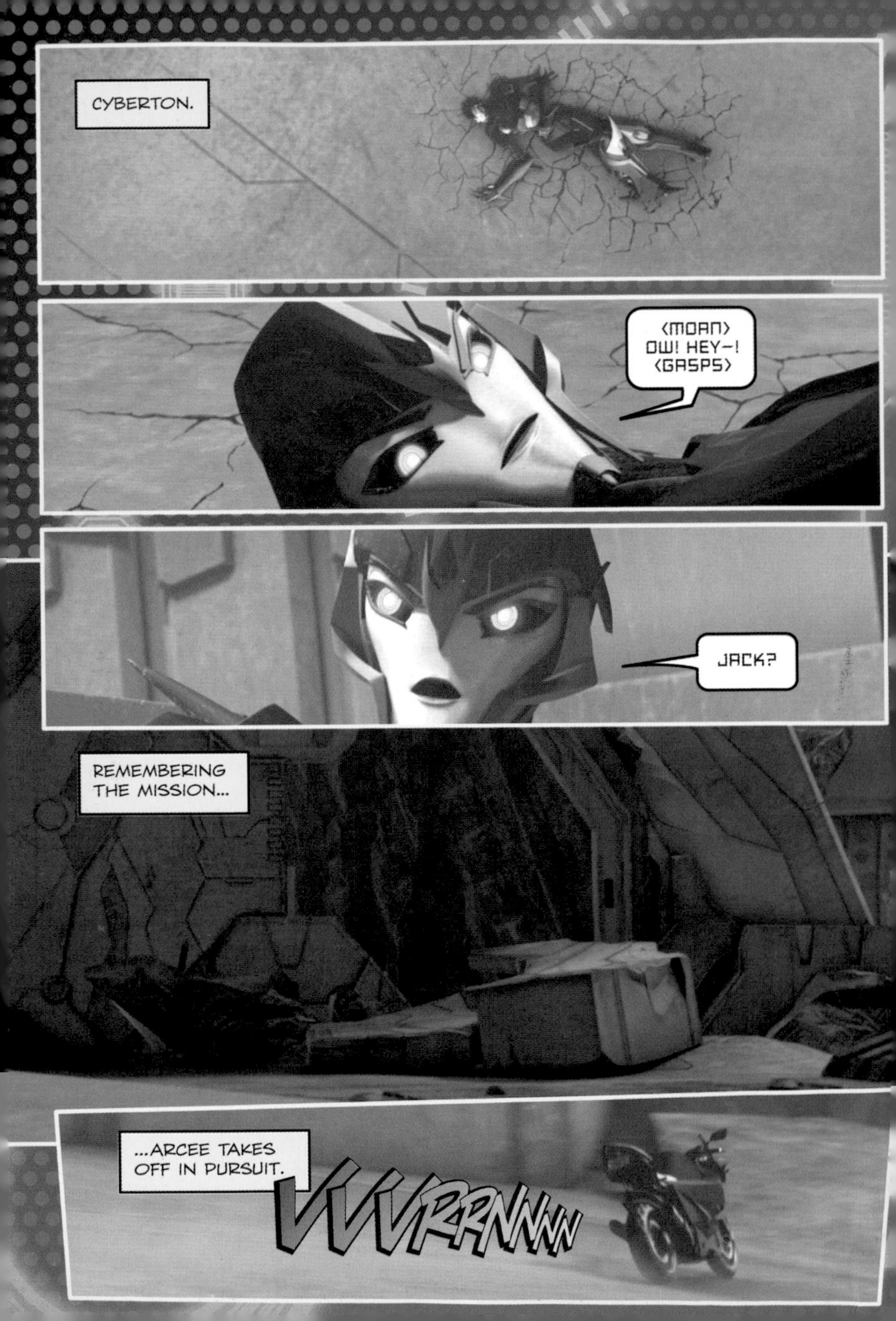

CYBERTON.
<MOAN> OW! HEY—! <GASPS>
JACK?
REMEMBERING THE MISSION...
...ARCEE TAKES OFF IN PURSUIT.
VVVRRRNNNN

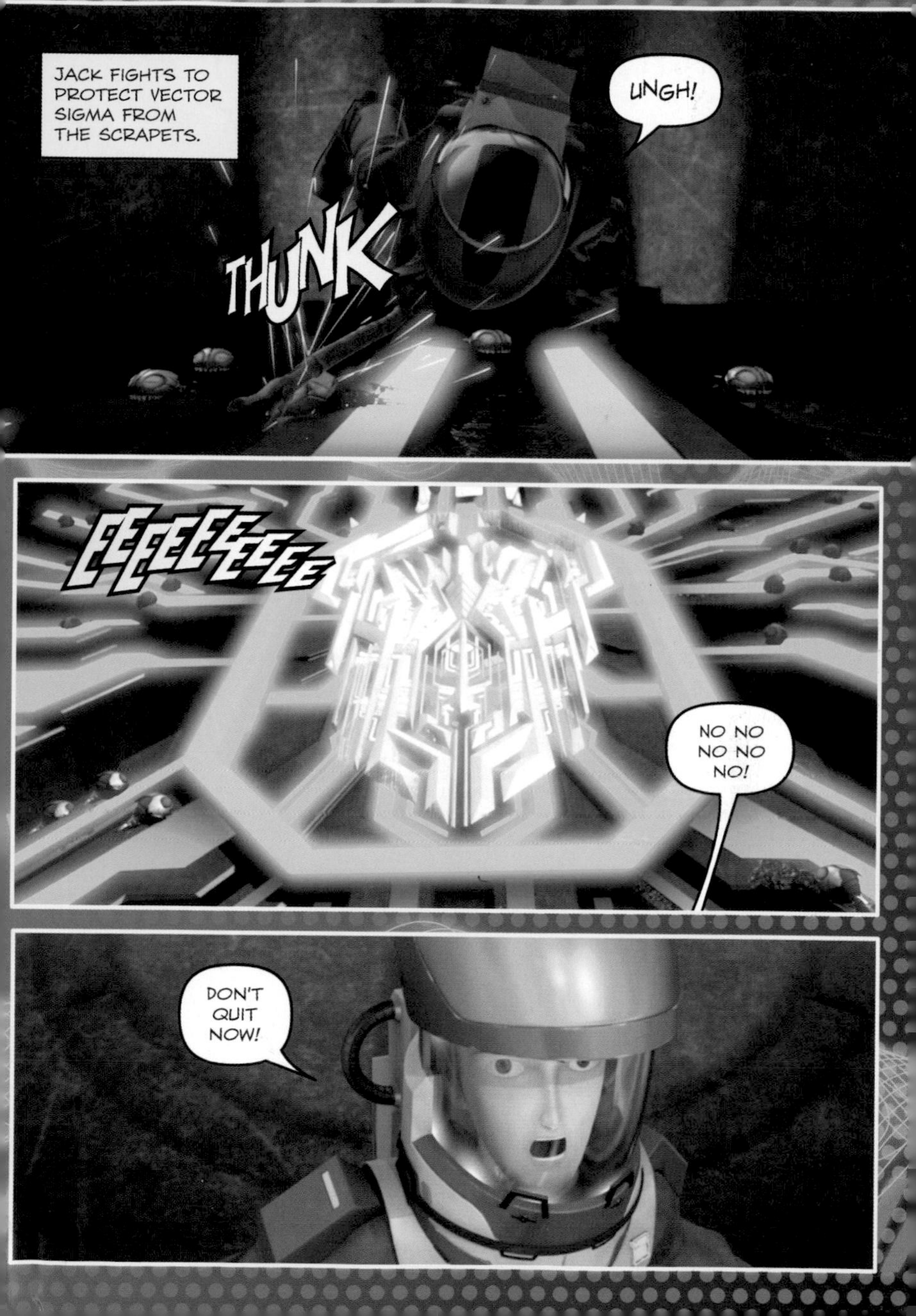
JACK FIGHTS TO PROTECT VECTOR SIGMA FROM THE SCRAPETS.
UNGH!
THUNK
EEEEEEEEEEE
NO NO NO NO NO!
DON'T QUIT NOW!

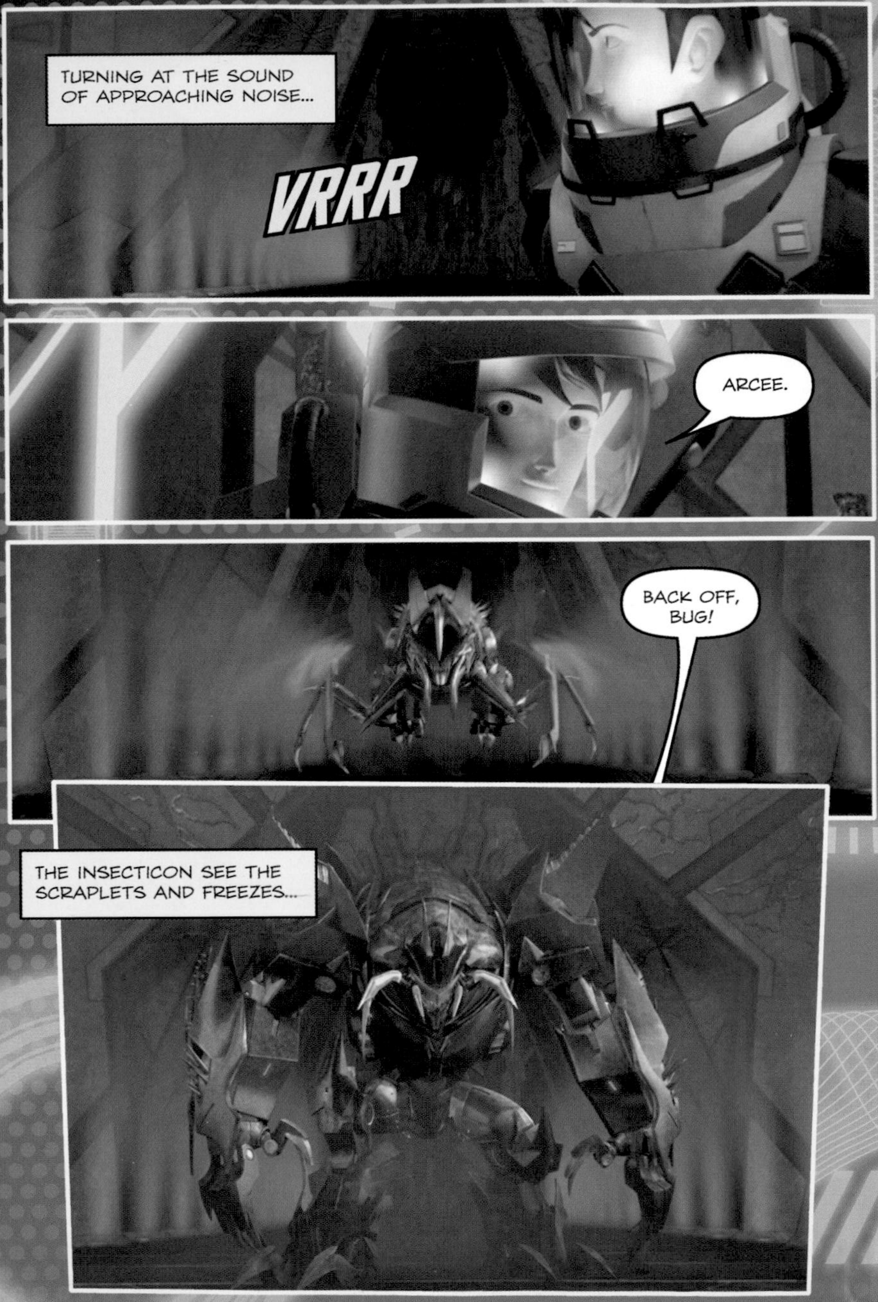
TURNING AT THE SOUND OF APPROACHING NOISE...
VRRR
ARCEE.
BACK OFF, BUG!
THE INSECTICON SEE THE SCRAPLETS AND FREEZES...

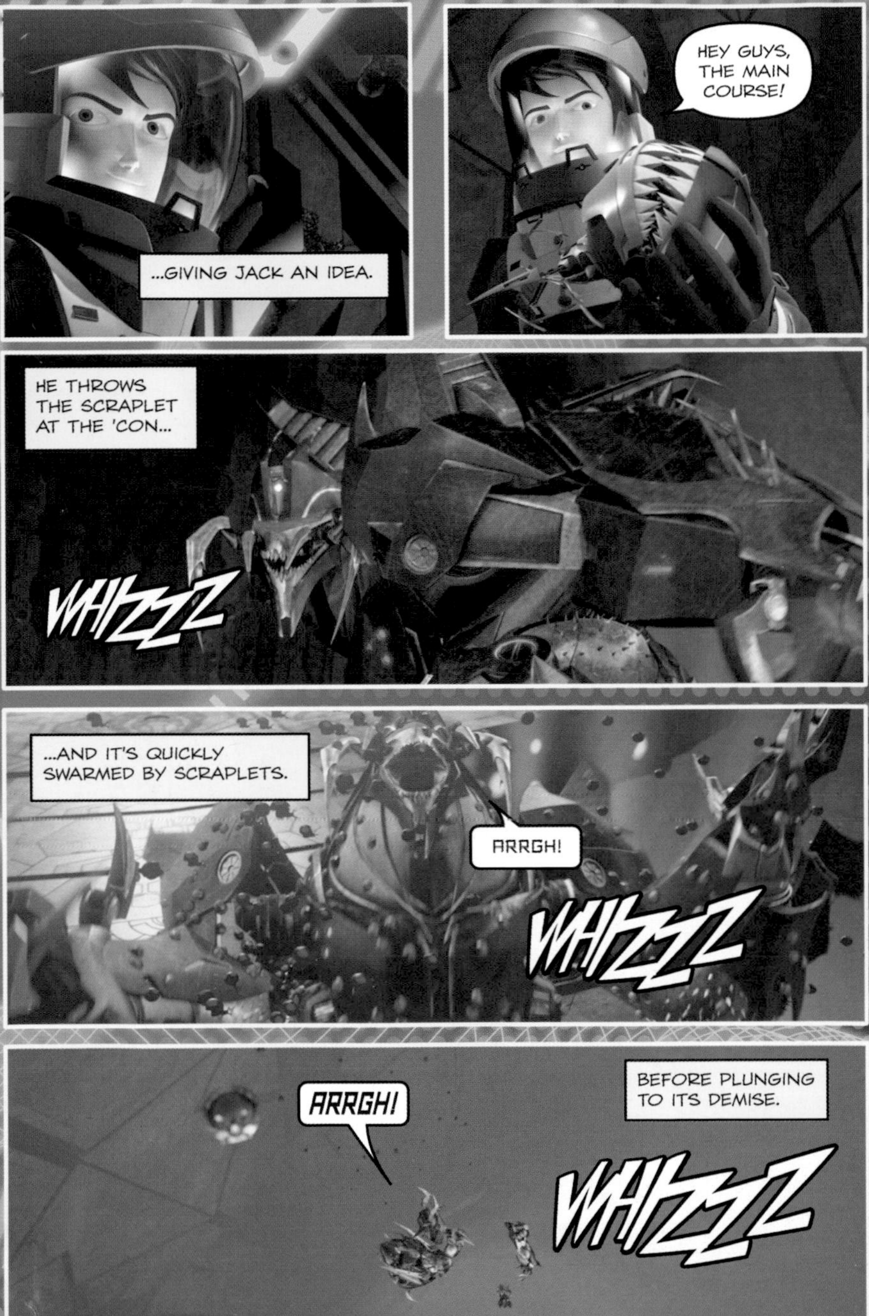
...GIVING JACK AN IDEA.
HEY GUYS, THE MAIN COURSE!
HE THROWS THE SCRAPLET AT THE 'CON...
WHIZZZ
...AND IT'S QUICKLY SWARMED BY SCRAPLETS.
ARRGH!
WHIZZZ
ARRGH!
BEFORE PLUNGING TO ITS DEMISE.
WHIZZZ

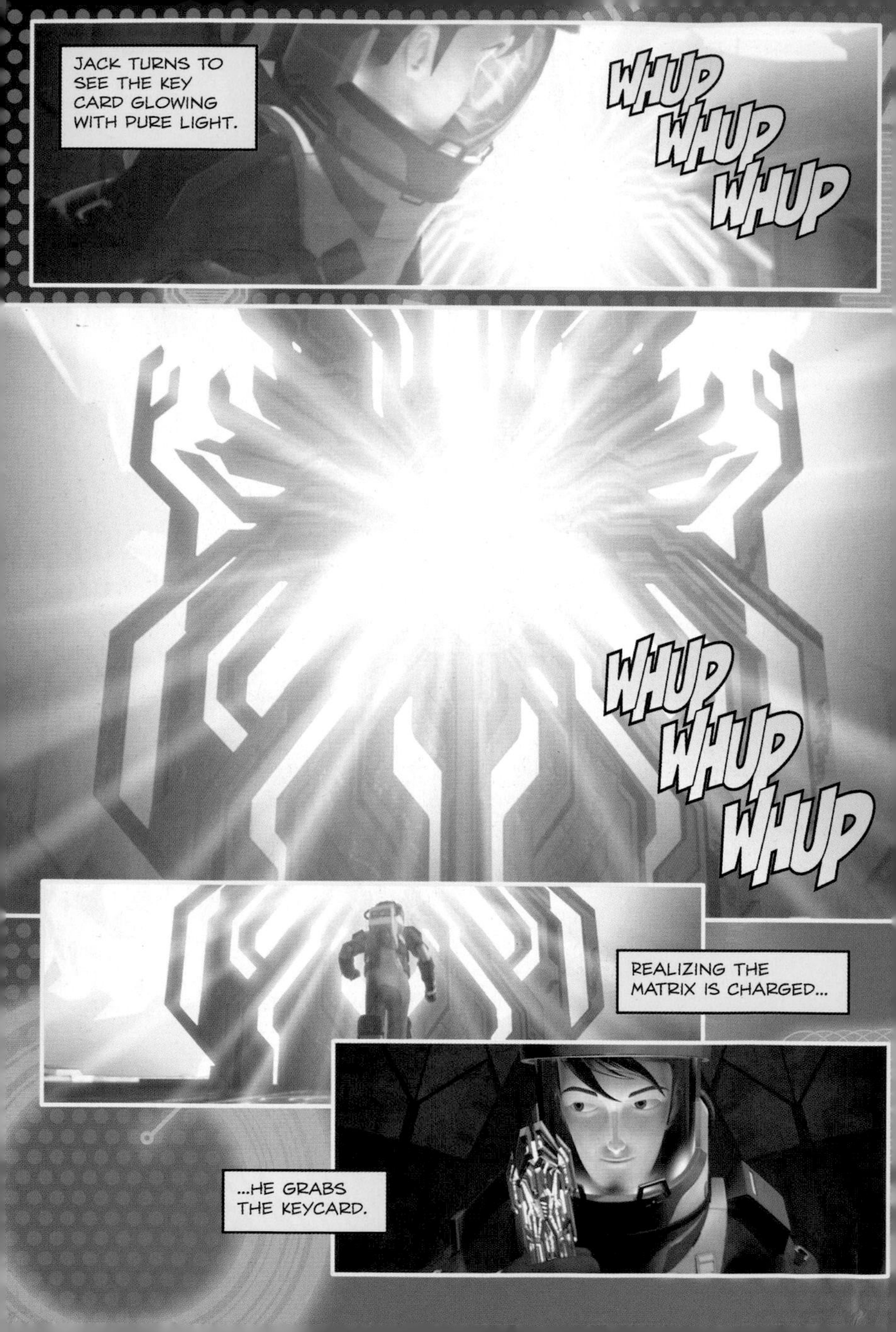

JACK TURNS TO SEE THE KEY CARD GLOWING WITH PURE LIGHT.
WHUP WHUP WHUP
WHUP WHUP WHUP
REALIZING THE MATRIX IS CHARGED...
...HE GRABS THE KEYCARD.

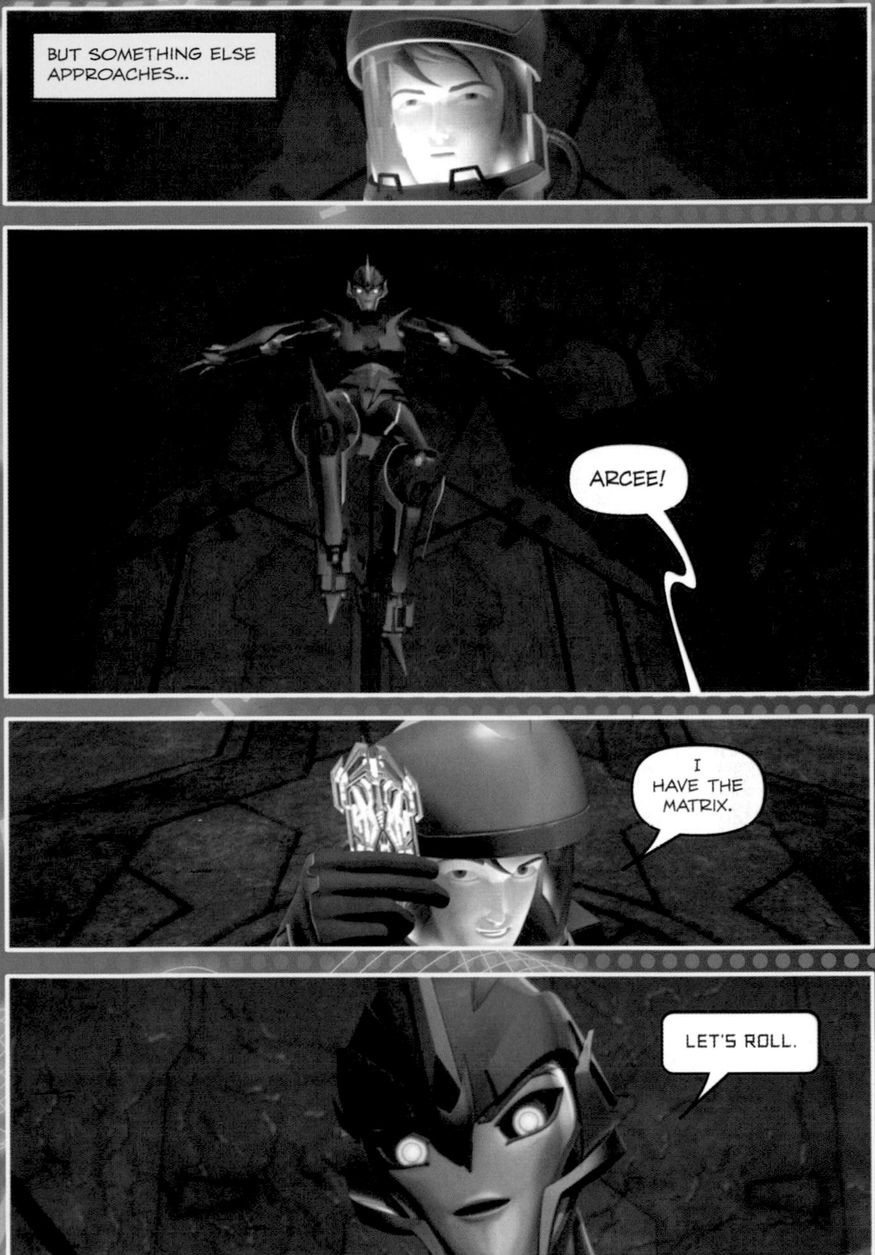
BUT SOMETHING ELSE APPROACHES...
ARCEE!
I HAVE THE MATRIX.
LET'S ROLL.

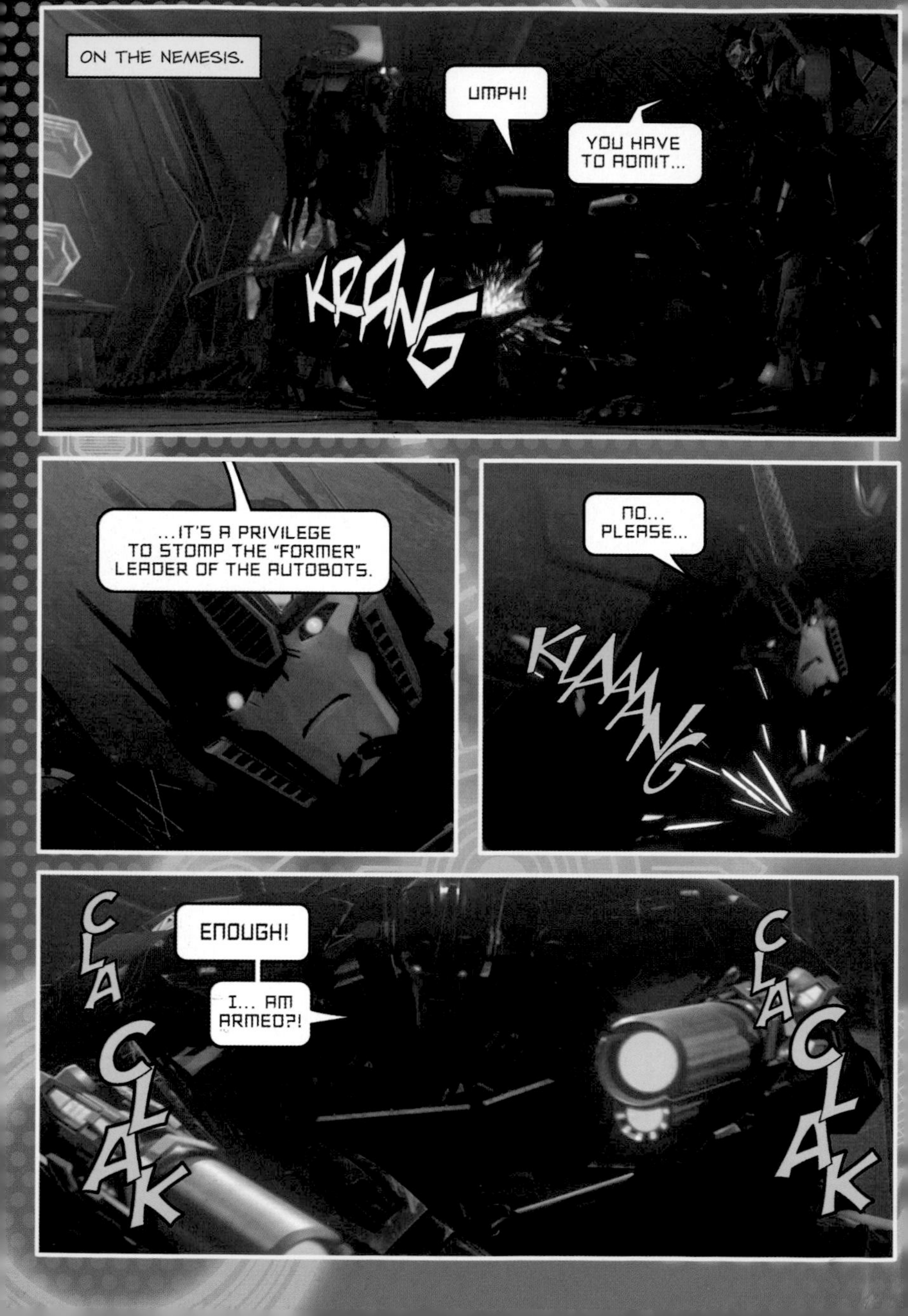
ON THE NEMESIS.
UMPH!
YOU HAVE TO ADMIT...
KRANG
...IT'S A PRIVILEGE TO STOMP THE "FORMER" LEADER OF THE AUTOBOTS.
NO... PLEASE...
KLAAANG
CLACLAK
ENOUGH!
I... AM ARMED?!
CLACLAK

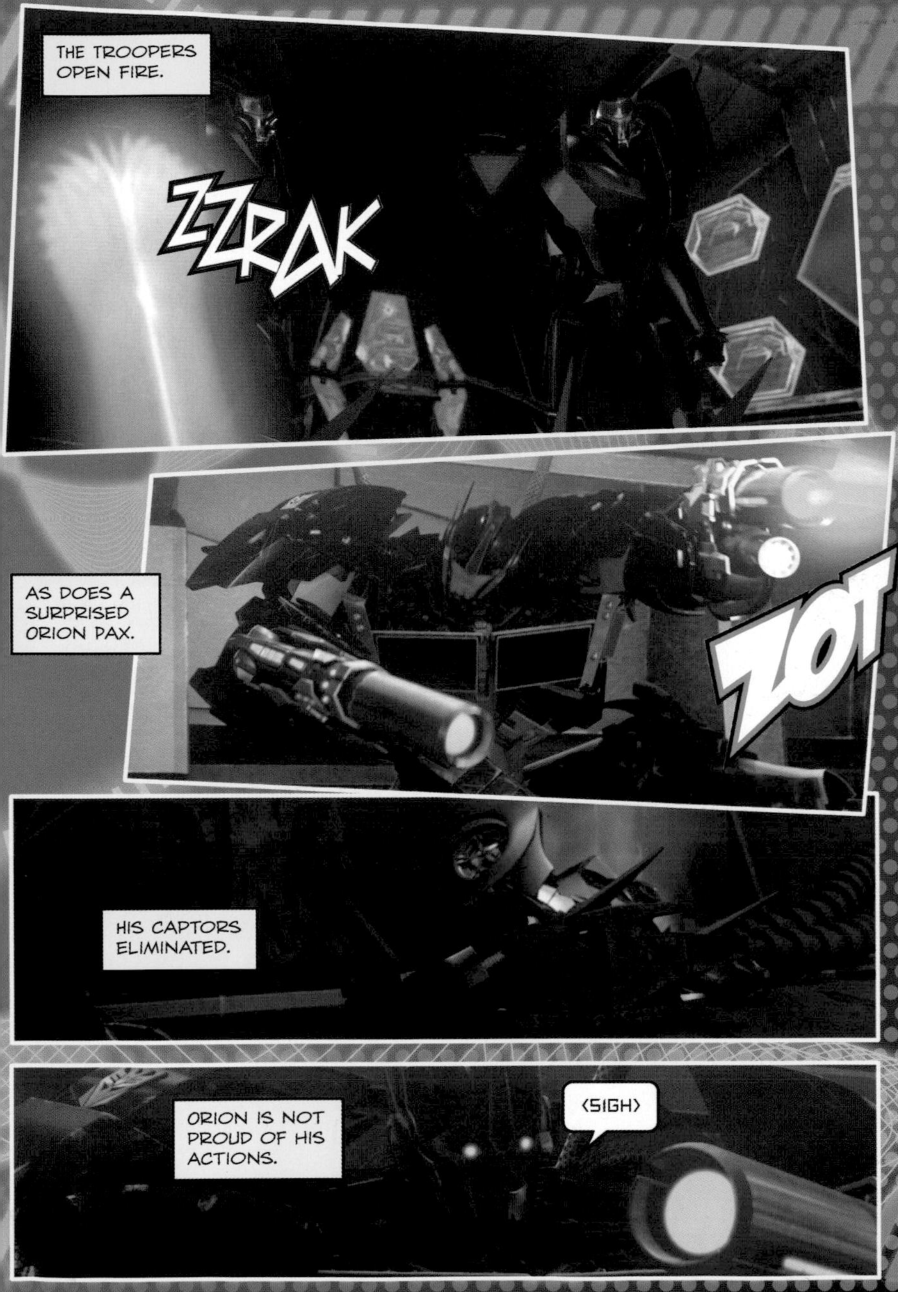
THE TROOPERS OPEN FIRE.
ZZRAK
AS DOES A SURPRISED ORION PAX.
ZOT
HIS CAPTORS ELIMINATED.
ORION IS NOT PROUD OF HIS ACTIONS.
<SIGH>

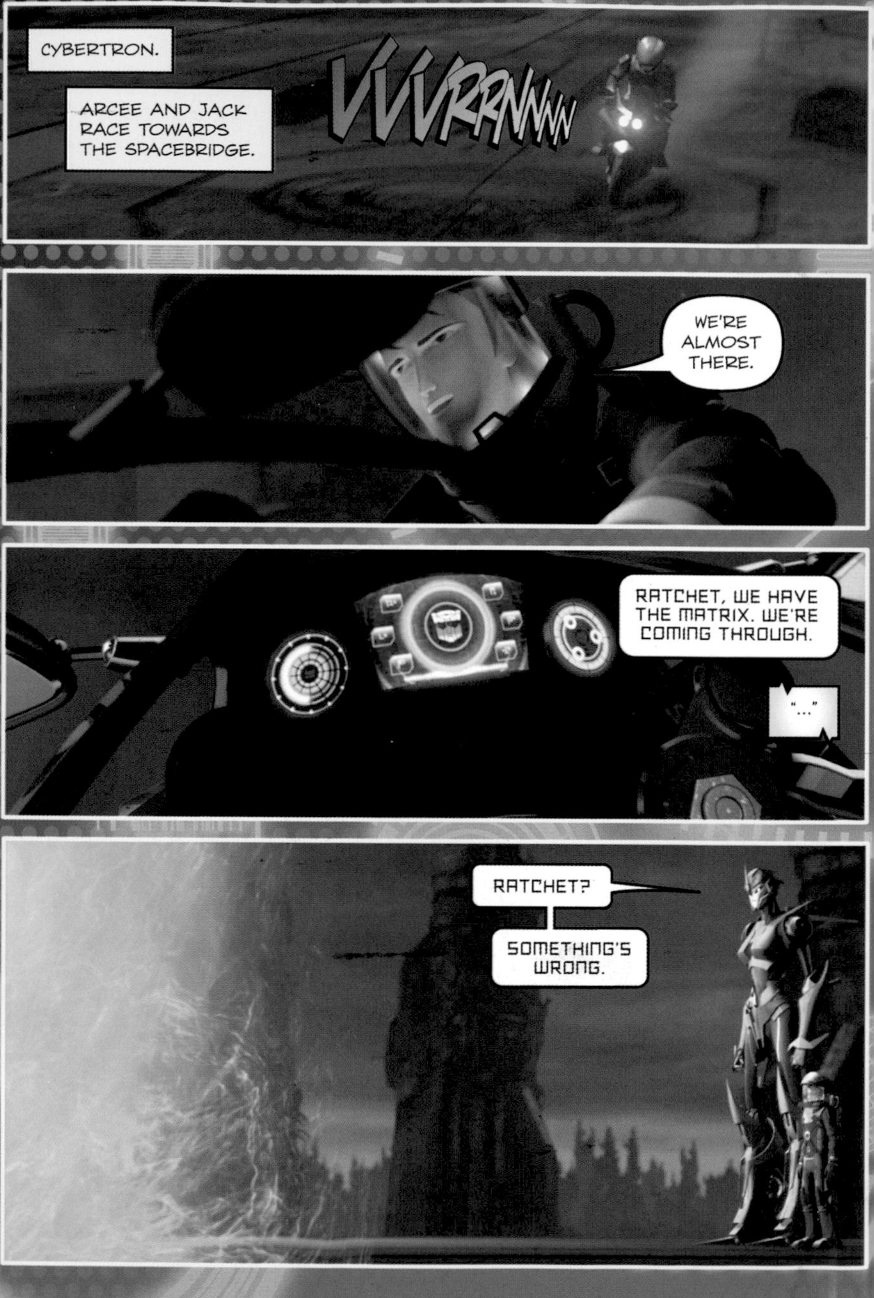
CYBERTRON.
ARCEE AND JACK RACE TOWARDS THE SPACEBRIDGE.
VVVRRNNNN
WE'RE ALMOST THERE.
RATCHET, WE HAVE THE MATRIX. WE'RE COMING THROUGH.
"..."
RATCHET?
SOMETHING'S WRONG.

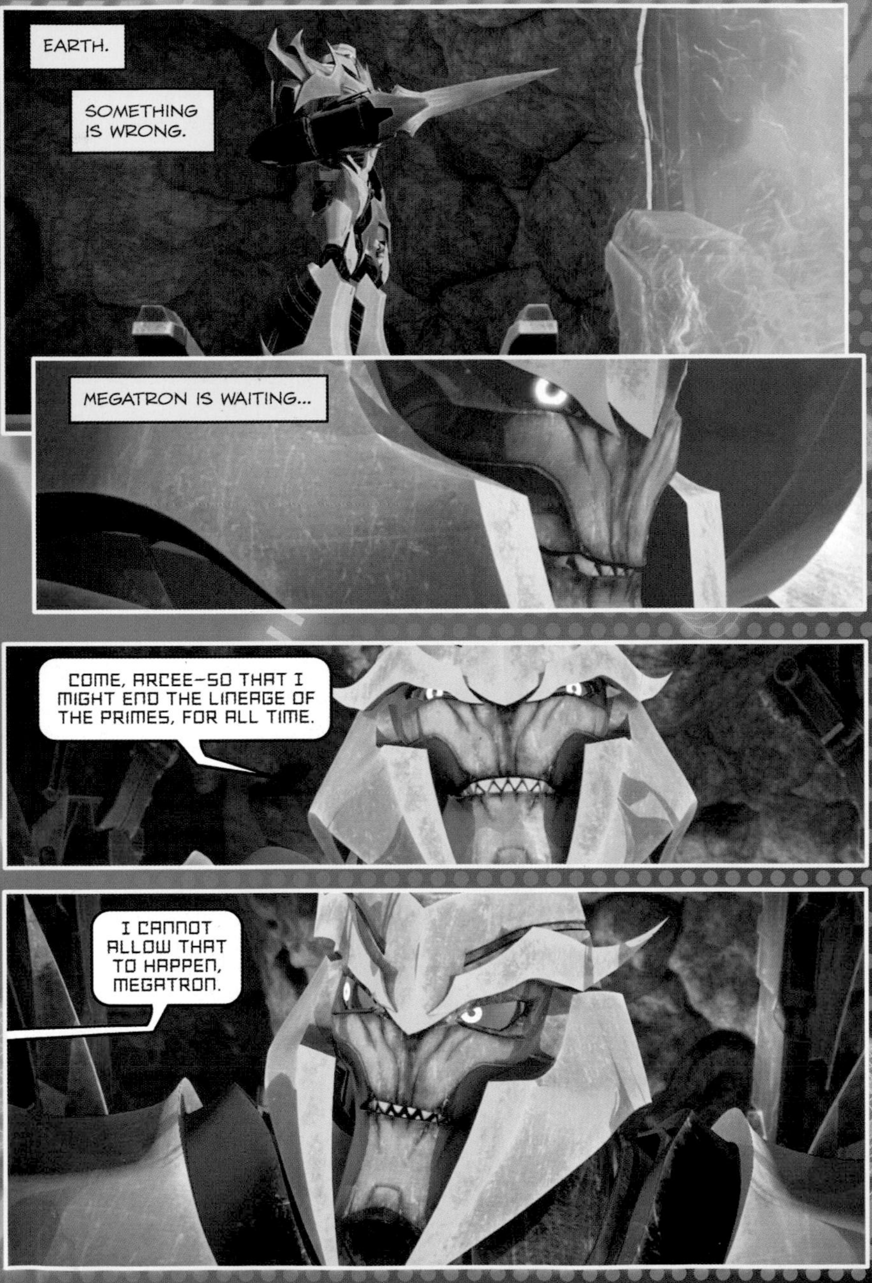
EARTH.
SOMETHING IS WRONG.
MEGATRON IS WAITING...
COME, ARCEE—SO THAT I MIGHT END THE LINEAGE OF THE PRIMES, FOR ALL TIME.
I CANNOT ALLOW THAT TO HAPPEN, MEGATRON.

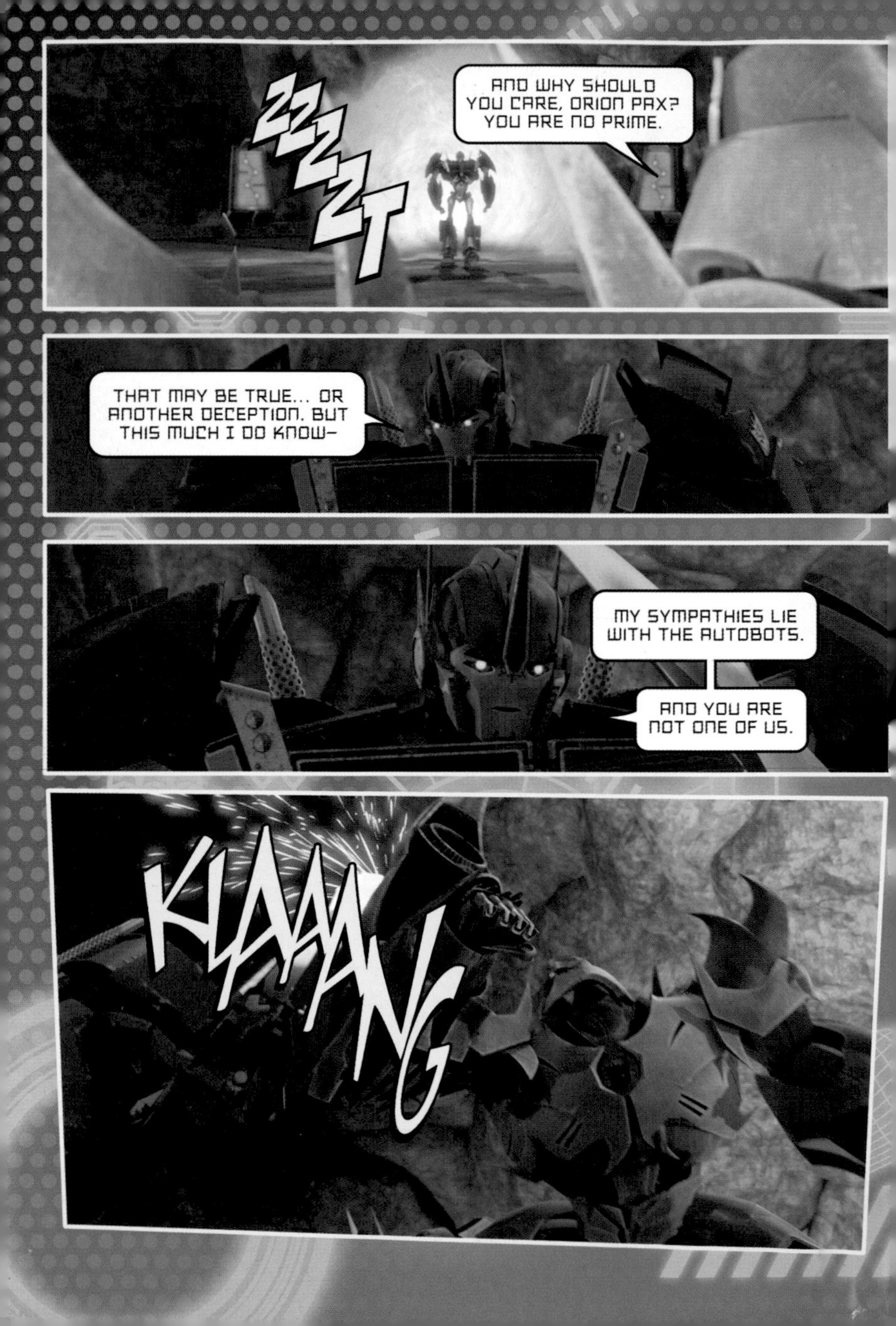
ZZZZZT
AND WHY SHOULD YOU CARE, ORION PAX? YOU ARE NO PRIME.
THAT MAY BE TRUE... OR ANOTHER DECEPTION. BUT THIS MUCH I DO KNOW—
MY SYMPATHIES LIE WITH THE AUTOBOTS.
AND YOU ARE NOT ONE OF US.
KLAAANG

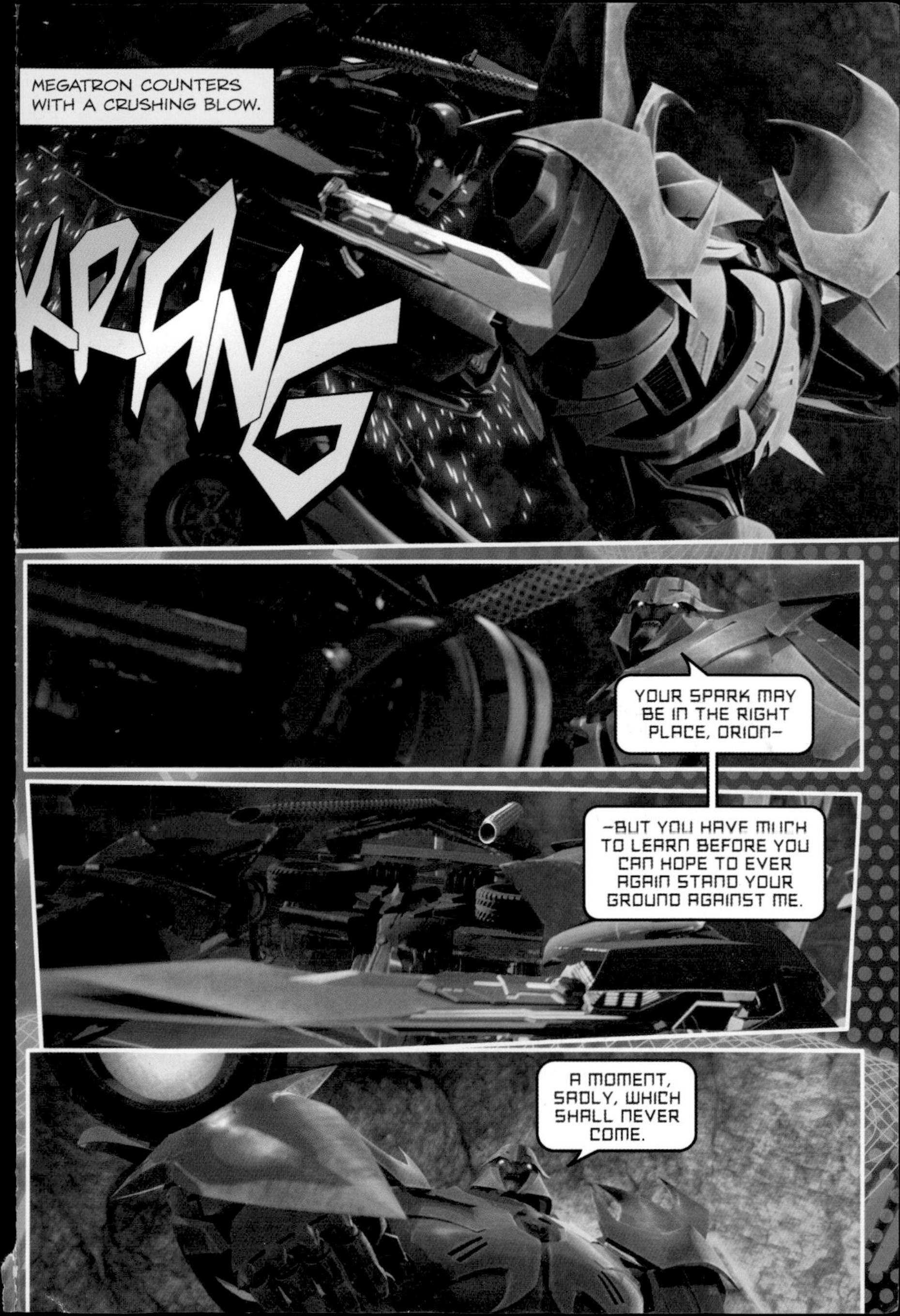

MEGATRON COUNTERS WITH A CRUSHING BLOW.
KRANG
YOUR SPARK MAY BE IN THE RIGHT PLACE, ORION—
—BUT YOU HAVE MUCH TO LEARN BEFORE YOU CAN HOPE TO EVER AGAIN STAND YOUR GROUND AGAINST ME.
A MOMENT, SADLY, WHICH SHALL NEVER COME.

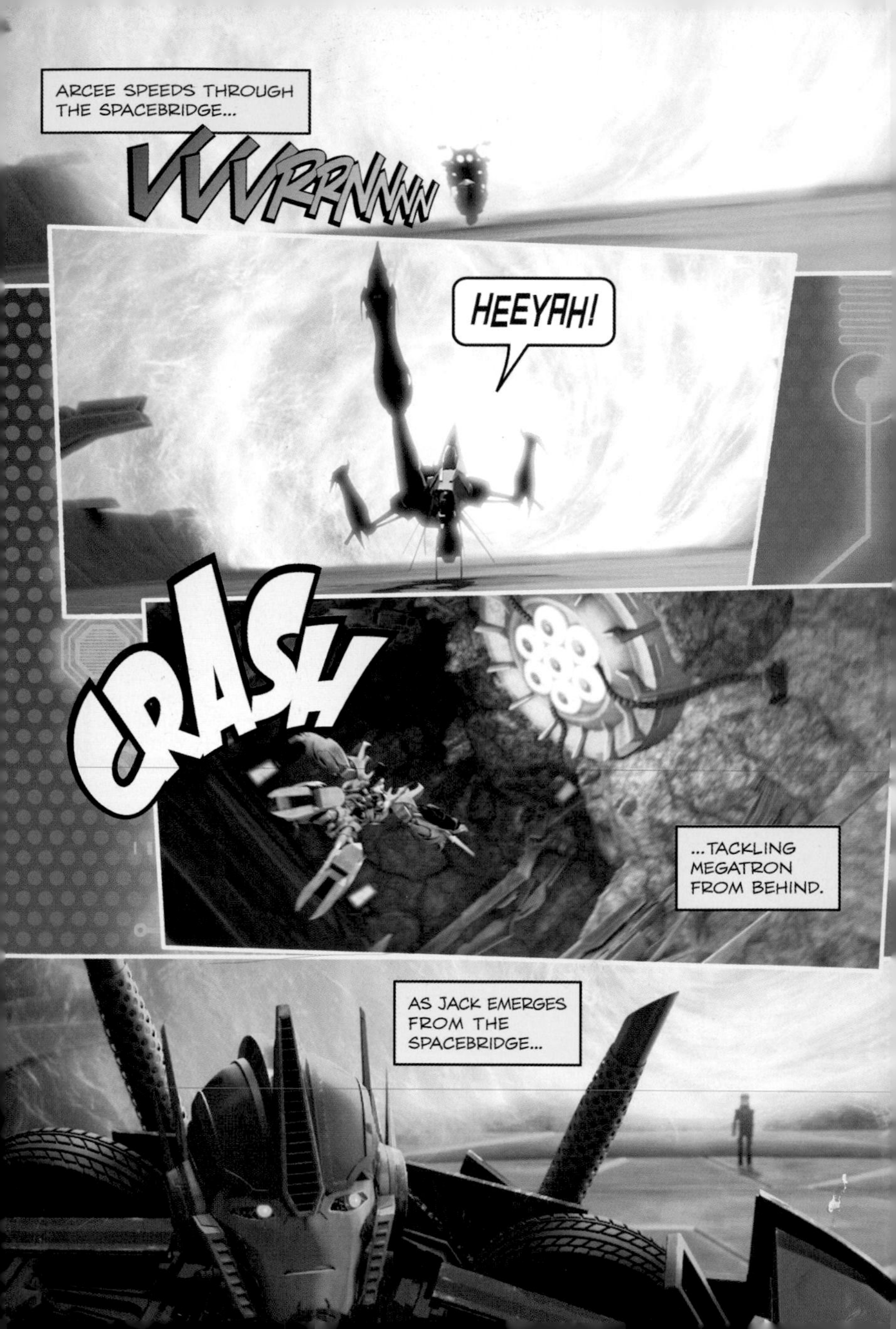
ARCEE SPEEDS THROUGH THE SPACEBRIDGE...
VVVRRRNNNN
HEEYAH!
CRASH
...TACKLING MEGATRON FROM BEHIND.
AS JACK EMERGES FROM THE SPACEBRIDGE...

...AND PRESENTS THE MATRIX TO ORION PAX.

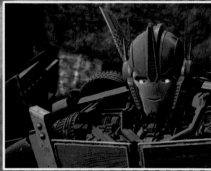

ARE YOU... CERTAIN I AM WORTHY?

EEEEEEEE

EEEEEEEE

YOU HAVE NO IDEA.

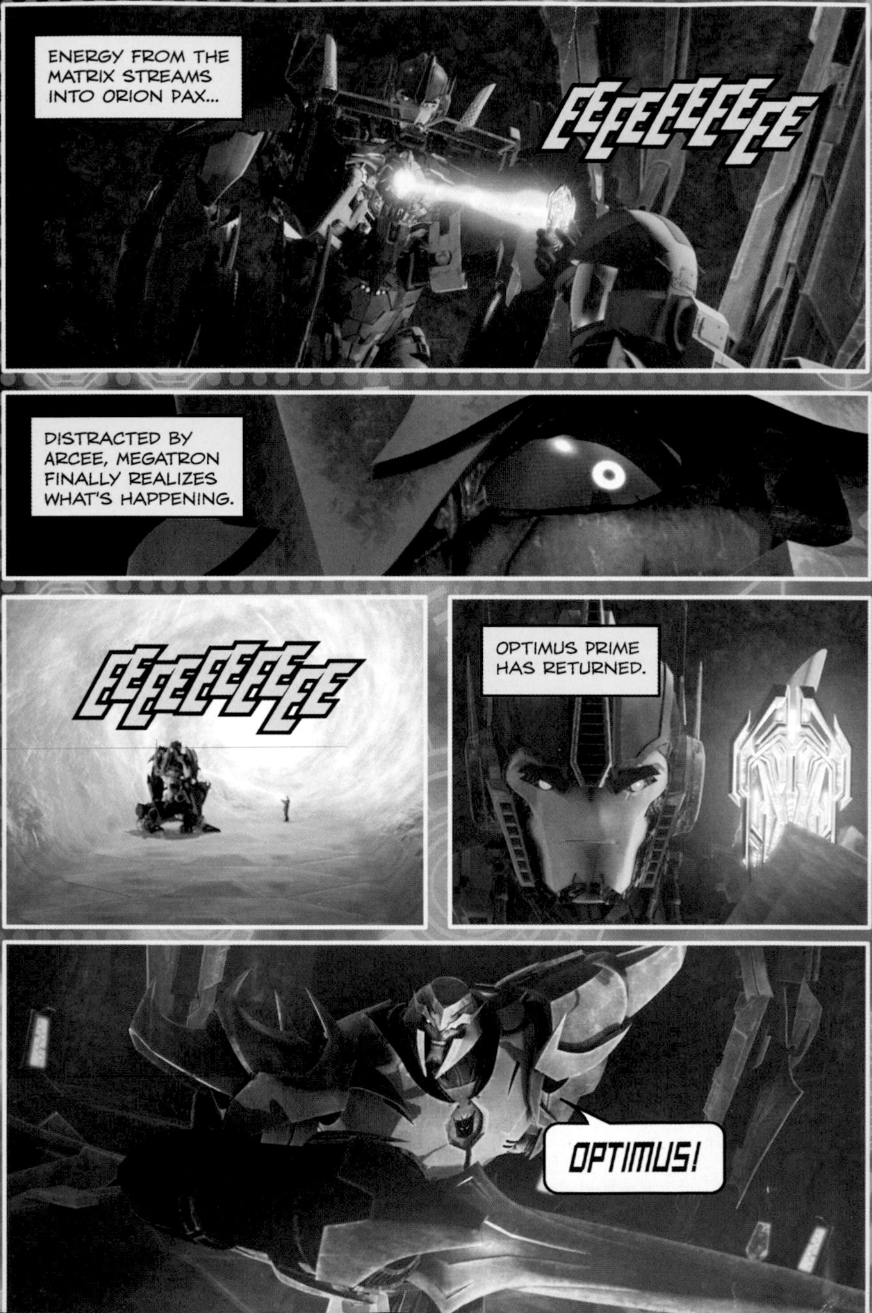
ENERGY FROM THE MATRIX STREAMS INTO ORION PAX...
EEEEEEEEEEEE
DISTRACTED BY ARCEE, MEGATRON FINALLY REALIZES WHAT'S HAPPENING.
EEEEEEEEEEEE
OPTIMUS PRIME HAS RETURNED.
OPTIMUS!

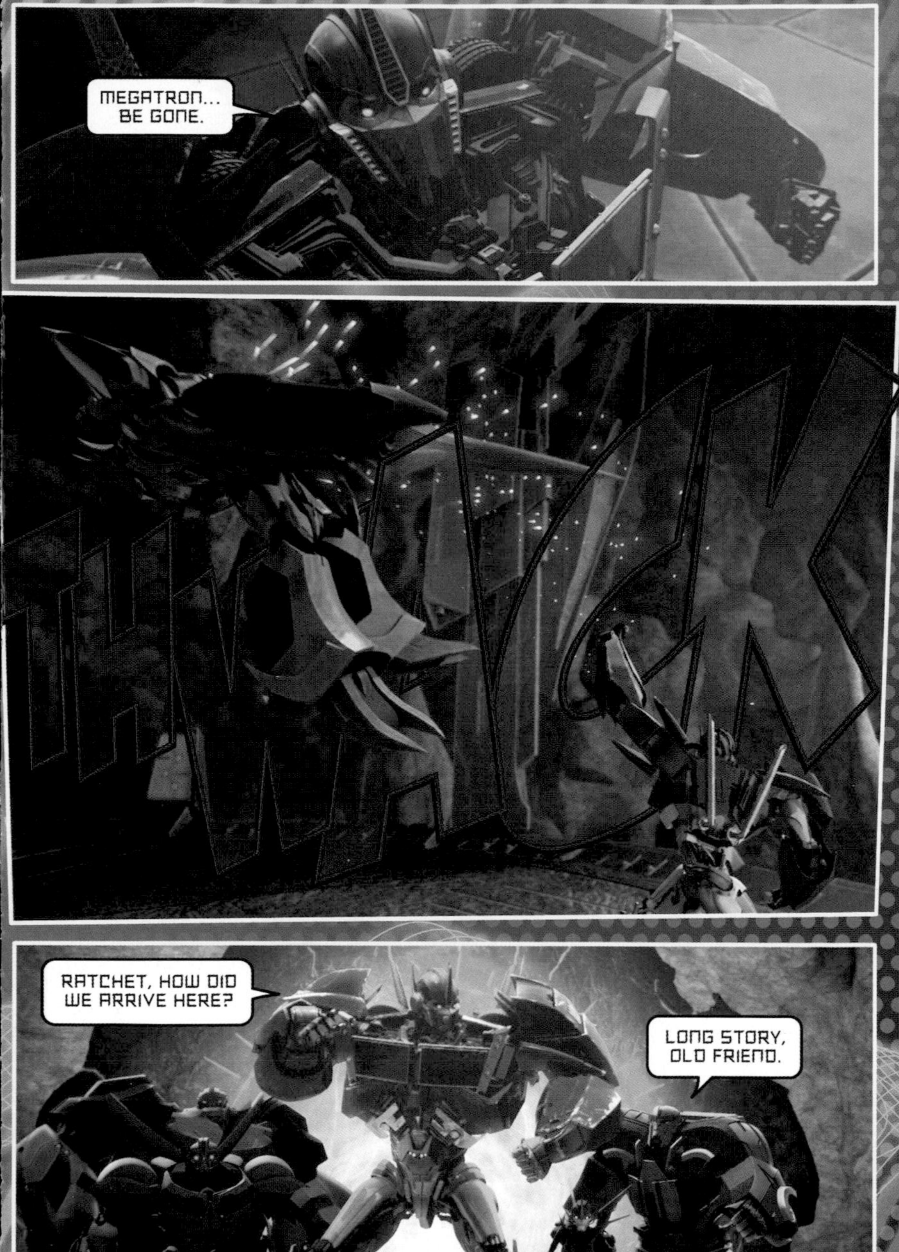
MEGATRON...
BE GONE.
THWACK
RATCHET, HOW DID WE ARRIVE HERE?
LONG STORY, OLD FRIEND.

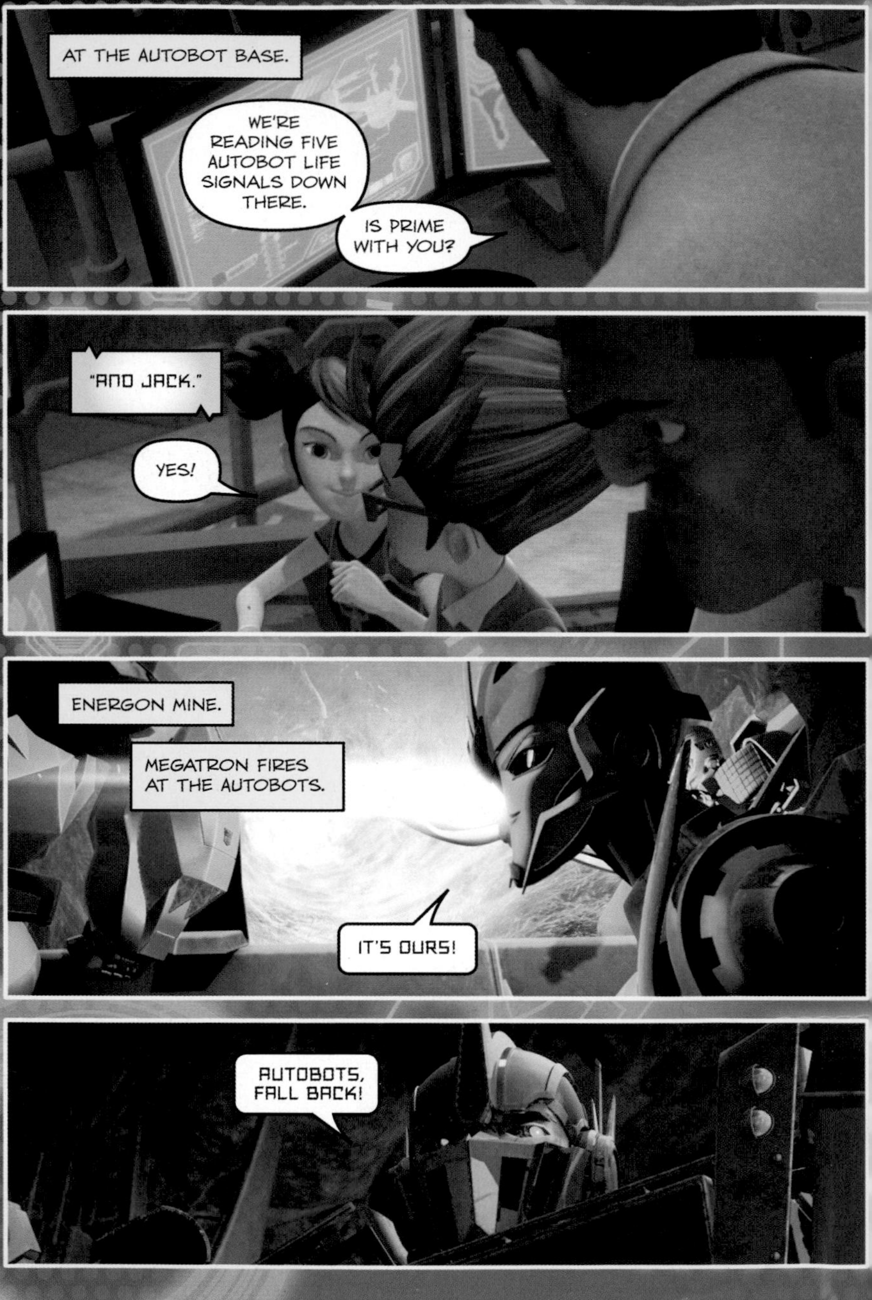
AT THE AUTOBOT BASE.
WE'RE READING FIVE AUTOBOT LIFE SIGNALS DOWN THERE.
IS PRIME WITH YOU?
"AND JACK."
YES!
ENERGON MINE.
MEGATRON FIRES AT THE AUTOBOTS.
IT'S OURS!
AUTOBOTS, FALL BACK!

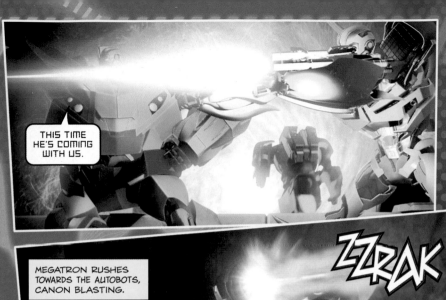

THIS TIME HE'S COMING WITH US.

MEGATRON RUSHES TOWARDS THE AUTOBOTS, CANON BLASTING.

ZZRAK

CHAWUM CHAWUM

ZZZT

BUT PRIME RETURNS FIRE AND IS THE LAST TO ESCAPE INTO THE GROUNDBRIDGE.

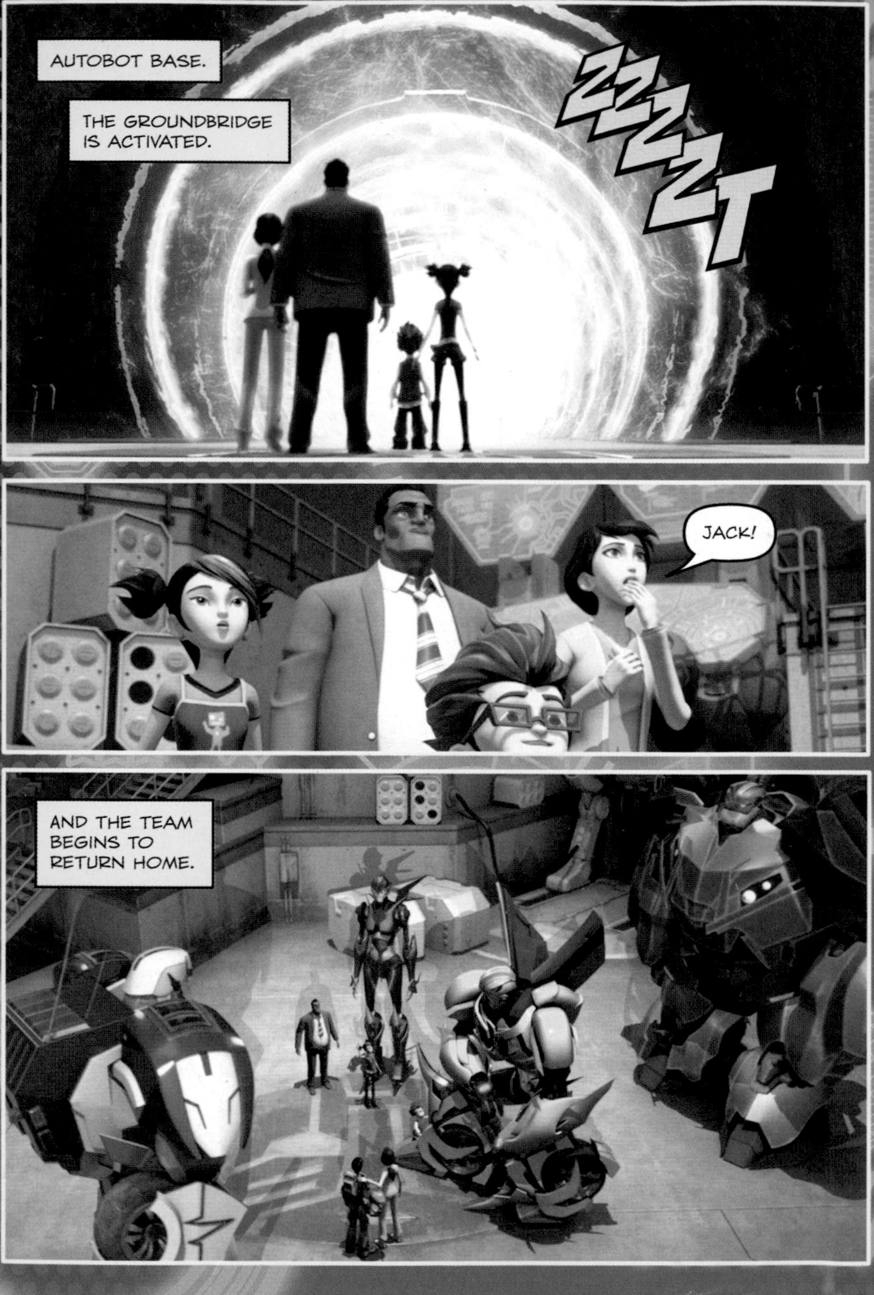
AUTOBOT BASE.
THE GROUNDBRIDGE IS ACTIVATED.
ZZZZT
JACK!
AND THE TEAM BEGINS TO RETURN HOME.

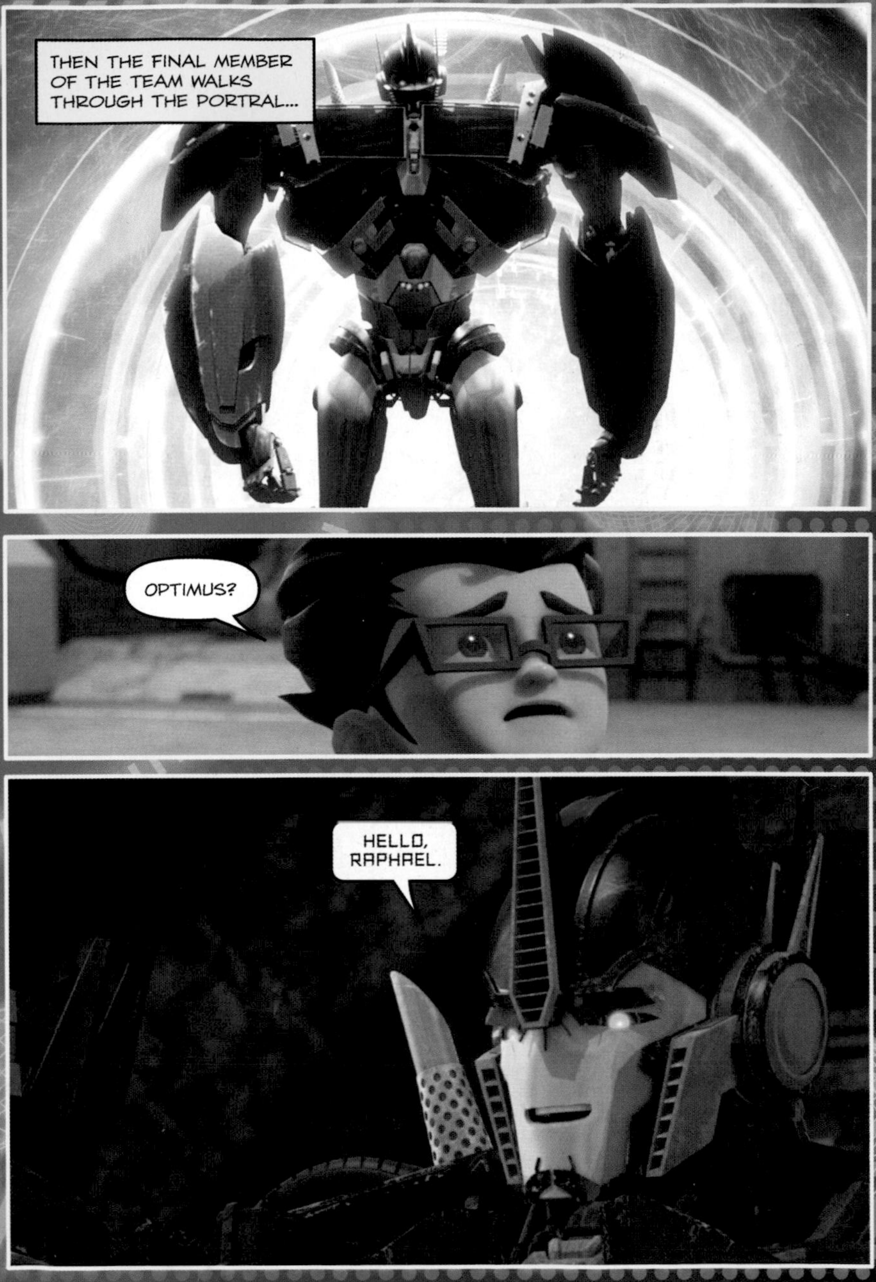
THEN THE FINAL MEMBER OF THE TEAM WALKS THROUGH THE PORTRAL...
OPTIMUS?
HELLO, RAPHAEL.

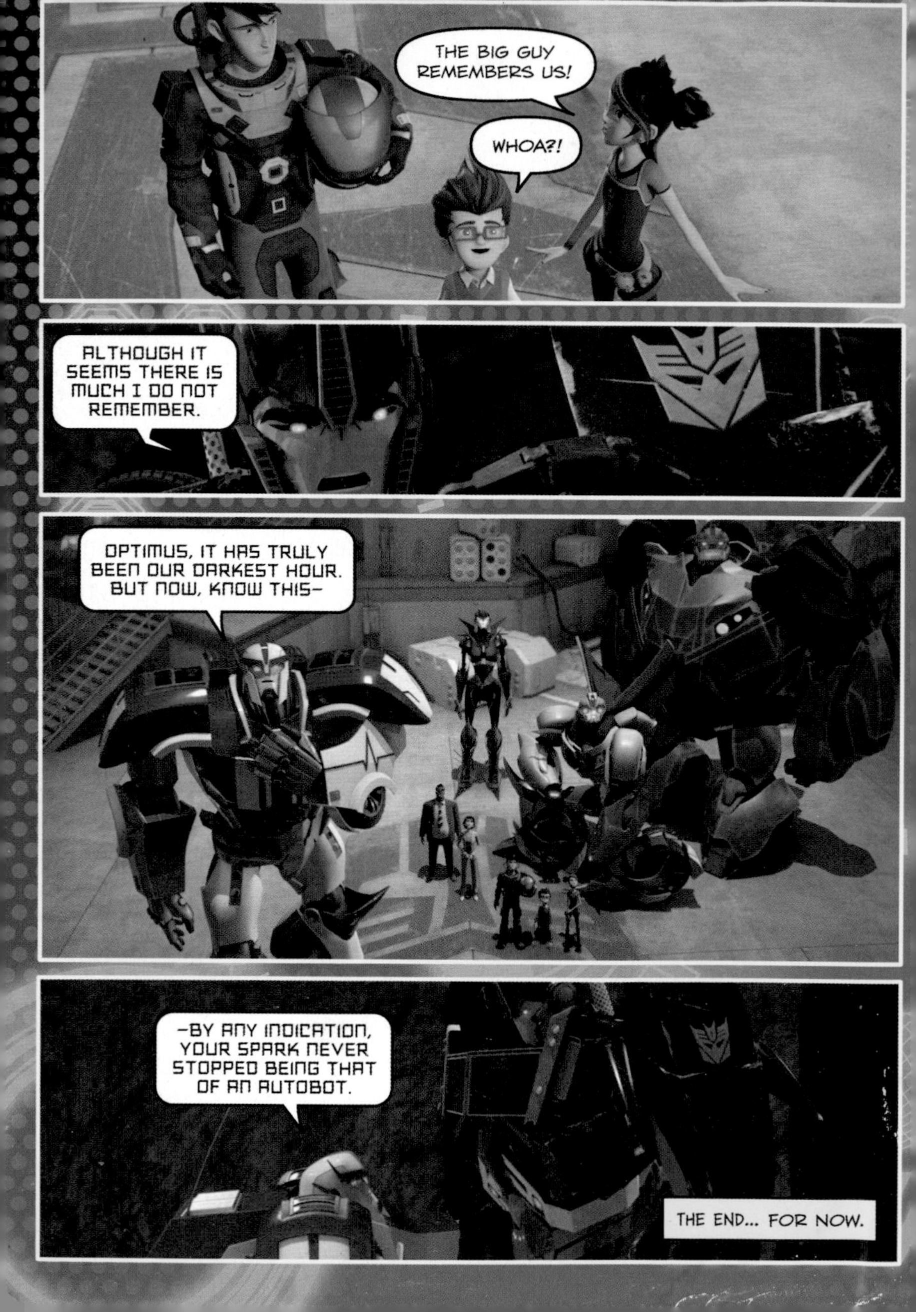
THE BIG GUY REMEMBERS US!
WHOA?!
ALTHOUGH IT SEEMS THERE IS MUCH I DO NOT REMEMBER.
OPTIMUS, IT HAS TRULY BEEN OUR DARKEST HOUR. BUT NOW, KNOW THIS–
–BY ANY INDICATION, YOUR SPARK NEVER STOPPED BEING THAT OF AN AUTOBOT.
THE END... FOR NOW.